PASSION'S BEGINNINGS

"Come here, Kirsten." To her amazement, Richard's voice was incredibly gentle. "What am I going to do with you?"

She gave him a wobbly smile. "Love me?" she whispered.

"Love." His tone was harsh. His eyes darkened to a deep troubled brown. "This is no time or place for love," he said gruffly. Richard reached for her then, encircling her slight form within the warmth of his strong arms. After gazing for a time into her blue eyes, he groaned. "There's time only for this . . ."

He kissed her brow gently. His lips moved down to her nose, where he nipped playfully, tenderly, at the tip. He kissed her cheek, nuzzled her neck. His breath quickened as he worshipped her throat.

Kirsten clenched her hands at her sides to keep from touching him, encouraging him. To caress him now would be like daring the devil. To kiss him now would be begging for heartbreak . . . But his scent assailed her nostrils, the woodsy smell tantalizing her. His skin was warm; his hands were gentle in their caresses—Kirsten gave up the battle and surrendered to the wonderful, pulsating feelings that flowed from nerve ending to nerve ending. She raised her arms, settling her hands at his neck.

Richard groaned and captured her lips in a kiss that seared her all the way to her toes . . .

CAPTURE THE GLOW OF
ZEBRA'S *HEARTFIRES!*

CANDACE McCARTHY
RAPTURE'S BETRAYAL

ZEBRA BOOKS
KENSINGTON PUBLISHING CORP.

ZEBRA BOOKS

are published by

Kensington Publishing Corp.
475 Park Avenue South
New York, NY 10016

First Printing: March, 1993

Printed in the United States of America

Chapter One

Hoppertown, New Jersey, May 1778

The moon cast a silver glow over the sleeping villages as a lone figure broke from the shadow of a large oak and ran toward the copse near the edge of the road. With a last furtive glance over her shoulder, Kirsten Van Atta slipped into the forest clearing ahead.

Her heart raced as she followed the familiar path. The trip was never more risky than it was this night; British soldiers were in residence at the local tavern. Alert for danger, her eyes sweeping the woods for any movement, she clung to the side of the road, moving stealthily from one hiding place to another. Overhead, moonlight filtered through the leafy canopy to make dusky patterns on the dirt lane. The night hummed with the song of summer's insects, and a warm breeze caressed her skin as she picked up her pace.

She had to get home. If her father found out she'd been out at night to see Miles, there'd be hell to pay. Cousins as well as good friends, Kirsten and Miles refused to sever their relationship, though their families were on opposite sides in the war. The Van Attas were Patriots, while William Randolph, Miles's father, was a staunch supporter of King George. Randolph had ordered his wife and son to stay away from his sister's family, and James Van Atta distrusted his brother-in-law enough to fear for his loved ones' safety. So Kirsten and Miles had no choice but to meet in secret, at night, when there would be no chance of discovery by their fathers. The cousins' affection for each other was so strong that they willingly risked attack by soldiers from either side.

The night blackened as Kirsten left the road for a footpath near the river, following the trail as it curved from its course parallel with the stream, heading deeper into the woods. The breeze rustling the treetops became cooler, and the moon slipped behind a cloud.

She had been gone much longer than she'd expected, longer than was wise under the circumstances; and each passing second intensified her fear. Her gaze now darting wildly from one shadow to the next, Kirsten clutched at the collar of her dark homespun shirt. She wore her father's shirt and breeches, both too large for her, the breeches held up by a piece of hemp. She could move freely through the forest in men's clothing, unhampered by petticoats.

An owl hooted in the distance. Startled, Kirsten stumbled and then righted herself. She seized hold of a nearby tree, struggling for breath, her pulse roaring in her ears.

Calm down. Use your head, she told herself. *No use getting excited over an old bird.*

Kirsten tucked back the silver blond tendrils that had escaped from beneath her conical, linen cap before she moved on. Suddenly, the woods had grown strangely quiet. She heard the roaring current of the Hohaukus as clearly as if she stood on the river's bank. Then lightning illuminated the sky, and she gasped at the great rumbling in the distance.

Thunder. It's only thunder! she thought. The advent of a summer storm . . . not British cannons.

As the first raindrop settled upon her cheek, Kirsten began to run. Within moments, the rain fell in torrents, soaking her to the skin. Her head bowed against the onslaught, she caught sight of a faint flicker of light through the trees. She froze. Someone was down by the river!

Once again, her feet flew over the uneven ground as she hurried toward home. Halting abruptly near a bend in the path, Kirsten surveyed the tangled underbrush. Ahead the path wound closer to the riverbank. Dare she venture off the trail?

Above, lightning streaked the sky and thunder shook the heavens. Kirsten decided there was nothing she could do but go on. If she didn't, she'd have to go back to Miles and endure her father's wrath. Hands shielding her face from the stinging rain, she plodded ahead determinedly.

Richard Maddox huddled beneath the tree, seeking shelter from the storm. Despite his cocked hat the wind whipped rain into his face. *Biv is long overdue,* he thought. Only a few minutes and he'd have to leave.

Richard waited, although he was chilled to the bone and hunger gnawed painfully at his belly. A twig snapped, and he stiffened.

"Maddox! Don't turn around, ye bloody traitor!" The guttural growl came from behind him.

9

Richard felt a jolt of surprise. How did the man know his real name? He cursed. He should have been more careful, watched his back. To lower one's guard was a dangerous thing in this time.

A gusty wind caught hold of his hat, and he grabbed for it.

"Don't move, I said!"

Richard froze as he felt the sharp edge of a bayonet, thrust through two layers of clothing, nick his damp skin. *One good clean strike and all will be over,* he thought. *This is all wrong! I won't die this way!*

He should have suspected that something was wrong when Biv changed the meeting date. *By the king's royal arse, I've been set up!* His body tensed with his anger. He wouldn't go down without a fight, nor would he be stabbed clean through like a skewered pigeon.

The heavy downpour continued as Richard slowly lowered his arms to his sides. He clenched his jaw as he anticipated the stranger's next move.

"That's it!" came the hateful voice. "Wouldn't want to frighten me and 'ave me slip."

"What do you want?" Richard asked.

"Want? Why nothing, mate." The man's harsh, mirthless laughter sent chills down Richard's spine. "You're the one who wants it. And the others thought I'd be just the one to give it to you."

"Where's Biv?" Had Biv been caught, too?

The man snickered. "Sorry, but Biv couldn't make it tonight. 'E sends 'is regards, though." He snorted. "Snivelin' coward if you asks me. Always wantin' me to do 'is dirty work."

Richard controlled his temper, his fists clenched at his sides. Damn, he'd been tricked by the man who was to have helped him!

Biv is one of them, he thought, his muscles coiling

in readiness to spring. *A whoring murderer like this bastard behind me.* He angled his chin slightly to the right, heedless of the bayonet point at his back. If he could just get a look at the man . . .

Suddenly, Richard sensed that they were no longer alone. From the corner of his eye, he spied a small figure farther along the trail.

The stranger inhaled sharply, apparently catching sight of the newcomer. "What the 'ell—"

Richard spun sidewise, smashing his fists against his assailant's face. The man staggered, but recovered quickly. Dodging the bayonet, Richard came back swinging. The stranger grunted under the force of Richard's fist and leapt back, brandishing his musket.

Rain fell in a deluge, blinding Richard as he fought for his life. He gasped, wavering, when the bayonet pierced his arm. Rallying, he landed a solid blow to his opponent's midsection. The man slipped in the mud and lost his weapon. Richard lunged for the gun, tripping in the slimy ooze. He fell on his injured arm. His head spun, and he could see spots before his eyes.

The pain was so intense, Richard knew he couldn't hold out much longer. He sensed that his opponent rose to his feet and retrieved the weapon. Richard's vision wavered as he fought to see him. He waited for the death strike. Suddenly, he heard a high-pitched scream and, on instinct, spun backward. Excruciating pain sliced through him as the bayonet penetrated his thigh. Richard's world went black as he lost consciousness.

Kirsten shrieked as she saw the bayonet plunge downward and sink into the felled man's flesh. In the eerie flash and fire of the storm, she could still make out the attacker poised over his victim. He looked up and stared at her.

Her heart skipped a beat. The man's face was horribly disfigured. When she realized that he was scanning the woods beyond her, she broke from her stupor and ran.

Terror kept her from looking back as hot tears mingled with rain on her cheeks. The wind howled a mocking litany: *He's coming to get you. He's coming to get you!* She tripped, rolling as she fell, a wet tangle of cloth and scraped limbs.

When she scrambled up, gasping, afraid, she searched for the disfigured man, but could find no sign of him. Where was he? Out there, waiting to pounce on her?

A twig snapped in the bushes behind her, and she held her breath. Seconds later, air left her lungs in a whoosh of relief. She saw two gleaming eyes in the darkness, before a deer, startled from its hiding place, turned and sped off into the night.

A loud crash reverberated overhead. Kirsten jumped, then fled for cover behind a huge boulder. She held a hand to her mouth as she crouched, swallowing against the bile of fear that rose to her throat.

She had no idea how long she huddled in her hiding place. Her legs were cramped, she'd lost her hat, and the rain drenched her hair and formed a puddle about her feet. She was cold, frightened, and wanted nothing more than to be home and in bed.

But despite her discomfort and the storm, she couldn't stop thinking of the murderer's victim. What if he wasn't dead?

She shuddered. How could she in all good conscience leave him, knowing there was a slim chance he might be alive?

She rose and then gasped as feeling returned to her sleeping limbs. A check of her surroundings showed there was still no sign of the disfigured man.

I have to get home, she told herself. *. . . But an injured man may be lying alone by the river!*

If he was struggling for life, she might be able to save him. Kirsten thought of the risk involved in returning to the clearing. What if the man's attacker was there? What if he'd come back to finish the job?

Go home, her common sense insisted. *Why risk your life for a stranger?*

Kirsten headed back toward the river.

Chapter Two

It was drizzling when Kirsten entered the clearing, clutching a solid tree limb. The man lay in the mud where he'd fallen. Still. Alert for danger, she approached the victim cautiously. She moved to within a few feet of his body and stopped, her stick raised, ready to defend herself against attack. She scanned the tree line before returning her gaze to the felled man.

Her eyes stung with the threat of tears as she studied him. He was a pitiful sight. Rain beat down on his twisted body. He appeared pale and lifeless.

He's dead! A tear escaped to trail down her cheek. *I'm too late!* She'd risked her life for a dead man.

Then, on impulse, Kirsten gave the body a nudge with her stick, and the man moved. Encouraged, she crouched beside him and placed a trembling hand on his shoulder. Had his chest risen or had she imagined it? She shook him lightly, and then again.

"Mynheer?" Her whisper was loud in the quiet after the storm. "Are you alive?" Was he friend or foe? She realized it didn't matter which side of the war he was on; he was someone who needed help—her help.

Lightning flashed across the river, followed by the low rumble of distant thunder.

Kirsten stood. *"Mynheer,* speak to me!" she pleaded. "You are alive, aren't you? Please . . . you have to be alive."

She glared at the man with frustration. "Move—drat you! Show me you're alive!"

Kirsten stared at him, wondering what to do. Whether the man was living or dead, she couldn't just leave him lying here! But if he had already died, what else could she do?

"Please," she whispered brokenly, "you can't be dead. You don't deserve such an end." She had a vivid memory of the struggle between the two men, and a chill ran through her as she recalled the hideous face of the one who'd wielded the bayonet.

Suddenly, the man on the ground groaned. Surprised from her thoughts, Kirsten bent closer and, with a cry of gladness, carefully eased him onto his back. She experienced an overwhelming rush of pity then. His face revealed that he was young, and she noted that he wore a fringed rifle shirt, which was muddy and torn, and breeches, which fit him snugly and were in worse condition than his shirt.

He's alive! Kirsten thought, and she grinned. She'd found him in time!

She sobered. *But now what do I do?* How could she move him if he couldn't walk?

After setting down the stick, she grabbed the man's shirt and tugged hard to get him to move. When he didn't respond, she tried again.

"Mynheer, speak to me," she commanded. "I'm a friend. I want to help." Instinctively, she spoke in Dutch, the language of her people.

The man mumbled, and Kirsten leaned closer to hear him. She gasped when he grabbed her wrist,

16

astonished by his show of strength. She fought to free herself, and he moaned, releasing her to clutch his arm in agony.

Kirsten was alarmed to see the slit in his sleeve near the shoulder. Fresh blood seeped from it. She stared at him, not knowing what to do. The man gazed back, his eyes wide, his lips moving soundlessly. Ashamed, she realized that he was only desperate to be understood.

"What is it? Tell me." She laid a hand on his brow and spoke to him soothingly.

"Bri . . . hide . . . me," he gasped.

She frowned. "I cannot understand you. Tell me again." She placed her ear nearer to his lips and was barely able to make out his next words.

"Please . . . hide . . . me . . . Brit . . . sh . . ." The man spoke English, and Kirsten understood him.

He wanted her to hide him from the British! She knew then that he was a Continental soldier. Remembering the redcoats at the tavern, Kirsten stood, terrified, half expecting to see that they were suddenly surrounded.

She mentally berated herself. It was foolish to think that the British would have to hide from a woman and a wounded man.

Her gaze returned to the injured soldier, whose eyes were open and glazed as he struggled to see her. Moved by his plight, Kirsten hunkered down and touched his arm. She started but didn't withdraw when his fingers latched onto her hand.

She reassured him in English. "I'm going to help you. Do you understand?"

The man nodded. She saw him relax and close his eyes.

Studying him, Kirsten bit her lip. "Can you walk?" she asked softly. There was movement, a barely perceptible negative shake of his head. "Then, I shall have to leave you for a while. To get a wagon." His dark eyes opened with alarm, and Kirsten patted his hand. "Relax. I promise I'll be back as soon as I can."

She searched the area for a place to hide him. "We had better get you into the bushes. That man"—she shuddered—"he may come back."

The soldier tried to sit up, and Kirsten moved to help him. He howled in pain, groping for his right leg. To her horror, she saw a second wound. Blood was spurting from his thigh.

"My God!" she breathed.

No wonder he can't walk, she thought. If he attempted it in his condition, he'd bleed to death. She'd have to leave him until she could return with the wagon.

But first she had to stop the flow of blood; he'd never survive until her return if she didn't. Kirsten tore two strips from the hem of her shirt, stopping once to breathe deeply. The sight of so much blood made her woozy. She brushed her hair back with shaking fingers. Then, using both hands, she pinched the edges of the leg wound closed and bore down with a steady pressure. His warm red blood drained between her fingers, filling her with alarm.

Finally, the stream slowed and then stopped. Kirsten breathed easier.

She'd done it! She'd stopped the bleeding! She bound the limb above the wound and then bandaged the gash itself. *Please God*, she prayed silently, *let him live!*

The soldier seemed to be resting quietly now. *A good sign*, she thought. Hopefully, in passing out, he had escaped the worst of the pain.

Kirsten felt shaky. She'd never had to hurt anyone before; it brought little comfort to her to know that

18

doing so had been necessary.

"I hate to leave you here, but I have no choice. You must save your strength." She spoke aloud, thinking that somehow, even though unconscious, the man would understand. "When I get back, we'll get you in the wagon. I don't know how we'll manage, but we will."

Kirsten was soothed by her own words as she made light of the upcoming struggle. "I'm sorry. I didn't want to hurt you, but I had to . . ." She went to the river and rinsed her hands.

The soldier needed her; she wouldn't let him down. "You are going to live," she vowed as she returned to his side.

She looked for a place to hide him, then decided she'd cover him up and leave him where he lay. She found several suitable branches with leaves intact, and shielded him with the leafy foliage.

After a last peek at the wounded man, Kirsten felt satisfied. She headed for home, her pace hastened by concern.

"Three o'clock and all's well!" The *klapperman*'s voice rang out in the silence of the rain-washed night. Kirsten was on the Ackermans' farm when she heard the familiar sound. She quickly hid behind the barn. The last thing she needed was to be discovered by the man making his rounds. Garret Vandervelt was a friend of her father's and would no doubt see that she got home—and that her father knew of her escapade.

Vandervelt carried his lighted lantern and a timepiece—a brass hourglass. Kirsten watched him set his hourglass on the Ackerman's *stoep* before he pulled out his rattle, or *klapper*, from his coat pocket.

He shook the *klapper* once, before putting it away. Vandervelt then proceeded to the neighboring farm, where he'd repeat the ritual. The sound of his voice would be heard at each home in Hoppertown every hour until dawn, Kirsten knew, and she was relieved to see him go none the wiser as to her presence. His deep cry was reassuring to the Hoppertown villagers, for it warned all, housekeepers and convicts alike, that he was on the watch to keep everyone safe.

Once the rattle-watch was out of sight, Kirsten left her hiding place. Moments later, she was home and inside her father's barn.

"Pieter?" Her voice was but a whisper in the dark interior of the stable. There was no sign of the groom.

A horse nickered from the nearest stall, and Kirsten smiled and slipped inside the cubicle to stroke the mare's neck. "Easy, girl. It's only me."

The sleek hair of the horse felt smooth against her palm. The mare snorted in pleasure at the young woman's touch, and Kirsten laughed softly, her spirits rising.

But dawn was fast approaching, and she realized that she had much to do before daybreak. The smile left her face as she gave the horse one more pat. "Sorry, girl, not this time."

The mare nudged Kirsten with her nose as she turned to leave. She studied the bay gelding snorting restlessly in the opposite stall, and then she glanced at the mare, whose big eyes seemed to plead with her.

"But you understand, Hilga, don't you?" she murmured to the mare. "If I let you come, you have to be quiet." She found the halter and slipped it over Hilga's head. "I'm depending on you now. Don't let me down. The man's life is at stake."

Closing her eyes, Kirsten rested her head against the horse's side. "He deserves to live, girl. No one deserves to die that way." She sighed and lifted her head, stroking the mare's chestnut coat. "He needs us, Hilga. It's up to us girls to see that he makes it."

The moon broke through the clouds as the wagon wheels creaked over the muddy road. Kirsten gripped the reins fiercely. It had been a hair-raising experience, hitching up the wagon and escaping the farm without sound. *But we did it!* she thought smiling at the horse.

The worst of it hadn't ended there, though. Twice the wagon had become stuck in the mud on the journey through the woods. Kirsten was glad she'd chosen Hilga; the mare's docile nature had made things easier. Both times, the young woman had climbed down from the wooden seat and had urged the horse on with soft words and a hard tug on the reins. Each time the cart had rolled free of the mire, Kirsten had made a silent vow to reward the animal.

The wind stirred the treetops, sending a cascade of cold water down upon woman and horse. Kirsten had no idea how much time had elapsed since she had left the Continental soldier. The treacherous condition of the turnpike forced her to a slow, steady pace, which made the journey nerve-wracking. She was anxious to get to him.

Was he all right?

Kirsten pulled the wagon off the road and onto the narrow path, silently praying that the cart would fit past the trees and bushes. She'd have to drag the soldier several yards if it didn't. She swallowed hard. Perhaps he wouldn't survive that ordeal.

The cart fit through the thicket easily. Kirsten halted the vehicle under a tree and jumped down to secure the mare. Moving toward the mound of branches she had left, she was shocked to find that they'd been disturbed. Her blood ran cold when she

21

spied a trench in the mud leading to a coppice.

Had the attacker come back to finish off his victim? That thought was just too terrible, too awful for her to take in. Kirsten's stomach heaved. Trembling, she advanced, parting the bushes to peer inside.

"Thank God!" A quick check told her the man was still alive. He must have dragged himself through the mud. Her relief was short-lived when she noted fresh blood on his pantleg. His thigh was bleeding again; the crimson stain appeared black against the muslin bindings.

"You fool," she scolded. She wasn't angry; she was too happy and relieved to find her patient alive. The wind had been fierce; no doubt it had disturbed his makeshift cover. The poor man must have awakened and sought refuge elsewhere.

Tearing a fresh strip from her shirt's hem, Kirsten rebound the wound. She didn't know how she'd explain the ruined garment, but she'd think of something. If not, she could always bury the shirt in the woods.

How was she going to move the soldier, though? Unconscious, he was dead weight. If she could wake him, she could help him to his feet. She tried rousing him with a light shake and then shook him harder when he didn't move. When she again failed to rouse him, Kirsten stood, tears of frustration coming to her eyes. *What am I going to do?*

There was a rope in the wagon. It could be slipped under his arms and tied so he could be hoisted onto the wooden platform. *It just might work!* She had to try; there was no other choice. Kirsten returned to the wagon and untied the horse.

She was so cold! The wind had died down, but she was soaked to the skin. She glanced at the man lying senseless. If she was cold, what about him? She shivered. There was no time to lose—he could be dying.

She sprang into action. Guiding the mare through the mud to the small copse and then crouching beside the injured man, she again tried to wake him. This time he moaned. There would be no help from that quarter, she realized. It was entirely up to her to save him.

"*Mynheer?* It's me—Kirsten. I'm back. I brought the wagon just as I promised. See?" The man blinked once and then his eyes closed. Kirsten rose, retrieving the rope. After directing a few gentle words to the faithful mare, she returned to him. His eyes were open.

"I have a rope," she explained, "and I'm going to tie it around your chest." The man struggled to sit up. Suddenly overwhelmed with a feeling of warmth, Kirsten continued. "I don't want to hurt you, but I'm afraid I have to. When I get you to the barn, I'll see to your wounds and you'll feel better." She paused. "Can you lift up this arm? That's it!"

Murmuring words of encouragement, she looped the piece of hemp about his body. She flinched when he groaned, but hardened herself against his body's protest. Finally the rope was secure. Kirsten's brow furrowed as she pondered what to do next.

She tugged on the rope. *I have to get my arms under his!* She cried out at first, staggering under his dead weight. When she tried again, however, her burden felt lighter. Utilizing his last ounce of strength, the man rose to his feet. Then, exhausted by the effort, he passed out.

He fell against the wooden platform with a thud. Kirsten inhaled sharply as she fought to keep him from sliding to the ground.

It was like a game of tug of war as Kirsten battled with the inert form of the Continental. Finally, she was able to push him halfway onto the wagon. Grabbing hold of the rope, she then moved to the front end of the vehicle, slipped the piece of hemp under the seat, and pulled it to her over the top. She heaved until her efforts warmed her.

There was a loud scraping noise as the man slid across the wooden platform. Kirsten felt faint with relief at her success. Time was precious; she had to hurry before the sun rose and the townspeople woke. She grabbed the reins, hopped up onto the wagon seat, and clicked her tongue. Hilga shifted and then obeyed the command. Soon the wagon was rolling along the road back to the Van Atta homestead. Fortunately, the wheels ran smoothly through the mud on the return trip.

Kirsten maneuvered the wagon beside a thicket near the edge of the Van Atta property. After a quick check to see how the man had fared, she jumped down and ran toward the barn. No one moved within its dark depths, save the horses inside their stalls. Soon, the groom Pieter would be rising, and the barn would be stirring with life.

She couldn't bring him here! A barn was not safe from the British, who often appropriated the horses and cattle of Hoppertown residents. And she couldn't risk endangering her parents.

On the far side of her father's land were the remains of the old Van Atta mill. It had been abandoned when Kirsten's grandfather had built one closer to the village. The ruin held fond memories for Kirsten. She and cousin Miles had played there often as young children. But that was before the war, before the bloodshed . . . Those days were forever gone.

I'll take him to the mill's cellar. Hurrying to the wagon, Kirsten then headed for the safety of the deserted mill.

The man, wrapped in several blankets, was sleeping peacefully on the dirt floor of the cellar when Kirsten made for home. He'd be safe until morning, shielded from the weather by the wooden floor of the room above.

His wounds would need more doctoring, though. Tomorrow she'd bring a bread-and-milk poultice.

It was near daybreak, with the birds chirping their morning song, when Kirsten crept past the room in which her parents' still slept and slid tiredly onto the soft feather tick of her bed.

Chapter Three

"Kirsten? Kirsten! Get up, you lazy daughter. There are chores to be done!"

Groaning, Kirsten sat up and yawned. She brushed back a tumble of platinum blond hair and blinked to clear the sleep from her eyes.

"*Kirsten!* Did you hear me?" Her mother's voice was sharp, even through the closed doors of the alcove bed.

"Yes, *Moeder*. I'm getting up."

"Well, be quick about it. Your *vader* has been up for over an hour." The door closed with a click; Agnes Van Atta had left the room.

Kirsten stretched and wondered why she was so tired. Her eyes widened as the memory of the injured soldier came to her. Was he all right? She hoped he was comfortable and that he hadn't somehow stumbled from the sanctuary of the mill.

He'll need the poultice . . . and something to eat. Kirsten began making a mental list of supplies for her patient. Then she gasped, remembering that she'd left her mud-encrusted shoes to dry on the front stoop. There would be an awful scene if her mother discovered that she'd been out last night.

27

"Kir-sten!" Her mother's high-pitched shrill made Kirsten flinch.

Drat. It was too late; her mother must have found the footwear. "I'm coming, *Moeder*."

Kirsten opened the alcove doors and peered out cautiously. As she'd feared, her scowling mother stood not far from the bed, a damp shoe in each hand.

"Good morning!" The young woman beamed at her mother. "A wonderful day, isn't it?"

"Don't you good morning me, young woman! Not when you can see what I'm holding!"

"You mean my shoes?"

Agnes Van Atta's lips twitched with annoyance. "Of course, your shoes!"

"Are you upset?" Kirsten padded in her bare feet across the cold floor to the *kast*, the wardrobe, from which she took out the day's clothes. She laid these garments carefully on the bed before she pulled off her nightgown.

"Of course, I'm upset!" her mother said. "You were out during the night again!"

"There was a storm." Kirsten sat on a chair to put on her stockings.

"What were you doing?" Her mother looked concerned. "Your *vader* will not like this."

"What are you going to tell him?" Kirsten blinked in pretended innocence. "That he should be angry because I saw to the animals? That I finished the milking before you rose from your bed?" She turned from her mother as she slipped on a second striped petticoat. Next, she donned a dress of blue calico.

"You've finished the milking?" Agnes asked, sounding surprised. Kirsten nodded as she slipped on her apron and tied the strings.

"And the chickens—they are fed?" her mother asked.

"Of course, *Moeder*. That reminds me—I must tell *Vader* that we need more feed." Kirsten straightened her bedding and closed the alcove doors. She could sense that her mother's anger had cooled as she put away her nightgown and shut the *kast*. The spring nights were cool, and the need for warmth made quilted bedcovers and light flannel gowns customary.

There had been no need for her lie. She had seen to the animals before going to bed so that she could sleep later in the morning. But Kirsten would have fabricated an excuse if necessary. A man's life was at stake.

She braided her hair and then pinned up her silver blond plaits. When she was done with her toilet, she grabbed a broom from the corner of the room and proceeded to sweep the bedchamber floor.

"And just what do you think you're doing?" her mother asked. She had not yet left the room.

Kirsten sighed as she met her mother's gaze. She was tired of being treated like a child. Her parents meant well—she knew they feared for her safety— but . . . "I'm doing my chores, *Moeder*."

"What about your shoes?" Wrinkling her nose with distaste, Agnes raised the muddy footwear. "Really, Kirsten, you should take better care of your belongings."

"I'll clean them." Flushing, Kirsten reached for her shoes.

Her mother shook her head. "Never mind, daughter. Go ahead with your sweeping. I'll put them outside—you can clean them later." She moved toward the door. "When you're done sweeping, you had best clean the hearth. You'll need a clean feather. I noticed yesterday that the last one mysteriously disappeared." And then, gesturing for Kirsten to continue with the broom, Agnes Van Atta left her daughter's bedchamber.

Kirsten thought the day would never end. As she worked quickly to finish her chores, she found her mind wandering to the wounded soldier.

What if he was bleeding again! She churned the butter with vicious pumps. He could be dying! She had to see him; she had to know.

When the butter was ready, Kirsten placed the store in the coolest section of the pantry. Later the firkin—the vessel that held the butter—would join others in the cellar under the house. Kirsten was outside picking early greens for her mother when she saw her father wave to her on his way to the sawmill. Smiling, she called out a greeting. She was climbing the steps with the basket of peas when the top section of the Dutch door opened.

Agnes glanced at her daughter's full basket. Her face softened as she met Kirsten's gaze. "There's suppawn on the table," she said gruffly. "You best come and eat while it's still warm."

"But, *Vader*—"

Her mother frowned. "Your *vader* is too busy to eat right now."

Kirsten stifled her disappointment as she sat down at the table board. She looked forward each evening to the family meal. By this hour her chores were done and she could relax and enjoy her father's attention.

She saw a plate of *olijkoecks* at the other end of the table, and her spirits rose. She'd pilfer an extra share for her patient! If awake, he'd surely enjoy the fruit-sweetened fried batter cakes.

Her heartbeat quickened. The man had to be alive—he had to! Night and the freedom to escape to check on her patient seemed a long way off.

*   *   *

The night was warm; the day's spring breeze had dried the dampness left by yesterday's storm. It was after the *klapperman's* second visit that Kirsten slipped out of the house. In the barn, she changed quickly, donning the breeches she'd worn the day before and a clean shirt. She had taken up the satchel full of provisions for her patient and was ready to go when she heard male voices outside.

"'Ey, Will, are ye in a mind for a tasty morsel this night?"

"Well, that depends now. What exactly do ye mean by a morsel?" The night reverberated with their shared laughter.

Peering through a crack in the barn boards, Kirsten tensed. *There are British soldiers on Vader's property!* She was trapped!

Clutching the sack to her breasts protectively, she envisioned the injured man at the mill. The soldier was defenseless in his condition; she had to get to him right away—before the British found him!

The Britons' voices receded as they left the barn area. "I guess we've been spared, Hilga," Kirsten whispered. She was startled when she heard a squawk and then angry clucks. "They're stealing *Moeder's* hens!"

She frowned as she peeked out into the yard. The two redcoats were heading toward the village; one carried a limp chicken. She glanced toward the house and was glad to see that the windows remained dark. *Thank God they didn't wake Moeder and Vader.*

Tugging her dark calico cap over her blond plaits, she crept from the barn and headed toward the mill where the soldier waited.

The old wooden structure was built a foot above

the ground on a brick foundation. The dirt cellar underneath had been dug out after the construction of the main floor, leaving a small storage area not quite high enough for a man to stand up in, though Kirsten had no difficulty walking about the room. The wooden walls of the main level were splintered and rotten, but the foundation was solid, giving the cellar stability and making it a safe place to hide. The only access to the cellar room was a break in the foundation wall, which her grandfather had blocked off many years before the abandonment of the mill. A few steps led down to the old entry. The dilapidated look of the entire structure made the whole mill seem unsafe, keeping away unwanted intruders. *An ideal place*, Kirsten thought, *for my Continental soldier*.

The makeshift door she'd wedged in the cellar opening refused to budge until she gave it a good swift kick, jarring the nailed-together boards loose so she could pry them away. Kirsten allowed her eyes to adjust to the dark room, her heart picking up its pace when she spied the wounded man lying against the far wall.

Is he dead? The hairs rose at the back of her neck as she crawled inside to feel the man's brow. Her patient was burning with fever. If she didn't work fast to bring his temperature down, he could die within days . . . perhaps hours.

She left the cellar room to rummage through her satchel until she found the tinder box. She needed light and a fire to heat the man's poultice. When the flint struck steel, it produced a spark which Kirsten fanned to flame amid the dried grass and bits of wood she'd brought along. She then pulled a candle from her sack, held its wick to the fire, and set the lighted taper near her patient.

To her delight, she found items left in the cellar

from her days of play there. She and Miles had come to the mill and had fished in the stream whenever they had finished their chores early. They had cooked their catch over an open fire in an old iron skillet provided by Aunt Catherine, Miles's mother. They had also heated water in a kettle Aunt Catherine had given them so they could make tea while they shared their fish feast.

Kirsten found the kettle where she'd hidden it years ago, beneath the bottom steps of the old staircase leading up to the main floor of the mill. Made of pig iron, the kettle was rust free.

She washed the kettle in the stream by the mill's waterwheel, and then poured the milk she'd brought in a small jar into it, and set the kettle over the fire she'd made. When the milk boiled, she added a few crumbs of bread. While the concoction simmered, she took a piece of linen from her satchel, as well as a container filled with lard. She coated the fabric with the lard, then waited for the bread-milk mixture to cool a bit before dipping the cloth into the milk until it was saturated.

The man lay as still as death, moaning only once when she carefully unbound his bloody bandages. Kirsten gasped; the wound had begun to fester and she had to cut away the crusty part of the bandage with the knife she'd brought. Next, she lowered the hot compress gingerly over the infection before returning to the fire to prepare a poultice for his arm.

Her patient was filthy. Her main concern, however, was not bathing him but saving him.

With the second compress in place, she rinsed out the kettle and drew fresh water from the stream. Then she doused the fire. Her lips twisted as she eyed the bottom of her shirt. It would be difficult enough to explain one of her father's shirts missing—but two? She cut through the cloth with one clean swipe of her knife.

She knew only one way to bring his fever down. She began to bathe his brow with the cool water from the stream. As the taper burned low, she lit another. Her vigil over the wounded man continued until, exhausted, Kirsten fell asleep.

Hours later, when the night was quiet, she awoke with a start. She blinked and focused on her surroundings. The taper had burned low, and the cellar air was rife with the scent of tallow. As she inspected her patient, she recalled that earlier he'd thrashed wildly in the throes of fever. It had taken all of her strength to keep him still so he wouldn't hurt himself further. Finally, exhausted by his struggles, he'd slept. She had continued to bathe him with the water.

Butterflies fluttered in the pit of Kirsten's stomach as she studied him. The newly washed male features displayed character and an odd strength despite his vulnerable state. The stubble of beard on his chin, she noticed, did nothing to detract from his handsome face. But he was thin, too thin. She had a feeling he had suffered much, more than at his attacker's hands.

A faint scar ran across his brow to disappear into his tawny hair. Lines of pain were etched on his face, and dark shadows encircled his closed eyes.

Studying him, Kirsten was infused with a sudden warmth . . . a feeling akin to tenderness. Hesitantly, she reached out to touch him, stroking his brow and running a finger along his jaw. Boldly, she smoothed the hair from his forehead. She gasped when her hand was caught within strong masculine fingers.

She glanced at the man and found him staring at her, awake. Kirsten tried to pull free of his grip, but he refused to release her. She stifled a rising panic.

"*Mynheer*, how do you feel?" She smiled, very aware of the heat of his touch.

He relaxed his hold of her hand. "Sore," he admitted in answer to her question.

She studied him with compassion. "Are you thirsty?"

He nodded, and Kirsten wet a clean cloth and placed it on his lips, which were cracked and dry. Their eyes met and locked, and she felt a new tension in the air as she moistened his mouth and squeezed the cloth to allow water to trickle onto his tongue, down his throat.

Kirsten swallowed and looked away. "Can you sit?" she asked, filling a cup. She felt shaky.

"I think so." He struggled to rise, and she helped him. With her assistance, he sipped from the cup.

"That scarred man—who is he?"

He scowled. "I have no idea." His gaze became hooded. He lightly ran his fingers over her wrist, the simple act sending frissons of pleasure up her arm and down her spine. She couldn't help staring at him. He seemed unaware of the way he was touching her, of the effect his touch had on her.

Kirsten flushed and looked away.

"It was you in the woods." The soldier's deep-timbred voice played havoc with her senses. She nodded. "Thank you for saving my life."

She withdrew her hand from his grasp. "It was no trouble."

His mouth formed a wry smile, one corner of his sensual lips curving upward. "You make a habit of rescuing strange men?" He chuckled at her look. His eyes were a warm shade of brown; she found their russet color striking. His gaze grew tender as he caressed her cheek. She enjoyed feeling his fingers against her skin, and she realized by his look that he enjoyed touching her.

"I'm glad to be alive." He shifted and winced with pain. "I never thought it mattered," he murmured, then stopped upon seeing her expression of horror, as if realizing he'd said too much. The soldier fixed her with his gaze and offered her a wan smile. "What were you doing in the woods at that hour?" Suddenly, he caught his breath and cried out, his face turning a ghastly shade of gray. "Sorry . . . I'm not up to conversation, I'm afraid."

Immediately concerned, Kirsten rose to her knees. "Don't talk," she urged. "Rest. You've had a bad time."

It was dark in the cellar with only a single candle, its wick sputtering in the melted tallow. The man lifted his hand, grimacing with pain, and dropped it back to his side.

Sympathetic, Kirsten took his fingers in her grasp. "You're burning with fever again!"

Dipping the cloth in the kettle behind her, she turned to find him struggling to see her, his eyes unable to focus. "Relax," she soothed. "I'm here, and I'll take care of you."

He lay limply while she bathed his face and neck.

"You're Dutch," he mumbled, his words slurring together. He closed his eyes.

"Yes. I'm a Van Atta." She said it with pride, for she was descended from the Hoppe family who had settled and built Hoppertown.

"A Van Atta," he repeated softly. He sounded amused.

"And you are?" she asked.

"Richard." He hesitated, as if debating whether to reveal his identity. "Richard Maddox. But you mustn't tell anyone." His forced laughter prompted a fit of coughing, and she had to hold him until the seizure passed. He lay back, his energy sapped, his breathing labored.

"That man—do you think he'll come back?"

"Not if he . . . thinks . . . me dead," he gasped.

Kirsten shuddered at the memory of the disfigured man. Richard Maddox was obviously a Continental soldier in an area presently occupied by British troops. He had every right to be wary of danger—wary of everyone, including herself.

Until the British grew tired of Hoppertown, no one in the village was safe. But she would shield and protect this soldier until he healed. With luck, the Britons would have left by the time Richard was ready to move on.

"Richard . . ." He didn't answer, and she thought him asleep. She caressed his bearded cheek, and he smiled, his eyes remaining closed.

"Kirsten?" he murmured drowsily, and she quickly withdrew.

"Yes?" She barely breathed, disturbed by the pleasure she felt at touching him, embarrassed by her own boldness.

His head moved, and he kissed her hand. She blushed, shocked by the sensations that flowed through her as his lips seared her skin, filling her with a strange warmth. "Thank you . . . for helping me." He sighed. His eyes opened then, and he smiled. "Angel," he whispered, his lashes fluttering closed again.

"*Mynheer?*" she said. When he didn't respond, she realized that he'd fallen asleep.

She felt an odd prickling sensation in her chest as she covered the sleeping man with a blanket. Something about Richard stirred within her feelings she'd never before experienced.

She stared down at him as she rose to her feet. Relaxed, he looked almost boyish. She studied his features . . . the long lashes that feathered against his cheeks . . . his lips, which were perfectly formed and very male . . . the tawny mane of hair that fell to his shoulders. She recalled the lean form beneath the blanket . . . his muscled arms . . . his flat belly . . . the firm feel of the flesh surrounding the wound on his thigh.

Heat rose to her cheeks. Startled by her thoughts, Kirsten tore her gaze from the wounded soldier and gathered up her things to leave.

Chapter Four

Concern for the soldier plagued Kirsten as she did her morning chores. Richard had been sleeping peacefully when she'd left him, but he had still had a low fever. She decided that she should check on him again before nightfall. Would she be able to escape from the house without raising her parents' suspicions?

The soldier's presence on the farm put their lives at risk. Anyone caught harboring a rebel soldier would be held accountable by the British, probably killed. Kirsten, therefore, thought it best to keep Richard a secret from her family. He was her responsibility, not theirs. If the British found him, she alone would suffer the consequences.

Kirsten had an opportunity to leave the house shortly after her father returned for the midday meal. In fact, it was her father who gave her the perfect excuse to go.

"The strawberries in the far field are ripe," James Van Atta said over the dinner table. "Kirsten, perhaps you'd like to pick some later, hmmmm?" He gifted his daughter with a bright smile.

Kirsten grinned back at him. "I'd love to." She

turned to her mother, for she still had some clothes to wash. *"Moeder*, you don't mind?" She hurriedly added, before Agnes could form an objection, "I'll do the *wassen* when I get back."

Agnes smiled at her husband and daughter. "Why not? I've been longing for strawberries." She placed a plate of *bollen* on the table. "But please, Kirsten, you must be careful."

"I will, *Moeder*. I'm aware of the dangers of war."

The older woman's expression lightened. "Be sure to take a big enough basket."

Kirsten nodded as she reached for a *bolle*. Biting into the warm bun, she had trouble concealing her delight at finding so easy an escape from the house. The strawberries grew near the mill; she'd be able to check on Richard.

When the Van Attas had finished their meal, Kirsten helped clear the table. Then, with her basket in hand and a smile on her lips, she left the house to pick strawberries.

The air was fragrant with the scent of wild flowers; the sky overhead was a glorious shade of blue. As she filled her basket with the bright red berries, Kirsten forgot the perilous times and the threat of the British in Hoppertown.

The sight of the mill ruins jerked her back to reality. This was a time of war, and a Continental soldier needed her. She hurried toward the cellar opening.

Richard awakened, his mouth parched with thirst. Daylight filtered through the cracks in the flooring above, relieving the gloom in the dark cellar. Vaguely, he wondered what time it was. There was no sign of Kirsten. Where was she?

He realized that he was hungry. Kirsten's satchel lay several feet away, where she'd left it. He smelled something in the air. Was it food? Had she brought him anything to eat? He tried to rise, but fell back, gasping for breath as pain ripped through his injured thigh. Dizzy, he lay still, sweat beading his brow, until his world stopped spinning.

"This is a fine mess you've gotten into, Maddox," he scolded. He hated feeling helpless! It was imperative that he regain his strength; he had a job to do. He couldn't stay here indefinitely.

Someone had tried to kill him, which shouldn't be surprising in time of war. Richard frowned. The man he was supposed to meet—Biv—having found out his real identity, had tried to murder him, which meant that the traitor responsible for Alex's death was someone within General Washington's own camp.

He'd been so close to discovering the treacherous link . . . Damn! He had to get to Washington. The general must be warned. Richard growled in frustration. He couldn't move four feet; how could he think of traveling the miles to camp?

While he was recuperating, he could trust no one, not even Kirsten. For all he knew she was a Tory, only pretending to be sympathetic to a Continental soldier. Her assistance might be a ruse to acquire information from him.

Richard recalled her soft urgent voice, her expression of concern. He shook his head. Kirsten, he decided, would probably never cause him any harm.

Just as he wondered how safe he was in his hideout, he heard a distinct movement outside. He froze, watching helplessly as the wood over the opening moved. When he caught a glimpse of silver blond hair escaping from a small linen cap, he relaxed. He observed Kirsten pull the boards back into place and then bend to pick up her basket.

When she turned, her blue gingham skirts rustling, Richard heard her gasp. He found himself staring. It was his first clearly focused view of his blond savior. Her hand fluttered about her throat as she gathered her composure before she approached him, smiling.

"You're awake," she said. "How are you feeling?"

Mesmerized by her lovely face and bright blue eyes, Richard continued to study her. She had full lips, a delectable shade of pink . . . a small straight nose . . . and the most disturbing but enticing look of innocence about her. She blushed under his regard. Intrigued, Richard grinned at her.

"I'm feeling thirsty," he said. "And hungry." His voice sounded husky.

Kirsten laughed. "That's wonderful! You must indeed be feeling better to think of food. After I check that leg, you can have what I've brought you to eat." She glanced teasingly under the linen square covering her basket, but when her gaze met his, twinkling blue eyes dimmed under his intent look.

"Is something wrong?" she asked. "Is it your leg? It pains you?" Setting down her basket, she knelt beside him.

"My legs hurts like hell, but I'll live." Richard winced when she pulled at the bandages. He shifted against the wall and was assailed by a strange, strong odor. "What's that foul smell?"

"Other than you, *mynheer?*" She glanced up from the exposed gash.

"I suppose it could be me, couldn't it?" His lips curved ruefully.

"It could, but it's not. The smell you mean is from those rags over there." She gestured to a small pile a

42

few feet away. "Your poultice."

Richard blinked. "You put that godawful thing on my leg? No wonder it burns like hell."

Kirsten stiffened. "It burns like hell, because you were stabbed in the leg with a bayonet. I assure you the poultice did more good than harm. It only smells because it's rancid—old."

As she spoke, she probed the wound gently. She was satisfied with its healing. Kirsten rebound the wound with a clean strip of linen fabric and rose to her feet. Collecting the offensive rags from the floor, she grimaced at the odor and then kicked loose the cellar board blocking the exit. She disposed of the rags where no one would stumble upon them and then returned to the cellar and her patient, who gave her a weak smile.

"Don't look so smug. The air in here is still not as sweet as it should be."

The man's face turned red, and she instantly felt contrite. She smiled an apology. He had been seriously injured and had no control of his condition. She'd help him bathe in the stream outside as soon as he was stronger. "Have you ever had *olijkoecks, myn*—"

"My name is Richard," he insisted.

Her face felt heated under his warm look. "Richard."

"No, what are olij . . . ?" He frowned, but his eyes sparkled.

"*Olijkoecks.* They are delicious batter cakes . . . and I've brought some freshly picked berries." She reached for her satchel and removed one of the cakes, which had become hard and unappetizing. "I'm afraid it is stale and won't taste very good now. I brought it last night, but you were too ill to eat."

43

"It will be fine," he assured her, reaching for the cake.

Kirsten watched the soldier take a tentative bite of the *olijkoeck* before devouring it. *He must be starving,* she thought. After lifting the cloth off the basket, she offered him the ripe, red strawberries.

Richard's eyes glowed with delight as he sampled the fruit. Warmth filled Kirsten as she sat back on her haunches. Watching him eat was pure pleasure for her. He popped a berry between his sensual lips, and a dribble of red juice ran down his chin. Kirsten had a sudden, strange urge to taste some of the sweet juice herself . . . to lick just below that masculine mouth. She shuddered, aghast at her own thoughts. Her breasts tingled, and she felt her belly turn over. Embarrassed, she looked away.

The light in the cellar room was relatively strong, and she could see the man clearly. His eyebrows were thick and darker than his tawny mane. There was whisker stubble on his square jaw in all shades of blond and gold. She met his eyes, which appeared to turn color, from russet to a warm golden brown. She was fascinated to realize that his eye color changed with his mood.

There was a small scar across his brow. *Where and how did he get it?*

Despite his present state of health, Richard appeared all male, with a power that disturbed her. Kirsten recalled the strength of his grip when she'd first found him. He might look slim, but his muscles were firm. When faced head-on, he'd be a worthy opponent to any man. But Richard Maddox had been hurt, he was ill, and evidently he hadn't eaten decently in a long while.

He was a stranger, but Kirsten felt as if she'd known him all her life. Richard stirred feelings within her that she couldn't explain. She was drawn to him, protective of him. While she'd doctored him, a bond had formed, a strong, intangible link that made her wonder if it was one-sided.

"Is there anything to drink?" His deep voice shook her from her trance.

"I'll fetch you water from the stream." She was startled to hear that her voice was hoarse.

Richard nodded, watching her closely as she went outside with the iron kettle. *Such a mystery this female,* he thought. She'd proven to possess courage. What had made her return to help him?

She came back with his water, hunkering next to him on the dirt floor, heedless of her petticoats and linsey-woolsey gown. He studied her face as she handed him a cup. Her lashes were long and dark, fluttering against her silken cheeks like the fragile wings of a moth. Their fingers brushed as she released the cup. Their gazes held fast. Kirsten offered him a trembly smile. Something kicked hard in the pit of his stomach.

He stared at her over the rim of his cup and watched her flush from the scooped collar of her dress upward.

"I have to go," she said.

"When will you be back?" He would be sorry to see her go.

"As soon as it's safe."

Richard frowned. "Tonight?" She nodded. "Why did you come today?" He could tell from her expression that she knew what he was asking. Why had she risked her safety as well as the discovery of his hideout?

"I . . . I was worried," she admitted, and Richard felt a jolt. "Last night you were in a bad way."

"About last night . . ." he said.

"Yes?" She refused to meet his gaze.

"Thank you."

She looked at him then, surprised. "You already thanked me."

"Lean closer," he urged. "I want to thank you properly." He had the strongest desire to kiss her.

She appeared confused, but she obeyed, apparently without thought.

Richard cupped her face with his hands and then kissed her, a tender soft meeting of lips that sent his heart tripping at a rapid pace.

"Why did you do that?" she gasped when he released her. He saw her flaming face and knew she, too, was affected by the kiss.

He grinned, pleased. "Why do you think?"

She rose, her basket in hand. "I must go," she said gruffly. She wouldn't look at him. "I'll be back tonight with more food and some of my father's garments for you."

He caught the hem of her gown, forcing her to meet his gaze. "He won't mind?"

She blinked. And then, to his amazement, she grinned. "He'll never miss them."

Averting her gaze, she muttered good-bye and slipped from the shelter. He watched her block the doorway, smiling, anticipating their next meeting.

A week later, in the middle of the night, Kirsten tossed and turned, trying to sleep. In a drastic change of temperature, the weather had become hot. The humid night air was stifling within her bedchamber. She'd left the door to her alcove bed open in an unsuccessful attempt to relieve the heat. Later, she'd discarded her bedgown; the thin linen had clung damply to her skin. Now perspiration dotted her forehead and breasts. Her hair, curling into moist ringlets, lay wet against her neck. She groaned, searching for a cool spot on the feather-tick mattress.

An owl hooted in the darkness, and a dog's bark echoed in the far distance. Kirsten gave up on sleep and sat up, blinking, as she heard the two o'clock call from the rattle-watch. Not a breeze stirred within the bedchamber. She glanced toward the open window and saw that the leaves on the old oak tree directly outside hung without moving.

She was so tired! As she'd expected, the sleepless nights spent at the ruin had caught up with her—time with Richard followed by chore-filled days. How could she not suffer from lack of sleep?

Richard . . . Her pulse raced as she recalled his kiss. She'd been unable to put it out of her mind, her reaction to it had been so strong.

She wanted to see him, to be certain that he was all right. It was impossible to sleep anyway when she could barely breathe in this hot room.

Kirsten rose from her bed and stretched, studying herself in the moonlight that filtered in through her window. Did he find her attractive? She gazed down at her small naked breasts, the curves of her hips and legs.

Good God, what was she thinking! She forced such thoughts away.

Kirsten reached for her dressing gown, taking it down from a hook near her bed and then slipping her arms into its voluminous sleeves. After a quick peek out her bedchamber door, she left her room to move quietly through the house. She crept past the door of her parents' room, silently praying that they, unlike her, were unaffected by the heat and were sleeping peacefully.

Kirsten breathed a sigh of relief upon exiting the

house. She couldn't forget the night when, over-confident about her ability to escape, she'd tripped at the bottom of the stairs, nearly waking her parents and giving away her nightly visits to Richard.

The night air was no cooler outside than in her room. Padding barefoot across the yard to the barn, Kirsten debated whether or not to ride Hilga. It was too hot to wear slippers on her feet, so the journey would be easier and faster on the gentle horse. Once inside the stable, she thought better of the idea. Horse and rider would be an easy target in the darkness. She'd be safer traveling as a lone figure on foot.

Insects buzzed and chirped in songful chorus as Kirsten followed the trail to the ruins of the mill. The after-dark sounds seemed magnified this night. Small nocturnal animals scurried through the brush, but the forest creatures didn't frighten her—it was the thought of meeting man.

The threat of British soldiers had ended two days ago when the troops had left Hoppertown, but she could never be too careful. There might be deserters about. British or Patriot, they would be dangerous. War-crazed and desperate, there was no telling what they might do to the unwary, especially an unprotected woman.

Kirsten's thoughts went to Richard. He wasn't expecting her tonight; there was a good chance he would be sleeping when she arrived. If so, she'd simply check to see that he was comfortable and return home.

Her steps faltered as she neared the mill. The memory of his kiss came back again; its gentleness haunted her. She continued along the path, recalling the tenderness of his caress. Would he make love as tenderly as he kissed? Or would he be a fierce, demanding lover? she wondered, and was immediately shocked by her musings.

Her dressing gown, which felt light and airy against her skin, suddenly seemed too sheer to be worn in male company. She'd been daring to wear it instead of her man's clothes, but it was so hot this night. *The garment is large and loose, and it's dark.* Surely, Richard wouldn't notice that she was naked underneath it.

She stopped in her tracks. She imagined the heat of his piercing gaze on her bare skin. The back of her neck tingled. Her heart thumped hard.

No need to worry. He isn't expecting you. He's probably sleeping. Kirsten moved on toward the mill, envisioning his brown gaze turning a golden color as he stared at her body.

Her nipples hardened in response to that image. *This won't do!* she thought, picturing how his lips would curve slowly into a sensual smile. She felt her legs weaken. No, this wouldn't do at all!

Kirsten admitted that Richard fascinated her. *Why?* It wasn't because he'd been charming to her lately. On the contrary, he'd become testy the last day or so, frustrated with his confines and the need to get about. Sympathetic to his feelings, Kirsten had tried to be patient with him. She understood that it wasn't easy for him to be trapped for hours on end in such close quarters.

A soft glow ahead drew her attention. She hesitated. Richard was awake! An inner voice warned her to go home and forget this visit. Anything could happen on this steamy, sultry night.

Nonetheless, anxious to see him, Kirsten ignored the warning and hurried toward the light.

* * *

Alex, it's great to see you! Have you heard from your wife Mary? Did she have the babe yet?

Alex . . . what's wrong? You look ill. Are you hurt? What happened? Alex? Alex! No! You can't die! I won't let you. I promised Mary I'd watch out for you.

I won't let them put you in that pit. You're going to live, damn you! You've got a wife and child to think about. Live! Damn it, live!

You British bastards! He was just a kid! You whoring sons of bitches! I'll see you pay for this! I'll see you belly-shot and hung before I'm through with you. Murderers! You swiving murders!

"I can't breathe!" Locked within the terror of his nightmare, Richard found himself at the bottom of a freshly dug dirt pit. "No, I won't let this happen."

It's hot! God, it's so hot! No! No! You haven't paid yet you bastards! No! No! "No . . . !"

Richard sat bolt upright in the dark, his breath rasping loudly in the night's quiet. His heart drummed painfully within his chest as he struggled to fill his lungs with air. He slowly became aware of his surroundings, his state.

Sweat dripped from his skin in dirty rivulets, along his neck and bare arms, on his chest. The air in the cellar hung heavily about him.

It was only a dream! he thought. *Thank God!* His terror, though, had been real enough. He blinked against the sting of tears. And his grief was real. It was no dream that his friend Alex was dead. That was a fact Richard couldn't change, although he desperately wanted to.

He closed his eyes and swallowed against a tight throat. *"Oh, Alex,"* he whispered, shuddering.

As if the floodgates had opened, the painful images rushed through. He was unable to keep them away. He saw Alex as a young boy; they'd been friends forever, since childhood, born and raised in the Pennsylvania Colony. A groan escaped Richard's lips as he recalled the times he and Alex had fished together at Barker's Creek. Alex, younger by three years, had looked up to him.

Trouble had never followed the gentle Alex as it had the more mischievous Richard, but Richard had always felt a sense of responsibility for his younger friend, a feeling that had not changed when Alex followed Richard to war. He had tried to talk Alex out of going; after all, Alex had a young, pregnant wife to care for. How could he leave her alone at home?

But Alex had been determined to go. Fired up with the Patriot cause, there had been no stopping him from joining the Continental troops.

Richard blamed himself in part for Alexander's death. Perhaps if he had stayed home and not joined . . .

If only the British hadn't raided Richard's grandfather's farm . . . If only they hadn't killed the old man, burned his house . . .

If only he and Alex hadn't become separated . . .

Now Richard was a Patriot spy, determined to find Alex's killer. He had taken his dead friend's place, working underground for General Washington.

Gentle Alex a spy? he thought. At first, Richard hadn't believed it when he'd been told by one of Washington's staff; Alex had hated deceit of any kind. But Richard had been informed that the war had hardened his childhood friend, and he had believed it to be true. That was the only thing that made sense.

As he began to breathe easier again, Richard thought longingly of the stream. He was thirsty. The running water would be cool and inviting to his parched throat. He groped for Kirsten's tinder box and tried futilely to light a candle. Tinder box in hand, he groped his way toward the blocked cellar doorway. The wound on his thigh throbbed, but he was able to bear the pain. Kirsten's attentions to his injuries had done wonders.

He missed Kirsten, he realized with surprise. Confined this past week, he'd come to enjoy her nightly visits. He'd hadn't kissed her again, but only because he'd controlled an almost irresistible urge to do so.

Shoving the boards away from the cellar opening, Richard stumbled outside. He inhaled deeply of the outside air. The night was humid and hot, but a welcoming change from the closeness of the mill's cellar. He returned inside to get a lantern. The moonlight allowed him to light the lamp easily, and he placed it on a rock near the streambed.

He dipped his cupped hands into the water, and then he drank, enjoying the cool wetness as it trickled down his throat. Next, he eyed the stream speculatively and decided that he felt well enough to bathe by himself. Until now he'd washed inside, Kirsten helping with a pot of water and bar of soap.

He grinned with boyish delight as he began to unfasten his breeches.

Kirsten slowed her steps as she came to the mill, for splinters of wood, rotting boards, and other debris littered the ground. She frowned when she came to the cellar entrance. The door was unblocked, and the soft glow of light she saw came from the other side of the ruin.

After checking the cellar's interior, she picked her way toward the soft illumination. The first thing she spied as she rounded the ruin was the lantern sitting on a rock. She scowled. How could Richard be so careless? Had he forgotten the dangers of war?

Kirsten scanned the tributary and found Richard several yards away, downstream. Her eyes widened. Naked, he stood in the current, cupping his hands and tossing water over his sleek, lithe body.

She stared at him in awe, heat suffusing her throat and face. She swallowed hard. She'd never before seen a man without clothes. The sight made her heart skip a beat, and a strange liquid warmth invaded the juncture between her thighs.

He was magnificent. He had filled out nicely with the food she'd brought him, and no longer appeared thin and gaunt. His sinewy back and tight buttocks appeared golden in the lamplight. His hair was wet and unbound, and the sleek, damp-dark strands that fell to his shoulders and back gave him a wild look that was extremely male. The water on his skin sparkled as it ran down masculine thews and tendons before dripping back into the stream.

A deep male groan rent the night's silence as Richard flung back his head. His expression of ecstasy fascinated Kirsten. She went hot and then cold beneath the filmy dressing gown as, mesmerized, she noted the sensuous pleasure Richard took in his bath.

Kirsten trembled with desire. She'd never before felt so womanly, so aware of another's body in conjunction with her own. The tips of her breasts tingled as they hardened against the linen fabric of her dressing gown. She froze, unable to move, unable to look away from Richard's naked splendor.

Her lashes fluttering shut, she lifted her hands to her blossoming nipples, felt the pebble-hard excitement of her body's response.

She opened her eyes and gasped when she experienced a pleasurable, erotic tightening in her womb.

Kirsten inhaled sharply. Richard had turned around, and she could see his shaft straining from its curly nest. He looked up and saw her. He did not seem surprised; perhaps he had been thinking of her.

Oh, God! she thought, aware that her face had warmed.

"Kirsten." His voice was husky, rich with meaning. His gaze flamed with desire as he strode from the water, his body dripping.

He stopped within several yards of her, studying her with an intensity that made her step backward in confusion.

"I . . ." Flushed with embarrassment, Kirsten didn't know what to say. She was startlingly aware of how her body had come alive, responding to Richard's look . . . his approach. "I have to go!"

"No!" He stepped forward and then checked himself when she stopped.

"Kirsten," he said, his eyes glowing, "come here."

Chapter Five

"You look well, *mynheer*." Kirsten wasn't surprised that her voice quivered; every nerve ending in her body hummed and trilled with life.

Richard laughed, the husky resonance vibrating in the distance between them. "I thought you weren't coming." He looked amused. "If I'd known . . ."

"I suspect you would have gone to greater lengths to shock me."

"Is that what I've done?" He gestured toward his naked body. "Shocked you?"

Kirsten's face flamed. "No. I'm a farm girl. I've seen too much of life."

"Oh?" A gleam came to Richard's gaze. He came toward her then with a look of intent.

"Stay back!" She panicked. She should have gone home! Hadn't she sensed a strange, new tension in the air this night? Why hadn't she listened to her own instincts? Why was her heart racing? Even as she acknowledged the danger of being near him, Kirsten felt a shiver of excitement shudder along her spine.

In several long strides, Richard was near enough for her to feel the cool dampness radiating from his wet skin.

"How are you feeling?" she asked. *Oh, God!* she thought. *Don't let me make a fool of myself!*

"Right now?" He chuckled, his eyes twinkling. "Right now I'm feeling fine . . . mighty fine."

"Richard—" She raised a hand to fend him off when he reached for her, gasping when she encountered the moist sleekness of his bare chest. Her fingers withdrew as if burnt, but his large hand caught hold of her wrist, placing her palm back on the damp skin.

"Say my name again," he prompted, pushing back the sleeves of her dressing gown with his hands.

"Richard," she repeated.

He smiled, enjoying the way she pronounced his name with the *ch* sounding like a *k. Ric-kard.* He studied her, marveling that she was here before him now, as if conjured from his dreams. She looked the picture of innocence and earthiness, seductive and alluring in her flowing robe. Her hair was loose, and the silver blond strands that fell to her shoulders caught fire beneath the glow of the lantern. Her skin looked dewy, her lips moist. Her blue eyes shimmered and grew round.

Richard couldn't stop himself from sliding one hand beneath her platinum tresses, from caressing the damp flesh at her neck. Her mouth opened, and the sight of her pink tongue between her open teeth made him moan softly.

She was so lovely! It took a great deal of his self-control to go slowly with her . . . carefully. He wanted to devour those pink lips, to bury himself in her silken body. She seemed to embody all that was innocent, good, and alive. A night in her arms would be heaven, banishing for a time his private hell.

He slipped an arm around her, impelling her against him with the hand at her nape, then lowered his head with lips parted, eager to capture her sweet mouth. She was so young. *Too young*, an inner voice cautioned. Ah, but she was all woman!

Richard felt her stiffen as the soft swells of her breasts pressed against his own hardness. He touched his mouth lightly to her lips. To his delight, Kirsten responded, melting against him, whimpering, her arms lifting to embrace him. He drank from her lips, sipping deeply of the honey inside. The taste of her was sweet. He'd been longing to kiss her again since that first day's brief, unsatisfying encounter. The reality of this experience far exceeded his expectations.

With his strong arms around her, Kirsten was unafraid to return Richard's kiss. Her robe was moist from his skin, the wet linen merely a thin film between male and female. She gasped as his mouth trailed hotly from her lips down her neck, nuzzling beneath the dressing-gown collar. Her hands fluttered against his back, and she arched her neck, encouraging him to explore her throat.

Richard's head lifted, and she felt his fingers on the buttons of her robe.

"Kirsten," he whispered. "I want to look at you."

She hesitated for only a second. "Yes . . ."

He made quick work of the precious buttons, parting the fabric and pushing the garment off her shoulders. As the robe fell to the ground, Kirsten experienced, for the first time, the excitement of having a man's admiring glance on her naked body. The knowledge that Richard found her pleasing to look at made her feel heady.

"Oh, Kirsten . . ." He cupped one of her breasts, worrying the nipple between his thumb and forefinger. "My angel . . . you're lovely . . . so beautiful . . ."

She was jolted by sensation as his lips encircled a tiny nub. She gasped, feeling all gushy inside, then sighed with pleasure when Richard's tongue laved her nipple before his mouth slid over to enjoy its twin.

"Richard . . ."

His head lifted from her breast. "Sh-h-h . . ."

He brought his finger up to stroke her bottom lip before he dipped inside to brush the digit across her teeth. Richard's eyes glowed with desire as he paid homage to the interior of her mouth.

Their eyes met as he trailed his hand along her jaw down her throat to recapture her breast, and his gaze held hers captive. Kirsten moaned, enjoying the magic of his touch.

Soon, a strange ache invaded her lower body. When Richard nudged her legs apart with his thigh, she accommodated him. The brush of his knees at the apex of her desire made her cry out and clutch at his shoulders. She felt she was drowning in a tide of sensuality.

The two clung in passionate entreaty, searching for that moment of sweet freedom. Lips met, opened; tongues thrust in desperation; teeth nipped lovingly.

As he lowered Kirsten to the ground, the wound in Richard's thigh throbbed, but he ignored the pain. The ache in his loins was far greater, and he sought relief from it with the woman in his arms.

Her eyes appeared round and trusting as he lowered himself on top of her. She felt so soft, her curves conforming to his maleness perfectly. He kissed the line of her throat, pleased when she opened her legs as if requesting that he further the intimacy. With a deep moan, Richard probed her feminine petals with the tip of his desire, until Kirsten cried out with denial and pushed him away.

"Kirsten?" The haze of ecstasy was receding from his brain. He cursed beneath his breath as he braced himself above her, wincing when the wound in his arm gave him pain.

Richard focused on the woman beneath him and was taken aback by the film of tears in her blue eyes. "Kirsten?"

She blinked, and he groaned with frustration. Carefully, he eased away from her and rose to his feet.

"Are you all right?" He extended a hand, aware of the hard pulsating core of him that still felt desire. He knew he'd been playing with the forbidden, but for God to have chosen to remind him in this way! He gritted his teeth as she accepted his hand, avoiding her glance as he helped her upright.

"I think I'm cut," she said.

He looked at her then, surprised. "Cut?" he echoed.

She gave him a weak smile. "The ground . . ."

Richard muttered a harsh oath. "Let me see." His breath hissed from his lips when he saw the small puncture wound below her right shoulder blade. He felt guilty, as if he were no better than a rutting animal. Good God, anyone could have happened by!

He found the culprit after a thorough check of the ground—a small iron nail protruding from a piece of wooden floorboard. He glanced at her with concern, pleased when she smiled in reassurance, secretly glad that her cry to stop had had nothing to do with the fear of making love.

"We'd best see it cleaned," he said, referring to her wound. "Come to the stream, and I'll wash it for you." He took her gently by the shoulder, though he wanted nothing more than to drag her back into his arms.

"I'm sorry," she said as she allowed him to seat her

59

on a rock near the water's edge.

"There's nothing to be sorry about," he replied gruffly. Reality had hit him hard, sobering his passion-clouded brain. He had no right to touch her. How could he have forgotten the situation he was in—this blasted war? He couldn't afford to become involved with anyone.

Startled by the sudden change in Richard's behavior, Kirsten gaped at him. He'd been so loving . . . so warm, but then . . . Had she somehow offended him? She knew nothing of a man's desire.

Kirsten watched wistfully while he retrieved her robe and thrust it in her direction with the words. "Cover yourself!"

Hurt, she blinked and turned away, clutching the dressing gown to her bare breasts.

Richard placed his hand on her shoulder, turning her to face him. "It's not what you think. Please try to understand."

"Understand what?" she replied, stung.

He sighed, closing his eyes. "It's too complicated to explain, little one, so I won't try." There was something in his eyes that tugged at her heart strings.

"Richard . . ."

He cleared his throat. "Show me your back and hold still, Kirsten, while I wash your cut." He dabbed at her cut with the moistened hem of the shirt she'd procured for him.

The wound throbbed, and Kirsten flinched. Richard apologized huskily for hurting her. He rinsed the shirt and bathed her entire back.

"All done," he pronounced. Then, he surprised her by placing a kiss between her shoulder blades.

"Thank you." She blushed as she turned to face him.

Richard watched, intrigued by the movement of her

lashes which flickered against her cheeks. His gaze went to her lips, and he felt a jolt of renewed desire.

"You'd best get home," he said.

"Yes, I suppose I should," she said. But she seemed reluctant to leave.

The imprint of her skin still tingled on his lips as she donned her gown and fumbled to redo the buttons.

"Here . . . let me help you." His tone was whisper-soft.

She glanced up, swallowing, and nodded. He hurried to fasten the robe, conscious of the urge to take her. His desire for her was still strong.

"Good night," she said when he had finished.

He bowed his head. "Good night," he echoed.

Once she had disappeared from sight, Richard picked up his breeches and began to dress. Sleep, he thought, would be a long time coming.

Once out of Richard's sight, Kirsten ran, heedless of her bare feet, her only thought to escape Richard and her tumultuous feelings for him. She was confused. The passion tightening her womb had been new and frightening to her.

It had felt so good being in his arms, knowing the magic caress of his lips. *But it was wrong,* she thought.

He was a stranger, after all . . . or was he?

She paused for a brief rest, gasping for breath. She was at the edge of the field not far from the mill. Here, out from under Richard's gaze, she allowed the tears that she'd held in check to fall freely. *I care for him . . . what am I going to do?*

Kirsten was mortified. What must he be thinking? She had offered herself like a wanton tavern wench, curling against him, purring like a kitten being stroked. The urge to return and demand an explanation for his behavior was great. The cut on her back hurt little compared to the strange ache inside her heart.

Straightening, Kirsten looked back down the path to the ruin. She shuddered pleasurably, remembering. On her breasts, Richard's hands had been large but, oh, so gentle! Her fingers rose to encircle a nipple, and her breath caught with the memory of his caress. That secret place between her legs grew damp, and her eyes closed as she imagined the feel of his intimate touch.

What she wanted of him, Kirsten didn't know. She was aware, though, that her body cried out for something only Richard could give her.

She was headed back toward the mill when a low feral growl froze her in her tracks. The hairs at the back of her neck rose as the rumble came again from behind her, loud and near. She turned slowly and saw two eyes beaming at her from the shelter of the woodland. There was a flash of white teeth as the animal snarled at her.

Kirsten feared she was in trouble.

Would the creature attack? Or would it tire of the game and run away? She waited, terrified, wishing she were back at the mill. *Oh, Richard!* she thought. If she were lying beneath him, she wouldn't now be in danger from this wild animal.

She breathed a sigh of relief when the beast moved forward into the moonlight. It was the Vandervelts' old farm dog, ordinarily a harmless canine.

"Koolsla!" she called to him, extending a friendly hand. Named after the cabbage dish he'd been found eating as a young pup, he was a mangy-looking mutt with big eyes. She beckoned him again, but the dog's back bristled menacingly.

"Koolsla! Go home, boy. Go home! It's Kirsten. Remember me? I won't hurt you."

The canine inched closer and growled, baring his teeth.

"Don't move, love," A familiar voice whispered. "The poor thing's hurt. There's no reasoning with a wounded animal."

"Richard!" she breathed and started to turn.

"I said, 'Don't move!'"

She froze, feeling the force of his anger hit her in thick, taut waves.

When Richard spoke again, his tone had softened. "Now, I want you to listen and obey me. No-no, love, don't be afraid. I'm here to help you."

Kirsten sensed when he moved; she saw him from the corner of her eye.

"I'm going to attract his attention."

"No!" She swung to him and then back to the animal, freezing when the dog began barking wildly.

"For God's sake, stay still or you'll get us both killed!"

"I'm sor—"

"Sh-h!"

Tears welled in her eyes. Richard was in danger because of her!

"Koolsla!" He tossed a rock toward the animal, and to Kirsten's surprise, the dog bolted in the opposite direction.

"Is it safe?" she whispered.

"For now." Richard moved up behind her and placed his hands on her trembling shoulders. She gasped as she was spun around. "God, woman," he rasped, "you scared the hell out of me! Don't you know enough not to tangle with a hurt and overexcited animal?"

63

An injured creature like you? she wondered. She should have known better, but she'd been careless, preoccupied with the memory of his kiss, his touch. She stifled the urge to clutch him tightly and beg him to love her.

A sudden fierce trembling seized her; and with a mild oath, Richard pulled her into his arms. She must have cried out, because he held her away. *He could've been killed!* Kirsten thought with horror.

"Oh, God, don't cry, sweetheart." He drew her against him. "I shouldn't have yelled at you, but I was frightened."

"And I—I—wasn't?" His tenderness was her undoing. She sobbed harder into his chest, and he cupped the back of her head with his hand, stroking her hair.

"It's all right," he murmured. "It's over, and you're safe."

Her body shook as she cried. What was the matter with her? She was not one given to crying, and certainly never one to carry on so!

Finally Richard released her and raised her chin with a finger. His gaze caressed her face before he kissed her deeply.

Moaning, she responded passionately, fusing herself into his length.

Suddenly Richard stiffened. "No!" He thrust her away, his expression tortured. "Don't look at me like that. I'm fighting myself, not you! We cannot get involved. There's this bloody war!"

She gaped at him, stunned. Then the pain eased with understanding. Richard wanted her, but was afraid! Afraid the pain would be unbearable if they became lovers only to have the war tear them apart.

She backed away from him, nodding in quiet agreement, but determined to love him at all costs.

He reached for her, his expression torn. "Kirsten, please try to understand—"

"I do understand." Her lips quivered as she tried to smile. "I have to get home." She hesitated. "Are you all right?"

To her relief, he nodded. In the horror of her encounter with the dog, she'd forgotten his injured thigh. He'd come a long way from the ruin; he must be in pain.

She eyed him with concern. "Your leg . . ."

"It's all right. I've been exercising it some each night."

She knew a sudden stab of alarm. "You're getting ready to leave?"

"Not yet." But the look in his eyes said, "Soon."

She bit her lip. "I'll see you tomorrow?"

He inclined his head.

"Good night, Richard," she said softly. "And thank you. I don't know what I would have done—"

"I'm only returning the favor," he replied, his voice sounding harsh. Then, he turned and walked away, taking the evening's magic with him.

Chapter Six

A summer shower fell on the Dutch village of Hoppertown, bringing the inhabitants relief from the heat. Kirsten stood at her bedchamber window, watching the rain as it saturated the earth, listening to it beating against the gambrel roof.

The yard below was awash with color, the June blooms in her mother's flower beds a riot of glorious hues. She found no comfort in the beauty outside; her thoughts were with Richard.

What am I to do? I've become obsessed with a man who'll be leaving soon, a stranger I'll never see again. Despite reason, she couldn't ignore her feelings for him. *I'll never forget him . . . never.*

Love? Was that having your stomach full of butterflies? An ache she couldn't name? She could understand his position. He had a war to fight; she'd just be a distraction in the bloody scheme of things. But, how could they deny what was so evident, this powerful attraction?

Richard said they couldn't become involved. Kirsten knew he was fooling himself. The glow in his russet eyes when he looked at her, the way his body hardened whenever she touched him, spoke the truth. It was too late—they were already physically and emotionally bound to each other.

And why not? she thought. *We could live for today and hang the consequences!*

She had moved from the window and was now flipping through the clothes stored in the *kast*. The next time she went to see him she wanted to be beautiful for him. She frowned at the meager selection of simple homespun apparel. Kirsten thought of the dresses that had been brought over from Europe, those belonging to her grandmother, others that were her mother's. The fancy garments were too grand for daywear, and Kirsten wondered if she'd ever have an occasion when she could wear one.

There is my Sunday best, she thought. The outfit consisted of a red and gold waistcoat, a scarlet petticoat, and a lace cornet head cap. She dismissed the idea. She'd never get out of the house wearing it, and if she did, her mother would be furious if she smudged or marred the fine ruffled hem.

She slammed shut the *kast* door, scolding herself for indulging in girlish fantasies. Richard wouldn't notice or care what she wore! She was kidding herself to think otherwise. She recalled the harsh way he'd left when she'd seen him last—two nights ago—and she decided that she was playing a fool's game in believing that he might care for her.

The best thing for both of us, would be to return to the mill and find him gone. She rejected the thought instantly. She wanted—needed—to see him at least one more time.

"Kirsten!" her father called from downstairs. "The rain is slowing. Are you coming? Your *moeder* and I are ready to go."

"Yes, *Vader,* I'll be right down!" She brightened. She'd forgotten that today they were going to

Peremus Kerk. The church not only served as a place of worship for the Hoppertown and Paramus communities but as a town meeting place and, on occasion, a hospital for Patriot soldiers. Today was not a day of worship but a time when members of the community were gathering to discuss how to handle the British when they returned. It would be a serious occasion for the adults, for the young a visit with friends.

Kirsten checked her gown and was satisfied with her appearance. She thought of Richard and longed to go to him, but her parents would get suspicious if she asked to stay home. The only thing to do, she decided as she peered into the looking glass and straightened her cap, would be to visit Richard later.

Peremus Kerk was an octagonal building located about a mile out of Hoppertown. The Van Attas' wagon pulled onto the dirt-packed turnpike, joining the procession of carts and buggies that meandered down the road. Some of the locals came on horseback; others had hitched a ride with friends.

Kirsten was enjoying the sights and sounds about her when suddenly she heard someone call her name. Glancing back over her shoulder, she saw Rachel Banta in a buggy two vehicles behind, waving vigorously. The Ackermans, directly in back, also hailed her heartily. Smiling, Kirsten returned their hellos.

No one would have known by the travelers' festive air that their mission was other than just a social gathering. Spirits were high with the temperature down, and with the Briton's leavetaking, there was something to celebrate.

As the Van Attas neared their destination, Kirsten saw the weathercock on the *kerk* spire. She was suddenly aware of the fact that the adults had become quiet. Only the children continued to babble with excitement. Soon, the youngsters were silent, too, noting the change in their parents' mood.

The vehicles pulled into the churchyard one by one, and the taciturn passengers alighted.

"Kirsten!" The hoarse whisper came from behind a cluster of trees that grew near the church entrance as she jumped down from the wagon.

Frowning, she glanced about and saw nothing.

"Kirsten! Over here." The last word rose with a croak.

She searched again and was startled to see her cousin Miles. She waved to him, before she turned to her father. "Vader? There is someone I need to speak with. I'll be inside in a moment."

James nodded as he helped his wife from the wagon, and Kirsten rushed over to see Miles.

"I thought you'd never hear me," he croaked, and she couldn't help chuckling as his voice broke.

"What are you doing here?" she asked, amused that her young cousin was finally experiencing the change that most boys of his age had already been through.

"Don't laugh." Miles glared at her.

"Oh, Miles. You so wanted to sound like a man, but you forgot you must be a frog first." She stifled a giggle.

"Kirsten, please!"

She apologized and then pressed him for a reason for his presence at the meeting.

His lips tightened. "My mother insisted we come."

"Aunt Catherine is here?" Kirsten was astonished. William Randolph, Catherine's husband and Agnes

70

Van Atta's brother, was a Loyalist, and everyone knew it.

"I told her it was foolish," her cousin said. "If my father finds out—"

"I know," Kirsten breathed. Her uncle was a cruel man when he was angry. By coming here, Aunt Catherine was placing herself at great risk. "Where is she?" She looked for her aunt.

"She's inside."

"Oh, no."

"Kirsten, *please*. You've got to help me. Somehow, we have to convince her to go home."

"But Miles if she truly wants to be here . . ."

"I love my mother. I don't want her hurt." There was a fierce light burning in her cousin's dark eyes.

The young woman sighed. "All right. I'll see what I can do. Maybe, after a time, one of us could pretend to be sick."

"Not me. Knowing how I feel, she'll never believe I'm not faking."

"Okay, me then." Kirsten grinned. "Come on. They're going to be starting shortly. Let's hope we can find seats together."

Miles looked worried. "Are you sure you want to sit with us?" he said. "Your father . . ."

The girl glared, halting his words. "You are not a Loyalist. And my *vader* is not the problem—yours is."

"I say it's time the people of Hoppertown do something to help the revolutionists!" John DeVore, a young lad of about eighteen, stood up from his seat across the room. "Or shall we wait until George's horned beasts return and rape our women!"

The boy's audience was a vast one. Several rows of

71

benches lined each of the eight walls, and each bench was filled to capacity.

"I agree!" Frederick Terhune chimed in from the front row. "We can't wait. Isn't it bad enough that the swine have threatened my poor Anna?" He was a portly man dressed in a green coat with silver buttons. His matching waistcoat and knee breeches along with his white stockings were made of silk. On his head he wore a gray goat's wig, powdered and in the latest style; the hairpiece looked ready to topple.

Murmurs filled the church as the villagers digested Terhune's remark. It was the first that Kirsten had heard of the incident. Curious, she glanced at the pale girl who suddenly become the cynosure of all eyes.

"What of the threat that's still present? What of the Tories?" The one who spoke was a gentleman Kirsten didn't recognize. "The enemy are among us, and we do little to crush them!"

"But they are our own flesh and blood!" a woman cried. "We have made our displeasure known. What would you have us do—commit murder?"

The comment caused an uproar. Kirsten glanced at her aunt and saw her stiffen. *Things are getting out of hand,* she thought.

It took several attempts by the *voorlezer*, rapping his fist against the pulpit, to regain peace. The man wasn't altogether successful, for an eerie disquiet had come over the group. Tempers simmered below the surface, and Kirsten heard the heated exchanges of neighbors and friends. She grew concerned.

Next, they would turn on her aunt. Catherine Randolph didn't deserve to suffer for her husband's loyalties. Kirsten's gaze went to her parents, who sat in the section across from them. She saw by her mother's expression that Agnes understood. Encouraged by that silent approval, Kirsten turned to her aunt.

She bent over, pretending to be sick. "Oh-h-h," she groaned, clutching her stomach. In the confusion about them, she hoped that no one but her aunt and cousin would witness her performance. "Aunt Catherine ... I ... don't ... feel well. I ... oh-h-h ... !"

"What is it, dear?" Catherine eyed her niece with concern.

"I don't know!" Kirsten gasped. "It must be something I ate." She cupped her mouth as if she were about to be sick.

"Oh, dear!" Catherine exclaimed. "We'd best get you outside—now. Miles!" The woman rose, and with her son's help, ushered her niece from the crowded church.

Once outside, however, Kirsten didn't know what to do. She was saved by Miles's quick thinking.

"Mother, is she all right?" he said. Kirsten secretly applauded her cousin's acting abilities.

"I'm afraid not," Catherine replied. "She seems quite ill."

Kirsten groaned for effect while holding her stomach. She must have overacted, she realized when she saw her aunt's eyes light up with suspicion.

"Perhaps we should get your mother—"

"No, no! I'll be all right in a moment. But *please* stay here with me for a while."

Catherine's eyes narrowed. "Perhaps Miles and I should see you home."

"Oh, yes!" Kirsten said a bit too hastily. "I should feel much better resting in my room."

There was a tense moment of silence.

Finally, Aunt Catherine chuckled. "You're a clever

73

girl, Kirsten," she said. "I'll eat my cap if you're truly sick."

"I . . . ah . . ." The younger woman flushed guiltily.

"Mother!" Miles said. "How can you say such a thing!"

"Miles Randolph," his mother said sternly. "Don't you dare tell me that this has nothing to do with me and your father!"

"But, Aunt Catherine, if Uncle William learns that you came today—"

"Don't fret, niece," Catherine said. "Do you think I'd have come if there was a chance he'd learn of this?" She stared at the two young people reproachfully. Then her expression softened. "So you decided to act on my behalf . . ."

Kirsten blushed. "I'm sorry."

"For what, child? For caring?"

Miles was impatient. "Mother, will you go home now or not?" he squeaked.

Catherine sighed. "After all the trouble you two have taken to convince me to leave, I suppose I had better go."

A short while later, Miles thanked his cousin for her help. He stood on the Van Attas' stoop, his eyes bright, his expression filled with warmth and respect for his older cousin. "You did it!" he exclaimed. "But then somehow you always manage to accomplish what you set out to do."

Kirsten smiled. "Not always, but usually," she teased. "You had best hurry and get your mother home before your father arrives there." During the ride to the Van Attas', Miles had confided that William Randolph had gone to visit a Loyalist friend.

The boy flashed a brief glance toward the waiting

wagon. "Can you make it tonight?" he whispered. His voice splintered on the word "tonight," and he cursed.

Smiling, Kirsten shook her head. "I can't. Not tonight." She immediately sobered. "But soon. I'll let you know." Her only desire this night was to see Richard.

"Let me know then," Miles told her, and she assured him that she would.

Suddenly, Miles hugged her tightly. "I hope you're not in any trouble."

Not because of either of you, she thought, her mind consumed with the image of Richard Maddox. She returned his hug and shook her head as they pulled apart. "I'm not," she said. "Don't worry. Now, get!" Kirsten waved at her aunt in the cart.

Miles returned to the cart, and the Randolphs left.

"I tell you, Randolph, it's the only way." Bernard Godwin inhaled a bit of snuff through his right nostril, before repeating the procedure with the left. "They're banding together. I've heard talk of a militia."

"It's true, William," said Edmund Dunley. "They're meeting in Peremus this very day."

"Do we have anyone on the inside?" William Randolph sat back in his chair and began picking his teeth with the edge of his thumbnail.

Dunley raised a pewter tankard to his lips. "Dwight Van Graaf," he replied before taking a healthy swig.

"Van Graaf," William murmured. "Good man?" When the other two gentlemen nodded, he said, "Then, what are you so concerned about? With Van Graaf as our spy, we can certainly handle a few

75

cocksure Dutch."

The three men sat in Randolph's study, avid supporters of the English king, George. English by heritage, they were satisfied with the way things had stood before the uprising, unable to understand what all the fuss was about. They'd paid their share of taxes to the King and yet had retained enough for a hefty profit. The land had been good to them, and so, too, they believed, had their mother country.

Randolph was a prosperous farmer, who gave gladly to the British troops. He was not only baffled by his neighbors' choice of sides, but his anger bordered on vengefulness.

Godwin and Dunely, his two cohorts, hailed from the Ramapo region to the north. Their motives were more clearly defined; they wanted to line their pockets with coin.

"You may be right," Godwin said. "But what of the forces coming from the south?"

"That's where Biv comes in, gentlemen," William replied with a wicked smile. "Now that the 'Mad Ox' is out of the picture, we have nothing to worry about."

"Are you sure the job was done? The man is dead?"

"So Phelps said. And you know Phelps." The man chuckled. "He so loves his work!"

A door slammed on the back side of the house. William rose from his chair behind a polished oak desk. "Gentlemen, I believe our meeting is over. Until next Thursday then?" He extended a hand to first one, then the other.

Voices could be heard in the corridor outside the study door. William frowned when he heard Catherine's laughter, followed by his son's shrill tone.

He threw open the door, surprising the both of them. Miles gaped in open-mouthed horror, while

Catherine blinked and then smiled in docile acceptance.

"Where have you been?" Randolph demanded.

"Why, William, whatever is wrong? I thought you were going to visit the Prevosts, so Miles and I decided to go for a ride."

The smooth way in which his wife offered an explanation took the wind out of Randolph's sails. "It was raining," he muttered gruffly.

"Good day, gentlemen." Catherine smiled at her husband's departing guests as she encircled his arm with a slim, white hand. "As you can see, dear, the rain let up, and I was feeling restless."

William was lost in his wife's guileless blue gaze, and one corner of his mouth curved upward. "Did the horses give you any trouble, sweetheart?"

His father's endearment brought a frown to Miles's face. He didn't hear his mother's response; he was watching William with the intensity of a hawk. His father's good humor was often followed by fits of uncontrollable rage.

Had his father learned of the church visit? Had someone informed William of his wife's betrayal?

Miles knew he'd have to watch his father closely—and guard his mother with an even closer eye. There was no telling what the old man would do when his temper finally erupted. The last time he himself had sustained a broken arm and his mother . . .

Closing his eyes, Miles swallowed thickly.

It won't happen again! he vowed silently. Never again would he allow his father to strike her . . . never again would his mother suffer!

Chapter Seven

Richard sprang up from beside the fire, his stance defensive as he grabbed for a log.

"Richard?"

"Kirsten!" He relaxed and dropped the chunk of wood. "You shouldn't sneak up on a body that way! You're lucky I didn't kill you."

Angered by his tone, Kirsten came into the firelight, her blue eyes blazing. He was in a wide clearing by the stream, a prime target for anyone. "You're the foolish one, Richard Maddox, having a fire. And here in this clearing! I'm surprised, *mynheer*, that you could be so ignorant! What if I'd been a British soldier? Do you think so highly of your skills that you can afford to leave your back unprotected!"

She was right, Richard knew, but it galled him to admit it. Twice now—no, three times counting the last when he'd been bathing openly—he'd been careless enough to lower his guard. A soldier—a spy—couldn't afford to lose track of the risks he was taking. To do so was placing oneself at death's door. It was a mistake, he silently vowed, that he wouldn't repeat.

He averted his glance. "You shouldn't have come."

"I know," she admitted.

At the husky resonance of her voice, Richard closed his eyes. He could see her clearly in his mind's eye . . . her shining platinum tresses that were silky to his touch . . . her luminous eyes that were the color of the sky on a sunny day.

The tension between them thickened as Richard threw a piece of kindling onto the fire, watching in fascination as the flames leapt and popped and crackled. His gaze met hers where she stood unmoving. He frowned. "Then, why did you come?" he asked.

Detecting no warmth or welcome, Kirsten swallowed against a painful lump. He was a beautiful man both in face and form. His light hair glowed golden in the firelight. He wore only his breeches, and her gaze riveted on his bare chest. His muscles rippled and moved with each breath. She blinked, and tore her gaze away as her heart began hammering within her breast. Her lungs felt tight with the need to draw air.

"Why?" she echoed. Kirsten looked up at him through long, thick lashes. "Because I had to . . . because I wanted to."

His mouth firmed. "Well, you can turn around and head home. I don't need to see you right now."

Richard took several steps toward her, his movements a testament of how disturbed he was by her presence. He seemed to stalk her as an animal would its prey. "Go, Kirsten. Leave!" A muscle pulsed near his temple. "Can't you understand that I don't want you here!"

"Fine!" she cried, stung. "So you don't want me! Well, I'm not finished with you, Mynheer Maddox,

80

and I don't intend to leave until I'm ready, so you can just go to the devil!" She spun from him, lest he should see her tears.

And after all she'd risked for him! She sensed his approach, and she whirled, her arms swinging. "Stay back, you *blather schuyten!* Leave me alone!"

"Kirsten, hold up." Richard grabbed her flailing wrists, but she broke free, clipped his jaw with her fist, and heard him mutter beneath his breath.

"Sonofabitch!" he growled when she struck him again. "Damn it, woman, stop hitting me!" Kirsten socked him in the arm and he bellowed in anger. "I said stop!"

As his cry echoed in the stillness, Kirsten sprang back, horrified at what she'd done. She raised a hand to cover her gasp of horror, her fingers trembling against parted lips.

His face taut, Richard clutched his arm, then rubbed his cheek.

"Oh, Richard! I'm so sorry!" She made a move toward him, but then stopped, afraid.

He shook his head and stared at her in astonishment. "Are you finished?" he said, his voice dangerously soft.

She nodded vehemently. "Yes." It was a whisper of apology.

His right arm bracing his injured left, Richard glanced down to check for signs of blood from his shoulder wound. The injury throbbed with pain, but there was no trace of blood. He winced as he carefully lowered his arm. The next thing he knew he was laughing. It began as a chuckle and built steadily to a full-throated roar.

"Damn if you aren't something!" he managed to gasp. He sensed Kirsten's shock, but couldn't seem to stop. "God, lady, what I wouldn't give to see you tangle with the general!"

Kirsten froze. Had Richard gone mad? She watched in helpless horror as he continued to chortle until his cheeks glistened with tears of mirth. "Richard?" She dared to venture one step closer.

His laughter eased, and he simply grinned at her, the wide stretching of his sensual lips making him appear boyish, appealing. He lifted his arm in invitation. "Come here, you foolish woman!"

Afraid to move, she shook her head.

"Don't tell me you're afraid of me? What do you think I'll do—retaliate? Hit back?" He chuckled. "What? And have you cripple me for life? I can only thank God you fought with your hands instead of your knees!"

Kirsten looked confused. Then her eyes widened with disbelief that he could suggest she'd hurt him in his tender man parts. "Oh no, Richard, I'd never . . ." The implication made her blush.

"Come here, Kirsten." He smiled, amused. "I promise you I'm not angry with you. Come here." His voice dropped to a husky entreaty. "Please?"

When he looked at her with such warmth in his russet eyes, how could she refuse? She approached him cautiously, her muscles coiled. She was ready to flee at any unexpected movement.

Richard noted her wariness with amusement, and his lips curved into a wicked grin. Damn, but she had a right to be wary! He was tempted to tease her, to teach her a lesson she wouldn't soon forget.

She had a damn good right clip, almost as powerful as any man's punch, stronger than many he'd had the pleasure of encountering. He pretended to glare at her, saw her start and then hesitate in her steps. His expression softening, he shook his head and beckoned her forward with his hand. His jaw hurt like hell but he had told her the truth. He wasn't angry; he actually felt proud of her.

When she came to within a yard of him, Kirsten paused, her chin down, her stance like that of a recalcitrant child.

"Oh, Kirsten." To her amazement, his voice was incredibly gentle. "What am I going to do with you?"

She gave him a wobbly smile. "Love me?" she whispered.

"Love." His tone was harsh. His eyes darkened to a deep troubled brown. "This is no time or place for love," he said gruffly. Richard reached for her then, encircling her slight form with his strong arms. After gazing for a time into her blue eyes, he groaned. "There's time only for this . . ."

He kissed her brow gently. Then his lips moved down to her nose, which he nipped playfully, tenderly, at the tip. "God knows why He made our paths cross, love." He kissed her cheek, nuzzled her neck. His breath quickened as he worshipped her throat.

"You're special, Kirsten Van Atta," he whispered as he raised his head, his russet eyes aglow. "Young . . . innocent . . . but more woman than child."

She could sense the restraint in him. He bent his head, his breath warm upon her cheek, and his mouth found her earlobe. His tongue swirled in the hollow of her ear.

Kirsten clenched her hands at her sides to keep from touching him, encouraging him. She felt confused, somewhat angry, while at the same time repentant for striking and hurting him with her fist. She shouldn't touch him; he'd rejected her, told her to go home. To caress him now would be like daring the devil. To kiss him now would be begging for heartbreak—and pain.

"Kirsten . . ."

His scent assailed her nostrils, its woodsy aroma tantalizing her. His skin was warm; his hands were gentle in their caresses. Closing her eyes, Kirsten tilted her head back. She shouldn't let him do this . . . she shouldn't allow him to . . . fondle her breasts.

Against all reasoning, she moaned softly in mindless pleasure as Richard cupped and palmed her aching flesh. Giving up the battle, she surrendered to the wonderful, pulsating feelings that flowed from nerve ending to nerve ending, that made her breathing uneven, made her heartbeat quicken. She raised her arms, settling her hands at his neck, beneath the thick, mass of hair bound at his nape. As she played with the soft silky strands there, she felt Richard's mouth everywhere . . . worshipping her neck, her ears, her face, following the movement in her throat when she swallowed.

"You shouldn't have come," he murmured, but he couldn't seem to leave her alone, not for a second.

Kirsten sighed with enjoyment. "But you're glad I did."

His head rose, but didn't say anything. She blinked up at him in protest of his stopping. He must have felt her dismay and shared the depth of her desire, for he groaned and captured her lips in a kiss that seared her all the way to her toes.

She opened her mouth to receive his thrusting tongue, imitating its movements with her own.

"Kirsten . . ." He tugged her with him to the ground, taking care that nothing hurt her, then pulled at the buttons of her homespun shirt. "What? No dressing gown? I liked your dressing gown." His eyes glowed and caressed each feminine feature.

The buttons came free one by one, but as the last opened, she covered his hand. "No, Richard."

"No?" He looked incredulous.

"You don't want me—you said it yourself."

"Hell, Kirsten, I want you. But love?" He scowled. "That's a different story."

"Get up, Richard."

"Don't fool me, woman."

"Me! I'm not the one whose behavior is in question. You turn hot then cold on me. I'm so confused!" She fought back tears. She'd never felt this way before; she was afraid.

"You want me." His tone was fierce as if daring her to deny it.

She nodded, her lashes fluttering against pale cheeks. "Let me up, Richard." She caught his gaze, saw something change in his expression.

He groaned as if in pain and then stood, presenting her with his back as she stumbled to her feet, fumbling with her shirt buttons. "Kirsten," he murmured, "I have to go." He faced her, his brown eyes searching the depths of her soul.

"Go!" She felt her chest constrict.

"I'm well enough to travel now," he began. "I have to get back. There are many who need me."

But what about me? she thought. *I need you! What about me?* She said, "So you're leaving Hoppertown . . . when?"

"Perhaps I should leave this night."

"When were you going to tell me this?" Her head lifted from the last of the buttons. She was angry. "You weren't going to, were you?"

He flushed. "I wouldn't have left without saying good-bye . . . and thank you." He shifted uncomfortably and studied the ground. Richard ran his hand through his tawny hair, tugging his club free with his awkward movements.

"You would have!" She sounded tearful.

He glanced up. "I wouldn't. I swear it! Although now, I wish to God I could have avoided this!"

"Well, pardon me, *mynheer*, if I make you feel guilty! This isn't easy for me either!"

Something moved in the woodland off to the right, catching Richard's eye, instilling alarm. "Hush!"

"I won't hu—"

He pulled her against him, clamping a hand over her mouth. He was conscious of her curves beneath the coarse muslin shirt, the full mounds that begged to be kissed and caressed.

Struggling, she bit his hand.

Richard cursed and regained his hold on her. "There's someone in the bushes, you little termagant! Bite me again and you'll be sorry!"

She froze and then slumped within his arms. "Act naturally when I let go of you," he warned her softly. "If they've seen us, we don't want them to know we've spied them."

"The fire!" she whispered when he'd released her.

"Forget what I said then and put it out—quickly! I'll get everything back inside."

Whoever was out there, Richard thought, was on the far side of the woodland separating the field surrounding the mill from the next one. They were probably unaware of him and Kirsten, a miracle considering the way he and she had argued. They? For some reason, he thought more than one person was out there. He hadn't wanted to alarm her, but this could be dangerous. He'd had no choice but to tell her.

Kirsten's hands shook as she ran to the stream, filling the kettle and returning several times from the bank to the fire to douse the flames. The water hissed and sizzled as it became steam.

"Richard, what of the embers? If they come this way, surely they'll know someone's been here."

"Get in the mill. I'll take care of it." He searched for the three-legged fry pan.

"What are you going to do?"

"Get rid of them." He began scooping up the coals in the pan. Sensing her presence, he looked up, scowling. "Didn't I tell you to get inside?"

She stiffened, and he sighed. "Please?"

Without waiting to see if she complied, he carried the filled frying pan toward the stream. He managed to get rid of the ashes in two trips. Before joining her inside the cellar room, he swept the area with a leafy branch from a nearby bush.

Waiting anxiously for him to join her, Kirsten began pacing the dark room. Who could be out there? The British? Tories? Just a friendly neighbor taking a walk? Come to think of it, the rattle-watch had been late making his rounds. Perhaps he'd only seen Garret Vandervelt moving from his last stop toward the next!

She scurried to her feet and moved to the doorway, her intention to relay her suspicion to Richard. She gasped, startled, when his form loomed in the opening before her.

"Kirsten! What were you doing?" He ushered her back inside, blocking the entrance, enclosing them in their own little world.

"Richard—out there—it may be the *klapperman* making his rounds."

"Afraid not, love. I saw them. In the clearing. They were definitely wearing bright red coats."

"British soldiers," she breathed fearfully. "How can you be certain?"

"I know George's men when I see them."

87

"What are you going to do?"

Richard drew her trembling form within the circle of his arms. "We're going to hide here and hope they don't find us." He stroked her hair, nuzzling his face in the silken strands. "We'll be fine, little one. As long as we stay here, we'll be just fine."

His quiet voice was reassuring to Kirsten. She felt safe and secure within his arms. Sagging against him, she listened to the sound of his heartbeat, enjoying the rise and fall of his chest as he breathed. His skin felt warm, comforting. He smelled so good and familiar to her. Content, she wanted to stay in his embrace forever. *But no doubt he thinks differently,* she thought.

Richard released her when she pushed herself away from him.

"There is something to eat," she informed him, keeping her voice soft. "I brought what we call *puffertjes*—they are cinnamon cakes—and some vegetables from our garden."

"You're amazing, woman." He was pleasantly surprised by her thoughtfulness. "What kind of vegetables?" It had been a long while since he'd eaten fresh vegetables.

"Peas and a *radijs* or two—radishes," she replied, and he heard the pleasure in her voice.

The thought of a tangy radish made Richard's mouth water. "We may as well get comfortable," he said. "It's going to be a long night."

Too long, he thought. How could he remain this close to her and not lose himself in her silken sweetness? When his eyes became adjusted to the lack of light, he could make out her form. She was sitting on the blanket on which he'd lain each night since his confinement. To his mind came an image of her lying there naked, all soft and willing, her warm hands touching him with passionate fervor. He heard a noise and spun toward the door in a raised crouch. His hand searched the cellar floor for a weapon and found the knife Kirsten had brought days before for his use. It would be a poor method of defense should they be discovered, but it was the only thing available.

"Richard?" She sounded scared.

"I think they're coming, love," he told her. "We must stay quiet."

Kirsten froze, the taste of fear on her tongue. She was afraid they'd hear the thunder of her heartbeat. Her ears picked up movement outside the ruin. A shuffling of feet. A man's chuckle. Footsteps clipping across the floor above.

Next came the low murmur of British voices, followed by the harsh exchange of angry words. Huddled with her chin to her raised knees, Kirsten was afraid to breathe. She buried her face in the crook of her legs, wishing Richard were closer, beside her, touching.

Something settled on her arm, and a hand muffled her startled gasp. It was Richard. She shuddered with a sigh of relief. Joy bubbled within her, brought on by his nearness, by the feeling of protection and security it gave her.

She relaxed, and he released her, his arm encircling her shoulders, pulling her against him. Kirsten went to him willingly, and the two strained to hear the sounds above them. *It is almost worth being in this dangerous position*, she thought, *to have him against me.*

"Shall we camp 'ere, sir?" someone said from the room overhead.

"Is it safe?"

Kirsten could picture the British officer eyeing the

room's rotting floorboards from the threshold.

"That beam looks sound, Major, but that one . . ."

"Perhaps we'll keep going as soon as I speak with that fool Biv."

Biv! Richard perked up, his ears tuned into the major's words.

"Who is this Biv, sir?"

And then, at the sound of splintering wood, "Sergeant! Get those two outside before the bloody floor caves in!"

There was a loud creak of buckling wood as the man complied. Then, "Sir? You were going to say, Major?"

"Biv, fool that he is, thinks he's a Loyalist. But the fact remains he's still just a colonial."

"Will 'e be 'ere soon?"

"Any moment now," the major informed his subordinate. "I'd get rid of him, but we may have need of him again."

"Whatever for, sir?"

"The Tories, Shadwell. We'll need someone to control them. Yes, I've heard he has the local Tories banding together. Later, these bands may be useful in taking the damn rebels unawares. If they kill one another, who cares? Biv and his kind aren't worth a damn anyway. They're all hoping that the King rewards them generously."

Footsteps sounded on the wood steps leading from the main floor of the mill building as the major and his underling joined the others waiting outside.

Kirsten released the breath she was holding. Richard gave her shoulder a reassuring squeeze. "Oh, Richard . . ."

He silenced her with a finger against her lips. She understood when she heard movement against the door to their hideout. Terror made her huddle against his breast. There was a *creak* as if someone leaned against the wood and then a clear and distinct British male voice.

"'Ey, mate! What do ye thinks down 'ere?"

Kirsten nearly gasped aloud.

"It's just an old ruin, Jake. It looks about to fall in, if you ask me."

"But what if the rebs 'ave something 'idden 'ere?" the man called Jake asked.

The answer he got was a short bark of laughter and some comment about God allowing the Yanks half a brain.

Kirsten heard with relief the sharp command from the men's superior officer and then disgruntled remarks as they moved away.

Neither man nor girl moved a muscle, waiting with apprehension for further noise. When none was forthcoming, they breathed easier, but Richard knew that the danger was far from over.

"I think they've given up and gone on, but we can't be too careful." He spoke in the softest of whispers. "It looks like we'll be spending the night here, Kirsten love. We can't risk leaving. There's no telling for sure where they've gone. For all we know, they could be camped just a hundred yards from here."

"But how can we stay trapped in here all night long?" she whispered fearfully. "What are we going to do?"

She could have bitten her tongue as soon as she asked the question. The air in the cellar room became fraught with tension. She was aware that he leaned closer to her, felt the warmth of his breath on her cheek. The hand that had been stroking her shoulder, glided sensuously down the length of her, slipped to her waist and than ran up and down, tracing the line of her rib cage.

91

Hundreds of nerve endings within her sprang to life, and she was once again overcome with breathless wonder. She shivered as his lips found the curve of her jaw, sensitizing her skin with kisses and gentle bites. His raspy breathing echoed the acceleration of her own lungs. She shouldn't allow him to do this to her! He was going to leave her, he'd said so! She was setting herself up for the worst kind of heartbreak.

But the way Richard gave her pleasure made denying him impossible. She wanted him. She loved him! And if loving him meant only one night in his arms, then so be it! She'd take her night and fight like hell to spend another with him.

"Will it be so very bad being trapped here with me?" he asked, his voice like silk. "I'm sure we'll keep busy. You seemed to enjoy my touch earlier."

"You don't want me," she murmured, trembling. "You—"

"Oh, Kirsten love, I do want you. Too much . . . too damn much! And if it weren't for this war—" He stopped, and then spoke again with more feeling. "I've tried fighting it. God, how I've tried! And I almost lost the battle two nights ago when you cuddled against me so sweetly."

He encircled her form with both arms, pulling her above him as he lay back. Her hair fell like a silver mantle, brushing his face with wisps of silk. He couldn't see her as he wished; it was too dark in the night-enshrouded shelter. But he could picture her as if it were daybreak. Her blue eyes would be bright with the light of love, her lips dewy and slightly open, and her platinum tresses would catch the dawn's light, brightening to white as the sun rose.

She inhaled sharply. She could feel the tautness of his muscles, could imagine the heat of desire straining against his linen breeches. His hands ran

92

the length of her arms, lovingly squeezing her through her sleeves, until they reached her wrists. His fingers played over her pulse points. And then his palms cupped her breasts.

"Oh, Richard." She was in danger of succumbing to desire. As his fingers fondled her breasts through fabric, they swelled to fill his hands. She reached out for his chest with her hands, exploring.

He stopped her. "No, love—not yet. I want you to feel . . . feel and enjoy." He undid each of her buttons until her breasts were bared for his loving hands.

"So soft . . ." she heard him murmur. "So sweet." He shifted beneath her so he could suckle her nipple. When one breast was wet with his kiss, his lips moved to sip deeply from its mate.

She moaned and arched to ease his position. His mouth was doing things to her she'd never thought possible. He moved again, sliding her a bit backward until his tumescence was cradled in the cleft between her thighs. As the tip of his staff pressed through his breeches, Kirsten gasped. Liquid warmth bathed her womanhood, and she experienced again a pleasurable ache that begged for Richard's touch.

"Kirsten . . ." His husky voice came from deep in his throat as he rolled them until they'd exchanged positions. "I can't wait much longer. Ah, woman . . . you feel like silk!"

His hands guided her breeches from her limbs, pausing now and then to fondle her legs. Instinctively, her legs opened, and she gasped and closed her thighs as cool air brushed against the warm wetness of her desire. She heard a rustling of clothing in the darkness as Richard shucked his breeches. Then she knew his hard, sinewy length as he stretched out above her.

"Kirsten, this may hurt," he gasped as his leg

insinuated itself between her thighs. "But only the first . . . time." His words sounded as if they came from between tightly clenched teeth. "Open up, sweetheart. That's it!"

His hard tip touched and teased her feminine petals. And then he was probing deeper and deeper, until she thrust upward, searching for . . . what?

He feels so huge! she thought, and knew a moment of fear. "No, we shouldn't!" She moved her head back and forth against the blanket, pushing against him, afraid.

"It's all right, love," Richard crooned. Taut with desire, he knew he couldn't stop; she felt so wonderful. "Easy now," he groaned, and drove into her deeply.

His kiss stifled her cry of pain. He forced himself to remain still, allowing her body time to adjust for him. "It won't hurt anymore, love. From here on in, it's sweet sailing."

Kirsten's eyes widened in wonder as, slowly, he began to move within her. The ache, the joy of having him touch her, intensified with each thrust of his male hips. Oh, something was building, growing inside of her!

She gasped and cried out as she climaxed. Her body went taut and then shivered deliciously. At that same moment, Richard groaned and spilled his seed into her.

Chapter Eight

"Are you all right?" Richard eased himself from the woman beneath him and drew her against his side. He cradled her head on his chest and allowed his fingers to play with her hair, enjoying the silken texture.

Kirsten nodded and nuzzled against him. "I am fine, *mynheer*." She stretched upward to place a kiss on his cheek.

Richard was only slightly relieved. The last thing he wanted to do was hurt her. He frowned. She'd been a virgin. It was too late; he had already caused her pain. He shouldn't have touched her! He had to leave on the morrow, perhaps never to return. He could never be the man Kirsten needed.

"Even if you hurt me—just a little," Kirsten murmured after a long moment of silence, "it was worth it. I have never before felt so . . . so . . ."

Richard couldn't help but smiling. "I know. It's never been this way for me before either."

"This is true?"

He could sense her surprise. "Yes," he admitted softly.

The two lay basking in the sweet aftermath of their

lovemaking. Trapped within the ruins, they shared their own private world. The soldiers might never have come there. The threat of the war seemed far away.

But soon reality crept in to haunt Richard, reminding him of the job he had to finish. While Kirsten slept, her naked form cuddled against him, he remembered the Briton's words. *Biv, fool that he is, thinks he's a Loyalist . . . I'd get rid of him, but we may have need of him again.*

Biv! Just as he'd thought! Biv was at the bottom of the treachery! Soon, Richard vowed, the bastard would meet his fate.

He must get to Washington's camp. This information was vital. Biv had had a hand in the attempt on his life. Was the man a direct link with the traitor who'd killed Alex?

Richard shuddered. For all he knew the traitor might now be laying a trap for Washington's army. He wondered if he could live with himself if this time with Kirsten meant the deaths of innocent young men.

Kirsten stirred in her sleep, and he tightened his embrace. Crooning softly, he rubbed her back until she settled back into a peaceful slumber.

Oh, woman, he thought. *What have you done to me that I'd neglect my duty for a night in your arms?* He ran a finger down her cheek, across her lips, knowing the exact moment when her mouth curved in joy at his touch.

She moaned and then opened her lips to draw his finger into her mouth. Richard drew a harsh breath when she tasted the digit, her tongue swirling about it with slow flicks.

He withdrew his hand to cup and caress her throat, before he captured her breast. Kirsten snuggled against him, her fingers splaying against his chest, discovering a male nipple, pinching it gently.

"Oh, girl!"

"What's fair is fair," she murmured groggily. When he retaliated by pressing a hand to the moist triangle of curls between her legs, Kirsten whimpered.

"Richard," she cried.

He laughed, the deep mellow sound becoming raspy when her fingers enclosed his rising manhood.

"We shouldn't, Kirsten, you—"

"It doesn't hurt much."

"Still, you're sore . . ." Richard hesitated, but the flowing tide of ecstasy was hardening his body, capturing his soul. He couldn't take her! She must be raw, he wanted it to be good for her. "I know a way, but you must trust me."

Trust him? Kirsten thought. She'd given herself to him. She trusted him with her heart . . . her life. "What shall I do?"

"Lie back." He slid down to kneel between her open legs.

"Richard?" Kirsten blinked and tried to see him. His hands skimmed over her thighs to the gateway of her desire. She arched off the blanket, shocked, when his head bent and his hair brushed against her legs. His warm, wet mouth kissed her intimately. She gasped. "Richard, what . . ."

He straightened. His eyes, glowing, held her gaze. "Trust me, Kirsten."

She did . . . and captured a moment of heaven in the arms of her Continental.

"Major! Sir, there's someone approaching!"

"Shadwell, get the men into position!" Major

Richard Thatcher was instantly alert as he barked orders, insuring the safety of his men and supplies. He stood outside the ring of the firelight, his small troop of men lining up, prepared to fight.

There was the pounding of hoofbeats.

"*Rea-dy* ..."

The soldiers hefted their guns into firing position.

"*Aim* ..."

Just then a lone figure on horseback came galloping through a break in the trees.

"Hold up, Shadwell. I think it's our man."

"Hold up!" The order was repeated for the line. A second command was issued, to keep position.

Suddenly wary of the soldiers' stance, William Randolph hesitated, his hands clutching the reins tightly as he pulled up his mount. But the horse, lathered by the gallop and the heat, reared, nearly unseating his master. Randolph skillfully brought the gelding under control and then his gaze fastened on the British commander.

"Major Thatcher?" he asked.

The man nodded, his expression stoic, and fingers of fear closed about Randolph's throat. The officer was a stern-faced individual of high rank, clad familiarly in the red coat and uniform of the British Army.

Randolph took off his hat and with his sleeve wiped his sweat-beaded forehead. After replacing his headgear, he climbed from his horse, his movements cautious. He was shaken by the lack of welcome. He'd not expected to be treated as royalty, but he'd hoped to have been greeted as a friend.

No one moved. The soldiers' muskets were trained on him as he approached.

"Major Thatcher." Trembling, Randolph held out his hand. When the officer made no move to accept the handshake, he lowered his arm, paling. "The King waits for his Queen." He saw that Thatcher recognized the passwords; and he smiled, no longer afraid. "I'm here to lend my services. I can be of tremendous help to you and your command."

Randolph extended his hand a second time, and this time—as if some message had passed between the two men—the major's hand lifted from his side.

"It's a pleasure to meet you, Major," Randolph said. "Please—call me Biv."

A warm breeze wafted in through the cellar opening, playing gently over Kirsten's bare back, lifting tendrils of her silver-blond hair. She stirred and then came awake in an instant at the feel of coarse wool beneath her, the absence of the alcove walls of her bed. A smile settled upon her lips, and she closed her eyes. Memories of the night infringed on her consciousness, making her body feel hot and tingly all over. She remembered Richard's touch, his kisses . . . his hard manhood entering her.

Kirsten rolled onto her back, searching for the warmth of his flesh, his muscled hardness. When her hand hit the empty blanket beside her, she frowned, then opened her eyes to find him gone. Her gaze went to the opening in the opposite wall, and she experienced a sudden, squeezing, gut-wrenching fear. The British—had they gotten Richard?

She scrambled to the doorway. There was no sign of him anywhere.

Her heart lightened. There were no indications of a struggle either, so wherever he was, he must be all right. She recalled his fierce determination to be on his way, and felt a jolt of alarm. *He's left me!* she thought. And after a glorious night of making love!

She fought back tears. *Oh, Richard, how could you have gone?* Kirsten sank to the ground, heedless of her naked bottom on the ragged boards of the makeshift door.

She sniffed. To catch a glimpse of heaven only to have it ripped away!

Curse you, Richard Maddox, you promised to say good-bye! She wiped her eyes and straightened her spine. Crying wouldn't bring him back. She would survive this; she was, after all, a mature woman of eighteen, and Richard . . . was the man she'd loved. But she would miss him!

Kirsten's lips firmed. She'd always known he'd have to leave. She'd surrendered herself to him anyway. Her pain now was her own fault.

Oh, Richard . . . why didn't you say good-bye? I never asked for gratitude. But, she realized, she'd asked him for more, more than he could give her. She'd asked for his love.

She stood, wincing at the stiffness of her muscles. Her body tingled wherever he'd touched her—and he'd explored her everywhere.

She gathered her belongings from the cellar room, folding the coarse blankets which had been Richard's bed . . . their bed of love. Next, Kirsten collected her basket. She began to cry when she spied the radishes, recalling his pleasure when she'd shown him what she'd brought.

But they'd never sampled the fresh vegetables or the cinnamon cakes. She caught back a sob. They'd become too involved in each other.

Without taking the time to dress, Kirsten moved about the cellar, wiping out all traces of Richard's stay. Soon, she stood with all her belongings at her feet, eyeing the shelter which had been their night's haven.

In a fit of anger, she picked up the iron kettle and hurled it against the wall. With a clank, the pot rolled into the corner of the room. Tears blinding her, Kirsten cursed, venting her fury.

And then she realized she was no longer alone.

Richard heard the commotion as he neared the mill. He became alarmed when he heard Kirsten's raised voice, and he threw down the wild flowers he'd gathered for her and rushed inside to see what had happened.

She stood in the center of the room, naked, muttering harshly in Dutch. She bent and, in her anger, began throwing things. Whatever she could get her hands on. A pot. A basket. Her tinder box.

Richard was startled. But soon the sight of her naked and beautiful, spitting like an angry kitten, brought him to the point of merriment. Eyes twinkling with good humor, he entered the room. "Kirsten?"

Taken by surprise, she spun about, and he saw her eyes widen in astonishment.

"Richard!" Her face became radiant with joy. "Oh, Richard, you're here!"

His chest was bare, and he was without boots. He wore the linen breeches that she'd "borrowed" from her father. The fawn-colored garment was loose in the seat, but fit him snugly in the legs where his thighs stretched the fine cloth taut.

Kirsten suddenly realized that she was naked. With a mild exclamation, she grabbed for her clothes and dressed. When she was done, she faced Richard and then flung herself into his arms. Her soft sobs filled the cellar room.

"Easy there. What's all this?" He pulled back to

study her. "Kirsten?"

"I . . . oh, Richard. I'm so glad to see you!"

"You act as if you thought I'd lef—" He felt a jolt. "You thought I'd left!"

She blushed. "When I woke up, I was alone. You were gone so long . . ." Her eyes flashed blue fire. "How could you scare me like that?"

Something squeezed his chest. He shouldn't have touched her. "Kirsten, you knew before we—before last night—that I'd have to leave." His voice was brusque.

She clutched his arm. "But not without saying good-bye! You promised you'd say good-bye first!"

He understood her pain. "So I did," he said, his tone gentling. "And I will. As you can see, I haven't broken my promise. I'm still here."

She didn't appear mollified by his reassurances. "You left and came back because you felt guilty."

Richard's eyes narrowed. "Guilty? Why should I feel guilty? You knew there was no chance of a future for us." He saw her flinch, and reminded himself that he'd only stated the truth.

"Curse you!" She came at him then in a whirl of fury. "Why did you have to come here, make me feel things I've never felt before! Yes, I knew!" Sobbing, she struck at his bare chest. "Why did I ever save you anyway?"

Crying, she hit him again and again. Richard stood, enduring the force of her blows, knowing that the pain of her fists was nothing compared to the anguish she was feeling.

Finally, he'd had enough. But apparently she thought otherwise. Despite his attempts to stop her, she continued battling him at arm's length.

"Stop it." Richard caught her wrists. "Kirsten, stop it!"

102

She sagged against him, and he thought if it were not for his hold she would have fallen.

"I'm sorry." She seemed ashamed by her outburst as she attempted to pull free.

Richard, sensing her new calm, released her.

"I apologize," she repeated. Her blue eyes pleaded for his forgiveness.

"You're no sorrier than I am." He muttered an oath when he saw how she whitened. "Not for making love, you fool woman." His tone became tender. "For causing you pain."

She cupped his face and caressed his smoothly shaven jaw. He was glad he'd used the razor she'd brought him.

"Kirsten . . ." He paused. "I have to leave. I can't stay."

Her hand on his face stilled. "I know."

"Love, forgive me."

She stiffened. "There's nothing to forgive," she said without feeling. "As you carefully pointed out, I knew beforehand that you'd leave when you were well."

He studied her tight expression, understanding the pain she was feeling, sharing the hurt because he himself didn't want to go.

She looked lovely and irresistible. He wanted nothing more than to lie with her on a patch of thick grass, to love her until those soft whimpers rose from deep in her throat. He loved the sound of those little cries.

Groaning, Richard captured her mouth, his lips hot and fiercely demanding. He enjoyed the taste of her, the scent of her; his staff swelled and hardened with his desire.

Kirsten clung to Richard as if her life depended on holding him forever. He was going to leave! These moments would have to last a lifetime.

His head lifted. His russet eyes were warm and glowing as he smiled. She returned his smile and saw his face change abruptly as he stared at her mouth. He released her, averting his glance as if unable to bear the sight of her kiss-swollen lips.

"You're leaving tonight," Kirsten said. The words were spoken without emotion, just as a statement of fact.

His gaze met hers as he nodded.

"Can I bring you supplies?" she asked and held her breath as she waited for his response. "Please . . ." She touched his arm.

"I don't know that it's wise—"

"Please. I promise not to cry and make things difficult." She squeezed his arm. "You'll need supplies."

He frowned. "You'll bring them tonight?"

She nodded and was rewarded when he agreed. *One more time,* she thought. *I'm going to see Richard one more time!*

"Kirsten!" Agnes Van Atta entered her daughter's room in good spirits. "Daughter, it's time to get up."

There was no movement behind the closed doors of Kirsten's alcove bed. Agnes frowned. "Kirsten!" She jiggled the door handles, gasping when they swung open to reveal a bed that hadn't been slept in.

"James! James!" she cried, running down the hall. "Kirsten is not in her bed. She's gone!"

James met his wife on the stairs. "Gone? Gone where?"

"How should I know? The foolish girl! Her bed's not been slept in."

"That does it!" he growled. "'Tis too dangerous

104

for her nightly escapades. Our daughter must be punished."

"Moeder?" The young woman's voice reached them on the steps.

James regarded his daughter with a scowl. "Kirsten, you've been out in the night. Miles again?"

She followed her father's gaze to her breeches. There was no denying that she'd been out when she shouldn't have been. She nodded, lying. *"Moeder . . . Vader*—I'm sorry."

"Hush!" Her father was angrier than she'd ever seen him. "Don't say a word, daughter. Go to your room!" He pointed toward the stairs. "It seems, young woman, that since you can't resist leaving the house at night, I must lock you in so you don't go wandering." He stared at her, scowling. "How could you foolishly endanger your life that way?"

"No, *Vader!* Please . . . don't lock me in!" She had to see Richard this one last time!

"I am sorry, Kirsten," he said gruffly, and she knew that no amount of pleading would change his mind. If only she'd had the foresight to rumple the feather ticks!

Eyes hot with tears, she climbed the steps toward her room. Lock or no lock, she had to get out. There must be a way to escape.

Dear God, please let me go to him. Please let me see Richard just one more time!

Chapter Nine

For the sixth time in an hour, Richard walked to the edge of the field, hoping to spy Kirsten. But, as on the first five occasions, there was no sign of her, and he returned to the clearing, disheartened.

"Fool!" he muttered under his breath. *I should leave now while I have the chance.* Seeing her again would only make things more difficult. He had enough food to last through the first two days of his journey. Why wait for supplies he didn't need?

Because you're not waiting for the supplies, old man, an inner voice taunted. *You're waiting to see her . . . Kirsten.*

He remained for a second hour before making the decision to go. He'd dallied too long already. Something must have kept her from coming; he couldn't wait to find out what it was. He was healed enough to travel—had been for a couple of days now. And it would be best to travel by night; the cloak of darkness would shield him from the enemy, making his journey to find his commander safer.

He took a last look about the old mill as he retrieved his satchel, and slipped the strap across his shoulder. As his gaze went to the cellar opening, his heart lurched. He'd never forget the sweetness of Kirsten's arms. His blond savior had made him feel things he'd never thought to experience. He'd never forget her.

He found a stick and went inside the shelter. Within seconds, he came out again and blocked off the cellar doorway. Then, with a wistful glance toward the field, he left, heading south, in the opposite direction from Kirsten's house.

Richard had said good-bye the only way he could. When Kirsten returned, she would find his farewell—a few words quickly etched into the dirt floor of the cellar.

Good-bye, love, his message read. Thank you.

Kirsten shook her bedchamber doorknob, only to find that her father had made good his threat to lock her in. Heart pounding, she hurried to the window to gauge the slope of the gambrel roof and felt a sinking sensation within as she she realized that trying to escape that way would not only be futile but dangerous.

Tears pricked her eyes. Richard was leaving, and she was unable to have her one last visit with him.

Oh, love! She'd promised to bring supplies; she'd promised to be there! When she didn't come, would he delay his departure for one more day?

She recalled with bittersweet pain their passionate lovemaking, the pleasure they'd found in each other's arms. It had felt so right, so wonderful! Surely, he'd thought so too!

"Please, Richard, wait for me," she whispered, "and I'll find a way to get to you." She climbed into her alcove bed, powerless to control her free-flowing tears.

He left! Somehow she knew it. She could sense him leaving, slipping away into the night.

Richard, you never said good-bye. Rising from the bed, she went to the window and looked longingly toward the stand of trees blocking her view of the field and the ruin beyond it.

"Oh, Richard," she sobbed, all hope of seeing him again vanishing. "You promised to say good-bye!"

The next morning she returned to the ruin and, as expected, found that Richard had gone. She saw the partially open door, but couldn't bear to go inside. She returned home, sad beyond measure.

The days that followed seemed empty to Kirsten, meaningless. Her parents had increased her workload, she suspected, in the belief that she'd be too exhausted at night to do anything but sleep. For a while, it worked; after so many chores, she was so tired at bedtime that her only desire was to rest her weary bones. Soon, however, Kirsten adjusted to the added labor, and she found herself lying awake at night, thinking of her lover . . . of Richard.

Two weeks passed without incident in Hoppertown. Kirsten's days went fast, but her nights were long and lonely. These were the times when she missed Richard the most. Her thoughts took on a carnal nature. Memories of Richard's lips devouring hers, of his callused palms on her breasts, and of his long, lean length crushing her to the blanketed ground returned to haunt her, invading her dreams when she did manage to doze off.

And, she became consumed with fear for his safety, wondering if he'd made it to wherever he was going. Where, he'd never told her. The fear gnawed at her, and her suffering began to show.

Soon she began to feel a new concern. She had lain with a man; it was possible that she was with child.

109

While she waited anxiously for the time of her courses, her eyes grew shadowed, her movements sluggish; and she could see her parents' increasing concern for her. *Dear Lord, what will I do if I carry Richard's babe?* She'd seen what had happened to a village girl who'd conceived out of wedlock. The young woman had been forced to leave Hoppertown. With her lover gone and her reputation ruined, no man would take her to wife. *The scandal,* Kirsten thought, *would kill Moeder and Vader.*

A few days later Tories arrived to disturb the peace of Hoppertown, and Kirsten was forced to put aside her concerns. She first learned of them from Miles. Her cousin had sent word begging her to meet him. Her door had been unlocked for over a week now. She left, knowing the risks she took venturing out at night, the consequences if she were caught. But Miles's note had sounded urgent. She met him at their usual meeting place in the forest.

"Miles." She smiled. She hadn't realized how much she'd missed her cousin until she'd seen him there anxiously awaiting her arrival.

His gaze met hers across the clearing. When he made no move to come forward, she went to him with a frown.

"You came." His voice was richer, deeper than before, all traces of boyhood gone from it.

"Did you think I wouldn't?" There was an odd light in her cousin's gaze that disturbed her. Since that day at *Peremus Kerk* where she'd seen him last, she had suspected that his voice hadn't been the only change in him. The innocent youth of her childhood had grown up, and something must have forced him to do it so quickly.

Kirsten waited, her tentative smile encouraging him to confide in her.

"I had no idea."

She waited with growing fear for him to explain his cryptic words.

"Something has happened," she said softly. "What?"

Her cousin's face seemed to crumble. "My father . . . Tories . . . A group of them coming to see Father."

Kirsten's brow furrowed. "Tories? How many?"

Miles sat down on the huge, flat rock, and a strange foreboding came over Kirsten as she joined him there. He seemed fascinated with a stone near his foot, kicking it, watching it bounce across the ground. Kirsten fought back a stab of irritation.

"I don't know," he said. "I heard Father talking with Mr. Dunley. He expects them any day." He stopped, raising his gaze from the pebble to meet her eyes. "They plan to use Hoppertown as their base of operations for a while. To build an army and—"

"Don't tell me. Let me guess. To crush the force of Dutch Patriots," she said, her voice sharp. She cursed at his nod, easily imagining her uncle's words.

Miles touched her shoulder. "Kirsten, I don't know what to do. I can't bear to see relatives and neighbors fight!"

"I know," she said. "Perhaps if I tell *Vader*—"

"No! You mustn't. If you do, Father will find out and he'll—" He clamped his mouth shut.

"He'll what?" Kirsten's tone was soft.

Miles shook his head. "Nothing." He begged her with his eyes. "Please . . . don't tell Uncle James."

Kirsten hid her shock. Her cousin seemed frightened, overly upset. "No. No, I won't if you don't want me to."

What had her uncle done to his own son to elicit such terror?

"Maybe there's something we can do," she said.

111

Miles brightened. "Do you think so?"

"Let me think about it." Kirsten offered him a smile. "Between the two of us, we should be able to think of something."

She silently prayed a solution would come to her quickly.

The Tories arrived at sunset during the last week of June. They entered the local tavern first to inquire as to the whereabouts of William Randolph. The innkeeper, who was Martin Hoppe, a distant cousin of Kirsten's, told the disreputable-looking group where to find the Loyalist. Unfortunately, the men did not immediately leave. They commandeered a table in the corner of the room, demanded to be served, then put up a ruckus when Martin wasn't quick enough for them. They were a sordid lot, their clothes dirty and sweat-stained, their unwashed bodies malodorous to those they passed in the common room.

The tavern was empty but for a few farmers and a family of six who had stopped for the night along on the way to the New York colony. Among the Harris family members was a beautiful, auburn-haired young woman with large green eyes and alabaster skin. She drew the Tories' notice instantly. She and her relatives were finishing their dinner when a few members of the ragged bunch sat down at the next table. The Harrises stood to leave, and Tom Harris, the eldest boy, eyed the men as his little brother and sister moved by them.

The lad's gaze narrowed when a Tory leered at his sister Megan. The lecherous man leaned over to whisper a suggestive remark in his friend's ear, and Tom clenched his fists, ready to fight. He saw red when the filthy scum extended his arm to block Megan's path.

"What's your hurry, pretty bird?" the offensive man said. He grinned wickedly as he reached into the pocket of his greasy, patched breeches and pulled out a few coppers. "Here. There's more where this comes from, if yer as pleasing on yer back as ye be to me eyes."

Tom went into a rage. "Tory bastard!" he yelled. He smashed his fist into the man's face and knew the pain of torn knuckles as he struck out a second time.

Chairs scraped across the floor as several Tories stood, and Tom saw the immediate danger to his family. "Get out!" he shouted to his mother. "Take Megan, James, and Mary, and run!" He ducked and swung wildly to keep two of the band from pinning his arms and rendering him helpless.

The local farmers came to Tom's aid, and the tavern erupted into a first-class brawl. Tankards sailed through the air to clank against the floor, tables overturned with a great rumble, while those too young or innocent to fight scurried for safety outside the tavern walls. There was a loud thud and a grunt as one Tory smashed into the wall before he slithered, unconscious, to the rough, wooden floorboards. Crude curses and groans of pain filled the common room as Tom and the Hoppertown residents fought to subdue the Tories.

Tom and the farmers prevailed in the end. Battered but triumphant, young Tom Harris grinned his thanks to the men who had fought beside him.

The leader of the Tories shook his head as if to clear it as he rose from where he'd fallen against a table. Glaring at the victors, he helped a comrade rise to his feet. "Dutch *boers!* Ye've asked for trouble, ye 'ave. Ye 'aven't seen the last of us, mark me words!"

He waited at the tavern door for his friends to join him, and then he grabbed up a dented tankard and threw it through the window, causing the glass to crack and shatter. "Just a taste of what yer in fer," he growled.

"You bastard!" Tom rushed forward to retaliate, but Martin stopped him, catching him by the scruff of his neck.

"Leave him be, son," the innkeeper murmured. When Tom protested, he said, "Damn riffraff. Let them think they've got us frightened. The next time we meet, we'll take care of the Tory scum."

The band left, and Martin called a meeting. An avid Partiot, Tom joined in, wanting to see if he could help while his family remained in Hoppertown. When the discussion was over, Tom and the farmers went their separate ways. Each farmer had a message to bring to the residents of Hoppertown. Danger had come to the peaceful village, and before morning everyone would be alerted—and prepared.

A heavy thundering noise startled Kirsten awake. She blinked groggily and instantly came alert when she heard her parents' voices outside her bed-chamber. Throwing on her dressing gown, she left her room and joined her mother on the stairs.

"*Moeder?* Who is it?"

Agnes spared her daughter a brief glance. "James, who's there?" she asked her husband.

James Van Atta peered out the window. He held a burning taper for light. "Why, it's just a boy!" he exclaimed.

"A boy!"

"Is he armed?" Kirsten tried to see outside.

Her father flashed her a startled glance before

looking out the window again. The thunderous pounding on the door continued. "No, I don't think so."

"*Vader,* shouldn't we let him in?"

Kirsten's mother moved up behind her husband. "Is it safe?"

"There's only one way to find out," James said, and he threw open the door.

"James Van Atta?" the youth asked. A pair of anxious brown eyes gazed up at James from beneath an unruly crop of bright red hair. His white shirt and dark weskit with matching breeches showed signs of a struggle. The young man looked as if he'd been fighting.

"Yes, boy. What is it?"

Kirsten was the first to notice the boy's injuries. "Why, he's been hurt, *Vader!* Tell him to come in!"

The youth's knuckles were split and caked with blood; he had a long scratch on his neck and a darkening about his right eye.

"Come in, boy," James invited.

"Tom, sir. Tom Harris." He entered the house and then stood awkwardly for a moment. "Your cousin Martin sent me. He said to tell you about the Tories in Hoppertown." His brown eyes glowed with anger. "One of them molested me sister. That's how I got this black eye." He gestured toward the injured eye. "I tried to take him, I did. I would've had him too if there hadn't been more than five of them. Thankfully, I had help—a couple of farmers.

"We're staying at the tavern, sir," he continued. "Me mother and us children are on our way north to me aunt's in Albany."

"These Tories—what can you tell me about them?"

Kirsten drew up a chair for the boy, who flashed

her a a smile of gratitude before he made his reply.

"Not much to tell, I'm afraid," Tom said. "There's several of them—mean sonuvabitches." He blushed as if suddenly remembering there were ladies present.

Kirsten stifled a small smile when her father snorted. "Tom, did Martin say anything else?" she asked gently.

The lad nodded his thanks as she handed him a damp cloth. "There's to be more of them." He held the wet linen up to his swelling eye. "They're to meet here in Hoppertown with some man named Randolph."

Kirsten heard her mother's startled gasp.

"He said to tell you there's to be a meeting tomorrow morning at the tavern," Tom went on. "And for you to be there."

"And that's all?" James's expression looked like thunder. The boy nodded. "Are you sure?"

Tom was clearly taken aback by the man's sudden brusqueness, and Kirsten took pity on him. "I'm certain he's sure, *Vader*," she said softly. She turned to the young man. "Are you hungry, Tom? Would you like something to drink?"

James's face softened. "You're right, daughter. Where are my manners. Have something to eat, boy. You must be hungry after your run." He frowned. "Do you have more stops?"

Tom shook his head. "None, sir. You're my last."

Kirsten's father nodded with satisfaction. "Eat then."

"Come on, Tom." Kirsten lit a candle from her father's taper and helped the boy to rise.

"Kirsten," her father called as the two headed toward the pantry at the back of the house, "give Tom a glass of brandy."

The youth's face brightened. "Thank you, sir."

116

Left alone with her husband, Agnes gazed at him with horror-stricken eyes. "James, about William— what does this mean?"

"Damn him!" James cried. "Damn that rotten Tory bastard!"

"James!" She reeled with shock. "He's my brother!"

"He's a lying, murdering bastard!" He regretted the outburst when his wife began to cry. He drew her into his arms and stroked her back, trying to comfort her. "Agnes, I'd give anything in this world if I could stop this from hurting you."

He had an inkling of what William was planning, and the thought of it forced a chill along his spine.

"Can't you miss the meeting? Forget all of this . . . ?" She stopped when she saw the thunderous look on her husband's face.

"I'm sorry, wife, but that I cannot do." He regarded his spouse with a worried gaze. "Not even for you."

"Your name is Kirsten?" Tom asked.

Kirsten nodded as she set down a plate of *olijkoecks* and then took a seat across from him at the scarred dining table. She smiled. Her brow furrowed when Tom stared at her thoughtfully. "Is something wrong?"

"No . . . no." He shook his head. "It's just that I met this man." He paused, gazed at her unbound hair. Self-conscious, Kirsten raised a hand to tame the wayward strands.

"No, you couldn't be the one," the young man said.

Man? she thought with a scowl. She perked up. Richard? "Man . . . what man?"

Her heart raced and her breath quickened. *Calm*

117

down, she told herself. *You're being foolish. It couldn't be Richard.*

Tom picked up a cake from the plate before him. "What if you're not her? I promised not to tell anyone but her."

She sighed, annoyed. "But I *am* Kirsten, didn't I just say so?" Tom hesitated. "Oh, never mind!" she burst out impatiently. "It couldn't have been that important."

She rose and returned to the larder to pour Tom a measure of brandy.

"*He* seemed to think so."

"He?" Kirsten froze in the act of raising the bottle. Despite herself, her curiosity was piqued.

"We came across him south of here, near Elizabethtown. There's an inn there where we stayed the night."

Tom bit down on a *olijkoeck* and continued his story with his mouth full. "This fellow appeared to hear that we was heading north. He comes by the table just as I was leaving. The others—they'd gone ahead to our room."

Kirsten bit her lip as he took another bite.

"This fellow seemed friendly enough. And he was alone, too. So, when he comes over to my table, I thinks to myself, 'this man's harmless, you can talk with him.'"

Tom gave her a funny look. "Can I have that brandy?"

Kirsten became aware of the empty cup in her hand. She poured him his measure and plopped the drinking vessel before him with a thud.

"The man?" she probed, clearly irritated.

Tom turned beet red. "Oh, yes, sorry." The boy's face lit up as he took a sip, shuddering as the fiery liquid slid down his throat. "This fellow says, 'If you

118

meet a fair-haired woman with eyes the blue of the sky and her name is Kirsten, give her a message for me. Tell her I'm safe. Tell her I said good-bye.'"

Kirsten paled as Tom spoke. The man had been Richard! Her eyes misted, and the room blurred before her. Sending that message had been a dangerous and foolish thing to do, and she loved Richard for it.

"Are you all right?" Tom said.

"Fine." Kirsten rasped. "Thank you for telling me this." She met his gaze.

Tom stared at her and then shrugged. "You've got blue eyes and light hair, so you must be the right woman."

Kirsten had to silently agree.

Chapter Ten

On June 27, 1778, General George Washington gave orders to General Charles Lee of the Continental Army to assume command of the American Advance Corps scheduled to attack Sir Henry Clinton's British troops. Lee scorned the assault as unimportant, and the Marquis de Lafayette along with Anthony Wayne moved out to do the job instead. Upon learning that the command was to include some 6,000 men, however, Lee changed his mind, ranting and raving that the job belonged to him. Washington reversed his decision; by military courtesy the right of command belonged to Lee. Shortly afterward, Lee set off to take the command from the Frenchman, Lafayette.

Once in control of the troops, Lee made no real effort to prepare for the battle. He blatantly disregarded his superior's orders. At 10 A.M. the next day, Lee's army clashed with British troops near Monmouth Court House. Faced with the enemy's rear elements, General Lee ordered his army to withdraw. In so doing, he gave the British commander time to engage his main body of troops.

Richard Maddox, who had left Washington's

company in Hopewell only two days prior to the attack, was stunned to hear of Lee's obvious cowardice. He knew how much Washington had relied on Lee. The man's failure to valiantly command the Continental Army, Richard felt, was treachery of the worst sort. What should have been a strong advance on the redcoats had been a hasty retreat instead. Richard understood the gravity of the situation. General Lee should be held accountable for his actions.

Richard had infiltrated a band of Tory soldiers, posing as a Loyalist, when he received word of the Continentals' losses. If not for Washington's sudden arrival on the scene, the rebel army would have fallen. The American troops had managed to hold their own despite the sordid heat, a temperature of a hundred degrees.

After indecisive action at the center of the Continental troops, Clinton's army had pulled back. General Washington prepared for renewed attack. But when the black of night ended the day's fighting, Clinton's army was gone. They'd retreated in the cover of darkness. Word had it the Britons had marched toward Middletown and then had escaped to New York by boat.

Was it possible, Richard wondered, that Lee had made a deal with the British, that he'd been aiding the enemy? Lee had been a British prisoner for a time, captured by General William Howe at Basking Ridge. Lee had later been exchanged for British prisoners.

By self-proclamation, Charles Lee was a master at the art of war; why did he then bungle the campaign by calling a retreat? Especially when the Continentals had no trouble holding their own . . .

When news came of Washington's decision to

court-martial Lee, Richard silently applauded his chief commander. Such behavior in an officer was a disgrace as well as a poor example for the enlisted men. It could also mean grave danger to all in the Continental Army. Richard thought of the soldiers he knew and wondered how many of them had been there, how many had escaped death.

Glancing toward the Tory riding beside him, he felt a fierce hatred for his kind—Tories and the British troops that used the Loyalists to further their own ends.

This cursed war! So many dead! When would it all end?

When he'd first joined up with the Tory band, it had been extremely difficult for him to stand by and watch the havoc it wrought on innocent people. But the success of his mission depended on the Tories' acceptance of him.

The band had joined up with another force in their travels, and Richard Maddox, alias Ethan Canfield, played his part well, laughing as raucously as the rest of them. He took up their nasty habits like chewing tobacco and spitting on the ground. He gained a reputation for making use of the wenches. Amused eyes watched him each time he carried a struggling woman off into the bushes or behind a barn to have his rutting way with her.

Once out of sight, Richard immediately released the frightened ladies after obtaining their promise to remain silent. It was some consolation to know that by playing the lecher he was actually serving to protect the women of the cause. If it were not for him, he realized, more innocent young women would have been raped by these men. Instead, the men seemed satisfied to hear "Ethan's" description of the act, to enjoy his malicious delight in using his captives.

Richard had a knack for embellishing a tale, and the Tories hung on to his every word. He wasn't certain how much longer he could get away with this ruse, protecting some women with his "legendary prowess." Lately, there were some who were looking to benefit from his experience, having expressed a desire to join in "Ethan's" fun. So far, Richard had been able to convince them that he needed to work alone, and that he was unable to perform with an audience.

Kendall Allen, though, might prove a problem. The man hadn't been easy to convince; Richard wasn't sure he'd been successful with that one.

He chanced a look in Allen's direction and was dismayed to find himself the target of the man's black gaze. He touched the brim of his hat in a mocking salute to Allen. Merritt Abernathy on his gray gelding reined in to ride beside him, and Richard saw Allen scowl before Abernathy's bulky frame blocked him from view.

"Canfield." Abernathy was in awe of the tawny-haired man who was so obviously confident about his abilities.

Richard nodded a greeting. "Abernathy. I hear there's to be a raid . . ." He trailed off, waiting for Merritt to fill him in.

"Tomorrow night," the man confirmed, "Near Hackensack. From there we go to Paramus to join up with Biv."

"Biv?" Richard kept his excitement in check.

Abernathy bent his head as he patted his restless horse. "A local man with connections. He's promised us recruits." He sighed. "We lost two good men before you came to us, Canfield. And one during that last raid near Springfield." He regarded Richard through clouded eyes. "Ambushed by that damned

124

militia! I can't believe it happened."

Studying Abernathy, Richard almost pitied the poor fool. The skirmish had caused the death of Reinold Van Norden, Merritt's best friend. Van Norden had been Dutch, a Loyalist forced by his family to leave home and join the band. He recalled the pain of losing Alex and felt sympathy for Abernathy. Of the lot, Abernathy was the most cultured and likable. He had joined the Tory band not because of greed but because of a strict belief that the King should govern the colonies.

Richard studied each of the other members of the outfit—Allen, Abernathy, three brothers by the name of Greene, and a Hessian called Heinerman. Abernathy was the only trustworthy one. The rest took too much delight in vicious raids, in taunting the helpless. They were often more cruel with their captives than was necessary.

Richard's eyes twinkled as he met Abernathy's gaze. "In Hackensack," he said, "are there any women?" He slowly fingered the leather reins, stroking the worn straps as a man would caress a woman's flesh.

Merritt's laughter rumbled out. "Hey! Canfield here wants to know if there are women in Hackensack!"

The air was rent with guffaws and cackles as all but Allen turned to regard Richard with vast amusement.

"Don't worry, mate," said one of the Greenes. "You can bet your tail won't be wasted."

"That's right, Ethan! There'll be plenty to fondle with your 'ot, grubby paws!"

"Paws!" Richard Maddox placed his hand over his heart. You wound me deeply, sir!"

The remark brought on another chorus of snickers.

125

"You'd best 'eal quickly then, Canfield," another Greene brother shouted. "Sid couldn't possibly 'urt as much as the feisty claws of some dear lady."

Richard grinned at the leader of the group. "You could be right there." He smacked his lips noisily in anticipation.

Weeks had gone by, and still Kirsten couldn't forget her Continental soldier. When her courses came, she was both relieved and disappointed. The last thing she needed in this time of war was to bring an innocent babe into the world, but there was something riveting about the thought of holding Richard's child . . . a tiny someone they'd created together in love. Now she had nothing from her relationship with Richard.

He'd been gone for a long while, but he could have left yesterday, her memories of him were so clear. She yearned to hold him again, to feel his warm lips capturing her mouth, his hard body pressed against her.

Kirsten was in the garden, picking vegetables, when she remembered Richard's delight in the food she'd brought him. She recalled when he'd eaten the strawberries . . . the way the juice had drippled down his chin . . . her urge to lick it away.

Blushing, she straightened and, with basket in hand, headed toward the house. Would she never get over him?

She mentally scolded herself for her obsession with Richard.

"*Moeder?*" she called out as she entered the house. She set her basket of fresh vegetables on the tableboard and then found her mother in the parlor mending a shirt.

Agnes looked up at her approach.

"*Moeder* . . . are you crying?"

"Of course not." Agnes sniffed as she plied needle into cloth. "Why would I be crying?"

Kirsten stared at her with concern. "*Moeder?*" A heavy silence descended as Agnes continued to work her needle. The younger woman sighed and then asked, "Where's *Vader?*"

Agnes exclaimed as she pricked her finger. When her daughter murmured with concern, the woman began to cry in earnest. Tears fell unchecked down her pale, age-lined cheeks.

"I told him not to go, but he wouldn't listen!" She sobbed. "There's going to be trouble. I can feel it! He doesn't know William. He doesn't understand!"

"Are you talking about the meeting at the tavern?" Kirsten sat at her mother's knee. "You should not worry so. *Vader* knows what he's do—"

"No, he doesn't!" Agnes burst out, interrupting. "William won't forget. He'll get even!" She dropped her stitchery and caught hold of her daughter's hand, squeezing it painfully. "He always does! He'll hurt James, he'll hurt you!"

Kirsten straightened. "Nonsense, how can he hurt .us? We can take care of ourselves." Certain that her mother was overwrought, she attempted to soothe away Agnes' fears, but her words had little effect, for her mother was beyond listening.

"I'm going to Martin's," Kirsten said. She would learn for herself of the men's plans. Without waiting for her mother's consent, she slammed out of the house and hurried toward the barn.

Her father had left on horseback. Kirsten, however, hitched Hilga onto the wagon, and within minutes, she was guiding the mare toward the Hoppertown tavern. She parked the wagon a good distance away and crept toward the building's open window.

"I say that we should form our own army!" Huddled beneath the open tavern window, Kirsten recognized the hoarse voice. It belonged to one of the Ackerman boys—John. "We have enough able-bodied men here!" he said. "Why should we rely on General Washington's army to provide protection? When was the last time Washington and his men stayed here? A month ago? Two months? Three?"

"He's right!" someone shouted, and a chorus of male voices agreed.

"But if we fight, who's going to farm in our absence?"

"We're not asking you to leave Hoppertown, Banta," John Ackerman said. "You'll be free and on hand to bring in your own harvest. What we're needing is a militia of local men to guard what is ours!"

"Why not simply join the county militia if you want to fight? They're always looking for recruits."

Kirsten jumped when her father answered.

"I suggest we contact the proper authorities and let them know we're forming our own detachment," James Van Atta said with quiet authority. "All of you who feel you can leave Hoppertown are welcome to join the county troops wherever their activities lead them. However, we need several men to remain behind and set up camp near the village. There's an area north of Hoppertown Road that'd do nicely. Whether you leave or stay, your efforts to help the cause will be appreciated."

A cramp seized Kirsten's leg, and she shifted to ease her discomfort. She was proud of her father and of the way the others listened to him. No one had said a word as he spoke.

"What of Randolph, Van Atta?" Kirsten heard the high-pitched whine along with scraping of a chair across the wooden floorboards. She'd know that tone anywhere! Dwight Van Graaf was a thin man with a hawkish nose and pale blue eyes that Kirsten felt could see right through you.

"He's your brother-in-law—what do you think he's up to?" There was a direct challenge in Van Graaf's remark.

Silence fell over the common room as all waited for Kirsten's father's response.

"I've had about enough . . ." Martin Hoppe began.

Peering through the slit in the curtain, Kirsten saw her father raise his hand. "It's a fair question, Martin. If anyone else doubts my allegiance, let him speak."

No one made a sound, and Kirsten grinned.

"Van Graaf?" James asked.

With an awkward movement, Kirsten saw the man shake his head and resume his seat.

"I love my wife," she heard her father say, "but I also love this land and what it stands for. I'd hoped and prayed that it wouldn't come to this, but I believe, gentlemen, that we have no choice. If I knew what William was up to, I'd tell you. Unfortunately, I'm just like the rest of you, wondering what the bastard is planning and praying we can somehow stop him before his plans are realized."

Moeder, Kirsten thought, *will not be happy about this.* But she understood and agreed with her father. Satisfied with what she heard, she stood to leave. Pain shot through her leg as blood flowed freely whereas before it had been restricted by her position. She gasped and the tavern became ominously quiet at the thud made by her falling against the outer wall.

There was a shuffling from within and then the curtain was wrenched aside. Kirsten found herself the object of several suspicious male gazes as men peered at her through the open window.

"Kirsten!" Her cousin Martin was the first to recognize her. "What are you doing listening outside the window?"

Her face flamed as she encountered the startled gaze of her father. Anger darkened James's countenance, and Kirsten knew she was in deep trouble. *"Vader—"*

"You had better be able to explain yourself, daughter." His stern tone made Kirsten turn pale.

"I wanted to know . . ." she began and then hesitated as she experienced the force of the anger that emanated from the room's occupants. "I want to help!"

James seemed taken aback, and his daughter sensed it. To have his sincerity questioned by a fellow Patriot and moments later to find her eavesdropping on their discussion! "Help?" he said.

Kirsten nodded. "Help. And I *can* help, *Vader*. I can shoot, and I can organize the women . . ."

She stopped when she heard first one male chuckle and then another as the men laughed at the notion of women helping.

"Stop it!" Kirsten cried. "Do you think I—we—take this war lightly? Do you believe it is only your honor that is threatened by enemy troops? Who has more reason to fear the lecherous dogs than we do? Do you think I relish thinking of what they'll do to me if I am caught helpless?"

The men's laughter ceased abruptly. Kirsten glared at them, the light of determination in her eyes.

Now that she had their attention, her tone softened. "You tell us nothing and expect us to stand

130

by meekly while you decide our fates. I—we women—want to know what you are planning!"

She stared at each man present, hard. "There must be something we can do. Because we are women, are we to stay in our homes while you fight our battles?"

"We'll need a hospital," John DeVore suggested, and Kirsten smiled at him as she nodded.

"And a way to send word from family to family should the need arise," another man said.

Kirsten brightened as several others spoke of ways in which the women could help.

"Vader?" She caught James's attention as the men left the window outside which she stood to resume their seats. "I'm sorry if I've displeased you." She was hard pressed not to cry.

Her father studied her a long moment. "You have not displeased me, daughter." He suddenly smiled. "Go home, Kirsten. I'll talk with you later. In the meantime, try to help your *moeder* understand what has to be."

Kirsten nodded and then left for home.

Chapter Eleven

The Tories settled in on the Randolph farm, and word spread through the village quickly. With the news came stories of cruelty and recruits. The Loyalists were building an army, and they cared not if their soldiers were willing.

His fists clenched at his sides, Miles stared at the two men before him. William Randolph was angry with his son, and the other man, the Tory leader, observed the scene between son and father, seeming to take great pleasure, Miles thought, from the tense exchange.

"You'll not shame me, boy!" William bellowed. "We need you. England needs you!"

"I'll not fight my friends, Father."

William's closed knuckles struck the side of his son's face, and the youth reeled backward under the force of the blow. "You'll join the ranks or pay for your disloyalty!" the older man sputtered. "I'm your father. You'll obey me or—" He narrowed his gaze, and then an evil smile turned up the corners of his thin lips. "You love your mother, don't you, boy?"

Miles felt a jolt of alarm. "Yes, sir." *Damn you, you old bastard! Someday I'll take Mother away from here. From you and your cruel ways!*

His father's smile vanished. "I'll give you the night to reconsider Greene's generous offer." He gestured toward the man beside him. "If you should still prove disagreeable in the morning . . ." His voice dropped off ominously, his implied threat hanging in the air. "Do you understand, son?"

Miles nodded. *Don't call me son! I'll never be like you. I'll never admit to being your son!*

The two older men turned, and the man called Greene slapped Randolph's back. "You're a man after my own 'eart, Will," the Tory growled. William chuckled and the two moved down the hall, talking earnestly, oblivious to the hate-filled gaze of William's son.

Listening, watching him go, Miles felt a wave of revulsion for the man who'd sired him. He wouldn't join the Tory army, he vowed.

His shoulders slumped. But how could he not when the man had virtually threatened his mother?

Kirsten, Miles thought. He had to talk to Kirsten. Soon. Tonight. He hurried to his room and scribbled a note. Next, he gave it to their stable boy, instructing Jims to take it to the Van Atta farm.

Then, Miles waited anxiously for Kirsten's answer.

Kirsten was on the turnpike to the tavern when she heard someone beckoning her. She stopped and turned toward the sound. To her surprise, she saw Jims, calling and waving for her to wait for him.

"Jims," she said by way of greeting, and as the boy came closer, she saw the note and guessed its source.

"Good day to you, Mistress Kirsten." The lad smiled, then handed her the note. "Miles sent this."

Nodding, Kirsten accepted and unrolled the piece of parchment. She scanned the message quickly and then thoughtfully eyed the dark-haired stable boy. "Tell Miles I'll be there."

Jims inclined his head and started to turn.

Kirsten stopped him. "Jims?" The boy glanced at her. "Is everything all right at the Randolphs'?"

The youth's face darkened for a moment. "As right as can be expected, I 'magine."

She gave him a wry smile. After a brief inquiry and the ensuing exchange about Jims's mother, the boy left Kirsten to continue toward her cousin's tavern.

The urgency of Miles's note lingered in Kirsten's thoughts as she went on to the inn. Miles had begged her to meet him in the usual place. He'd told her it was a matter of the utmost importance.

Kirsten frowned with concern as she entered Martin's establishment. She anticipated the night, anxious to find out what was bothering her younger cousin.

Martin Hoppe came out of the back room as Kirsten stepped inside. He grinned when he saw her. "Kirsten. I see your *vader* has spoken to you."

She nodded. "He said you wanted to see me."

The innkeeper inclined his head and then gestured toward the back door and an outbuilding in the rear yard. "Come into the summer kitchen. I'm making *oblyen*." He saw Kirsten's eyes light up. "You would like one?"

"Yes, thank you." She loved the way Martin made the wafer-cakes. In fact, she enjoyed most Dutch sweets.

He smiled and helped her to find a seat in the cluttered workroom. When he had poured her a cup of cider and set a plate of fresh-baked *oblyen* before her, Martin placed a second batch of the cakes into

135

the brick oven and then turned to gaze at his young cousin.

"I have been thinking about what you said, Kirsten."

She blinked up at him as she took a bite. "About what?"

"About the women wanting to help. I have spoken to Margaretha about it, and she agrees." Margaretha was Martin's younger sister. She was pretty but frail, the apple of her brother's eye.

"I told her of my concerns, and together we thought of a plan," he continued. "She came up with the idea."

Kirsten paused in the act of chewing. "A plan?"

He nodded. "We were discussing what to do if we were attacked by British troops . . . how we could keep the children and"—he paused—"women safe. And we realized that we needed a shelter for all to flee to. That's when Margaretha thought of the Van Voorhees' place."

The Van Voorhees' farm was miles outside of the village—a huge brick structure that was solid and sound. Kirsten found Martin eyeing her intently.

"That would be a good place to hide the children," she said.

He didn't correct her by adding and women. He simply gazed at her and agreed.

"You want me to speak to the Van Voorheeses?" Kirsten guessed. There must have been some reason for his summons.

Martin shook his head. "I spoke with the family myself last night. They are Patriots—unlike those that have chosen to be neutral or loyal to the King. They have agreed to help us."

Kirsten was puzzled.

Her cousin grinned at her. "Can you not guess why

136

I have asked you here?"

She frowned and told him no.

"What would happen if the British attacked this day, this very second?"

"We'd be helpless," she said.

"Not entirely. But surely you can see the need to prepare." He drew a breath before he went on. "Kirsten, I need you to meet with the women and to decide how best to gather supplies to leave at the Van Voorhees' farm. Also, there should be some kind of system to alert each Patriot family should the need arise."

"I see," she said, her heart pounding with excitement. Here was work to help the cause! "You want me to handle this, be in charge."

"Yes. We'll need food and linens, clothes and utensils. We can't expect the Van Voorheeses to feed everyone for any great length of time."

She agreed. "We'll need medical supplies in case anyone is wounded on the way. And, if any of the militia men are hurt . . . It might be wise to bring them to the farm rather than the church."

Martin frowned. "I don't know about that. That's something we'll have to think about." He had gone back to his baking, and now he wiped his flour-covered hands on a linen cloth. "Come downstairs to the cellar. There are some things down there I want you to see. You might find them useful."

Kirsten followed Martin outside and back into the main part of the inn. The door to the cellar was in the winter kitchen attached to the tavern common room. Martin went down the steps first, his way lit by candlelight. Kirsten was close on his heels, watching her feet to avoid tripping on the wooden stairs.

The room smelled musty. At first, she could see nothing and wondered what it was that Martin had spoken about. Then, her cousin moved toward the far end of the cellar, and the glow of the burning taper lit up the corner.

Kirsten's jaw dropped open. Stacked in the corner were wooden crates of various sizes. At least twenty of them, she guessed. Maybe more. Her gaze shifted to the right, and she caught sight of several large barrel-shaped casks.

"How did you get all this down here?"

Martin looked at her. "We managed."

The cellar had a low ceiling. She could just stand upright, while Martin, she'd noticed, had to bend slightly for he was too tall.

"What is in the crates?"

"Fabric, guns, ammunition, and other necessities. The barrels hold flour and grain, as well as other foods preserved in brine." He hesitated. "For you," he said. "For the shelter."

She blinked up at him. "But aren't these supplies for the inn?"

He shook his head. "These are gifts, compliments of the British Navy." His teeth flashed white in the candle glow. "I've a friend south of here who's a privateer."

"Booty?" she said, and then laughed when he nodded, his dark eyes twinkling. "Wonderful! It's kind of George's men to be so generous with their things. Remind me to thank them someday." And then she and Martin began listing the supplies.

As Richard stared at the familiar landscape, his heart lurched. Kirsten was only miles away. He'd had no idea when he'd joined up with the Loyalists that his travels would again take him toward Hoppertown.

How was she faring? he wondered. A single day hadn't gone by since he'd left her that he didn't think of her, that he didn't recall the sweet scent of her, the taste of her soft flesh. The first days after his departure from Hoppertown had been the worst. She'd filled his every waking hour, her image consuming his dream-filled nights. After a time, the ache left by her loss had eased some, and he'd convinced himself that he was better off without her. His feelings, he was sure, had been rooted in lust. He'd been a long time without a woman, and he'd been vulnerable, ripe for her charms.

But the knowledge that she was only a short distance away now brought back memories of their time together, of the caring she'd given him while he'd healed. She had saved his life, so he simply wanted to show her he was fully recovered, to thank her one last time. The way he'd been forced to leave had been less than desirable.

"Canfield?" Merritt Abernathy interrupted Richard's thoughts. "We're nearly there. The Greenes sent word they've taken up residence on a farm belonging to William Randolph." Elias and John had gone on ahead, while Allen, Heinerman, and the others, including Maddox, had stopped for a time to rest and wait for word.

Randolph. Richard wasn't familiar with the man. "How long will we be staying?" Except for the brief mention of Biv, he'd come no closer to discovering the man's identity.

"Only a few days I reckon."

Richard was aware of Abernathy's stare and felt slightly unnerved by it. But the man's attention was only fleeting. Richard relaxed as they traveled on. He should be cautious, he decided. But he had to be careful his imagination didn't get the best of him.

*   *   *

The night was clear, but the moon was only a golden sliver in a star-studded black sky when Kirsten slipped from the house for her meeting with Miles. The temperature was mild; and the forest sounds were somehow soothing and familiar this night as she followed the path to the small clearing known only to her younger cousin and herself.

Miles was waiting when she arrived. His eyes lit up at the sight of her, and he rushed forward to greet her. Detecting anxiety and strain in his expression, Kirsten grew concerned. Heart thumping with anticipation, she followed him to their favorite sitting place and sat down beside him on the flat rock. She removed her linen cap and cradled it in her hands.

"What's wrong?" she asked after waiting several moments for him to speak.

He hesitated a moment, then said, "My father, he's been pressing me to join the Tories."

"Oh, no."

He nodded; his face went taut in the moonlight. "I don't want to go, Kirsten, but he's—" He stopped abruptly.

"He's what?" she encouraged softly.

"He'll not take no for an answer. I've got the night to think about it, and if I don't do it then . . ." Turning to face her, he grabbed her hands, clutching them tightly. Her cap tumbled to the forest floor unnoticed. "I'm afraid, Kirsten, afraid of what he'll do if I don't join them, afraid of what will happen if I go."

He drew a deep breath, releasing it in a shaky sigh. "Damn them all! Why are we fighting anyway? Why can't we live in peace?"

140

Kirsten stared at him with compassion. She understood the battle inside him, but she believed in the cause—the right to live freely without the dictates of King George. "What are you going to do?" she said.

"I don't know." He held her gaze. "I was hoping you could help me. I don't want to join that army. I don't want to leave Mother in the hands of that ba—" With a look of horror on his face, he clamped his mouth shut.

Kirsten felt shocked. "He's threatened your mother?"

Miles sighed, and his shoulders drooped. "He's hit her before, Kirsten. I won't let him do it again."

"My God!"

"Please—help me find a way out of this."

"Is someone pressuring your father?" she asked. "Why would he want you to leave when you do so much work on the farm?"

Miles looked thoughtful. "Well, there's a man—Elias Greene—he might be influencing him."

"Have you tried talking with Greene?"

Her cousin gave a bark of harsh laughter. "That animal? He's as bad as . . ."

Kirsten turned to stare at the forest thicket. "I'll talk with him."

"Are you mad? I can't let you do that! Besides what good would it do? He'll never listen to you."

"Perhaps if I appeal to him like a sister to you," she suggested.

Miles grunted. "The man is scum, so are his brothers. I can't let you speak with him. I forbid you to approach him."

Kirsten's hackles rose. "What will you have me do then?"

He shook his head. "Nothing. There's nothing

you can do, I see that now. I don't know why I've involved you in this anyway. It's a family matter."

"And what am I if not family?" She was angry.

"I didn't mean—what I meant was . . . Please don't be mad. I may need you to watch out for my mother."

"Then you intend to go with them?"

He blushed. "What else can I do?"

"Not go!"

"Then what do you suggest?" His tone was mocking. "Stand by while he beats my mother?"

Something in his voice caught Kirsten's attention. "He's hit you, too."

Miles nodded. "I can live with that. I can't abide his abusing Mother."

Kirsten hugged him. "I'm so sorry," she whispered. She pulled back, her eyes full of tears. "What if you come to us? My father will take the two of you in."

For a moment, his face brightened. Then a shadow fell and he gazed at her with despair. "He'll come after us. He'll kill your father, hurt you, hurt your mother. I couldn't bear that."

"Think about it," she pleaded. "Discuss it with Aunt Catherine."

"She'll not leave him."

"Why ever not?" Kirsten couldn't understand.

"Because she loves him. When he's not angry, he's most charming; and in his own distorted way, he actually returns her love."

"Oh, Miles . . ."

His eyes glistened. "Damned ugly state of affairs, eh?"

Kirsten nodded; and a short time later when they split up to return to their homes, she vowed silently to find a way to help him.

The more she thought about her cousin's dilemma, the more she felt the need to do something. Kirsten found little sleep that night after she climbed into her bed. Her mind was too active, trying to find a solution to Miles's problem. How could she keep Miles from having to leave without arousing his father's anger?

The only thing she could come up with was to confront the leader of the Tory army and somehow convince him that Miles was inadequate for soldiering, that he would be ineffective for their cause. But how? What could she say to get her point across? And was the man as bad as Miles made him out to be? Would she be placing herself in danger if she went to talk with him?

She'd heard the Loyalists occasionally went to the tavern to drink Martin's ale and eat his food. The inn would be an ideal place to meet Greene. She'd be able to call out to her cousin Martin if she needed help.

Time was running out for Miles. Could she dare hope that Greene would visit the tavern for the morning meal? She hoped so. She'd have to visit her uncle's place if he didn't. Knowing what she now did about her own mother's brother, Kirsten thought she'd rather take her chances with the Tory leader, Greene, in the forest than in William Randolph's home.

The thought stayed with her when she dressed the next morning and headed toward Martin Hoppe's inn. Either luck was with her or her prayers had been answered. A group of Tories were in the common room of the inn.

Her hands were clammy, her heart thumping with fear as she entered her cousin's establishment.

Several heads swiveled in her direction. Her nervousness increased, but so did her determination to help Miles.

143

"Greene!" she called. "Is there a man here who calls himself Elias Greene? A King's man?"

There was the scraping sound of a chair as a large, hefty man rose from his seat. "You're looking at him, sweets. What can I do fer you?"

Kirsten's knees trembled as she approached his table, aware of the three men who sat around it. She wondered if some of them were Greene's brothers. "I need to speak with you, Mr. Greene."

His eyes glowed, and his mouth split into a toothless grin. "Come join us then."

"In private, Mr. Greene," she said sharply.

The man's amusement faded, and his gaze narrowed.

"Please," she added, softening her tone.

"Hoppe!" Greene called, and Martin came out of the back room. "The little lady here wants to speak with me in private. Got a place we could be alone?"

Martin glanced from Greene to his young cousin. He frowned at Kirsten, his expression questioning.

"May we use your back chamber, Mr. Hoppe?" she said. It wouldn't do for Greene to know that Martin was her cousin and thus would come to her aid should she need help. As her eyes met Martin's, she silently pleaded with him to trust her.

"Come this way," Martin said after several seconds.

Greene mumbled something to his friends, who laughed at what he said, and then he followed Kirsten into the workroom of the tavern.

144

Chapter Twelve

The back workroom was actually the inn's winter kitchen, where Martin and his servants baked during the cold months. During this time of year, it was used as a serving kitchen and storage room. Dried herbs hung from the huge wooden ceiling beams. Boxes and barrels were stacked in haphazard fashion about the floor. There was clear path to the door outside, for Martin needed access to the summer kitchen, an outbuilding several yards away from the main tavern. Dishes were stacked at one end of a long worktable, and tankards, which were newly washed, stood ready to hold the customers' ale. Except for the path which went straight through from the common room to the outside, the only other clearing seemed to be the space before a door leading to the cellar below.

Martin seemed reluctant to leave after he escorted Kirsten and Greene into the summer kitchen.

"Thank you, Mr. Hoppe," Kirsten said. "If we need anything, we'll call you."

Catching her look, he nodded, and Kirsten was sure he understood that he should stay nearby.

"So," Greene said. His gaze took on an unholy

gleam as he studied her from head to toe. He looked unkempt with his tangled red hair and untrimmed beard. His fingernails were dirty, his clothes unclean. There was a large stain on his shirtfront, and several splatters of grease darkened his Durant breeches.

Kirsten shifted uncomfortably and motioned for him to sit down in the only chair in the room. She paced from one corner of the kitchen to the other, wondering how best to broach the subject. Finally, her resolve firmed, she stopped and met his intense green gaze.

"I understand you have a brother, Mynheer Greene," she began.

He narrowed his gaze. "I do."

"Younger?"

He nodded.

"And I imagine that when you were children you looked after him."

"On occasion." He seemed impatient as he continued to watch her. She was conscious that she looked very feminine in her barley-corn gown. The dark blue and white squares in the fabric contrasted attractively with her light hair, and deepened the natural color of her eyes, or so her father had often told her.

"I have a cousin—Miles Randolph," she said. "I hear you're interested in him as an addition to your army." She hurried on under his intense stare before she lost her nerve. "I'm asking you to let him go, *mynheer*. He's just a boy without the stomach for fighting. His *vader*—my uncle—doesn't understand this."

Greene grunted. "He can pick up a gun; he can fight."

"But his mother needs him. The farm—"

The Tory scowled. "He put you up to this, did he?"

"No!" Kirsten denied, shaking her head. "He doesn't know about my coming to see you." In her anxiety, she clutched his sleeve. "Please, *mynheer*, I beg of you to forget Miles. Convince his *vader* that the boy would be better off at home."

"And where do yer loyalties lie, mistress?" Greene rose from the chair. "Are ye a rebel or loyal to the King?" He was in command of the situation and seemed to enjoy his power.

"I'm a Van Atta," she said. "I'm loyal only to myself."

He came toward her then, and she stepped back, suddenly overwhelmed by the strong, unpleasant odor of his unwashed body.

"You seem fond of yer cousin," he said, his eyes gleaming. "How fond, I wonder?" He stalked her about the workroom.

"What do you mean?" Her voice trembled as Kirsten fought back a rising panic.

"I'm asking ye to what lengths ye'll go to help yer cousin." He reached out to lift an unbound lock of her platinum blond hair. "I can be persuaded to help him . . ."

He grabbed her arm, and she gasped. She fought to break from his hold, but couldn't escape his powerful grip. *"Mynheer,"* she said, *"please* . . . let go of me." She heard the desperation in her own voice and was appalled by it.

Greene grinned. "I enjoy it when a wench begs. Please what?" He jerked her against him, forcing the breath from her lungs. "Ye're a soft bit of flesh."

His head lowered and she turned away so that his wet mouth glanced off her cheek instead of her lips.

147

She suppressed an urge to vomit when he dipped his head once again.

"*Mynheer!*" She wanted to shout, to scream for Martin, but in her fear her voice had lost volume.

"A wild thing," he growled. He pressed against her intimately. "Fight me. I like that."

"Leave me alone," she said in a strangled whisper.

"Ye don't mean that."

She found the strength to attempt to push him away, but was unsuccessful. "I said, 'Leave me alone.'" She was surprised at how firm she sounded just then.

Anger darkened his expression. "Ye want it, I can feel it. Tell me ye want it or know yer Miles will be the first in the line of fighting."

"No." Kirsten was aghast. How could she have allowed things to get so out of hand? Cousin Martin was in the next room. If she could just call him . . . She twisted free, elbowing Greene in the stomach. He grasped her arm and hauled her into his embrace.

"Bitch!" Greene's breath rasped against her cheek, before he bit her tender flesh. Kirsten gagged as he captured her mouth.

Repulsed and finding new strength, she fought him. "Martin!" she called, but knew she'd have to cry louder to gain her cousin's attention over the noisy patrons in the inn's common room. Her senses swam dizzily. *Martin*, she screamed silently. *Where are you? Help!*

She broke free and kicked out at Greene's legs. When her attack had no effect on him, she swung her fists at crates and barrels stacked on the wooden kitchen floor, dislodging them so they fell in Greene's path.

The Tory cried out when a wooden box glanced off

148

his shin. His green eyes turned dark with menace, his malodorous breath became rasping. He caught her by her skirts and dragged her toward him. Kirsten pulled back and heard the tearing of fabric. Suddenly, her bare shoulders were trapped by his bruising fingers. He jerked her against him.

"There," he gasped. "That's better. I've got ye now!"

Winded, she could only stare at him. He stroked her jaw, and she shuddered. He squeezed her chin until she cried out involuntarily with pain. Her alarm grew at seeing the change in his expression. The light in his eyes intensified, his nostrils flared with pleasure in the conquest.

"Martin!" she shouted. He clamped shut her mouth with his hand, and she continued yelling against his palm, her screams muffled shrieks.

Then Greene tugged her toward the cellar door. She thought of the dark, dank area below the common room and knew immediately what this brute had in mind for her. She feared not only being raped, but the Tory's discovery of the goods downstairs.

She was able to free her mouth. "Help!"

He caught her and kissed her into silence. With one hand between their bodies, he groped her left breast, pinching the fleshy mound. Her struggling body was pulled so tightly against him that she could feel his hardening manhood straining against her skirts.

Then, mercifully, she was free and tumbling to the floor.

Eyes closed, she lay gasping for air and heard male voices raised in anger.

She lifted her head, sought the source of the

argument, and was astonished by the sight of her savior. It wasn't Martin. It was Richard Maddox. Her beloved.

It took Kirsten a full minute to realize that something wasn't right, that Richard wasn't fighting Greene, that they were angry but apparently familiar with each other.

She gaped in horror as the men continued their argument. There was a tolerance between them that suggested these two were not opponents. *Richard . . . a Tory?* She felt heartsick. Had she been wrong to believe him a Patriot soldier?

She studied Richard, noting the change in his appearance, the rough stubble on his chin, his worn, dirty clothing.

Oh, God! Have I lain with the enemy? Had he tricked her, made her falsely believe he was a champion for the cause? Damn, but it looked that way.

"You!" she whispered, giving voice to her thoughts. "How could you?"

Richard stared at her, saw the horror in her expression, and realized what she must be thinking. His heart sank, but he could do nothing but continue the charade.

"You!" she said.

"Ye wish her for yerself," Greene spat. "I found her first. She's mine, Canfield."

"She is a child," Richard said, grateful that she hadn't called him by name, giving away his cover. "Let her go. She's barely worth the time. If it's a woman you want, I'll point out the worthy ones." He saw Kirsten's face contort and turned away, lest he reveal his own feelings.

150

The thought of Greene's hands on her lovely body made him physically ill. He had to convince Greene to leave her alone, but he couldn't let Kirsten know that he wasn't anything other than the Tory scum he was pretending to be.

"Go," he told her.

Greene stiffened. "No!"

Richard caught his arm and gripped it hard. "Let her go. She's not worth it." He enunciated each word carefully, with an implied warning. Then softened his tone. "I'll let you in on some of my fun with the wenches. Trust me. I know what I'm about. Here, you'll only anger the villagers and ruin our cause."

Greene looked at him for a long moment. Richard forced himself to regard the man pleasantly with a sly, conspiratorial smile on his lips. The Tory's mouth spread into a lascivious grin as he no doubt recalled Ethan Canfield's exploits. "Ye'll include me in yer games?"

The tension left Richard as Kirsten fled the tavern kitchen. He only hoped that she went directly home and did not remain to speak with him.

Greene was waiting. "I will show you how to enjoy the ladies," Richard said. He silently vowed to find another way to appease Greene later. No innocent woman would suffer at the man's hands.

Richard had to control the urge to beat the Tory leader to a bloody pulp, for the brute had touched Kirsten. And no one had a right to touch her but himself. He didn't want to think about the depth of his feelings for her. He didn't want to think at all. The only thing he wanted to do, dreamed about doing, was hold Kirsten and kiss her until she was breathless and clinging and moaning his name.

*   *   *

The shock of learning that her beloved Richard was actually a Tory instead of a Patriot soldier remained with Kirsten as she headed home. At Richard's command, she'd fled the kitchen, not waiting to speak with him, not stopping to glance at him, her only goal to escape.

As her footsteps conquered the uneven ground of the trail, Kirsten relived those horrifying moments when it seemed as if Greene's strength would overcome hers. She would never forget what it felt like to be vulnerable to a lecherous man's power.

She'd been so glad to be free at first, so happy to see that her rescuer had been Richard, it had taken her a while to realize the implication of Richard's arrival in Hoppertown . . . at the tavern. And when she'd seen the argument between Greene and Richard had lacked heat . . .

She hugged herself and quickened her pace. It was nearing the noon hour. The day was warmed by the sun, a bright orb whose yellow light filtered through the trees. She remembered the days Richard had spent at the old mill, recalling the heightened response of her senses to everything in the world around her, everything beautiful. Now with the knowledge of Richard's deceit came sadness, an awareness of the imperfection of her surroundings, a sensitivity to pain—her pain.

She glanced about and saw the scarred bark of an old oak tree, the leafless limbs of its dead branches. A breeze had picked up, rustling the foliage, tugging Kirsten's hair, and creating a chill down the back of her neck despite the day's warmth.

Richard, she thought. *Oh, Richard. How could*

152

you have lied to me? Was his name really Richard? Or had that been a lie, too?

Tears held in check during her months of loneliness fell now, soaking her smooth skin. Her throat tightened until the lump at its base threatened to choke her.

She sobbed out loud for a love lost, a dream destroyed. She felt used, humiliated, betrayed. How could she ever face him again? A part of her wanted to gouge his eyes out; another part wanted to lie beneath him and experience his tender, fiery touch.

When she arrived home, she went to the barn and took a shawl from a peg to cover her torn gown. A good thing, for her mother was sweeping the front stoop. Now Kirsten remembered the reason for her visit to the tavern. Miles. There was still the problem of Miles.

"Kirsten? Where have you been?"

"At the inn, *Moeder*."

Agnes seemed old beyond her years. There was a constant hint of sadness about her brown eyes now, caused by worry for her brother, her husband, and her child. "Is Margaretha ill?"

A good assumption, Kirsten thought. Martin's sister tended to be sickly. "No, I went to speak with Martin."

"Daughter, what is the matter?"

"The Tories," Kirsten said. "When will they leave? Why have they come?" she cried. Why did Richard join up with them?

"Kirsten, child . . . you are all right? Did something happen?"

The young woman looked at her mother through dulled eyes. "I'm fine, my *moeder*." She lowered her voice. "But I wish this war were over."

"The wench came to me," Greene said.

Richard studied the man over the worn table. Greene was deep in his cups, his mouth wet and slack, his eyes glazed and unable to focus. The two men were sitting with three comrades—Abernathy, Greene's younger brother John, and a new man, Samuel Joseph, recently recruited from the Hackensack area.

"What did she want?" Richard asked.

"To save her cousin, or so she said." Greene grinned. "I think she was enjoying my attentions."

Richard wisely held back a nasty comment, though his anger was intense.

"What's to be done when the old man wants his son to join us?" Greene commented.

"A cousin, you say?" Richard was careful to keep his tone light.

"Miles Randolph. A skinny whelp if ye asks me. Not worth his weight in coin, but since his pa's our host . . ."

"Ah!" Richard nodded with understanding.

"The old bastard gives me the shivers," Merritt Abernathy said.

"Randolph," the new recruit said. "I agree with you there. He's a way of looking right to your soul."

"Pah!" Greene said. "He's a fool, but a powerful one. There's nothin' to be afeared of." He glanced toward the innkeeper and raised his hand to draw the man's attention. "Hoppe! Another ale here!"

"Make it a round," John, Greene's younger brother, shouted.

Martin came for the empty tankards and then left to refill them. Moments later, he returned with mugs brimming with foam. After serving the ale, Martin didn't immediately leave the table.

"The girl," he said.

"She's gone home," Richard said, startled by the man's interest in Kirsten. Their eyes met, and Richard was surprised to see the venom in the innkeeper's gaze. What exactly was this man to Kirsten? he wondered. He felt a jolt of jealousy.

"Scrawny wench, right, Canfield?" Greene said. "Not worth the effort."

Richard inclined his head. The innkeeper seemed to relax, he noted, and Richard's feeling of jealousy grew.

"You want to eat?" the innkeeper asked. "Food's on. Full meal—five coppers."

"Five coppers!" Kendall Allen said. "Why that's robbery!"

"I'll eat and be glad to pay," Richard said quietly.

"And I," Abernathy intoned. Soon all agreed to buy supper.

Richard was thoughtful while he waited for his meal, thinking that concern for her cousin had brought Kirsten to see Greene, just as concern for him had caused her to save his life.

He knew what she must be thinking, knew the pain she must be experiencing because of him, but there wasn't anything he could do about that. He couldn't very well go to her and confess he was a spy for the Continental Army. He'd not only be putting his life in danger but hers as well—and the lives of Washington's men. If the Tories found out there was a Patriot in their midst, his work would be finished and so would he. He had to find the traitor—the one responsible for his friend Alex's death. Somewhere lurked an informant, a tie between General Wash-

155

ington's army and this sorry band of ragtag Loyalists. The success of his mission depended on secrecy.

He couldn't ease Kirsten's pain regarding himself—he knew she was in pain because he'd glimpsed it in her eyes—but he could help Miles.

This night Richard was to stay at the Randolph farm. The Tories wanted only able-bodied men. It would be simple enough to stage an accident.

Richard frowned. Kirsten wouldn't appreciate his methods, but it was the only way to keep Miles from being forced to join the Tory ranks. It wouldn't be a serious accident, just a small one.

Richard began to plan . . .

Chapter Thirteen

Word reached Kirsten of Miles's accident by way of the Randolphs' groom, Jims.

"He what?" she asked when he'd finished his tale. She couldn't believe she'd heard correctly.

"A crate stored in the barn loft fell on the young master, Mistress Kirsten. Broke 'is arm and hurt 'is ankle, but otherwise 'e was none injured."

Kirsten shook her head. "A crate in the loft, Jims?"

He shrugged. "A funny thing. I know nothin' about no crate. Never seen one up there, but then who's ta say with the bloody Loyalies about. They's leaving, though, I 'ear. It's not like we gotta worry for much longer. And good riddance, I say."

"Are you certain Miles is all right?"

Jims's brown forelock bobbed as he nodded vigorously. "'Is arm hurts 'im some and 'is foot, too, but 'e's right as a fox's tail."

Kirsten longed to visit with Miles, but knew that her cousin would never be able to escape the farm to reach their familiar meeting place—not with an injured ankle. She entertained the thought of going to the Randolph residence, but then she promptly dismissed the idea. The last thing she wanted was to cause an uproar between the families. Her parents might have allowed her to sit with Aunt Catherine and Miles at the *kerk*, but visiting the home of her Loyalist uncle was a different matter entirely. Besides, she wanted to avoid encountering that lecherous Tory leader, Elias Greene.

And Richard. It had been two days since she'd seen Richard Maddox, and the emotions she felt were both disturbing and overwhelming. She didn't trust herself to see him again. How could she could hate him in one breath yet long for him in the next?

Memories of their shared passion devastated her. She'd not seen him since the episode with Greene, but she could envision him clearly in her mind's eye . . . as he'd been by the waterside . . . his unbound tawny hair . . . his glowing brown eyes . . . his sensual smile as he'd left the stream to approach her . . . his body glistening from the cool, crystalline waters.

Kirsten's chest constricted with pain. She wished she'd never met him, that she hadn't gone back to the river to save his deceitful hide!

Liar, an inner voice taunted. *Those days with him were the best moments you've ever shared with anyone. Admit it—he may be your enemy, but you still love him. If he came to you now, you would willingly surrender to him.*

Love? Yes, she loved him, loved a man on the opposite side of the war.

And that is the real reason, Kirsten thought, *I can't visit Miles at his home.*

"Jims, can Miles make it to the river?"

The groom nodded. "With my 'elp."

"Can you bring him tomorrow? After the noon meal? At the clearing not far from the Ackermans'."

Jims agreed, and they went their separate ways.

*　　　*　　　*

Richard crouched at the edge of the Van Atta property and watched the house for signs of Kirsten. The Tories were preparing to leave Hoppertown the next morning. He couldn't go without seeing Kirsten again, without speaking with her, although he had no idea what he was going to say.

His plans for Miles had been successful. The boy had suffered a broken arm and a twisted ankle when he'd fallen under the weight of the crate. The crate had been almost empty. He hadn't wanted to seriously injure the youth. In fact, he hadn't been certain the crate would work. He'd been aware of the possibility of failure, for accuracy in timing and position had been imperative. Miles could have escaped totally unscathed, and Richard would have been forced to create a second accident and then another if that had failed until the boy was stricken from the ranks of the able-bodied. Fortunately, his first plan had worked perfectly.

It hadn't been easy finding the right equipment, carrying the crate up into the loft without someone seeing. He'd rigged up the accident with sticks and string and careful thought.

The barn loft had its own exterior door. The drop to the ground was substantial; someone trying to escape that way would have to jump at least fifteen feet to run for cover, a difficult feat when the yard outside was empty and wide open. Anyone trying to flee would surely be caught.

After deciding it would be too risky to remain in the loft to ensure his plan worked, Richard elected to stay in the barn but downstairs. Merritt Abernathy had spoken earlier of the fine Randolph horseflesh. It wasn't hard for Richard to learn that Miles came to the barn daily to attend his own mount, Dark Wind. It seemed the lad enjoyed grooming the horse himself each afternoon, often chatting with Jims if the groom happened to be there to tend the other animals.

Richard set up the crate so it would fall and then climbed from the loft to wait for his unwary victim. He'd pretended an interest in cleaning his flintlock rifle.

Richard's thoughts were forced back to the present with Kirsten's sudden appearance. His heart pumped hard, and his muscles tightened. He strained to see her as she exited the house and was fascinated by the way the sun glinted off her platinum blond plaits, making her appear an angel with a halo.

She wore a plain homespun gown of gray linen with a white muslin scarf about her shoulders. A matching white apron was tied about her small waist. The drab color and simple cut of the garment should have made Kirsten appear washed out and unattractive, but it didn't. Her beauty was enhanced by the contrast, her loveliness shining above the severity of the gown. A portrait of radiant grace, she left the stoop and crossed the yard, carrying a basket. The woman stole his breath away.

Kirsten must be on her way to the vegetable garden not far from the Van Atta house. Richard stared at the house, taken with the unusual Dutch design . . . the small windows with crescent moons cut into the shutters . . . the balcony that ran across the front of the house on the second floor. Except for Kirsten, he saw no sign of life anywhere. Not even a slave or servant.

He wanted to run to her, to lift her high in his arms. Chuckling, he'd spin her around and around until she was dizzy and laughing and the world whirled by her in a blur of colors.

He would stop then and bring her slowly back to earth. He'd lower her so that she brushed close against him, their bodies touching. And they'd both become aware of how well they fit together, like two halves formed into one. Their world would right itself. They'd gaze into each other's eyes with laughter lingering on their lips and their hearts singing with joy.

And then they'd kiss. Everything about them would cease to matter as their passion ignited and they clung to each other fiercely, unwilling to relinquish the ecstasy of the moment.

Richard had become immersed in a daydream so real that for a moment he actually believed it was happening. But with the freshening of a summer breeze, reality set in. He saw Kirsten in the garden, oblivious to his presence as she bent to pick tomatoes from the tall, lush bushes planted in neat, even rows. He stared at her clothed buttocks, his palms itching to cup their curves. His desire for her was hot and instantaneous. He sensed the bulge in his breeches and heard the wild thundering of his heart.

Drawn to her by a strong force, he came out of his hiding place. As he headed toward the garden, he realized he was playing with fire, but he couldn't stop himself.

No one came out of the house as he passed it. He tried to cool his ardor, for what would she think if she saw?

Fortunately, Kirsten still hadn't seen him, and he paused, breathing deeply to calm himself. He thought of winter . . . cold water . . . anything to keep him from making a fool of himself by grabbing her and kissing her hungrily.

He was more composed as he continued on, until

he was at the edge of the garden. Kirsten glanced up as if sensing his presence. A startled look flickering across her face, she straightened and studied him, but she didn't say a word.

Richard stared, fascinated. Her skin was smooth and flawless, a pale shade of honey gold. Her lips were pink and lusciously full, and he had the most powerful urge to taste her mouth. She looked away. When their gazes met again, emotion flared in the blue depths of her eyes, but he couldn't read her thoughts.

He swallowed, feeling his loins tighten again. His breath quickened as she started toward him. But then she stopped. For a brief moment, she'd looked almost happy to see him. He watched as her features clouded, her eyes dulled, and she frowned.

"Richard." His name was but a breathless whisper on her lips. And he was charmed again by the way she pronounced it. *Ric-kard.* The Dutch accent was faint, delightful.

"We need to talk," he said.

She averted her eyes as if the sight of him was too painful. "I think you should leave here."

"Kirsten, please—"

"Go! You're one of them. You lied to me. You're a Tory—a bloody Loyalist. The enemy!"

Richard looked at her. "Did I actually claim to be a Patriot? Did I intentionally mislead you?"

"Yes!" Tears hovered on the fringes of her thick lashes. He felt an answering jolt of pain in his gut.

"You know what I thought," she cried. "Why didn't you admit the truth? I cared for you! Did you think I would turn you in?"

"It was a chance I couldn't take," he said, his voice soft.

He wished he could confess the truth now, to ease

162

her mind, but he couldn't. Would she forgive him if she knew that he was lying to her now?

But he had no choice. Someday, perhaps, he could tell her everything. For the present, he had to allow her to believe in his deception, no matter how painful it was for the both of them.

"I'm leaving tomorrow," he said quietly. "I wanted to—needed to—say good-bye before I left Hoppertown."

"Why?" She sniffed, wiping her eyes. "You left before without saying good-bye. Having a sudden attack of conscience?"

Richard stiffened. "I waited for you as long as I could. Where were *you*?"

She looked away. Tugging a silver braid, she stared off into space. "I was home, locked in my room." She faced him, her expression a mirror of her pain. "My *vader* found out I had left the house during the previous night. He was furious with me."

"Kirsten . . ." He came forward, his hand outstretched to touch her. He wanted to embrace her, to offer her comfort.

"No! Don't!" she cried. "I won't allow you to do this to me! Go away!"

He stopped, dropped his hand. "You want me to just leave?"

Face frozen, she nodded.

Richard sighed. "Fine. If that's your wish, I'll go." He couldn't move, didn't want to. "Good-bye, Kirsten . . . and I did say it before. Good-bye. Have you been inside the old mill?"

She stared at him blankly.

"You haven't since I left, have you?"

Her lashes fluttering, she shook her head.

He turned to leave. There was still no sign of her parents, he was grateful to note. Richard guessed

163

they were out visiting friends or relatives, a strangely ordinary thing to do during a time of war.

But were these people actually at war? The area was considered neutral by some. There were Patriots and Loyalists among the Dutch families who lived here; there were also those who refused to take sides. Kirsten, he knew, was a true believer in the Patriot cause.

He took several steps away from her before he turned one last time. "I thought you'd like to know that your cousin—Miles—he'll not be leaving the area. In his present condition, he's of little use to the Tory army."

Kirsten blinked. "How do you know about Miles?"

He smiled slowly. "I have my methods." He stared at her lips, overcome a second time with a sudden urge to taste them. "One kiss to see me gone?" he dared to ask.

"No."

"Afraid?" he taunted.

"Uninterested."

"Liar."

And with that he left, the memory of her loveliness forever imprinted in his mind.

Kirsten watched him go with an ache in her heart. She clutched the tomato she was holding so tightly the fruit burst and juice trickled between her fingers. Seeds spewed over her hands and gown.

She cursed as she looked down at herself. Tears blurred her vision as she tossed the tomato away and wiped her hand on a cloth she had tucked into her apron waistband.

She sniffed and blinked to clear her vision. Richard was walking away, at the edge of the forest. Soon, he'd be beyond her sight, swallowed up by the bushes and grass and trees of the woods.

Soon, he'd be gone from Hoppertown to a fate unknown . . . perhaps a deadly fate. And she would never see him again.

She dropped her basket and started to run. "Richard!"

He froze. She could see the tension in his broad shoulders and back as he turned. There was a question in his gaze that tugged at her heartstrings . . . a look of hope . . . of joy . . . as she rushed toward him.

"Richard," she gasped as she stopped before him. She suddenly felt shy of him. "Please be careful."

His look was an intimate caress touching her flesh. Her skin tingled. Her face burned. She felt physically alive.

"This is a time of war, Kirsten."

She nodded in understanding, her eyes filling with tears. It hadn't been his intention to hurt her. "I know," she said, her tone revealing her anguish. "It's only that—" She caught back a sob, for she knew a future with him was out of the question.

Richard groaned harshly and pulled her into his arms, his mouth demanding, his tongue delving deeply between her lips. Her brain spun, and her body pulsed with feeling. The man she loved was holding her as if he didn't want to let her go.

He lifted his head and held her close, burying his face in her hair. "Good-bye, Kirsten."

"Good-bye, Richard," she managed to choke out. He released her, his hands lingering. He touched her cheek, and her tears fell; she couldn't control them.

And she whirled and left him to fight the war on the wrong side. He was her enemy, but she loved him.

I'm glad Richard's gone, Kirsten thought on her

165

way to meet Miles. The man wasn't what he'd seemed. Greene had called him Canfield. *My God, he even lied to me about his name!*

The Tories had left as Richard had predicted. Word had reached the Van Atta homestead during the early morning. A member of the militia had been on watch last night at the road leading from the Randolph farm. The news spread through the village like wildfire as runners went to all Patriot homes. The residents of Hoppertown could rest easier at night.

The day was a hot one, the July sun searing, and the humidity was at an all-time high. Perspiring heavily by the time she reached the clearing, Kirsten looked longingly at the river. The Hohaukus was a narrow body of water. Its crystal clear depths looked cool and inviting.

She tugged off her footwear and, skirts hiked to her knees, waded into the refreshing stream. She was careful not to slip or hurt her feet on the rocks scattered about the river bed. Splashing with her feet, she knew that Miles and Jims would find her at any moment.

Time passed. Kirsten gingerly walked about, enjoying the cold water on the hot day. Branches hung overhead, shading the area, and she moved a distance upriver to a spot where the bottom was rock free and soft. She waded there for a time, watching for Miles. But still he didn't come.

She made her way to a flat boulder near the shore. Although she longed to shed her clothes to fully enjoy the water's depths, she knew that would be unwise in full daylight. Perhaps one night soon she'd return alone to swim . . . armed. Kirsten knew a moment's sadness. How could she swim here while a war was going on and she could be accosted by any bloodthirsty, crazed soldier who came to Hoppertown?

Where is Miles? She was concerned, for it was a long while after the arranged meeting time. Had Jims forgotten to tell him? Was Richard mistaken? Had Miles left with the Tory band?

She waded out of the water, watchful of her footsteps over the rocky ground. By chance, she found a man's cocked hat—made of black fur felt—caught in the branches of a thick forest bush. Curious, she reached in and retrieved it, noting the military cockade and the silk band. It had a drawstring. She turned it over and saw tiny lettering inside the brim, but couldn't read it. Someone had stitched on the soldier's initials.

"Kirsten."

She looked up at her cousin with relief. Without reason or thought, Kirsten tucked the hat into a fold of her skirts, out of Miles's sight. "I'd begun to fear that you weren't coming."

He hobbled toward her, grimacing. "Tough to get about these days."

"So I heard." Kirsten studied his arm, which was in a sling, before her gaze dropped to his feet. "I'm glad."

He raised his eyebrows.

"Well, you're here in Hoppertown, and the Tories have left."

Miles found a perch on a tree stump. "Bit of good luck—that falling crate."

"Do you know how it happened?" She was mildly curious.

The youth shook his head. "No one about but that fellow Canfield. He was cleaning his rifle. Said he didn't see anything."

Kirsten jerked with surprise. "Canfield," she echoed. *Richard?*

"Yellow hair, brown eyes. Good-looking sort. The others say he's a reputation with the ladies."

"Oh?" Her heart skipped a beat. "What kind of reputation?"

Flushing, Miles shifted uncomfortably under Kirsten's gaze. "It's not something a man likes to discuss with a female. Not with his cousin anyways."

And Kirsten understood. Her chest felt tight. How many other women besides her had Richard lain with? Five? Ten? Twenty? She was appalled.

"Father went into a rage when the accident occurred," Miles told her. "Furious about my injuries, and because I couldn't fight." He shuddered. "I'm no soldier, and I never will be one."

"I know," she said softly.

"Word has it that Washington and his men are coming."

It was the first Kirsten had heard of this. "Who told you?"

"Jims. He was at the tavern when the messenger came."

General Washington here? Kirsten was astonished and excited by the prospect of meeting the great general of the Continental Army. There would be some folk, however, who wouldn't be gladdened by the news. "Does your father know?"

Miles shrugged. "I doubt it, but he'll learn soon enough."

Kirsten put on her stockings and shoes. "Where are you going?" Miles said with a scowl. "I only just arrived!"

"To tell *vader* about the general."

"He's probably heard about it already," her cousin grumbled, but Kirsten wouldn't be swayed. "When will I see you again?" he asked.

She finished and rose, brushing dirt and dead

leaves from her skirts. "I'll send word."

Kirsten turned, still carrying the cocked hat she'd found, unwilling to leave it to decay in the woods. She had no idea why she wanted it. *It's a perfectly good hat,* she reasoned.

Miles stared at her, scowling. "Damn it, Kirsten. If you think I'm going to walk here with this foot for just a few minutes of your time—"

Kirsten turned back and regarded him with hands on hips, the hat caught by a few fingers. "Where's Jims?" she demanded.

Miles blushed. "Back on the farm. I wanted to come alone."

"Then suffer, Miles Randolph, if your pigheadedness and pride prevents you from accepting Jims's help!"

Chapter Fourteen

Paramus. To the Dutch known as *Peremus*. It was there, a mile out of Hoppertown, Washington's men made camp. They came on July 10th and made their quarters on the flats not far from the *kerk* where the Dutch residents gathered to attend religious services. Kirsten rode her mount along the turnpike through the forest and past homes. She was on her way to see the great Patriot leader, General George Washington.

Excitement welled within her breast as she neared the encampment and saw the tents and the men wandering about. She frowned after a moment's study of them. The soldiers looked a sorry lot, not like great heroes of war. She'd expected the troops directly under Washington's command to be resplendent in fancy blue and buff uniforms with shiny brass buttons, sporting well-kept muskets and gleaming sharp swords.

The men she observed were without shoes and stockings. A few had footwear, but their clothes were threadbare and, in many cases, torn. Still, they seemed a proud bunch and held their heads high. Hungry and tired they might be, but they were true

171

Patriots, dedicated to liberty and freedom's cause.

Here in Hoppertown, the soldiers' hunger would be satisfied, for the land was rich and plentiful, the villagers more than willing to share their cherished supplies. Kirsten was glad Washington had elected to stop here in his journeys of war. It was a good place for the soldiers to renew both their bodies and spirits.

Kirsten was conscious of the soldiers' curious gazes on her as she entered their camp. Dressed in a riding habit of forest green, she rode Hilga, her faithful mare. She was hot, but dignity forced her to wear her jacket. However, she left open the buttons and felt somewhat cooler for it. Otherwise she looked most proper in her weskit and white linen shirt. She rode astride, unlike most women. Her full skirts accommodated the girth of the horse.

She reined in Hilga before a tent where a guard was posted. The tent probably belonged to someone of importance. From her high seat, she called out to the young man who stood sentinel.

"Mynheer," she said. "Could you direct me to the general? I must speak with him."

"And who are you?" he asked, eyeing her suspiciously.

"I am a resident of Hoppertown. My family is well known in the area. My ancestors, the Hoppes, came across the seas from the low countries. They settled this region." She brushed back a lock of silver blond hair, wiping her damp brow with the back of her hand. "I have come to offer the general some assistance. May I please see him?"

Just then another man came forward from beyond a row of tents. There was purpose to his stride; his manner displayed self-confidence. An officer, Kirsten decided.

"Is there something amiss, mistress?" he inquired, eyeing her with the wariness of one who trusts few. The officer turned to the guard. "Rhoades?"

"The mistress would like to speak with the general, sir."

The newcomer looked at her. "I'm Lieutenant Colonel Hamilton. Lieutenant Colonel Alexander Hamilton."

Kirsten stared. She'd heard about Alexander Hamilton, of course. He was the general's aide-de-camp and confidential secretary. Was this truly Washington's most trusted man?

"Mynheer," she said, "I'm a Patriot with great respect for General Washington. I assure you that I mean him no harm. I simply wish to speak with the commander."

"Your name, mistress?" Hamilton asked.

"Kirsten Van Atta. My cousin, Martin Hoppe, owns the tavern under the huge elm trees. Perhaps you are familiar with it?" He nodded. "My father is a *boer*—a farmer. Many come to us because of our mill. You can ask anyone in Hoppertown of us."

The lieutenant colonel's face softened. "A moment, please."

The man slipped into the tent, and within seconds the flap opened once again behind the guard to reveal the commander of the Continental troops.

"General," Kirsten breathed. "Mynheer Washington."

He was a big-boned man, tall, very tall. A bout with smallpox had marked his face, she noted, but he was still a surprisingly attractive man.

"You have a need to see me?" His voice and manner were pleasant.

Kirsten glanced about, suddenly conscious that she'd drawn the attention of the men. Her gaze

173

returned to the general. "May I speak with you—in private?"

"Are you armed?" the young guard said. "Sir"—he addressed Hamilton—"could she be armed?"

She was shocked and outraged. "Indeed I'm not! What need have I to bear arms here?"

The general appeared to stifle a smile as he waved her inside his tent. "Come in then—Mistress Van Atta, is it?"

She nodded and then preceded General George Washington into his temporary quarters.

Once inside, the commander was the perfect gentlemen. He obviously believed that she was no threat either to himself or his men. He pulled up a chair for her, the only seat available in his quarters. When she started to refuse his offer, he insisted that he'd been sitting for too long, penning letters, and needed to stretch his legs.

Kirsten's first thought upon hearing this that the inside of a tent was hardly the place for the general to stretch his legs. But she wasn't in a position to contradict him. "Thank you, General," she murmured and took the seat.

The tent was furnished Spartanly with just a cot and one blanket, a wooden, lap writing desk and the chair upon which she sat.

Her impression of the commander, upon closer inspection, was that he was larger than any other man of her acquaintance. He wore his brown hair in a ribbon-tied bag. His eyes, she noted, were startling, being a clear, sparkling shade of gray-blue. And he was dressed better than some of his subordinates. She couldn't help but see the contrast. His blue uniform jacket was finely cut, as were his breeches. And his boots were polished. She gasped. Such large boots!

He watched her and must have read her thoughts

about the difference between his appearance and that of his men, for his expression suddenly became dark.

"I'm sorry, General. I couldn't help but notice . . ." She bit her lip, aware of her blunder. One didn't insult the commander of the rebel forces, not intentionally or otherwise.

He nodded, his face softening. "My men. It is true some of them—many of them—need clothes, uniforms. Those you first saw are from a regiment which lost its command. We stumbled upon them after the battle at Monmouth."

Pain was evident in the general's gaze, regret for the outcome of the battle which had taken many Patriot lives.

Kirsten made some appropriate response. What she actually said she had no idea, for the moment was an uncomfortable one.

Washington seemed to shed his gloom then. "Now, my dear," he said, "how may I help you?"

"*Mynheer*—General—it is not what you can do for me that brings me here. It is what I can do for you. I want to help the cause. I'm a Patriot, a true believer in independence from the English king. I am here to offer you my services. Whatever I can do to assist, please tell me, and I shall endeavor to accomplish it."

The man's eyes twinkled. "That is most kind of you, dear lady. I must say I am surprised by your offer. It is not often that a young woman of your sort comes to me offering anything."

Kirsten gasped, affronted. "I did not mean—"

Washington held up his hand. "My words were not meant to insult. I speak in all sincerity. If I could think of something for you to do, I would do so and gladly, for I would have the utmost confidence that by your willingness and determination and dedication to the cause you would get the job done."

175

She nodded, mollified by his words of praise. "Name it, *mynheer.*" Her eyes glowed with the fervor of her convictions. When a mental image of Richard Maddox rose to haunt her, she firmly pushed it away, unwilling to be taken in by his lying, deceitful Tory charm. *Freedom,* she thought. Only then would they live in happiness and peace.

The general paced the tent floor, his head bent slightly as he reached each end to accommodate his height under the slope of the roof. "You will watch and listen and report if you suspect treachery."

"Treachery?" she echoed.

"A good officer finds his most valuable assets in the loyalty and honor of those who work under him. If, Mistress Van Atta, you could keep your eyes open and your ears alert for signs of betrayal, I would be ever in your debt."

Disappointed, but hiding it well, Kirsten nodded. *What does he mean by that?* But she didn't want to question him, for she was unwilling to appear ignorant. What kind of servant would she be if she seemed ignorant?

"Thank you, General. I will do what I can. And if I hear anything?"

"Report to my man—Hamilton. I believe you've met?"

Glancing in the aide's direction, Kirsten nodded, and with a soft word of farewell to both men, she left the general's camp. As she rode Hilga home, she felt strangely disappointed with General Washington. While his size was impressive, he seemed an ordinary man to her, not the great master of war, the man to lead the Patriot forces to freedom and liberty.

He found my offer amusing, she thought with indignation. "As if a mere female couldn't possibly do anything to further the cause," she said aloud.

176

She climbed off the mare before the stable, handing the reins over to Pieter, who would see to Hilga's care.

Stopping the groom when he would have turned away, she said. "I saw General George Washington today. Have you seen him?"

Pieter shook his head. "They say he's a great man. What manner of man is he?"

Kirsten shrugged. "A man . . . just a man." Would he be able to win this war? "Where's *Vader?*" she asked.

Pieter looked at her a long moment, obviously confused as to the direction of their conversation. "He's in the house with your *moeder.*"

"Thank you."

He nodded, eyeing her as if she were addlepated. She smiled at him and headed toward the house.

"Moeder . . . Vader."

"Kirsten," her mother exclaimed, "where have you been? Pieter said you took Hilga. Where did you go?"

Kirsten glanced toward her father. "To the soldiers' camp."

Agnes gasped, and her father frowned.

"It's all right. I spoke to the general. He was . . . most kind." She faced her father. "Have you met with him, *Vader?*"

"You shouldn't have gone there," he told her. "It is not proper for a young woman of your background to go there alone."

She stiffened. "I wasn't harmed."

"When you left here, you couldn't know that for certain," he said, scowling.

"But they are Patriots, *Vader!*"

"They are soldiers. And first and foremost they are men—flesh and blood men who have been a long time without their women. Many of them have seen

177

too much fighting. You could have been apprehended in a secluded area—ravished or worse."

Kirsten made a disparaging sound. "He is supposed to be a great leader. Do you think he'd allow his men to touch an innocent woman?"

"No, Kirsten, I know he would not. However, by the time the men were caught in their misdeed, it might have been too late. You must not return there, daughter."

"Yes, *Vader*." She had already decided that she wouldn't return to the camp alone. Next time, she'd take Pieter with her. Better yet, Martin Hoppe.

"Jonathan is to speak to the general tonight," James Van Atta said. "He's to offer the services of our militia. Our men are eager to assist."

His daughter stifled a grin. She had thought of it first. Her smile faded. Washington wouldn't find Jonathan Hopper's offer amusing, she mused.

"What is the general like?" her father asked, unable to contain his curiosity.

And Kirsten proceeded to relate her experiences with the man. She left out the embarrassing parts. Like when he'd assumed she'd come offering herself as camp follower.

"Hell and damnation!" Edmund Dunley bellowed. "The man's presence here will ruin everything!"

"Not to mention the troops he brought with him," William Randolph said. He appeared thoughtful as he studied his two cohorts. Edmund Dunley and Bernard Godwin were beginning to get on his nerves with all their caterwauling and complaints. They had a job to do and they would do it, whether General George Washington was in the vicinity or not.

178

"What are we going to do?" Godwin asked. He twisted his hands in his lap, clearly anxious at this new turn of events.

"It may be to our advantage that he's come," Randolph said. "Have you forgotten our connection? There are others like him among the general's troops, I'm sure. Disgruntled and tired wretches, they wish only to go back to their homes, and forget they ever encountered their 'great leader' and his bloody so-called cause."

"You think this true?"

"Yes, Edmund, I do." Randolph drew deeply from his pipe. "I do, indeed. Why don't you go back to your homes and relax. I'll send word in three days. It'll give me plenty of time to make contact with Rhoades and find out what he's learned. Who dares to guess, but this may actually speed up the war, bringing victory to us once and for all!"

"I hope you're right, Will."

William Randolph regarded Godwin steadily. The man was obese, a true glutton. He himself had been disgusted by the amount the man devoured at a meal and the manner in which it was consumed. "Am I not usually right?"

Dunley nodded, while Godwin apparently had decided not to comment. Randolph glared at the fat Tory until the man rose to his feet, clearly discomfited.

"On second thought, Bernard," William said. "Meet me here tomorrow night at ten o'clock. You'll go with me."

"I? Go with you?" Godwin said, his gaze becoming wary.

Randolph smiled wickedly. "Into the arms of the enemy. Afraid?" he taunted.

"Of course not!"

179

"Good." He slapped his hand on his knee. "Edmund, we'll see you here in three days' time. I'm sure you can make it." It was a command not a request, with implied consequences should he decide not to come.

Edmund Dunley inclined his head. He would come.

"Until then," Randolph said, rising to see his gentlemen friends to the door.

And the meeting of the Tory minds was ended.

Richard was tired of the charade. Thus far, his act had gotten him little or nothing. He was weary of the game, of pretending to like the fools who accompanied him on his travels. Would the ruse ever be over? Would he ever gain any clues as to the identity of the man he searched for, the unknown, faceless cur responsible for Alex's death?

The band had been on the move steadily for three days since leaving Hoppertown. Richard was annoyed that Greene had remained closemouthed about their mission. They wandered aimlessly through the Ramapo Mountains and later the region to the north in the colony of New York.

Finally, that night, a messenger arrived after they made camp. Richard recognized the man as one from Hoppertown and realized he must be one of William Randolph's men. His interest caught, he strolled over to where Greene stood with the messenger, deep in conversation. Their words were hushed, low. Greene looked over at Richard's approach.

"Trouble?" Richard asked politely.

The Tory leader scowled at him. Lately, he'd been exceedingly rude to Richard, his irritation evident and no doubt attributable to the fact that he'd yet to indulge in "Canfield's" games with the fairer sex. But in their wanderings, they'd come across few women, all of whom were, luckily for Richard, either too old, too ugly, or too fat for either man's tastes. So it was a great surprise to Richard when Greene decided to answer his question.

"General George Washington is at Paramus—near Hoppertown. In fact, a woman—Mrs. Prevost—is giving a party in 'is honor. Strange, actually, since the lady's a wife of a British officer. Well, in any event, Randolph wants us to return. Sends word 'e 'as news vital to our side. 'E wants us to deliver the message to the British army, to a Major Thatcher. Only the devil knows where that bastard is stationed."

Richard held back his excitement. "Surely, he doesn't expect us to take on the rebel army! We number what—fifteen men? How many does Washington have there? Did Randolph say?"

Elias Greene shook his head. "Do ye know?" he asked Randolph's messenger.

The man shrugged. "Thirty? Fifty? It's right hard to judge. He suggests you come to . . ." And he described a secluded area not far from William Randolph's farm. "Near enough to be reached by Randolph, far enough away to be safe from rebel attack.

"It will be safe to meet the night of this party at the Hermitage," he continued. "What with Washington and his officers being entertained by Mrs. Prevost . . ."

Greene frowned. "Don't like the sound of 'er. Don't like it at all."

Richard's insides froze. "Perhaps she's a spy for the King," he suggested. If Greene refused to return, then Richard's hopes of finding the traitorous link between the contact Biv and Alex's death would be dashed. Here was the chance he was waiting for. Randolph had gained his information from someone. Who?

"We've been idle these past days," Richard pointed out. "A return might herald some action. The wenches in Hackensack are comely. 'Tis only a few miles away from Paramus. Perhaps you and I can slip away one evening, seek a bit of entertainment there." His eyes gleamed as he gave Greene a wicked smile.

Greene jumped at the bait. "Yes . . ." He returned Richard's smile with a lecherous grin. "Fine, then, Canfield," he said to Richard. "Alert the others. Tell the sorry bastards that we leave for Hoppertown at first light."

Richard inclined his head and abruptly left to do the man's bidding. Soon he'd have the information he needed to complete his mission—and with Washington on hand to receive it!

His heart thundered in his chest. And he'd be near Kirsten again. Would he see her? Did he dare hope he would? If he did, it would have to be by chance, by an act of fate; for he could surely not risk seeking her company. The danger would be too great for both her and himself.

Still, he could dream—envision her sweet face, the smile on her lips when she saw him, the honey taste of her mouth as he kissed her, the soft whimpers as he stroked and caressed her silken skin . . . He imagined the throaty sound of her wild passionate cries as he made love to her and drove himself into her willing warmth.

He paused and closed his eyes. He was glad it was dark for his loins were on fire, his manhood hot and throbbing against the front of his breeches. It wouldn't do for the others to see him, to suspect the direction of his thoughts. There were a few among them so desperate for a woman that in their hunger they'd be less discriminating in their choice of sexual partners.

It was for this reason that Richard went into the thick of the forest on the pretext of relieving his bladder. After a few moments, he composed himself, then returned to camp to carry out Greene's orders.

The sun was but a faint glow in the sky when the Tories broke camp and moved out. They had traveled about for days, but the return trip to Hoppertown would take only a day, the direct distance being shorter than their earlier, seemingly aimless route about the countryside. Greene thought they would arrive at William Randolph's suggested meeting place by sundown.

Richard knew that he should concentrate on the meeting with Randolph, on the importance of his mission, as he walked along in the others' wake. But all he could think about was Kirsten Van Atta and how much he'd missed her. How much he wanted to see her again.

A dangerous state of affairs.

Kirsten was shocked when the invitation came. She stared down at the parchment that had recently been delivered. Her mouth open, she reread the carefully written words from Mrs. Theodosia Prevost, inviting her to attend a "small gathering" held in General Washington's honor, where there would be "dancing and other forms of amusement."

A party! She'd never been to the Hermitage, but she was familiar with the Prevost home. It was a modest but lovely house just north of her father's property.

The invitation was a great surprise to her, because Mrs. Prevost was the wife of a British officer. Major James Prevost was away, somewhere across the sea on business for the King. Why would his wife entertain General Washington? Could she be trusted? Was Theodosia Prevost neutral in the fight for freedom, or was she loyal to King George?

Kirsten was puzzled by something else also. She hadn't known the woman was aware of her existence. Why did Mrs. Prevost invite her and not her parents? Was it possible that the lady had made a mistake? Or had General Washington himself requested Kirsten's presence?

She became concerned that she wouldn't be allowed to go. Her father had been dismayed to learn of her visit to the Paramus encampment. Would he refuse her permission to attend her first real party? She wanted so badly to go.

And what did one wear to such an occasion?

Kirsten recalled the fine English and French gowns stored in the hall *kast* upstairs, brought over from England by her mother's mother—her grandmother, Elisabeth Randolph. Would *Moeder* understand? Would she let her borrow one of the fancy garments? And what if the gown needed to be altered? The ball was in two days—a hurried undertaking. Would there be hours enough to make the alterations?

She felt her heart lurch with an odd emotion. How wonderful it would be to attend such an event on a lover's arm! She thought of Richard, and her breath caught as she wondered what he was doing. Was he all right? Alive? She swallowed hard. *Dead?*

He couldn't be dead, she decided, for she would know it, would somehow sense it if he was. After all, hadn't she detected that special bond between them, a bond formed while she was nursing him back to health?

Nonsense! she thought. He was a Tory, and she'd never guessed it. She'd believed him a hero for the cause! *Ha!*

Pain lanced her midsection. There was no bond between them. She'd have no way of knowing if he were dead or alive.

Tears stung her eyes, and she brushed them away as they escaped to wet her cheeks.

I mustn't think of him. I'll go mad if I do. There is the cause to think about. Richard Maddox—Canfield, whoever he is—is a traitor. I have to forget him. Think only of Washington and Mrs. Prevost's party.

"*Moeder!*" she called, hurrying into the house. "*Moeder!* I've been invited to a party at the Hermitage! It's to be in honor of General Washington." She paused for breath on the stairs. Her mother had indicated that she was in the room above in the loft.

"Can I go?" she asked as she entered the chamber where the ladder reached up to the attic floor. "I'll need your help. There's a gown to select. Tucks to be made. Oh, *Moeder*, please! Make *Vader* see that I must attend. I'll be safe, I promise. I've never been to a party before!"

Chapter Fifteen

The summer evening of Mrs. Prevost's gathering was clear and lovely, the temperature pleasant, the sun an orange globe in a cloudless sky as Kirsten stood at her bedchamber window, waiting anxiously for her cousins. Martin and Margaretha Hoppe were coming to take her to the Hermitage. They, too, had been invited to the party.

The Van Attas had also been invited, their invitation arriving separately hours after their daughter's. But one of their horses—a gelding—had become sick, and James wanted to remain near to watch him. So the couple had elected to stay home.

Kirsten's fears that she wouldn't be allowed to attend were unfounded. Her mother had been excited for her, hurrying from the attic loft to open the *kast* in the hall below, pulling out not one but several dresses that she deemed appropriate.

Kirsten had stared in awe at the lovely gowns, and had felt her own excitement about the event grow.

A party! She knew it wouldn't be so grand as those held in her mother's England or in great places like Philadelphia, New York, or that city in the Virginia

Colony, Williamsburg. But it would be a fine occasion nevertheless, she decided as she tried on the first gown. And she'd meet all manner of illustrious people.

"Kirsten, stand still while I fasten the hem." Agnes Van Atta wanted to ensure that her daughter's gown fit perfectly.

Since the affair was a Patriot event, Kirsten had chosen from among her grandmother's and mother's dresses a gown of red silk. This particular garment had belonged to her mother, and it had been made for her only weeks before her departure to the New World.

The low-cut garment had elbow-length sleeves, each with a detachable white ruffle, and a long train attached to the back of the neck. This last could be removed if desired, affording the garment a somewhat different look should the wearer decide she needed one.

The bodice was long waisted, lined with linen and boned for form. The overskirt was gathered on drawstrings to add fullness in the back and was sewn to the bodice. The gown fastened in the front much like a jacket, with a opening to display the dress's petticoat.

Kirsten's petticoat was white and had tiny seed pearls stitched onto the skirt in a floral pattern. The fancy petticoat would look stunning under the bright red gown.

"Kirsten," her mother said, "come away from that window. Over by the looking glass. I'm not finished with you."

She turned restlessly and went back to her parent's side.

Kirsten's hair had been arranged artfully, fastened up in the back in a cascade of curls, several silvery strands having been left to hang in feathery wisps about the sides of her face.

"I thought this would look lovely in your hair." Agnes smiled down at her daughter with affection. In her hand, she held up a jeweled hair comb, diamonds set around a glistening red ruby gem.

"It was my mother's," she explained. "The only treasure left us from a family of wealth. Your grandmother wore it to her very first dance."

Kirsten squirmed impatiently while her mother added her grandmother's ruby hair ornament. *Dance . . .* she thought vaguely as her mother fixed a pin holding up a curl.

"Moeder," she gasped with a sudden realization, "what if I can't dance! I'll look a fool."

"Nonsense," Agnes said, standing back to view her handiwork. "Remember that charming little dance you and Miles used to do when we all went on picnics together?" She seemed pleased with her daughter's appearance.

"But we made that up!"

"Shall I call your *vader* then? He's a most accomplished stepper. He can show you how to dance."

Kirsten agreed. "Please hurry. Martin and Margaretha will be here soon!"

The doors to the alcove bed were open. On the feather tick mattress lay Kirsten's night rail, a spare petticoat, and various other discarded garments. Her slippers rested on the floor by the bed. Ignoring them, she pushed the clothing on the bed aside and carefully sat down.

James paused on the threshold of his daughter's room and gawked at her. Kirsten stood up, feeling suddenly shy and nervous. Her father's opinion meant a great deal to her.

"Kirsten," he said in a whispered voice, "you look beautiful."

"Oh, *Vader*, do you truly believe this?"

He nodded and came into the bedchamber. "You are a most attractive young woman. You'll be the belle of the ball."

"Even when I cannot dance?"

"But you can dance, dear daughter. I taught you once before, remember? When you were but six years old . . . at the Ackermans'?"

Kirsten frowned. "At the Acker—Ah! That? It wasn't a true dance, was it?"

"It was. It is. It's a Sir Roger de Coverley. Dance only the country dances, and you'll be fine."

She rushed into her father's arms and hugged him tightly. "Bless you, *Vader!*"

He laughed and held her slightly away. "You will mess your hair, daughter, if you are not careful. It's a calm night; no one will believe you weren't out dallying with some handsome beau."

James Van Atta suddenly scowled. "I want you to listen to me, Kirsten, and listen well. There is a war. Many of the guests will be true Patriots, but there may be those among them who only pretend to be so."

Kirsten wondered if he was referring to her hostess for the evening. "Mrs. Prevost is a pleasant woman, *Moeder* says."

His expression softened. "She is. You will like her. She is most charming."

The sound of horse hooves on the packed earth of the yard filtered up through the open window.

"They're here!" she cried.

Her parents smiled at her. "Slowly," her mother instructed. "Slowly."

James nodded. "You will get there soon enough."

Kirsten was barely able to contain herself as she went downstairs to greet her cousins. She wanted to run, but did not.

Night came after the sound of the *klapperman's* ninth rattle, so the sky was still bright as the three cousins drove up before the Hermitage at half-past seven. The Prevosts, unlike the other villagers who were farmers or *boers*, were mill owners and considered to be wealthier than other Hoppertown residents.

Kirsten studied the Prevost home, saw the modest building with a door flanked by a single window on each side. It was a two-story house with a flat roof as compared to the gambrel roof of her own home. There was certainly nothing too stately or grand about the residence, and the realization made her wonder how much of what she'd heard of the family was true. Did the Prevosts possess great riches? Were there hidden jewels in secret rooms?

She and the Hoppes had arrived at the same time as some of Mrs. Prevost's other guests. Kirsten recognized familiar faces in the group as she alighted from Martin's conveyance. She saw Rachel Banta and her family. And there were the Bogerts and the Van Voorheeses, the owners of the farm outside the village.

The sight of the last family reminded Kirsten that she had a job to finish. The day after the Tories had left, she'd begun the task of transporting the goods from Martin's cellar. With Martin's help, she'd managed to move several crates and one cask. Tired and sore after that, they'd decided to wait until they could get more help, before they attempted to transport the rest.

"Kirsten," Margaretha called. "Come. Mrs. Prevost is waiting to greet us."

Kirsten smiled at her cousin. Margaretha looked

ethereal in a gown of gold silk brocade. Her stomacher was embroidered with fine gold threads in a pattern of roses and laurel leaves.

Martin, too, looked smart this evening in a coat of military cut. His navy frockcoat had shiny brass buttons, and his buff breeches tapered down to white silk stockings. His silver-buckle shoes had been polished to a bright shine. Studying him more closely, Kirsten saw her cousin as one would view a man who wasn't a relative. Martin, she realized, was a handsome fellow.

Upon seeing Mrs. Prevost, she was surprised to recognize her hostess as a woman she'd seen at the *kerk* a few times. She'd had no idea that the woman who attended religious services on rare occasions was the wife of a British major, the lady who lived with her three servants in the Hermitage up the road.

As she and her cousins approached their smiling hostess, Kirsten detected some wonderful smells in the evening air. The scents of cook-smoke and baked goods and roasting meat made her mouth water in anticipation.

"Martin," Theodosia Prevost said, "how wonderful to see you again!" The dark-haired lady wasn't an attractive woman. Her features were much too plain, and she had a scar across her forehead that couldn't be hidden by face powder. But there was something about her that drew one to her, an inner glow that showed in her eyes, a charm and friendliness that immediately grabbed and held one's attention.

Of course, she'd know Martin, Kirsten thought. Everyone in the area knew the tavern owner.

"Margaretha," the woman said. "How lovely you look this evening! You appear well. Are you feeling better these days?"

The younger woman nodded. "Much improved.

TO GET YOUR
4 FREE BOOKS
MAIL THE COUPON BELOW.

FREE BOOK CERTIFICATE

Heartfire Romance

GET 4 FREE BOOKS

Yes! I want to subscribe to Zebra's HEARTFIRE HOME SUBSCRIPTION SERVICE. Please send me my 4 FREE books. Then each month I'll receive the four newest Heartfire Romances as soon as they are published. Free for ten days. If I decide to keep them I'll pay the special discounted price of just $3.50 each; a total of $14.00. This is a savings of $3.00 off the regular publishers price. There are no shipping, handling or other hidden charges. There is no minimum number of books to buy and I may cancel this subscription at any time. In any case the 4 FREE Books are mine to keep regardless.

NAME

ADDRESS

CITY _____ STATE _____ ZIP

TELEPHONE

SIGNATURE

(If under 18 parent or guardian must sign)
Terms and prices subject to change.
Orders subject to acceptance.

HF 111

GET 4 FREE BOOKS

HEARTFIRE HOME SUBSCRIPTION
SERVICE
P.O. BOX 5214
120 BRIGHTON ROAD
CLIFTON, NEW JERSEY 07015

AFFIX
STAMP
HERE

Thank you, Mrs. Prevost."

"Theodosia," their hostess insisted. "After all, we've known each other forever it seems."

She addressed Kirsten next, fixing her with an intent gaze. Kirsten expected to hear her say, And who is this? But she didn't. She said, "Why, Kirsten Van Atta, how grownup you are! You have your mother's eyes and your father's smile."

"You know who I am?"

Theodosia inclined her head. "So does the general, it seems. Do you know he specifically asked for your presence? I assured him that, of course, you would come. A young girl doesn't forget the first taste of berry pie."

Kirsten blinked. "That was your pie?" When the woman told her it was, Kirsten blushed. She remembered an occasion when a strange woman had visited the Van Atta homestead, bringing a delicious berry pie. While the adults had been otherwise occupied, little Kirsten had been unable to resist eating most of that pie, sharing the rest with the family dog, Ralph. When it had come time to share some pie with the lady guest who'd brought it, there'd been none left to eat. Agnes Van Atta had been horrified at what her daughter had done.

"Oh, dear, what you must have thought."

Mrs. Prevost chuckled. "I was extremely flattered. Your mother told me afterward that you had a bellyache for days."

"It was worth it," Kirsten said. "It was the best treat I'd ever eaten."

Theodosia Prevost appeared pleased by the compliment. "Then you'll appreciate some tonight. And don't worry, we've baked plenty. Six."

The Bantas were waiting to be greeted, so Kirsten, Martin, and Margaretha went inside, at Theodosia's invitation, and joined the other guests milling about the house.

"Look!" Margaretha murmured to Kirsten. "Isn't that Frederick Terhune and his daughter Anna?"

Kirsten studied the two persons in question. She recognized the heavyset man's garish choice of garment colors. And as usual, Frederick Terhune's powdered gray goat's wig sat crookedly on his head. Anna looked pathetically thin in her gown of faded green. "Yes, that's the Terhunes," she said. Her gaze continued on about the room, and her face brightened. "Oh, see, Margaretha! There's Mr. Hamilton—Alexander Hamilton, the general's aide."

Margaretha beamed. "He's an attractive man, isn't he?"

Is he? Kirsten wondered. She found the only man to her liking was Richard, a veritable stranger she'd probably never see again.

"What's this?" Martin exclaimed, raising Kirsten's chin with his index finger. "Why such a long face? Has the party palled for you already? And when the music has barely begun?"

She gave him a slight smile. Her grin became genuine as she heard the first strains of music above the conversation of the guests. There was one musician, a man at the pianoforte. The house was small, and Kirsten wondered how many people Theodosia had invited. The parlor seemed to be the main room. Guests took up every available chair; and a few stood at the parlor's perimeter, leaving a place for dancing in the center of the room.

Kirsten saw only four soldiers from Washington's army. She was surprised to see that they were well dressed for the occasion. Brought or borrowed clothes? she wondered, recalling the worn clothing she'd seen at the camp. And then she realized that the four men were officers, one of them being the general himself.

Her attention was drawn away from Washington as the three cousins were joined by friendly neighbors. Rachel Banta eyed Kirsten with admiration, before turning the force of her charm on Cousin Martin.

"Sir, would you escort me to the refreshment table?" the young woman said.

Martin gave Kirsten a twisted smile, then he and Rachel strolled off, leaving Kirsten and Margaretha in the company of Rachel's brother. Margaretha and Thomas Banta began discussing the changing weather. Kirsten stared after Martin, debating whether she should leave Margaretha and Thomas alone.

"She has a tenderness for him, you know," a voice said in Kirsten's ear. She turned to find John Ackerman by her side, grinning down at her.

"Who?" she said blankly.

"Rachel. She has a tenderness for Martin."

"No," Kirsten replied somewhat stiffly, "I didn't know." She'd never liked John Ackerman, and this evening's encounter with the man hadn't changed that.

He studied her thoroughly from shining blond tresses to bared upper swells of breasts to soft leather slippers. Kirsten shifted uncomfortably beneath his ogling gaze, glad that her mother had altered the hem of her gown to a length that modestly hid her ankles.

Ackerman continued smiling, despite his lukewarm welcome. "You're looking incredibly lovely this evening, Kirsten."

"Thank you, Mr. Ackerman."

He raised an eyebrow. "Mister?"

She nodded.

"I see." He looked disappointed. His gaze scanned the growing number of guests. "Miles here?" he asked casually.

Kirsten tensed, knowing the innocent question for the cut it was. As the son of a Tory family, Miles wouldn't be invited to this Patriot function, and Ackerman knew it. "Excuse me, Mr. Ackerman. I see someone I must speak with."

Margaretha and Martin had both disappeared. Kirsten hurried from the irritating young man's presence, her direction unknown, her excuse feigned to be free of him.

She brightened upon seeing the evening's guest of honor again, and she advanced toward him, her skirts rustling as she moved. The number of guests was quite large for the size of the house; therefore, people could be found in virtually every room on the first floor but the kitchen and servants' quarters. She paused at the threshold of the dining room. General George Washington had moved into that room as it offered more space, and was deep in conversation with Hans Bogert, a young man with an aptitude for being a total bore. The general looked distracted, impatient. She moved forward, after deciding that Washington needed to be rescued from the young man.

The general had spied her when she'd paused. He brightened as he saw her direction, and smiled gratefully.

"General," she said. "Hans. May I borrow the general for a few moments?"

After a look at Kirsten that spoke volumes, Washington excused himself to the young Bogert and then caught Kirsten's arm to escort her from the dining room. "Mistress Van Atta. How enchanting you look this night!" In a low tone, he added,

"Thank you, dear lady, for the most charming rescue."

Surprised by the compliment, Kirsten remained silent for a moment. "You're welcome," she said after a lengthy pause.

And then she said without thinking, "You cut a fine figure yourself, sir."

He laughed, and she blushed at her own boldness. "Now, now, dear lady, don't be embarrassed. I find your candor most refreshing, I assure you." He leaned close, bending his tall frame to whisper in her ear. "So many simpering females. Do they always behave this way?"

She gazed up at him with a half-smile. "You are referring to whom?"

"That one over there. She and her sister both. Oh, and see the one in green? She fairly gushed over my frockcoat. I thought I'd surely have to wipe up a puddle of sweet syrup."

Kirsten couldn't help herself; she chuckled. "You have a way with words, General Washington."

"Ah, but alas not the fairer sex?" His eyes twinkled as he stared down at her.

She blinked. Such banter seemed strange coming from the commanding officer. Was he actually flirting with her? She studied him and decided not. He was merely being gracious, she decided, trying to liven what, for him, must seem an ordinary evening. Wasn't he from the Virginia Colony? She'd heard they did a lot of entertaining there.

"It's been days since you came to our camp. Mr. Hamilton tells me you've not been to see him. Does that mean you've heard nothing unusual?" He seemed tense all of a sudden.

Kirsten shook her head. "You spoke of betrayal, sir. Do you refer to the Tory families in the area?"

"Are there many?"

She shrugged. "Some." *Including my own uncle. Does that make me suspect?*

"It is my custom to take a Tory home for my quarters. This way if the British attack . . ."

"I see," Kirsten said. And she did indeed. If the King's men attacked Washington and his men, they'd be raiding their own people's houses, perhaps destroying goods that they themselves would have used. "Is that why you're staying here?"

He shook his head. "A few of my men and I are here at Mrs. Prevost's most generous invitation."

Someone drew the general's attention away, and although she would have liked to question him more, Kirsten used the opportunity to excuse herself so she might search for Margaretha. She found her pretty cousin accepting compliments from a Continental soldier named McHenry, one of Washington's aides.

Margaretha's color was high, her eyes were sparkling, as she and McHenry conversed. She was obviously enjoying the man's presence. Unwilling to intrude, Kirsten moved on to mingle with Theodosia's other guests.

"You seem at a loss, dear cousin." Martin Hoppe appeared at her side as if by magic.

"And you? No lady to tickle your fancy?"

Martin grinned. "I know all—at least most—of the women here. Should I have suddenly become enchanted with one?"

The music from the pianoforte changed from a minuet to a lively country tune. Smiling, Martin touched his cousin's arm. "Shall we?"

She stared at the couples beginning the dance and hesitated, assailed by doubts. "I'm not very good."

"Come, Kirsten. Let's dance. You can do it."

She stared up at Martin and then suddenly grinned. "All right. But don't blame me if I step on your toes."

Moments later, she was grinning up at her partner as they executed the dance steps. Kirsten enjoyed herself so much that when the musicians began a second number she and Martin stayed on the floor for another go-around. When they were finally done, Kirsten was happy, but warm and out of breath.

"Oh, look, Martin!" she said, her blue eyes twinkling. "Anna Terhune is approaching. Didn't I hear you promise her a dance?"

Martin groaned softly as he spied the pathetically thin woman who was most definitely coming his way. "You're cruel, Kirsten."

"What?" She grinned up at him, pretending innocence, then placed a hand on his arm. "I think I shall go outside for a breath of fresh air so that you and Anna can have your dance." Her voice dropped to a whisper. "She's nearly here. I believe I detect the scent of her heady perfume."

Night had fallen when Kirsten left the house. The sky was clear, a star-studded black canopy with a partial moon. Struck by the beauty of the heavens, she gazed upward as she strolled the grounds.

Behind her rooms were lit with burning tapers placed so as to afford the most light. The glow filtered through the windows to softly highlight the lawn. Picking up the clean floral fragrance coming from her right, Kirsten directed her steps toward the garden, following a path.

She heard low voices and paused in her walk. A couple was standing amidst the greenery—a tall man and a young woman. She watched as the gentleman in dark coat bent over to kiss the lady's hand. His head lifting, he brought the woman's fingers to his lips in a gesture that Kirsten found extremely romantic.

Kirsten's pulse raced as she recalled a different time and place, when the flame of desire had been in Richard's eyes, when it had been Richard who pulled her into his arms for a kiss.

A firefly shone nearby. She stared at it unseeingly, her thoughts with a Tory she had no right to be daydreaming about, for no good could possibly come from such woolgathering.

She glanced back at the house, knew she should go in, but wasn't ready to face anyone yet with her emotions so raw from memories of Richard. Instead, she turned away from the garden, retracing her steps to a trail that led off from the yard, away from the house.

She started down the worn foot trail and then paused when she heard a noise behind her. Waiting for several heartbeats, she listened and wondered if she had been seen departing from the festivities. Could someone be following her? If so, was the person friend or foe? Her encounter with John Ackerman had been most irritating. Perhaps he had come after her.

Silence reigned for a moment, and Kirsten became aware of the night sounds about her . . . a mosquito buzzing near her ear . . . the leaves in the trees stirring ever so slightly on the gentlest of summer breezes. Then came the intrusive noises. A footfall on dirt. A person's breathing.

Without waiting to see who followed her, Kirsten bolted past a stand of evergreen bushes, as fast as her skirts would allow. She peered through the pine needles and saw no one. She waited a few seconds and then eased out from her hiding place. As she moved toward the house, she was glad that her gown was a dark color, not easy to see in the night. Her path took her from one hiding place to another, from a huge oak to another pine.

And that's when she saw him—a man with dark hat and coat. Not a guest, she knew instantly, for he was alone and skulking about as if he didn't want his presence known. He gazed through the open window, his interest caught by the happenings inside.

Good God, Kirsten thought. Was no one safe these days—not even with the Continental Army present? Not even for one night?

She searched the ground and found a rock. She picked it up with the intention of using it as a weapon.

Keep your eyes open and your ears alert . . . Had Washington known of enemy spies in the area? Was this man someone he'd hoped to apprehend?

Kirsten clutched her weapon so tightly that her fingers hurt and her whole hand grew cramped. Her breath quickened, and her heart pounded.

It would be wise to go back inside, pretend she was unaware of the man's presence, and, once safe, alert Washington and his men.

She gazed at the man's cocked hat. He had his back to her, which was to her advantage. But his position gave her no clue to his identity, for the back of his hat met the turned-up collar of his coat—an odd garment to be wearing on a summer night.

Go inside, an inner voice prompted. *Tell Hamilton or the general about the intruder. It's too dangerous to capture the enemy on your own.*

Kirsten moved forward, the rock in her raised hand. She had offered the general her help; now that she was needed, she wasn't going to shy away from the danger involved.

Chapter Sixteen

Her hand shook as she approached the stranger, and raised the rock high to bring it against his head.

He appeared to be unaware of her presence, so intent was he on his study of the people inside the house. Suddenly, he tensed. Kirsten realized that he must have heard the soft rustling of her skirts as she moved closer.

Her heart pounded as she wondered what to do. Run? Scream for assistance?

She then thought that she must have been mistaken, for he went back to his vigil. Seconds later she knew she was wrong. He spun, and his image blurred as he jerked back from her attack. The rock in her hand wavered in the air and dropped to the ground as her prisoner escaped.

She picked up the rock and rose in time to see him run toward the back lawn and disappear beyond the formal flower garden.

Undaunted by the skirts of her gown, Kirsten followed him until she came to where he appeared to have vanished. She paused at a hedge of tall evergreens, wondering if he was hiding only inches away, behind the thick dark needles of the shrubs.

She leaned closer, listening with her breath held, her body trembling. She was afraid to move a muscle for fear of discovery. She wanted to be the one to effect a surprise.

Kirsten's blood chilled. She'd heard a faint sound. The wind? she wondered. The soft noise made from a man's breathing?

She released her breath slowly and drew in another cautiously. Gripping her rock, she edged closer, one step at a time, to the end of the shrubs. Each rustle of her skirt seemed loud in the night's silence. It was attack now or lose the advantage in this deadly game. Kirsten burst out from her hiding place and stepped around the evergreens, the rock raised to strike.

He was there, right where she'd thought. The man gasped and reacted instinctively. He caught her hand seconds before the rock made bruising contact with his shoulder. He held fast to her wrist, and they struggled briefly as Kirsten fought to pull free. A minute later she pretended to give up, but really was gathering her wits for renewed attack.

Their breaths rasped loudly in the darkness. It was a dangerous moment. They were out in the open, their struggles having brought them from the man's place of hiding.

Kirsten's thoughts raced as she pondered what to do next.

"Good God!" It was the voice she'd once held dear.

Her head jerked up with shock. "Richard?" Her mouth gaped as she found herself staring into familiar brown eyes. *"Dear Lord in heaven, Richard!"*

"Kirsten!" he whispered.

"What are you doing here?" she gasped. "This is a private party . . . a Patriot party." Her face darkened. "You were spying, you traitor! On the general!"

204

Richard grabbed her arm. "Softer, love. We don't want to be noticed." He glanced about nervously. "At least I don't." He drew her behind the bushes and settled her before him, gently holding her by the wrists. She pulled away.

"No, love," he said. "It's not what you think. Nothing's been what you think. I'm not spying . . . I'm searching for someone."

She regarded him through narrowed eyes. It was dark behind the greenery, but there was enough light for Richard to detect her glittering blue gaze, the white glow of her bare shoulders above the gown.

"Why?" she asked.

He shook his head. He couldn't tell her. No one but General Washington and his confidential secretary, Hamilton, knew of his identity—his mission.

"Fine!" she said. "We'll see what Washington has to say about secretive intruders!"

"No!" He caught her arm to halt her leaving. "You mustn't." He pulled her back and caressed the silken skin beneath his fingertips.

"A spy! Isn't it bad enough that you lied to someone who helped you? Lied to me? You're a Tory—the enemy! How can I let you go free? This is war! Oh, why couldn't you have done your spying elsewhere? Why did you have to come back?" Her voice revealed her pain.

"Kirsten . . ." he pleaded.

"Give me a reason why I shouldn't call out for someone."

He maneuvered her until he could better see her. A parting in the bushes allowed enough light from the burning lamps of the great house to light up Kirsten's face. His pulse roared in his ears. He saw the bold, defiant look in her blue eyes, the firm line of her lips, and knew he had to tell her the truth. He had to

205

prove that he could trust her to keep silent. But would she believe the truth?

"Come . . ." he said. "Let's walk away from the house, and I'll tell you why I'm here. I'll tell you everything."

She refused.

"Kirsten, I swear on my soul that I'll not lie to you. I'll not betray you."

She glanced back at the house as if debating the action, and then she gave him an abrupt nod.

They went several yards before Kirsten stopped.

"What do you want to tell me?" Her tone was clipped.

For a long moment, he studied her in the darkness, straining to gauge her expression. He could see her clearly in his mind's eye. Her beauty was enough to take any man's breath away, and he was jealous, knowing that others must have noticed this.

Feathery strands of bright hair framed a face he had yearned for, it seemed, forever. Her smooth white shoulders and lush breasts rose above the red gown in a tantalizing display of femininity that drove Richard to distraction.

The gown was tight at her waist, a waist he now spanned with his hands, and her skirts flared out at her hips to fall in thick silken folds to the lawn beneath her feet. She was everything a man could ask for in a woman—that he could ask for—with her spirit and courage and . . .

He scowled and released her. "You fool, do you know you could have been hurt sneaking up on someone like that? What if it hadn't been me? What if it had been"—he thought quickly—"Greene?"

Anger flashed in her blue eyes. "I can defend myself."

"Can you?" he challenged. Richard recalled her

weapon. "God's Teeth!" he cursed. "With a bloody rock?"

Chin raised, she drew herself upward. "I can manage, *mynheer*. Better even than you, it appears."

The knowledge of how they'd met hovered in the air between them. And of this occasion in which she'd taken him by surprise.

"And you?" she said. "What if the one who came up behind you hadn't been me? You could have been killed!"

She turned with a swish of her skirts and walked several steps before spinning to face him. "You play a dangerous game with fate, Richard. You risk too much too often."

His face softened. "Say it again."

Her brow furrowed. "What?"

"My name," he said huskily. "Say it."

Kirsten blinked. He smiled, enjoying her reaction, for she was taken aback. She seemed nervous all of a sudden. He had the satisfaction of realizing that she still cared.

"Please," he whispered.

She hesitated. "Richard."

Ric-kard. He grinned and moved toward her.

She stepped back. "I don't understand . . ."

"The way you say it has a unique effect on me."

And he could tell that she blushed as they played their game of cat and mouse.

"You're trying to confuse me," she said. "To make me forget my reason for being here with you."

"Can I?" he breathed. "Can I make you forget?"

Kirsten inhaled sharply. Yes, he could make her forget. Her heart raced as she met his glowing brown gaze. He wore that little half-smile on his sensual lips, that look that brought up her temperature and made her melt inside.

207

She couldn't allow him to fool her a second time.

She gathered herself together and then held her ground. "Richard," she said with firmness, then raised a hand to check his approach.

He paused and sighed with defeat. "What is it you want to know?"

She was both surprised and wary of his change in manner. "Everything," she said, and he walked toward her again, taking her by the arm as he continued his steps.

And so they walked, arm in arm, as Richard began his tale.

Kirsten listened with incredulity as he spoke of the British raid on his grandparents' farm in the Pennsylvania Colony. She felt sympathy for his loss when he described the old couples' deaths at the hands of the King's men. Then, he told of his friend Alex and of their enlistment in the Continental Army, and she knew real pain for all he'd suffered.

Richard continued with the telling of his mission, of how he'd come to need her care at the old mill, and she felt a reawakening of joy in her heart. Richard Maddox was a Patriot spy!

Then, she recalled how he'd acted with Elias Greene, how he'd been traveling with the Tories, and she knew a resurfacing of doubt.

When he was done, she had no words for him. Was he speaking the truth? She recalled the look on his face when he'd sworn not to lie to her.

"Richard," she murmured, bowing her head. She didn't know what to say.

He caught her chin, tilting her face upward for his inspection. "Kirsten, tell me you believe me."

She nodded, and she realized it was true. "I believe you."

"And you won't tell a soul?"

"I won't turn you in," she said. "Your secret is safe."

He pulled her into his embrace, capturing her willing lips with a fierceness that took her completely by surprise.

He groaned as he raised his head. "This is foolish." But he couldn't seem to keep from caressing her . . . her throat . . . her bare shoulders. He buried his face in her hair, inhaling her fragrance. She smelled of lavender and sunshine.

"Richard."

"Hmmm?"

"Will I see you again? After tonight?" She wanted—needed—some reassurance that what was happening between them wasn't a dream, but something special . . . something eternal.

Kirsten felt him tense and experienced a pull in her stomach muscles. He released her and put a distance of a few feet between them. That he could do it so easily hurt.

"Kirsten, nothing has changed since I left the mill. There's still a war to be fought, and I have yet to find Alex's killer."

"And then? After it's over, and we're all free?" She waited breathlessly for his answer.

Richard shook his blond head. "I can't say . . . can't promise."

"You mean you won't say."

His lips firmed.

It would hurt to part on bad terms. What if she never saw him again? Her heart thumped. What if he died?

She gazed at her beloved's features . . . at tawny hair drawn back as was the style of most men . . . at the thin, white scar that ran across his forehead and disappeared from view.

On impulse, she touched the scar and saw emotions flicker across his face. "How did you get it?" she asked. She ran her fingertips gently over the mended flesh.

"Not in the war, but as a youth. Alex and I were fishing. I slipped on a wet rock and fell into the river. My head hit a tree stump that was buried under the water." He looked rueful. "The cut was deep. My mother nearly suffered a bout of apoplexy when she saw me. My father—he had to stitch me up."

"Oh, dear," Kirsten said. "Your poor *moeder*. I can understand why." Without thought, she had continued to stroke his forehead, and now she caressed his cheek. She placed a finger against his lips.

His mouth opened to kiss that dainty digit, and a bolt of desire struck in Kirsten's nether regions, the sensation spiraling upward and out to every part of her body. Her nerve endings hummed with life; her skin tingled. Her breasts swelled, the nipples straining against her shift.

"Richard . . ."

"Yes, love?" He gazed at her from beneath lowered lids. His brown eyes appeared slumberous, glazed with passion.

Kirsten wanted so badly to lie close to him, to feel his kisses searing her everywhere. She wanted to love him and have him love her in return.

She remembered his mission, the danger involved in his work for the cause. "You will be careful?"

He frowned. "Careful?"

"Of the King's men? Oh, Richard, I keep remembering the night I found you. That man who attacked you . . . the one with the disfigured face . . ."

Richard froze. "You saw his face?"

She nodded, and then realized that her description of his attack might in some way help him. "Yes, but only briefly. It was dark, but there was lightning. I saw him as he raised his musket to—" She caught back a sob. "Oh, Richard, it was terrible!"

He touched her cheek and gave her a tender smile. But there was still an air of tension about him, tension brought on by the knowledge that Kirsten had seen something of the man who'd attacked him. It had been dark. He'd been blinded by the rain. His own recollection of the event was hazy. Mostly, it was of pain.

"What do you remember?"

"Only that he was disfigured, horribly so. His face was twisted. His mouth seemed huge and pulled up at one side. He looked evil . . . dangerous."

Richard nodded. It wasn't much to go on, but it helped to know that the man was disfigured. And the man knew Biv.

Laughter filtered back to their secluded spot. Laughter and conversation. Richard studied the woman before him, sadly realizing that it was time for them to part. She'd been gone from the gathering for a while. Even now, she might be missed. Someone might be searching for her.

"You must go back, love."

"Oh, no."

He gripped her shoulders. "Yes. Before you're missed. Before I'm discovered."

"What about Hamilton? Shall I get him for you?"

Richard shook his head. "There's no time now. I'll have to contact him later. I've been gone from camp too long myself. Greene and his men could be suspicious."

She leaned forward. He released her shoulders to draw her fully into his arms. The feel of her soft curves pressed against him was nearly his undoing. Suddenly, his mission seemed unimportant. The only thing he wanted to do was hold Kirsten, to bury himself deep inside her—to love her until the end of all time.

But he couldn't. He pushed her away. "Come. I'll escort you back to the house."

Now that Kirsten knew the danger he was in simply by being here, she wanted him to leave quickly. She'd be all right without company on her way back.

"No," she said. "I'll go alone."

"I insist."

"It's too dangerous."

He glared at her. "Kirsten, I'll not take no for an answer."

She sighed. It was pointless to argue with a stubborn man, to exchange words that might draw the attention of the very people Richard wanted to avoid.

They returned the way they'd come, past the line of evergreens. Richard stopped at the edge of the garden, and pulled Kirsten into his arms.

"Kiss me," he ordered.

She blinked and then did so. The warmth of his lips sent heat throughout all of her, and she pressed against him, wanting more from him, much more.

He lifted his head, looked past her to the door of the house. Kirsten suddenly realized that while her response had been abandoned, genuine, his kiss had been controlled. She was irritated. Then a feeling of foreboding replaced her annoyance.

"What?" she whispered. "What is it?"

"Someone is at the door watching us."

Kirsten started to turn. "No!" he exclaimed in hushed tones. "Don't move!"

"But I must see—"

"All right, then, but do so slowly. Pretend an

interest in a bush or flower. I'll turn first so you can get a look."

They changed positions by pretending to study a garden plant, and Kirsten glanced toward the house and saw the shadow at the door. The shadow changed as the man moved.

"He's coming this way," Richard said. "Quick! Kiss me again."

Kirsten reacted instinctively, slipping into his arms as if she had been made to be there, which she believed she was. She knew she should tell Richard of her discovery. She had seen the man's face as he'd stepped back into the light. It was Martin Hoppe, her cousin.

They broke apart. Richard pulled her farther into the shadows. Her head reeled dizzily as he captured her mouth once again. She sensed the change in him as he devoured her lips, and she rejoiced in the knowledge that he, too, was caught up in the magic.

She clung to his arms and felt his muscles tighten. He groaned as he came up for air and then returned to playing havoc with her lips, nose, cheeks, and chin. Taking her mouth, he deepened the intimacy of their kiss, parting her lips to stroke inside it with the tip of his tongue.

In the heat of the moment, they forgot the war, forgot their surroundings. Passion reigned over all else. Kirsten moaned as Richard strung kisses down her throat to the valley between her breasts, paying special attention there. His damp breath seared her skin, her nipples tightened in response.

He raised his head. His gaze holding hers, he cupped the curve of her bodice where her flesh throbbed and ached to burst free of linen and ruby silk. She gasped at the pressure, arching her back and thrusting her breast up and into his hand. She had

213

the strongest wish that he'd tug all cloth from her pulsating bosom.

A feminine giggle rent the air, making them spring apart. Kirsten blushed as she remembered Martin. Her cousin must have seen everything. Would he ask about the man in her arms? Would Martin condemn her for such a wanton, public display?

Her gaze went to the house. Fortunately, Martin was gone. Had he gone back to the party before Richard's kiss?

There was no one at the door, but the giggle she'd heard sounded again. It came from the other side of the smokehouse on the other side of the garden. Apparently, some other female guest was dallying with a beau.

"Go," Richard said. His breath seemed loud in the surrounding night. "We shouldn't have . . . I must leave. Go back inside."

"Richard . . ." Her eyes stung with tears. She didn't want to say good-bye to him. She wanted to be with him, to follow wherever he led. The yearning in her heart warred with reason, and logic won in the end.

"I love you," she said. It was barely a whisper. A soft sound on a puff of air.

He heard it. She saw that immediately. Emotion flamed in his deep russet eyes. "I—" He turned away and shook his head. Again, he faced her. "I can't. I'm sorry."

And then he was gone into the night, and all that remained of him was the tingling imprint of his kiss and the masculine scent of him lingering on her clothes and skin.

Kirsten headed toward the house, pausing once on her way to wipe away tears. By the time she reentered

214

the front parlor, she was composed and smiling again.

She searched for Martin and saw him chatting with their hostess, Theodosia. His gaze met hers across the room, and she tensed, expecting censure. She was startled to see Martin grin.

Encouraged, yet still uncomfortable, she moved to his side.

"Hallo, cousin," he greeted her. "Enjoying the night air?"

She nodded, feeling her face heat from the neck upward. Her blue eyes shot daggers at him.

"Are you having a pleasant time, dear?" Theodosia inquired.

"Yes, thank you, I am." Kirsten pretended a sudden interest in another occupant of the room. Actually she looked at no one in particular, until a man came into her focus. The handsome gentleman was heading their way. He had eyes only for Theodosia.

"Mrs. Prevost," he said. "I believe this is our dance."

"Mr. Burr," Mrs. Prevost murmured, and Kirsten saw Theodosia's cheeks turn a delightful shade of pink. "I believe it is."

And with that their hostess left the cousins' presence. Martin asked Kirsten to dance, and she agreed. The remainder of the evening passed quickly; and for a while, Kirsten was able to put Richard from her mind. But only for a short time. That night, tired from the party and the late hour, Kirsten climbed into bed, prepared to sleep.

She dreamed of Richard Maddox.

Chapter Seventeen

Richard sat before the campfire, staring into the flames that crackled and spit with the dripping juice of roasting meat. Beside him, Merritt Abernathy tended the spit, turning the stick to cook the rabbit evenly. It was late, but that didn't matter to Abernathy who always seemed to be hungry and never turned down an opportunity for food.

"Where were you?" the Tory said to Richard. "I had a devil of a time convincing Greene that you were out looking for a wench."

Facing the man, Richard grinned. "My thanks to you. In a way, I was. But not for him if that's what he thinks. You know of the Hermitage and a Mrs. Prevost? I heard that she's been doing a bit of entertaining lately."

"Patriots!" the man replied with a grimace. "Isn't Washington staying at the Hermitage?"

Richard nodded. "Did you ever get so close to fire as to dare it to burn you? That's what I did."

Abernathy looked at him blankly.

"I stood out back and stared at the bloody rebs through the window."

"You didn't!"

"I did." Richard appeared smug. "Caught me an eye and an earful, too. Told Greene 'bout it when I got back. Overheard the rebel general's going to leave Paramus soon . . . in a couple of days or so. It seems the troops are heading north. Thought it might make things easier for us if Greene was to know."

The Tory eyed him with respect. "Daring bloody bastard, aren't ye."

A flash of white teeth was Richard's only answer to him.

Silence reigned between the men for a time. The only noises were the pops and hisses of the fire, the rustle of underbrush as some animal scurried in search of food.

"Did I miss anything while I was gone?" Richard asked, managing to keep his tone light.

Abernathy didn't respond immediately. He rose up to poke a stick into the rabbit to see if the meat was done. It apparently wasn't cooked enough for his taste, for he sat back with a look of impatience. "We 'eard of Randolph's plans. It seems the King's men need food supplies in New York, and we're to be the ones to transport the goods."

"No joking? We're going to New York?"

The other man nodded. "As soon as the dear rebel general decides to leave. In a week's time is my guess."

Richard whistled through his teeth. "A real challenge for us, eh?"

Abernathy inclined his head.

The other members of the Tory band were scattered about the forest clearing in various positions of repose. Greene had gone to meet William Randolph, the man who'd summoned the group to the area, to discuss plans further.

Richard knew this type of smuggling operation well. He himself had been involved in the transportation of supplies, back in the early days of his enlistment, before Alex's death.

He hid a smile. He'd learn the routes the Tories used for smuggling. That knowledge in the right hands should give the Patriots an advantage.

They'd be gone for some time, he mused. The thought gave him pain, for he wanted to see Kirsten again. But he couldn't let her know, not when doing so would make her hope, believe, they had a future together. And it wouldn't be fair for her to wait for him. What if he didn't make it back? At any time his double life could be uncovered. If the Tories knew the truth, they'd kill him . . . perhaps torture him first to learn what he knew.

Kirsten . . . The image of her wounded expression when he'd left her made his insides twist painfully. He'd departed from her only hours ago, and he could still smell her sweet feminine fragrance.

She'd looked a vision in her scarlet gown. He'd never seen her wear her hair up that way; the style gave her an air of elegance. The jeweled haircomb in her silver blond tresses was impressive, but it hadn't sparkled as much as her glistening aquamarine eyes had.

If only he could hold her again, lie with her one more time.

He became angry with himself. What good would it do to prolong the torture of their final parting?

Remember how it was when you left her the last time. Those days that followed . . . the longing for her company . . . the comfort of her arms. And what if a child came from their joining?

He drew a sharp breath. Dear Lord, was it possible that she was with child from their time together at the mill?

Closing his eyes, he pictured her curves and was somewhat comforted by the memory of her in her red

219

silk gown. Her waist had been small. Hadn't he encircled it with his hands?

Then came the startling realization that even if she were pregnant her body wouldn't have changed in so short a time, at least not her waist.

Her breasts? He vaguely recalled hearing that a woman's breasts changed when she was with child. They swelled, became larger. Kirsten's breasts had nearly spilled over the top of her gown. *Dear God,* he thought. The mental image of full honey-colored flesh above her red bodice brought him terror at the same time it seared his loins with fresh heat.

He had to know. He had to return to Hoppertown someday if only to find out if he was a father and could help the babe. It could be months from now . . . years, depending on this blasted war and the enduring strength of both sides. What if there was someone else in Kirsten's life then? He swallowed against a suddenly dry throat. At least he could see them happy and comfortable in their circumstances. It was the least he could do for not being there when she gave birth to his child.

Richard felt the strongest desire to hurry toward the Van Atta farm, and confront Kirsten with the one question that would forever haunt him until he knew the answer. Pushing to his feet, he moved toward the woods.

"Canfield, where are ye going?" Abernathy inquired, his eyes narrowing.

Richard stopped in his tracks. Where in heavens was he going? He couldn't leave now! Not after being gone for over an hour earlier—and missed.

Damn! He had to forget his concerns. He had to forget Kirsten! He faced the Tory with a raised eyebrow. "I'm going to take a piss," he said.

* * *

A Patriot spy! Gazing up at the top board of her alcove bed, Kirsten smiled into the darkness. It was late, hours after the party at the Hermitage; and yet her mind still spun with the exciting events of the evening. Her first dance. Her conversation with the general. Her meeting with Richard . . . and his kiss.

She'd left the doors to the bed wide and opened her bedchamber window. Glancing toward the raised sash, Kirsten saw the stars twinkling in the night sky, the moon's soft glow over a distant field.

She sat up, and hugged herself. She imagined she was with Richard again. They were dancing as she and Martin had done. It was a country dance—the Roger de Coverley.

Did Richard know how to dance? She decided that he most probably did.

In her imaginings, she wore a different gown for the occasion, a lovely creation of blue satin with a cream stomacher and a neckline that plunged to just above her nipples. Her skirts made swishing sounds when she walked or moved . . . or pressed up against his lean, hard, masculine body.

The music in her dreams was divine. There were three musicians instead of one—a woman with a harp, a man on a pianoforte, and a second gentleman with a violin. The lulling tune lured her into a land of enchantment where love and Richard were all that mattered. There was no war—no King George. Only her and Richard and the musicians playing the song.

An owl hooted from somewhere in the distance, bringing her attention back to the present. The call was sad and lonely, as if the bird were on its own, beckoning for its lost mate.

Kirsten giggled softly and shook her head. An owl sad and lonely? She was truly getting fanciful to think such nonsense. The smile left her face as it occurred to her why she was entertaining such thoughts. It was because of Richard. Her every thought since learning the truth about him came back to the wonders of love. Now the land seemed greener. The stars twinkled brighter in the black sky. The soft summer breeze caressed one's flesh like a gentle lover's hand . . .

Kirsten climbed from her bed and went to the window. Her room faced the back of the house. There was a tree directly outside, but she could see past it to her father's fields. A ribbon of dark glistening water threaded its way from her left, the south, to the north on her right.

Where is Richard now? It was a strange, thrilling experience knowing that he was nearby. Were the Tories camped in the forest? Or a field?

Richard had said that he must leave. He wouldn't say when he'd return, if he'd return, but she knew he would. She'd seen the look on his face after they'd kissed. He loved her; he must!

She had to have patience. He had a mission to complete, and she had her own work to do for the cause. Tomorrow when she arose, she would go to Martin's tavern. With Washington and his aides at the Hermitage and his troops encamped at Paramus, she'd be able to transport the rest of the supplies to the Van Voorhees' farm in relative safety . . . as long as she and Miles didn't stumble into the path of the departing Tories.

Kirsten turned from the window and went back to bed. Richard was gone. All she could do now was hope and pray for his safe return and continue with her work as before.

She had best get a good night's rest. There was a great deal to be done on the morrow. When he'd brought her home from the party earlier, Martin had told her he'd found her someone to help in moving the goods to the Van Voorhees'.

*   *   *

The next morning Kirsten left the homestead for her cousin's inn. When she arrived, her help was awaiting her. Among the four men that Martin had asked to come was John Ackerman, who had so irritated Kirsten the evening before. He grinned at her when he spied her, his expression smug. Stifling annoyance, she smiled at him politely before she addressed the group.

"Thank you, kind gentlemen, for offering to assist us."

Each man had brought a wagon from his farm. An hour after Kirsten's arrival, each wagon was full, and the drivers were headed down the road to the Van Voorhees' place.

They traveled along together in single file. The area was occupied by Continental forces, but there was no telling who else might be about. There were hungry deserters and small enemy bands roaming the countryside. The supplies were a valuable cargo that must be protected.

Kirsten had her own wagon to drive. Her father's flintlock musket lay next to her on the seat. She kept a careful watch on the surrounding woods as the group moved on to their destination. Her vehicle was the second one in line. Thomas Banta, Rachel's brother, was directly ahead of her, in the lead. His cinnamon brown hair glinted in the bright rays of the summer sun each time he passed under an opening in the green canopy above them.

They had gone about a half-mile when the road was blocked by a group of soldiers. A man stepped forward, clearly in charge. Kirsten recognized him as being the same soldier who had guarded Washington's tent when she'd made her visit that first day.

The young soldier stood in front of the line of six

vehicles. His arms folded across his chest, he glared at Thomas, before his narrowed gaze moved slowly to each one of the drivers.

"Who goes there? And what have you in your wagons?" The soldier held up his rifle.

Kirsten recalled the state of the men at camp and felt a faint flicker of unease. She rose up from her seat. "You! You were the guard at Mynheer Washington's tent."

He stared at her, raising an eyebrow. "And you are the wench who dared to venture into our camp alone."

She stiffened, insulted by the implication. "I had business with the general."

He approached, passing Thomas' wagon until he was beside her and looking up at her. Placing a hand on the wagon, he leaned against it casually and studied her boldly from head to toe. She met his gaze, refusing to be intimidated. He straightened, transferring his attention to the goods in her wagon.

"And what business is this?" he asked. He fanned his hand over her load, wooden crates. "You are perhaps denying the general supplies?"

Kirsten scowled. "We deny our Patriot brothers nothing! Have not your bellies been full since you came? Your thirst quenched? You have been offered our finest *kost* and *drank, mynheer.* Do not dare to suggest we do anything but!"

The young man seemed taken aback by her vehemence. The other drivers had climbed out of their vehicles to rally at Kirsten's side.

"We are merely preparing for a British invasion," Hans Bogert said shortly, and Kirsten was surprised at his show of firmness. "Our village is small, but there are women and children to be protected."

John Ackerman came forward, pushing his way past some of the other drivers. "You have food

224

aplenty in your camp. When you leave here, we will see that you have more than enough to last for weeks. Why take what you cannot use, what would be put to better use in the safekeeping of women and children against the King's men!"

The guard eyed them narrowly. "I sincerely hope you tell the truth, dear lady."

Martin came up from behind the others. "Lieutenant Rhoades!"

The soldier's face brightened. "Mr. Hoppe! I didn't see you there."

"Obviously," Martin said dryly, and the man blushed. "This lady you question is my cousin. Will you not allow us to pass without incident? She tells the truth, as do my friends here." He gestured toward Hans and John.

The man nodded, apparently happy to trust the owner of the local tavern. "Certainly, Mr. Hoppe, if you vouch for them."

"I ride with them," Martin pointed out dryly. Lieutenant Rhoades gave a sharp command to his comrades, and the soldiers cleared off the road.

Returning to their vehicles, the drivers climbed back into the wagons. Kirsten's fingers gripped the handle of her rifle as she clicked to her horse and the wagon began to move. She felt the soldiers' eyes on her as she passed by. It wasn't until they'd reached the Van Voorhees' home that Kirsten was able to relax. It disturbed her to have felt so threatened by men under General Washington's command. The fear brought home the fact that war did strange things to men—all men. Would she ever truly feel safe again?

The Van Voorhees' home was large, with a double front door flanked by two windows on each side and five windows above it on the second floor. There were several outbuildings on the property—including a smokehouse, a summer kitchen, and a huge barn. All were kept in good order by Samuel Van Voorhees and his two sons, Johannes and Jacob. Sarah Van Voorhees, Samuel's wife, was a short slim woman with golden hair and a gentle disposition. She greeted Kirsten and her male helpers with a pleasant smile. It was quickly obvious to Kirsten that she had this lady's support in the work they were doing, that Sarah was sincere in her efforts to help the Hoppertown residents, her neighbors and friends.

Samuel Van Voorhees was a contrast to his wife, being tall and large boned with rippling muscles. The man was active in the local militia as were his fifteen-year-old twin sons. Seeing Samuel and his wife together, one would think them a strange pair, but it was obvious to Kirsten how taken they were with each other. The big, hefty man treated his small wife like fine-blown glass, while he showed his children brusque affection.

With the Van Voorhees males' help, the wagons were unloaded in record time, the goods stored in the cellar under the main house. Soon the Patriots were on their way home. After hearing about the encounter with the soldiers, Samuel and his sons insisted on escorting the wagons for part of the journey. When it appeared that Washington's men had returned to camp, the Van Voorheeses left for home.

Back in the safety of her father's house, Kirsten still couldn't forget the attitude of the guard, the implied threat of the soldiers' blockade. She had half a mind to speak to the general! Such behavior in his men wasn't right. The Hoppertown Patriots had been nothing but hospitable to his troops.

She would seek out General Washington in the morning, she decided.

Chapter Eighteen

A shot rang out in the night, and Richard ducked as the musket ball whizzed past him.

"To the other side," he bellowed at Elias Greene. "Now!"

The man didn't move, but crouched, frozen in fear, behind a thicket on the left side of the dirt road, a few feet ahead of where they'd deserted their wagon of goods.

"Elias, for God's sake, move your arse across the road!" Richard shouted. He was positioned several yards away on the same side.

The man turned to look at Richard blankly. Richard cursed, wondering what to do next. At the first sign of Continental forces, they'd abandoned the cart of goods to take cover in the woods. Richard had run for an old oak with a huge trunk, while Elias had blindly fled until he'd reached a thicket of small evergreens. Richard and Greene had been on foot, guarding the left side of the vehicle, while Greene's brother Sid and the newest man, Joseph, flanked the right. The youngest Greene, John, drove the wagon with Merritt Abernathy. Kendall Allen and the others in the band stayed back at Randolph's farm, preparing a second run of goods to New York.

Richard rose up to glance across the dirt trail to the other side, but could see nothing. It was either fight or die like a helpless lamb. He raised the stock of his rifle to his shoulder, leveled the barrel, firing the flintlock toward empty space. These men were Patriot soldiers, and while they knew nothing of his work and would no doubt kill him if they got their hands on him, he couldn't shoot them.

He glanced back to the spot where Greene cringed like a coward, saw that he'd finally moved to the edge of the road. Gunfire rained beyond a thicket. The fighting was heavier on the other side of the road, and young Greene needed assistance.

He sighed as Elias slipped from behind one tree to the next and crossed the road. Richard knew he could hold this area on his own. If he got caught . . . He didn't dare think of that now, for he was a long way from General Washington's camp. There was no one here to vouch for him.

A nearby bush crackled as it moved, and Richard raised his rifle, training it on the swaying branches. *Go away*, he thought. *If you're a Patriot, I don't want to kill you. And it's too soon to destroy my cover.* The leaves rustled again, and then the action stopped. Whoever—whatever—it was had left.

Lowering his gun, Richard released a pent-up breath. The Patriots had climbed into the cart, and were now driving it away. The exchange of gunfire continued, but Richard watched with a half-smile. The Continental officer was a smart one. He'd gotten the message Richard had left him at that inn, had found the trail marks Richard had made.

Now if only I can get out of this mess alive!

The cart creaked as it rolled over rocks in the forest path. It was the noise of the wheels that had alerted the troops to the exact location of the smuggling party. Richard ducked low and moved back several yards, keeping himself hidden much as Greene had done. Most of the Patriot troops had gone; only one, or perhaps two, remained to continue the rain of rifle fire. Soon, the shooting stopped and the noise died down. It was quiet for a moment or two, and then Richard heard a cry of pain. Someone in the group must have taken a bullet.

Greene? He was a cocksure fellow, much like his older brother. Richard frowned, recalling Elias's earlier behavior and surprised to have seen marked fear in the man.

Richard crept through the woods and across the road to see what had happened to the Tory smugglers. He heard the soft murmur of voices . . . and the moan of a man in agony.

He skirted a copse and saw them—three men huddled over a fourth. There was one missing. Dead? Who had died and who was injured?

He gave their secret call before he approached.

"Canfield," someone said. "Thank God you're all right."

"Who's down?" he asked.

"Sid's dead. Abernathy here is hurt. Taken a ball to his left leg."

Richard bent over the man to take a look. Abernathy had taken the piece in his thigh, and it didn't look good. Examining the open wound closely, Richard wondered how best to treat it . . . if it was worth trying. Could they remove the ball? The leg muscle had been ripped wide open; the ball must have hit the flesh in just the wrong way. Already the poor victim looked half dead.

"Joseph?" Richard glanced up at the newest member of the band for a second opinion.

"I don't know," the man replied, his gaze doubtful, his brow creased into a frown of concern.

Greene looked shocked, his gaze unseeing, and another man—Greene's youngest brother John— was vomiting in the bushes after seeing his dead brother's body.

"Elias?" Richard asked.

"His brother is dead," Joseph said. "No sense talking to him."

He sighed. War was such a waste of human life. When would it be over? Would it ever be over?

He turned his attention to Merritt Abernathy. "Merritt? How are you feeling?"

The man didn't immediately answer, a testament to how hurt he was. Finally, his lips moved. "Like I've been skewered by a red-hot poker," he managed to gasp. He attempted to crack a smile, but his grin resembled a grimace. "Damn, Canfield, but it hurts like hell."

Recalling his own injuries, Richard felt sympathy for the man. These men might be Tories, but he'd come to know them. And in the end, they were just ordinary men like himself. He reached into his weskit pocket and removed a small bottle. "Here— drink this. It'll help ease the pain."

Elias came alive at the sight of the liquor. "Give me that!" He made to snatch the bottle from Richard's grasp, but Richard clamped onto Elias's arm with his free hand, stopping him.

"The man's dying, you fool," he hissed, his voice low. The shock of seeing Abernathy lying there had brought back the frustrations and horrors of the war. "Allow him a restful sleep."

Greene stared at him hard. He had bloodstains on his shirt, and lines of pain ran from his eyes and across his forehead. He made a pathetic picture. His

230

mouth quivered as he gave in to tears. Immediately, John Greene went to his brother, holding Elias as they both surrendered to grief.

Richard turned back to his injured Tory friend. He helped Abernathy take a sip of the fiery liquor. The dying man swallowed, coughed, and sipped again. Finally, exhausted, he lay back, his eyes closed.

"Canfield?" Merritt opened his eyes and rose up on his elbows in a surprising show of strength. "Thanks."

Richard grinned. "At least the bloody rebs didn't get everything."

Merritt Abernathy started to smile and then groaned and fell back. Blood poured from the man's wound, soaking his breeches, staining the ground. Before their eyes, he lost his life force. Richard watched, feeling helpless. Moments later, Abernathy was dead.

The Continental forces were long gone. Elias now cried out like a wild animal. His eyes feverishly bright, he let his gaze follow each of his men in turn.

"I'll kill the bastards," he vowed. "I'll kill each and every one of them for this. No bloody reb will escape us—ever gain!"

So it was that Richard saw another man turn mad with the death and destruction brought on by war. And he knew the danger of his position had intensified.

A month passed and then another. July became August and soon it was autumn. Life in the small village of Hoppertown had gone on peacefully during those remaining July weeks with the Continental Army gone and no sign of British or Tory troops.

With the Van Voorhees' farm ready for sheltering two days after they'd transferred the goods, Kirsten returned to the daily routine of helping her mother in the kitchen and garden, mending clothes, and feeding the farm animals. She'd never had a chance to speak to Washington about his man—the rude guard who'd blocked the road. And the next thing she'd learned was that the Continentals had left.

Kirsten had been busy with the local women from Patriot families, planning for enemy attack and for the safekeeping of the children. The day after the goods from the inn were moved to the Van Voorhees', she had called a meeting of the women to discuss plans in case of an attack. She had explained that there was already a place to flee in the event of a British invasion, and she had asked for linens and other supplies, including soap, ammunition, and onions and apples from their storage cellars.

These women were wives and relatives of the local militiamen. During their meeting, they came up with a system of alerting each family in the event that such an emergency should occur. There was a brief discussion on whether to include any of their Tory relatives. Most felt that since those families had chosen the King's side, they would have to suffer the consequences if their English friends turned against them.

With September came another raid—an attack by Greene and his party. The band left, however, before they could do much damage. Garret Vandervelt's home was torched one night, but the fire was found early and quickly brought under control.

Once a day, early in the morning, the militiamen drilled with their rifles. Other than an occasional attack from a small, ineffective Tory band, it could have been a time of peace.

Harvest time arrived, and the farmers ceased their drilling to bring in the balance of their crops. The Van Atta family began to prepare for the winter months with the beginning of November.

Kirsten and her mother were out in the yard working over a hot fire. That morning James Van Atta had slaughtered a cow and a sheep; and while he butchered the meat which would be cured in the smokehouse, the two women rendered the animal fat for various household uses. They'd built a large fire in the yard early that morning. A large iron kettle hung over the flames, held in place by a specially constructed frame made by Kirsten's father. Kirsten stood near the steaming pot, stirring the mixture of melted beef and mutton tallow. Agnes added chunks of animal fat to the hot cauldron.

"You seem quiet, daughter," she said, looking at Kirsten with concern.

Kirsten glanced up and wiped an arm across her forehead. Then, for a moment, she stared into the bubbling tallow. "I am fine, *Moeder*."

She gave her mother a slight smile, aware of the picture she presented. Her simple gown of muslin was stained with animal grease. Despite the cool November weather, she was soaked with perspiration due to the steaming heat of the iron pot.

Her mother studied her with a look of concern, and Kirsten had to reassure her parent a second time. Her only problem these days was that she couldn't stop picturing Richard and wondering when he'd return . . . *if* he'd return. She had begun to doubt his sincerity, whether he'd told her the truth the night of Theodosia's party. And her doubts hurt her deeply.

What if he'd been lying to save his skin? Had she let him free only to have him cause countless Patriot deaths?

233

She turned from the pot. A small table was set up nearby. Kirsten took a cup of water from the table and quenched her thirst. If Richard had deceived her . . . She closed her eyes as she experienced a wave of pain.

If he deceived me, she thought, *then by God I'll see that he pays!*

November 15, 1778

Richard returned to Hoppertown in the company of Tories. Kirsten was at the tavern at Martin's request, helping her cousin with his stores. Her work at the Van Atta home was done. The candles were made, the meat was smoked. The family was ready for winter. That day the Tory band returned to Hoppertown. There was a great stir among the local patrons as these unwelcome men entered the inn's common room. Elias Greene sat down at a table, and the others followed suit, noisily taking seats wherever it suited them.

Greene slammed his fist on a scarred tabletop and in a loud voice demanded a drink. "Innkeeper! Some ale for a group of poor weary travelers!" The man seated beside him laughed.

The cousins heard the call from the back room. "I'll get it," Kirsten said. "It's the Ackerman boys most likely."

She poured three ales and placed the tankards on a tray. She entered the common room, carefully balancing the tray on one arm, as the last of the men sat down. Kirsten froze when she saw who it was. Her heart began to pound, her pulse roared in her ears, for she'd seen him immediately . . . that bright blond head with hair fastened back into a club held by a black velvet ribbon. Richard Maddox.

As if in a trance, Kirsten moved to the first table and set a tankard before Elias Greene. She stepped back quickly. She'd not forgotten her unpleasant encounter with the man. But all the while, she was conscious of eyes on her . . . russet eyes. Richard's.

She went to the next man, placed a mug on the table, and got her arm grabbed as she pulled back. She gasped and tried to free herself. The tray in her other arm wobbled and started to fall.

And then everything happened so quickly she wasn't sure what was occurring. Richard must have jumped from his seat across the table when the tray started to topple, for the next thing she knew he was there, catching it and steadying her, his grip firm on her arm.

Kendall Allen had released her with a muffled curse. One of the pewter tankards had spilled, and ale had washed over to soak his shirt and stain his breeches. The other men in the room laughed, teasing their friend. Allen glared at her.

"Are you all right?" Richard's low husky voice reached her ears through the outburst of merriment.

She turned to him slowly, reluctant to meet his gaze. She was convinced he'd lied to her, and she didn't want to see his face—to find that she still wasn't over her love for him . . . that she would never be over him.

Their eyes met. Kirsten saw the tender warmth in his brown eyes, and as her insides churned with longing, she became angry not only with herself but with Richard. Why had he come back to disrupt her life? She wished she could forget him.

He'd been traveling for weeks with the Tory band. How long could it be before his convictions changed and mirrored theirs? The more she recalled about that evening at the Hermitage, the more she grew puzzled. If Richard had truly wanted to see Washington, he should have allowed her to get the general for him. Instead, he'd made up some excuse about there not being enough time.

He looked good, she noticed. Too good. His skin was a rich bronze from the summer sun. His body had filled out. Richard wore his sleeves rolled up over his elbows, and she could see that his arm muscles were well developed, rock hard, as he shifted the tray within his grasp.

"I'm not paying for it, wench!" Allen boomed. "In fact, we'll not pay for the round. It was your carelessness what did it."

"You'll not pay for the spill, but you'll pay for the round!" Kirsten said. "My cousin serves no cheaters!"

Allen's chair scraped the floor as he rose. "And if I refuse?"

"Easy," Richard said. "The lady wants only to be fair to her employer."

"Stay out of it, Canfield."

"Kendall Allen." Richard's voice had become a warning growl.

"Hoping to bed this one, too? What's the matter? All those others not enough to satisfy you?" He raked Kirsten with his bold gaze. "She's a scrawny thing . . . not like the last one."

Others? Kirsten thought, and her throat closed up. She blinked back tears as she took back the tray. It wouldn't do for Richard to know that the man's comments hurt.

"Kirsten," Richard murmured.

She refused to meet his gaze. "Thank you, sir, for your kind help."

Hands clutching the tray, she hurried toward the back room. Martin had come to the doorway to find

236

out what the commotion was about. Kirsten passed him with her head bent; she didn't want him to see her tears, to realize how humiliated and betrayed she felt.

Martin came into the workroom as Kirsten was preparing to leave by the back door. "Going somewhere, cousin?"

She froze.

"Kirsten, look at me." His tone was soft.

She glanced up and was unable to contain her tears.

"It's all right. What harm is some spilled ale?" When she shook her head, he said, "If not that, then what's bothering you?"

Kirsten held his gaze, and his eyes narrowed. "The man," he said. "The one with the fair hair—good God, he's the one you were with at the Hermitage!"

Martin shook his head as he went to her and touched her arm. "A Tory, Kirsten?"

She nodded, and there was a lengthy pause. She stared at the floor through her haze of tears.

"Cousin," he said slowly, "you wouldn't . . . ah, you . . ."

Her head snapped upward. "I'm no traitor to the cause, Martin, if that's what you're asking!"

He looked guilty.

"I have to leave," she choked out.

"I understand."

"Do you?" she asked, her expression displaying her skepticism.

Martin inclined his head. "I once knew a woman. She was the kindest, most sweet creature on the face of the earth. I fell in love with her within hours after meeting her. Everything was wonderful . . . until I learned she was married." His face contorted with pain. "A little something she had neglected to tell

237

me." He sounded bitter.

Kirsten wore her hair in braids, and he stroked a stray tendril away from her face. "I understand what it is to feel betrayed," Martin said.

She sniffed. "And what did you do? How did you learn to get over her?" She didn't deny her feelings for Richard, for she couldn't deny the truth.

"Day by day," he told her. "I took each new moment as it came. I still do." He smiled, but his expression told of a lingering sadness.

"Oh, Martin, I'm sorry."

He brightened. "Don't be. It was good while it lasted." After moving to the long worktable, he grabbed a plate of cinnamon cakes and placed it on a tray. Then, he turned to her. "Forget him, Kirsten, if he's the reason for your sadness."

"But, you said—"

"I know what I said, but this is different. This is war."

"I'll try," she murmured. "But it won't be easy."

She left by the back door, unwilling to chance meeting Richard in the common room. But there was no avoiding him. He stood outside, leaning against a large elm tree, his arms folded across his chest. Upon seeing her, he straightened, his mouth curving into a tentative smile.

"Hello, love."

"Don't 'love' me!" She walked by him.

He fell into step behind her. "What's wrong? I'm still here . . . and when I wasn't sure I would be. I thought you'd be happy."

She stopped, her body rigid. Glaring, she said, "You're still with them. Why? Because you lied! You're one of them—a Tory! A traitor to the cause!"

Hushing her, he glanced about. "Do you want to see me killed?"

"By whom?"

He scowled. "I'm working for General Washington—I told you that."

"I'll bet you are." Her blue eyes flashed angry fire. "Wenches in every village!" Her voice caught on a sob. "Tell me was I as good as those others you tumbled?"

"There were no—"

"Don't lie to me!" she hissed and then stomped away.

"Kirsten?" Martin was at the back door, staring out, scowling at Richard. "Is this *gentle*man bothering you?"

She nodded, averting her glance. Martin moved his arm, displaying his grip on a flintlock pistol. "I suggest you be on your way, mister. Now."

Richard blinked. "Kirsten?" She wouldn't meet his gaze. *"Please."*

The click of the hammer was loud in the ensuing silence.

Kirsten sighed. "Go away, Richard." Her heart thumped wildly beneath her breast as she studied him from beneath lowered lashes. He seemed about to protest, to stand firm, but then his shoulders slumped with defeat.

"I'll go . . ." His words were soft, full of hurt. "But I've not tricked you. I swear this on my grandmother's grave."

Kirsten stared at this avowal, and Richard returned with slow steps to the tavern. She met Martin's gaze as her cousin lowered his weapon. "Do you think he's sincere?" she asked.

Martin searched her face as if delving into her soul. "He seemed genuine enough."

She blinked back tears. "Then why is he still with them? They're Tory scum! If he's a Patriot, how can

239

he stay with them?"

"He's not one of them?" Martin raised his eyebrows.

She glanced at the house and checked the yard before signaling to her cousin to follow. Martin joined her only after returning inside to lock up the tavern. The Tories had finished their ale and left.

"Let's walk," Kirsten said. "I'm feeling restless." She led him some distance from the house, stopping under a large shade tree, away from prying eyes. Agitated, she picked off a leaf, pulled it apart, and dropped it to the ground. She pulled off another leaf and began twirling it by the stem.

"He says he's a Patriot," she began, her voice thick. "A spy."

Her cousin froze. "A spy, you say?"

She grabbed his sleeve. "You mustn't tell anyone. If he's telling the truth, he'll be killed. If he's lying . . . I don't know what will happen to him."

"He was the one in the garden," Martin said. "Wasn't he?" She nodded. "What was he doing at the Hermitage?"

Kirsten threw away the leaf and watched it sail in the air before it floated to earth. "He was there to see the general—or so he claimed. He says only Washington and his aide Hamilton know of his true identity."

"And did he see the general?"

She bit her lip. "No . . . he never got a chance. I caught him by the window staring inside. I didn't know who he was at first."

"You met then and became so familiar?" Martin looked disapproving.

Kirsten shook her head. "We met weeks before actually. I found him in the forest. He'd been injured, bayonet wounds. I saw the attack; I saw everything.

The man who hurt him took Richard by surprise. Richard never had a chance."

She took a deep breath and released it slowly. "I couldn't leave him there, Martin," she said, begging for understanding, for some sign of her cousin's approval. "The man who attacked him was horrible . . . his face was disfigured. I'll never forget that face."

"So what did you do?" Her cousin appeared fascinated by her tale.

She told him quickly of her efforts to save the injured man, how she would have taken him to the farm but for the danger she'd have placed her family in by doing so.

"So I took him to the old mill." She explained about the cellar, about how she'd nursed Richard back to health. She said she'd believed him to be a Continental soldier.

"Imagine my shock when he came back with Greene."

"Yes, I can." Martin was thoughtful. He paused for a moment to regard her intently. "And he told you what? That he was a Continental soldier? A Tory?"

"Well, no. He didn't say what he was. But you see when he was hurt badly he managed to tell me to hide him from the British. Because of that, I assumed he was a Patriot." Martin nodded his agreement. "When I found him at the Hermitage," she continued, "he seemed surprised but glad to see me. I threatened to turn him in, and he told me about his mission. Said he was working for Washington, trying to learn the identity of a traitor. His friend was killed while working as a spy. Richard is determined to find the traitor and to see the murderer pay."

"It's someone under Washington's command?"

"Richard thinks so."

Martin whistled softly. "And so he goes with Greene."

Kirsten nodded. "Hard to believe, isn't it? But I believed him . . . all too easily."

Her cousin smiled. "It's hard for you to know what to believe, I'm sure. But I can tell you one thing, his story seems too odd not to be true. Whether you believe in him or not is up to you." He steered her back toward the inn. "Whatever you decide, though, just be careful, Kirsten. I see there's more at stake here than just what side of the war a man's fighting. It seems to me that you care for this Richard. It's your heart I'd watch out for. Lose it to one you're unsure of and you risk pain and heartbreak . . . perhaps death."

Chapter Nineteen

A heavy pounding on the Van Attas' Dutch door woke the entire household. Kirsten reached toward her bed table and found her tinderbox. With a strike of flint against steel, she managed to nurture a flame on some threads in a small glass. To this, she quickly placed the wick of a candle.

The room came alive with a soft flickering glow. The knocking continued, and Kirsten set the candle in the holder and climbed from her bed. As she donned her dressing gown, she could hear her parents' voices in the hall outside her bedchamber. Hurrying to the door, she flung it open.

"*Moeder? Vader?* What's wrong? What is it?"

James stared down the staircase. "I don't know." He started down the steps. The thundering on the door took on a more distinct pattern. "It's the signal! We must be under British attack!" he exclaimed.

Clutching the edges of her garment together tightly, Kirsten followed her father while her mother hung back in the upstairs' hall.

"I should pack some things," Agnes murmured, her voice quivering with fear.

Kirsten's heart had started to pound at her father's words. Was it true? Were the British invading? She thought of Richard. Was he with them? He and his Tory friends?

James had opened the door to let in Thomas Banta.

"Hurry!" Thomas urged. "The militia are going for the Tories. We must join them!"

Kirsten's father seemed stunned. "Now? In the middle of the night?"

The young man nodded. "Ackerman found their camp near Zabriskies' old burned cabin. They sleep even as we speak. What easier way to take prisoners than to get them when their guard is down and they are most vulnerable?"

Over James's shoulder, Thomas regarded the two women. Agnes had come downstairs and stood behind her daughter, her expression revealing mixed emotions. "You women are to go the Van Voorhees' as planned in case of invasion. The Tories' number are few, but we know not if they are truly alone or whether the British camp is within distance. It's a precautionary measure, for your safety. All the Patriot families are going."

Kirsten frowned. She knew the Zabriskie cabin; it was far enough away. "But's that ridiculous. We'll be fine here."

"Don't argue, daughter. Dress and gather your things," James Van Atta ordered. "Agnes dear, worry not. I will see you there when this is over."

"Oh, James!" his spouse cried. "Must you go?"

He nodded. "You know I must." They stared at one another, knowing that there was much that wasn't being said. James knew his wife's pain; he understood that she was torn between the husband and daughter and the side they'd chosen, and the brother with whom she'd traveled to the New World. "Go, love." His voice was gentle, and she nodded. With tears in her eyes, she climbed the stairs to get ready to leave.

Kirsten followed her up the stairs. She dressed in her father's old shirt and breeches, uncaring of others' reactions at the sight of her in men's clothing. While her mother filled two satchels with clothes, she ran to saddle Hilga. When she was done, she found her mother waiting for her on the stoop.

"Can you ride with me, *Moeder?* It would be easier, swifter if you could." Her mother didn't say a word about her garments.

Agnes inclined her head. "Where's Pieter?" she asked.

Kirsten climbed down to help her mother up onto the horse. "He went with *Vader.* Come," she said. "We must hurry lest we get caught by those who might escape." She saw her mother settled and then mounted herself. "Hold on tight."

She waited a few seconds before she kicked the mare into a gallop. Her mother gripped her waist tightly; Kirsten was aware of fingers digging into her ribs. She could understand her mother's fear, and she didn't blame her. Agnes Van Atta had a husband going to war and a brother who was a Tory—the enemy of her husband. Either way, the outcome would hurt her.

The Van Voorhees' farm was bright with torches and candlelight, and other families were arriving as Kirsten and her mother did.

"Moeder?" Kirsten said, once she'd helped her mother down. "I'm not staying."

"What?" Her mother gasped. "Of course, you're staying!"

Kirsten shook her head. "I can't. And I can't say

why. But you must trust that I know what I'm doing."

"Catherine," her mother murmured as if in a daze.

Her daughter started in surprise. She hadn't thought of her aunt. How would Miles's mother be affected by all of this? "Yes, you're right . . . someone must get to her. Help her to escape."

"You can't." Agnes seemed to become more alert. "William's a Tory. You heard them at the meeting. They'll not allow her to come."

"They'll allow it," Kirsten stated, her voice firm.

Richard woke up to the shrill cries of men at war as the militia descended upon the Tory camp. He scrambled to his feet and took up his gun. All hell broke loose as the Tories reacted to the attack with panic and musket fire.

There were at least fifteen local militiamen, Richard guessed. He watched as Kendall Allen fell, a musket ball in his side. What should he do? He reacted on instinct then, helping the Patriots who appeared to need assistance, hoping against hope that the Tories wouldn't win; for he had displayed his true loyalties. He had picked sides against Greene and his men, joining the militia to fight them in hand-to-hand combat.

A young lad of about sixteen years of age was engaged in fighting Elias Greene. Richard saw the look in Greene's eyes as the big man knocked the youth to the ground. There was murder in the Tory's expression. Richard sprang to help the boy, pulling Greene off him and smashing the Tory in the jaw with his fist.

Greene saw who'd struck him and fell back, looking stunned. The boy rose to his feet, found his rifle, and trained the barrel on Greene's prone form. He flashed Richard a smile of gratitude, which froze on his face with his disbelief.

Richard grinned at the lad and went on to search for anyone else who might need aid.

A harsh cry caught his attention. He spied a familiar face, that of the innkeeper from Hoppertown. The man was in trouble, for Joseph had wrestled away Hoppe's pistol and had the gun trained on the tavern owner's chest.

Richard briefly recalled Hoppe's behavior toward him and felt a faint stirring of anger. By acknowledging that Hoppe had only been looking out for Kirsten, Richard cooled his head.

"Joseph!" he shouted, distracting the gunner's attention.

That provided all the time Martin needed to recapture his gun from the Tory's grasp.

Martin's gaze met Richard's across the clearing, and Richard nodded, then turned away. Suddenly, he heard someone call his name. A woman. Kirsten.

He saw her at the edge of the camp, crying out for him, her expression frantic as she searched amongst the fighting men.

Damn! How could she have been so foolish as to come here? She must have learned of the attack. She should have stayed home!

His breath caught as a pair of combatants fell near Kirsten's feet. With a gasp, she jumped back, out of their path, the two men tussling on the damp ground.

Richard hurried toward her and took her arm. "What the devil are you doing here?" he growled. "Are you eager to die?" He was angry, fearful of the harm that could come to her.

She seemed taken aback by his rudeness and jerked

free of his grip.

"Go home, Kirsten, before someone hurts you."

Her lower lip trembled. "Like you?"

He inhaled sharply, and tried again to urge her away from this dangerous place. But now he used a different tactic of persuasion. "Please, love. You don't belong here. You'll only get hurt."

"But I had to see you, to see if you were all right." Her gaze swept the campsite. "My *vader*, is he . . . ?"

"Your father's here?"

She nodded, holding his glance, her expression one of concern. Suddenly, her face took on a look of horror. *"Vader!"* she screamed.

Somehow Elias Greene had gotten free of the young gunman and was charging James Van Atta with raised sword. Richard raised his gun, and fired against the Tory, wounding him in the arm.

Greene jerked as he was struck. He swayed and his face turned white. He stared at Richard as he clutched his injured arm.

"Canfield," he mouthed, his eyes full of fury. Then he transferred his gaze to the woman at Richard's side. His lashes flickered as he looked beyond them, and a wild grin suddenly lit up his cruel mouth.

"Take him!" he ordered. "Get Canfield! The bastard betrayed us!"

Kirsten turned and then gasped. Several men were at the edge of the forest, newly arrived, it seemed, from out of nowhere. She cursed as someone caught her arm. Prisoners! She and Richard were prisoners of the Tories!

The battle raged on while Richard and Kirsten were taken from the skirmish and urged into the forest. The Patriots were so busy fighting that no one had witnessed the arrival of Kirsten or of the additional Tory soldiers.

Kirsten thought with wry humor that her father would kill her if she escaped her captors alive. As things stood, it would take a miracle for them to get free. And Richard . . . he didn't show it by word or deed, but he must be furious with her.

"I'm sorry," she said to him, her expression begging for forgiveness.

But Richard refused to look at her. She touched his arm, trying to draw his glance, but the direction of his hardened gaze never altered. He was tight-lipped and tense, and it was her fault.

"Move!" A strange, frightful man prodded her in the back with a rifle. Another Tory did the same with Richard, and she saw with a feeling of horror that it was her uncle, William Randolph.

"You!" she whispered.

He smiled when he met her glance. "Why, if it isn't my dear niece? Who's this?" he said, poking Richard a second time. "A friend?"

Greene came up from behind and gave Randolph an order. Stunned, Kirsten's uncle looked at him. There seemed a silent battle of wills as the two men fought to be the one in charge.

"This one's mine," Elias Greene said. Clutching his bleeding arm, he glared at Richard. "I've a score to settle."

"What are you going to do with us?" Kirsten asked.

Their captors refused to answer. They shoved Kirsten and Richard down the footpath until they reached a wide trail on which an empty wagon stood.

"Get in!" the strange man behind Kirsten commanded. He waved his gun in her direction.

A smirk settled upon Randolph's face. "Easy now, Joseph. 'Tis my niece you're escorting."

Kirsten glanced at Greene several times as she climbed onto the back of the wagon. The red-haired man made her nervous. He was mad, she was convinced of it. His green eyes darted about wildly without focusing. His movements were sudden and unpredictable—dangerous. *What if he pulls the trigger?* she thought. *What if he shoots Richard?*

Their captors climbed into the vehicle, and the horse pulling the wagon moved. Richard and Kirsten fell back against the wagon platform with the force of the start. Greene was in the driver's seat alongside William, while Samuel Joseph rode in the back to make sure the prisoners didn't escape.

"Where are we going?" Richard asked.

"Silence!" the guard barked.

Kirsten addressed Richard in a whisper. "To my uncle's farm, I think." He looked at her and nodded. His expression no longer seemed as fierce.

The man in back got upset with the whisperings. "Stop yer talking now!"

Once again, Kirsten inclined her head, pretending a meekness she didn't possess. Her jaw clenched with the strength of her anger. Her hands itched for a weapon with which to strike the guard dead.

The forest was dark and filled with the sounds of the night. A twig snapped in the brush, drawing Richard's attention. *Someone is out there,* he thought.

Kirsten met his gaze, silently mouthing *who?*

He shook his head. *I don't know,* he mouthed back. *Pray it's not the British.*

As Kirsten had predicted, the Tories took their captives to the Randolph farm. Kirsten's heart lightened. There she'd see Aunt Catherine or Miles. One of them would help them escape.

But she saw no one as they came into the yard. The wagon stayed out of view of the house's front windows, skirting the building until it reached the smokehouse out back. There, the driver reined in and got out. The three men then conversed briefly. Kirsten frowned, wondering what they were saying, what their plans for them were.

The guard had joined his cohorts, but kept his rifle trained on the two prisoners. He returned to the wagon a second later and ordered Richard and Kirsten to get out, poking Richard and then Kirsten with the gun to make them move more quickly. Kirsten, startled by the jab in her side, tripped and fell.

"Get up!" the man hissed as if he'd had nothing to do with her fall.

She scrambled to her feet and shot him a menacing glance. *"Bloody Tory!"* she muttered angrily. She could no longer pretend that she was afraid of him. Hearing her, Richard grinned, and the sight of his grin lifted Kirsten's spirits.

"What'd ye say?" the guard asked.

"I said, Sorry," she replied.

The man nodded, apparently too dumb to know when he was being made of fun of. Or else he'd not credited Kirsten with enough courage to ridicule him openly.

Her uncle stood by the smokehouse door. With a wicked grin, he gestured for the two captives to enter the outbuilding. "Your chamber awaits you."

The idea of such close quarters filled Kirsten with alarm. "My father will kill you for this," she said between clenched teeth.

But her mother's brother only laughed at her.

She stepped inside, and Richard followed her.

"Wait!" Greene said. "They could escape. Tie 'em up first."

"No!" Kirsten felt she'd go mad if she were bound.

Greene nodded to the guard. "Do it—*now!*"

Joseph tied Kirsten up first, roping her wrists behind her back and then looping another piece of hemp about her ankles. The smokehouse was specially constructed, with a platform above the area where a fire was usually lit to produce the smoke. The guard shoved Kirsten onto the platform, before he turned his attention to Richard. He tied up Richard in a similar manner, but made his bonds tighter than Kirsten's. Pushed, Richard fell onto the platform beside Kirsten.

"Sweet dreams, niece," Randolph said, and he shut the door.

The door slammed closed, and she heard the scrape of wood and metal as she and Richard were locked inside.

The odor inside the smokehouse was vile. It smelled strongly of burnt wood and ashes combined with the lingering scent of smoked meat.

Kirsten could feel Richard's thigh pressed against hers. The room was small. She could hear him inhale and exhale.

"Richard . . ."

"You should have stayed home where you belonged."

"You fool! I was concerned for you!"

His chuckle was loud in the small smoke-scented area. "We've been locked up in a smokehouse, have no idea what the Tories have decided is our fate—whether we'll live or die—and all we can do is argue. What a waste of precious time."

Kirsten didn't respond, but thought on his words.

"And what shall we discuss then," she asked, "the weather?"

"Kirsten," he warned, his voice suddenly sharp with anger.

"I'm sorry." She was sincere. "But I hate this place.

I feel I can't breathe in here and the smell is awful."

Richard sighed. "Is it my fault that we're here?"

She flushed. "I told you I was sorry!"

A moment of tense silence followed her apology. "I couldn't have picked anyone else I'd rather be locked up with," she said in an attempt to lighten the mood.

There was a moment of charged silence. "Thank you," he said, but he sounded amused.

"How are your ropes?" Kirsten asked. They'd become quietly contemplative for a time, but she feared he might be in pain.

"Tight and uncomfortable. And yours?"

"Mine aren't too bad," she said. "Can you turn your back to me?"

"For what?"

She sighed with impatience. "I thought I'd try to untie you, but if you'd rather spend the entire night here . . . Maybe you're anxious to see Greene again?"

"Wench!" he muttered, but she heard him shift in the darkness and felt the warmth of his body as he brushed against her in his efforts to move around.

Kirsten shifted about, turning to the side to give him her back. "Try to untie me first."

"No good," Richard said after one attempt. "I can't move enough."

She wiggled her wrists. The rope bit into her skin painfully, but she could still move her hands. Determined to get free, Kirsten rolled over and stretched out her fingers, feeling for the knot of Richard's ropes.

She couldn't find it. "I can't feel it," she said. "This will never work!"

"Wait," Richard bade her. "And keep your voice down! I'll wager our gentleman guard is not far off."

They both kept silent, their ears alert for any foreign sounds outside the smokehouse. After a time of quiet, Kirsten said, "I don't hear anything."

"Keep your voice low anyway," he urged. "He may be sleeping."

She nodded and then realized that he couldn't see her in the dark. "All right," she whispered.

They struggled against each other for what seemed like hours, but in actuality it went on for only about a half-hour.

"I give up," Kirsten said. "It was a dumb idea anyway."

"No, I think it's loosening. I can move my hands more. Try again."

Kirsten was disgusted. "One last time. And if it works, you—"

"What?" Richard's voice turned husky. "Owe you something? My life perhaps? My arms? A kiss?"

She swallowed. The air between them had become fraught with sexual tension, and she didn't know what to make of this sudden shift of feeling. She was afraid to believe him . . . to trust in him. He had saved her father's life, but could she trust him with her heart?

Gritting her teeth, Kirsten attempted to free Richard of his wrist bonds. She leaned against him, her muscles straining as she groped for Richard's rope. With a cry of gladness, she found the knot and was able to insert the tip of her middle finger in it.

"I think I've got it!" she breathed. She was afraid to say it too loudly, for fear that doing so would somehow jinx her ability to undo his bands.

The piece of hemp started to slip beneath her fingertip. Soon, she was able to place her entire finger in the opening. She fit two fingers in next, but she grew dismayed when she found she had no leverage. There was not enough room to pull.

"I can't free it!" she wailed. "I can't move enough

to tug it!" Frustrated, she relaxed her efforts. To have come so close!

"Hold on, love," Richard said. "I'll help you. Perhaps if I move in the opposite direction from you. Between the two of us, we should be able to manage it."

Richard jerked his body forward while Kirsten did the same. Finally, the knot came undone, and Richard's hands were free.

"Good girl!" he exclaimed. And he bent to untie his feet.

"Now me," she said. She felt him hesitate. "Richard?"

He chuckled as if the hesitation had been a joke, and soon she felt him undoing the ropes at her wrists. Kirsten flinched as he worked at the knot. "Am I hurting you?" he asked, his voice husky.

"A little. But it's all right, keep trying."

It was difficult for him. Her movements as she attempted to free him had tightened her bindings, and it was too dark to see.

Finally, Kirsten's hands were free and she bent to undo her feet. The knot wasn't as tight at her ankles.

"Richard? What shall we do now?" Freedom from the ropes added some hope to what had seemed an impossible situation. But Kirsten was suddenly and distractingly reminded of the old mill and the night they'd spent hiding from the British soldiers, waiting for them to leave.

Richard didn't immediately answer her. She heard him shift in the dark and then heard a noise along the inside wall. She thought he had risen to his knees. "What are you doing?" she asked.

"I'm searching for loose boards . . . for any way we can get us out of here."

"It won't help," she said with dejection. "This

building is too new. Uncle William is meticulous in his upkeep."

He cursed and the noise stopped. "Locked up tight," he agreed. "Why in hell would Randolph secure a smoke house?"

Kirsten's reply was dry. "There's a war on, haven't you heard? There are always soldiers about looking for food. Uncle William might be willing to share his grain but not his meat."

"I wish there was meat here now."

"You're always hungry," Kirsten said without thought.

The mood changed from one of light bantering and became emotionally charged.

"Kirsten, come here." His voice was low, seductive.

She tried to recapture the lightness of moments before. "I'm right here, Richard. This room is hardly large enough to travel far."

His low, husky laughter filled the smokehouse, rippling along Kirsten's spine. She hugged herself and felt gooseflesh rise on her skin.

"Tell me again why you came to our camp," he said.

She refused to answer, for fear she'd reveal her love for him.

"Kirsten?"

Suddenly, he was too near. She could feel his breath at her neck and ear, stirring the tiny blond hairs there. "Something about being concerned?" he said.

She was nervous. She didn't want to be hurt again, and since she'd met him, it seemed she'd experienced nothing but emotional turmoil—and pain.

Richard leaned in close to the woman beside him and detected a fragrance about her that was familiar . . . and sweet. Either the smell in the smoke-house was gone, or he was getting used to it, because all he could sense now was Kirsten's alluring scent.

He felt her tension and was somewhat puzzled by it. They'd been lovers before. She was no shy, inexperienced virgin. And it was obvious to him that she cared for him. If it wasn't exactly love she felt, there was at least a physical attraction. That was evident. That she couldn't deny.

Richard couldn't forget the time they'd made love . . . Kirsten's passionate responses to his touch . . . her wild cries as he thrust into her. Did she regret it? Had it been as good for her as it had been for him?

The memories brought heat throughout his body, hardening his loins and tightening his muscles. He had the most overwhelming urge to take her sweet lips and ravage them tenderly with his mouth.

He searched for her arm and found it, and heard her gasp as he ran his fingertips lightly over her skin. He felt the tiny bumps that had formed on it, and he couldn't help smiling.

"Are you cold?" he asked.

There was a moment of silence. "No."

His sense of touch was acute in the darkness, as was his imagination; for he could envision her expression as he continued his wandering caress. He stroked the curve of her neck and imagined her eyes closing in sensual enjoyment; he fondled her nape and then slipped a hand around in front to trace the fragile column of her throat.

She didn't say a word, but he was encouraged, because there was no sign that she wanted him to stop.

Richard moved closer and bent his head until his mouth grazed the warmth of her cheek. He nuzzled her there, then moved down to kiss her throat. He was rewarded when she moaned and dropped her head back.

"Kirsten," he gasped. His ache for her was intense, reaching new heights of desire. "Kirsten," he begged, "kiss me."

He shifted toward her fully and leaned closer until he felt sure that his mouth was nearly touching hers. She didn't kiss him, and he was mildly disappointed but not put off.

He sought her breast and gently cupped the mound, intending to stroke it until it swelled in his hand. When the breast budded, Richard bent his head and encircled her nipple with his lips, moistening the fabric over it, nibbling the tiny nub until she cried out with pleasure.

He withdrew his mouth to pull up her shirt. He wanted no barrier between them. He wanted to taste her bare skin, to lick and suckle her sweet breasts until she was whimpering with desire.

Kirsten gasped as he caressed her flesh through the linen cloth. It had been so long since he'd touched her. It seemed like forever. She felt her nipple bud beneath his questing fingers. She reached out to find him, having the strongest desire to touch his warm skin . . . his hard muscles.

She found his shirt, tugged it from his breeches, and slipped her hands beneath the hem. The heat of his chest spread to her own quivering flesh as she delighted in letting her palms wander from male nipple to male nipple, then dipped her fingers to his navel and lower . . .

Richard rejoiced in her response, his groin tightening and his manhood stiffening. "Kirsten, Kirsten, love . . . touch me. Yes, that's it. Now, let me touch you . . . everywhere." He raised her shirt, touched one nipple with his lips, and then the other.

258

Emboldened by her response, he caressed her leg, running his fingers from thigh to ankle and back to thigh.

And then he found her most private area, cupping that feminine mound, rubbing it with his fingers.

Kirsten stiffened until Richard's soft words of encouragement made her relax and glory in the intimate caresses through cloth. Richard encouraged her with soft loving words. He praised her beauty, the soft texture of her breasts, the wonderful, sweet taste of her. And then he was dipping his fingers inside her breeches.

She let out a muted cry as he found her most sensitive spot. Her pleasure was intense. She wanted to share it, to be joined with Richard, to feel him deep inside her.

"Richard," she begged.

They struggled briefly to adjust their garments to make the joining possible. Then, he reached for her and shifted her to a more comfortable position, until she was lying on the wooden platform with him above her.

He kissed and fondled her. She touched him everywhere, rejoicing in his groans. "Now," she said.

He impaled her with his staff, thrusting inside until Kirsten felt the earth spin and her whole body explode with pleasure. Richard cried out, signaling that they had reached the pinnacle together. Afterward, they rolled over and lay joined, side by side, enjoying the sweet aftermath of their union.

After a time, when he began to suspect Kirsten's discomfort, Richard pulled away to fasten his breeches. He then helped Kirsten to dress.

Suddenly, Richard sensed a change in her. She seemed tense, afraid. "What's wrong?" he asked.

"Sh-hh!" she said with a sense of urgency.

"There's someone outside!"

He froze and listened. And he heard footsteps on the earth, the brush of a body against the outer wall of the smokehouse.

"Hell and damnation!" he muttered. He shifted on the platform, getting into a fighting crouch.

Chapter Twenty

Someone was at the door to the smokehouse. Richard grabbed Kirsten by the shoulders and pulled her against him in a protective embrace. She heard his legs shift as he prepared to attack.

Kirsten heard the sound of the iron lock. She stared at the door. Who was on the other side? Her uncle? Greene? She shuddered. Were they coming to kill them? Her uncle was capable of murder; she was sure of that now that she knew he'd frequently beat his wife and son.

Her pulse quickened with fear. Were they coming for Richard, to torture him for information?

She heard wood scrape against wood as the person outside raised the bar. The door squeaked and slowly swung in. Kirsten caught her breath. A lone man was silhouetted against the opening.

Suddenly, Kirsten found herself tossed to one side as Richard lunged.

The intruder cried out as he fell back under the force of Richard's weight, and Kirsten scrambled from the platform, watching as the two rolled across the ground in a deadly tussle. Then she recognized the stranger.

"Richard!" she cried. "Stop! Please! It's Miles!"

Richard didn't hear her as he slammed a fist into the youth's face. Kirsten gasped as her cousin fell back, knocked senseless.

Richard, seeing his victim out cold, rose and, with a cocky smile of victory, turned to Kirsten. Then his smile disappeared.

"*Spitterbaard!*" she exclaimed, kneeling at her cousin's side. "I told you to stop. It's Miles. He's come to help us."

The guilty look on Richard's face might have appeared comical to Kirsten if she'd been in a different state of mind. Richard cursed as he bent down at the boy's other side. "I'm sorry, love. I didn't realize."

"Obviously," she snapped. "Tell him you're sorry when he wakes—*if* he wakes up."

Richard scowled. "I didn't kill him if that's what you're implying. I didn't even hit him that hard."

Kirsten grunted with disbelief.

Richard tried to revive the boy. He could see now that it was indeed Kirsten's young cousin, Miles Randolph; and although the lad's father was a Tory, Miles certainly posed no threat.

"Come on, fella," he urged. "Get up!" He gently patted the boy's cheek. "Wake up!"

Miles stirred and groaned. He opened his eyes, saw Richard, and flinched.

"It's all right," Kirsten said. "He didn't know it was you." She sensed Richard's gratitude for her support, but chose to pretend otherwise.

Miles turned his head in Kirsten's direction. "Kirsten! It was you I saw from my bedchamber window! I couldn't believe it when they brought you in! What happened? What did you do?"

262

"It's not what she did," Richard said, and Miles glared at him.

"Miles," Kirsten said gently, "he's a friend, but don't listen to him. It was my fault as well as his. He's only trying to protect me. The fact is, Richard was with the Tories who were attacked this night by our local militia."

Her cousin blinked. "I'm aware he's a Tory, but what are *you* doing with him?" He continued to regard Richard with suspicion.

"Trust me," Kirsten said, "he's a friend. He's told me so, and . . . I believe him."

Richard touched her arm, squeezing it lightly. "You must get home," he told her. "The militia—I must speak with them. There'll be others coming. Tories . . . British troops. Smugglers transporting goods to the King's men to the south."

"From New York?" she guessed.

He nodded.

Kirsten glanced at her cousin. Miles lay on the ground, looking better. His color was good, and he seemed none the worse for Richard's fists. "Your mother . . . ?"

"She's all right. She's sleeping."

She sighed with relief. "I was planning to come for her, to take her to join the others at the Van Voorhees'."

"Your family is at this farm?" Richard asked with raised eyebrows.

She inclined her head, studying his handsome features.

"Go there then," he said, "where you'll be safe. I'll be back to see you again." His voice deepened. "I promise."

"I don't know . . ."

"There are many I must talk with. Now that

Greene and the others realize I'm not one of them, I must work quickly to complete my mission. I suspect that Greene and your uncle are somehow involved with Biv—and perhaps someone in Washington's command." He scowled. "If only I had more time!"

"Richard, don't go," Kirsten pleaded, rising to her feet. "Or, at least, let me go with you. What if the militia won't believe you're one of us? What if they take you prisoner?"

"Then, I'll send for you." Richard stood.

"And if they won't wait? Won't listen?"

"It's a chance I must take." He grinned. "If that happens, I'm sure you'll hear about it. I'll expect you to rescue me."

Afraid for him, Kirsten shook her head. "Please, Richard, no." Her eyes filled with tears as she memorized his beloved features. She had a feeling that something terrible was going to happen to him, but when he was so determined to go, how could she convince him to stay?

Miles cleared his throat, drawing the attention of the two lovers. "You'd best go," he said as he scrambled to his feet. "Before Father or one of the others hear and come." He brushed the dirt from the seat of his breeches.

Kirsten eyed her cousin with concern. "You will be all right? Your father must not learn of this."

"I'll be fine. My father doesn't know I'm aware of your presence here. He'll not guess I was involved."

She nodded. "He'll blame one of the others." She patted his cheek lightly. "Thanks, cousin, for the rescue."

Miles's gaze held affection. "I should let you free and lock him up." He jerked his head in Richard's direction.

"But then Uncle William will know."

The youth sighed. "Go then—the both of you—and hurry. The morning sun will be up before you know it, and you'll be caught before you've had a chance to flee."

Kirsten kissed his cheek. "If ever you need me . . ."

He smiled at her. "I know."

"Be careful," she whispered. She hoped Miles was right in that his father wouldn't learn he'd helped her escape. She couldn't bear it if Miles was punished by William Randolph.

Miles nodded as he turned away. "Go."

And the two lovers fled into the dark night.

They traveled to the Van Atta farm first. Richard thought to check there, because it was closer than the Van Voorhees' place, and there was a good chance that with the time they'd spent in the smokehouse, Kirsten's family might have returned home.

He was wrong, however. When they arrived, the house was dark. Despite the hour, Richard could tell that there was no one home. There was no sign of a return, not a wheel track in the yard or a footprint in the soft dirt. Nothing.

Kirsten went to the barn to see if the animals were still there. Their cow was, but someone had come back for the horses. Pieter must have returned to take the animals away for safekeeping, or else the horses had been stolen by fleeing Tory soldiers.

Richard wouldn't allow Kirsten to go to the Van Voorhees' farm by herself. And so, despite the added risk he was running, he escorted her to the Patriot shelter. With Greene and the Tories free, there was a chance she might be apprehended along the way, and if that happened, he feared Kirsten would suffer because of the men's anger at "Canfield."

He stopped in view of the Van Voorhees' house, but out of sight of those who hid there. It was time to part, the moment Kirsten had been most dreading.

"Richard." A painful lump clogged her throat. "You'll be careful?"

He looked at her, and she could see well enough to glimpse the tenderness of his expression, the glow of his russet eyes.

"I'll be fine," he said. "And you? You'll be all right? You won't again take any foolish chances?"

She nodded. "You will come back."

"When I can. I don't know exactly when. I must speak to your militiamen. Then, I must find General Washington and report what I've learned. I've no idea what he wants me to do next."

"Richard, I don't know about the militia. There are those among them who are obsessed. Some saw you with the Tories, know you as one of them. I don't believe you'll be as safe as you think."

"It's a risk I must take."

Her blue eyes glistened. "Find Martin then. Talk to him first. You know who he is?"

He inclined his tawny head.

"Make sure he knows I'm well."

She and Martin had become close in their efforts to help the cause. Almost as close as she and Miles were.

Miles . . . She frowned. She hoped he was all right. If his father had learned of his part in their escape . . .

"What's wrong?" Richard asked, his brow furrowing with concern.

"I'm worried about Miles."

"Don't be. He's a smart young man. I'm sure he'll cover his tracks well."

"I hope you're right," Kirsten murmured.

Richard drew her into his arms. "A kiss to hold me until my return?"

She was thrilled with his mention of returning, and she raised her chin happily, offering him her lips. He bent his head and touched her mouth lightly, sipping her sweetness as one would sip a glass of fine wine, savoring the flavor, the moment of pure sensual enjoyment.

Suddenly, the kiss changed. Richard's arms tightened, and Kirsten reacted accordingly, moaning softly, leaning up into his kiss. There was a desperation to their embrace. The threats of war and an unknown future hung over them like clouds blocking out the sun. They fought to get closer, to feel the warmth of their own special sun, the light that came from being near the one most cared about.

Would they be reunited? Kirsten wondered. She clung to him, unwilling to let go.

The two lovers disengaged. "'Bye, love," Richard said softly, holding her lightly within the circle of his arms.

She could hear his labored breathing, feel the thunder of his heart beneath her fingertips. She stroked the hard muscles of his chest before slipping her arms about his waist in an attempt to bring him to kiss her again. When he wouldn't, she settled for leaning against him in a quiet moment of companionship.

Kirsten raised her head. "I don't want you to go," she said.

"I don't want to go, but I must. Many depend on me."

She nodded, blinked back tears.

And then, with a last, quick kiss, Richard urged her toward the Van Voorhees' residence. After he saw that she'd entered safely, he went on his way.

*   *   *

When Kirsten returned to the Van Voorhees' farm, her mother was frantic with worry.

"Daughter, my God! Where have you been? I've not seen you or your *vader* for hours. You are all right? You have seen your *vader*? He is all right?"

"I saw him earlier, but that is all. I'm afraid I don't know if he and the others are safe. I believe so, though. When I left them, the militia were holding their own."

There was a knock on the Van Voorhees' door. Mrs. Van Voorhees rushed to get it for a second time. As if conjured by magic, James Van Atta stood on the stoop, swaying tiredly but otherwise unhurt.

"*Vader!*"

"James!"

The two women cried out in unison.

Smiling, Mrs. Van Voorhees stepped aside to let her neighbor in. "Please come in, James."

"Thank you, Sarah."

Kirsten and Agnes sprung at their loved one to hug him. Behind him, still on the stoop, another member of the militia, George Zabriskie, waited to see his family. The Zabriskies' cries of joy echoed the feeling of happiness in Kirsten's heart.

She stepped back to better study her father. Had Richard spoken to the men yet? There had barely been time . . .

Her father had brought the farm wagon, and it was dawn when the Van Atta family climbed into it and headed for home.

"*Vader*, where are the horses?" Kirsten asked as they rolled and bumped over the dirt road. The faithful mare Hilga was with them, tied to the back of the wagon, while a gelding pulled them along.

"Pieter has them. He went back to get them when some of the Tories escaped."

268

Kirsten nodded. It was just as she'd thought. She silently thanked God that the Tories hadn't stolen them. "The other men—are any hurt?"

James shot his daughter a glance. "Minor injuries only. Thomas was grazed in the arm by a musket ball. Nothing serious as long as it's treated proper. The others including myself suffered a few cuts and bruises, nothing more."

She smiled at her father, glad.

Suddenly, he scowled at her. "You were out this night, daughter."

Kirsten's heart pumped hard. He was going to punish her. "Yes, *Vader*," she said meekly.

"You could have been killed!"

She inclined her head.

"Why?"

She blinked. "Why? Ah . . . because I couldn't stand by while you all fought elsewhere. I had to see, had to know, in case I could help."

He looked at her as if she were crazy. "Without a weapon how did you propose to do that? Stare them to death?"

"I—"

"You will not venture out like that again! The next time you are told to go to the Van Voorhees' farm, you will go and stay there! *Is that clear?*"

"Yes, *Vader*."

"James," Agnes interjected, "do you truly think this will happen again? That we'll be forced to hide? Sarah and Samuel are wonderful people, but—"

"This is war, Agnes," he said, his voice sharp. "How many times must I tell you?" He saw her face and was immediately contrite. "Dearest, no one will truly be safe until this terrible time ends."

And Kirsten had to agree, silently.

*   *   *

After he'd left Kirsten, Richard slipped into the cover of night and headed toward the tavern under the elm tree. He had a hunch that it was there the militiamen would gather to discuss their raid. The local inn was popular with the Hoppertown men, and Richard knew that Martin Hoppe, the owner, was truly dedicated to the cause.

Would Martin believe him as Kirsten had suggested, or would he follow along with the others and consider him a Tory trying to save his skin. If so, who could blame him?

The tavern was up ahead, lit only with a single taper in a window of the common room. Richard crept stealthily toward the door, unsure of his welcome. He knocked softly on the heavy door. There was no sound of movement inside, and he thought that he might have been mistaken about the gathering place. The militia must have met elsewhere—at one of the member's homes perhaps.

Then he heard the click of the door latch. He stood back, his heart beating wildly as someone opened the door.

Martin's eyes widened as he saw who it was. "Come in," he invited after a long moment. He didn't take his gaze off Richard as he stepped aside to allow him to enter.

"You're Kirsten's friend," he said.

Richard nodded. "And yours, I hope."

The man didn't comment, but turned and moved toward one of the tables, where he pulled out a chair and sat down. "You have something to tell me?"

"Yes, I do," Richard said, "but first I must confess something, and I must have your word that you'll not speak of it before a living soul."

270

Martin looked wary, but he inclined his head. "You saved my life. Why?"

"Because I'm a friend—a Patriot. I'm a spy working for General Washington. I've been traveling with this particular band of Tories for weeks now. My usefulness there ended last night when your men attacked us. I couldn't fight you. I had managed to get out of combat with Patriot or Continental forces until last night. Then I was forced to make a choice. An easy one, I might add. I couldn't kill your men. We are, after all, brothers fighting on the same side."

"So you say."

Richard nodded. "I can understand your skepticism. And I realize it's up to you whether or not you choose to believe me."

"Kirsten does, but then, my cousin is in love with you."

Richard started. In love, Kirsten? And after everything he'd put her through.

"I agree," Martin said, accurately reading his thoughts. "You probably don't deserve it."

Richard flushed, but he also experienced a secret burst of joy. Kirsten loved him! Her cousin was staring at him. He returned the man's gaze.

"Kirsten trusts me because she senses I speak the truth."

"Perhaps." Martin's gaze didn't waver, and the piercing look went right through Richard. "This is what you wanted to tell me? What you wanted me to keep silent about?"

"That I'm a spy, yes. I'm searching for a man . . . his undercover name is Biv. I don't know what he looks like. Before, when I first came to Hoppertown, I was to meet with him. I got word by a messenger. He was the key informant for a friend of mine—a dead friend. Alexander Brooks. Alex worked

271

for the general in a similar capacity as I. Only his main function was the acquisition and transference of British battle plans."

Martin blinked. "This was done?"

Richard shrugged. "I said it was Alex's job, not that he was necessarily successful at it. Alex met this man Biv and supposedly gained some very valuable information about the King's troops. Unfortunately, Alex didn't live long enough to tell what he'd learned." He paused. "He was murdered in cold blood." He couldn't suppress a small shiver.

Richard had remained standing since his entry. Now he gestured toward a seat. "May I?"

Martin nodded. "An ale?" he asked, rising to his feet.

"Thank you, yes."

Richard waited patiently for Martin to leave the room and return with the ale. It took Kirsten's cousin longer than he'd expected, and he wondered if he'd made a mistake in confiding in the man. Martin could have left to alert the others of the presence of a Loyalist.

But Martin had only found some food to go along with the ale. He came back holding two tankards by the handle in one hand and balancing two plates in the other.

"Hungry?" he asked.

Richard smiled. "Starved."

Martin sat down and took a drink. "Thought I'd betrayed you, didn't you?"

He nodded, not bothering to deny it.

"I'm not an unreasonable man, Canfield—Canfield, that is your name? I heard Greene call you Canfield, but I assume now that it might not be."

"You assume correctly. My name's Maddox. Richard Maddox."

"The Mad Ox?" Martin bit into a piece of bread.

Richard was stunned. "You've heard of me?"

"No. You mean you're actually called that?"

Richard gave him a slight smile. "I'm known to some by that name."

"I see." But the man looked puzzled. "As I started to say, ah . . . Maddox—"

"Richard."

"Richard, then. I am not an unreasonable man, nor am I too obsessed to see that what you're saying has got a ring of truth to it."

Richard, who'd raised a slab of bread to take a bite, paused before placing the crusty piece between his lips. "I thank God for that."

The two men grinned at one another, suddenly at ease.

"So, all right now, tell me about this Greene," Martin said. "He's one of the men who escaped?"

Richard nodded. "'Fraid so."

Martin cursed. "And my cousin?"

"Safe at the Van Voorhees' farm. I took her there myself."

Her cousin sighed with relief. "Good. She's a foolish girl at times."

Richard stiffened, believing that the man was referring to her involvement with him. But Martin was regarding him with amusement, and Richard knew he'd misjudged the man.

"She tends to run toward battle instead of away," Kirsten's cousin said.

Richard's mouth split into a grin. "I know. Damn her."

And then he told Martin of his experiences with the band of Loyalists and the threat of more troops, and the possible arrival in Hoppertown of the King's men.

Chapter Twenty-one

The men rushed out of the forest surprising the Van Atta family on their journey home. They were Tories; among them were familiar faces—Edmund Dunley's, Bernard Godwin's, and that of William Randolph, Agnes' own brother.

James bellowed an oath when he saw them. He reached for his rifle only to have one of them fire at him first, grazing his arm.

"*Vader!*" Kirsten exclaimed as she scrambled to her knees to check his injury, but he pushed her back, ordering her to stay down.

"Randolph," James growled. "Bastard!" Beside him, his wife began to cry. "Tories! Bloody Loyalists!"

The five Loyalists stepped out of the woods onto the road. Kirsten's gaze never left her uncle as the men moved in to block the Van Attas' wagon. William Randolph looked smug. He was dressed much like the others, in dark coat and matching knee breeches, only Randolph's clothing was obviously a class above the garb of the others in quality and cut. His shirt was pristine white and neatly pressed.

Kirsten knew her family was virtually trapped. Because of the dense thickets on both sides of the trail, it would be impossible for her father to drive on or turn around with any speed. The mare Hilga, tied to the back, would further hamper any escape attempt.

William Randolph approached the cart, grinning, an evil light in his familiar brown eyes. "You're going to turn this vehicle around, Van Atta, and head back to the Van Voorhees' farm."

Kirsten was startled. "Why?" she said. How did he know about the Van Voorhees' farm?

Her uncle shot her an exasperated glance. "You escaped unharmed, I see." He scowled; clearly he'd been upset to learn of her disappearance from the smokehouse. "As to your question, dear niece, you're going to obey because I command it. And because by now the others will have captured your rebel friends there."

"But William, why?" Agnes sobbed. Tears fell down her cheeks, a testament to her confusion and pain. "Why are you doing this? We're family—"

"Family!" Randolph said with loathing. "You've chosen sides; you're not my kin." He looked at his sister with disgust. "I told you not to marry him. He's been nothing but trouble for the Randolphs."

"No," she cried, stung by his words. "It's not true. He's a good man! For God's sake, he's my husband, the father of my child!"

"*Silence!*" Randolph leveled his gun in James's direction. "Or I'll shoot him dead before your eyes."

Agnes blanched and kept still. She knew her brother meant business. Somehow, during the past years, he'd changed into a monster . . . a cruel, inhuman being.

"Godwin. Dunley," Randolph called. The fat man and his cohort came forward. Their guns raised, they waited for orders.

While Randolph spoke to both men, he didn't

allow his gaze or his gun's bore to veer from his brother-in-law. "I told this Dutch *boer* here to turn around. See that he does it."

Godwin nodded, his jowls bobbing. Edmund Dunley left his friend to walk toward the rear of the wagon, keeping a careful watch on Kirsten. William lowered his gun and began to walk about.

"You'll never win," Kirsten taunted, raising her chin. "You may think you can, but you won't! The King will never give you what you want. He'll demand more from you until you're bled dry. And then he'll ask for more still."

"You know nothing," Dunley said sharply. "You're a child."

"Don't I? Am I?" She gave him a grim smile. "And I suppose your leader, Elias Greene, knows all?"

"Pah!" Dunley retorted. "Greene isn't our leader. Your Uncle William is."

"You heard him," Kirsten retorted. "I have no uncle."

Her uncle firmed his lips. "Elias Greene is hardly a leader, girl," he said as he approached her. "The man's useful is all. At this moment, he's got the wives and children of your wonderful militiamen. Think we can't win when your men are consumed with concern about the safety of their loved ones?"

"Pig!" Kirsten cried, and her uncle slapped her.

Randolph laughed and stepped around to the front of the wagon, where he folded his arms and stared up at the driver.

James Van Atta had no choice but to do what his brother-in-law ordered, although he thought the man was crazy. With a scowl on his face and a vein pulsating at his left temple, he rose angrily and started to climb down from his vehicle.

"Stop!" Randolph ordered.

Kirsten's father froze.

277

"Stay in the wagon." William held up his gun in warning.

His gaze flickering toward his leader, Bernard Godwin fingered the trigger of his rifle. "Shall I shoot him?"

James turned slowly. He looked at his brother-in-law and then down at his gun, glanced toward Godwin and then back to William as if he believed the whole lot of them had gone mad. "How am I to turn my horse about if I don't get down? The road here is narrow."

William Randolph gazed at him through veiled eyes. "Mr. Joseph!" he shouted. A man who had been watching the exchange from several steps behind, came forward. William signaled to him with a wave of his arm. "Take the horse's reins and help my sister's husband to steer this claptrap about."

Samuel Joseph hurried to do as he was bid. Then he returned the lead to James Van Atta.

"Let's go then." Randolph had climbed onto a mount that one of his men had brought to him. He rode before the wagon, his head held high. Dunley and Godwin walked alongside, while another Loyalist followed on foot in back.

"You won't get away with this, William," Kirsten's father said heatedly. He placed an arm about his sobbing wife to offer her comfort. "You're mad! You don't know what you're doing!"

William glanced back over his shoulder. "Oh, you think not?" His thin lips curved upward. "I think I shall . . . with your help. We shall see. We shall see . . ."

The group headed toward the Van Voorhees' farm. Kirsten rubbed her smarting cheek. What was to become of them? she wondered.

*　　　*　　　*

Richard and Martin were surprised at their conversation when John Ackerman and several members of the local militia burst into the common room of the inn.

"What?" The innkeeper started to rise. "What's wrong, John? Has something happened?"

John nodded. "I'm afraid so, Martin." He stopped as he noticed who sat with his friend.

Richard stood, feeling the sudden tension in the room. He eyed the Patriot group warily, for he knew the men did not know he was one of them. They thought him a Tory. The enemy.

"The bloody Tories!" John spat out, staring at Richard. "Their leader Greene—that red-haired bastard—and his men have taken the Van Voorhees' place."

"*What!*" Richard exclaimed. He stiffened with rage. "When? How?" *My God*, he thought, *Kirsten's there. And now Greene!*

"Over an hour ago. Perhaps longer. Sometime in the night," Ackerman said, his eyes narrowing. He addressed Martin. "We'd stopped at Vandervelt's on the way there." He gestured toward Garret Vandervelt, the *klapperman*. "After that fire the last time, he wanted to check his house. We knew our families were safe . . ." His voice trailed off. "At least, we'd thought them safe."

"Damn!" Martin knocked back a chair as he moved from the table. "Margaretha's there. Like you, I'd thought she'd be safe. I planned to bring her home later."

"And my *moeder* is there," John Ackerman said.

Several men spoke of their loved ones who'd been sheltered at the Van Voorhees' farm and who were now in the hands of the enemy.

"Kirsten," Richard murmured, and Martin met his gaze, sharing his concern.

279

"There's ammunition in the cellar," Martin said. "Load up. We're going to need it."

Many of the men followed him from the common room to the workroom and the cellar stairs, but a few of the militiamen hung back. One was staring at Richard; Richard could tell from the man's angry expression that he was in for a bad time.

"Tory," the man growled. "You're one of them. Thomas! John, don't let him go free! He's the enemy. He was with Greene!"

With Martin gone, Richard lacked the support of the only man who knew his true identity, so he was unable to stop those who grabbed him roughly and shackled him.

"All right, Canfield, what are their plans? What are you doing here?"

"I don't know their pl—" Richard's words were cut off when someone struck him across the mouth. His head snapped back under the force of the blow, and his lip split, spurting blood.

"The truth, Canfield! Tell us the truth!"

"I tell you, I don't know!"

The man raised his fist.

"He's telling the truth, Banta. Put down your fist and release him. He's one of us."

The men turned at Martin's entry. "But, Hoppe—"

"I said, let him go. He's a Patriot working for Washington. We'd just been discussing his work when you came in." He raised an eyebrow. "Why do you think he was here—alone? We were having a calm and pleasant discussion of his mission, of why he was with the Tory troops."

"You believe Canfield?"

"His name's not Canfield. It's Maddox. Richard Maddox."

"The Mad Ox," one of the men said. "I've heard the name." He stared at Richard. "Yours?"

Richard nodded, feeling relieved as John Ackerman undid his shackles and he was able to stand and rub his wrists. His flesh was tender there for he'd been bound twice in the past twenty-four hours. He bent to soothe his sore ankles.

"What do we do now? How do we know how best to handle them?"

"Richard?" Martin asked.

"Greene is a madman. We'll have to move cautiously. I don't trust him at all."

There were various muffled comments from the group.

"Can we do it?" Garret Vandervelt said. "Can we free our families?"

Richard studied each of the men. "Will you trust me to help? Do you believe in my loyalty?"

The men became quiet as each thought on his words and tried to decide.

"I trust him." Martin was the first to speak up, and Richard grinned at him, pleased. Martin didn't return his grin, but looked at the others grimly, waiting for each individual's answer.

"I don't know," Jonathan Hopper said. He was the commander of the militia, so his opinion held a lot of weight. He eyed his cousin. "You believe him?" he asked Martin, who nodded. "I shall trust him also."

Richard sighed with relief as each of the men followed their commander's lead.

"Arm yourselves," he said after the men had looked to him for direction. "We'll travel together to the Van Voorhees' farm. There we'll split up into two groups, one to approach from the front of the house, one to attack from the back. We can break into four groups if necessary." He picked up a knife from the table, the one Martin had used to cut the bread. "Bring knives as well as guns. You may need them.

The Tories are a cunning lot. Get your weapons and return here quickly."

"Hurry!" Martin encouraged.

And the men left to equip themselves.

Kirsten and her mother were separated from Kirsten's father and thrust into the parlor of the Van Voorhees's house, where the Tories had imprisoned a number of women and children. The chamber was a fairly good-sized one, but even so, it was too small for the number of occupants. Every available chair was taken. Kirsten and Agnes were forced to sit on the floor near the fireplace. Since it was November and the weather was cool, there was a fire burning brightly. As her mother went to sit down, Kirsten made sure she was a safe distance away from the threat of escaping sparks.

To Kirsten's relief, the men hadn't tied them, having felt there was no need to. Perhaps they thought women and children too weak and vulnerable to be capable of escaping under any circumstances. Whatever their reasoning, Kirsten was grateful. Her wrists and ankles still pained from being bound earlier.

She studied her mother with concern. Agnes had nearly gone out of her mind when James had been dragged from her side. She looked haggard. Her eyes were dull, their expression lifeless.

"They'll kill him!" Agnes wailed. "I know they will."

"You don't know that, *Moeder*," Kirsten responded, stroking her parent's arm.

"They will if William has a say about it! You heard him—William never liked James!"

That explained some of those strained moments, Kirsten realized, when the two families had picnicked together during Kirsten's early childhood. She recalled a time or two when a happy outing had been destroyed by an argument between the two men. Probably over something minor. She didn't remember exactly. In fact, until now, she'd not thought of the angry exchanges at all.

It had grown chilly outside with the coming of the new day, and Kirsten was grateful for the warmth of the fire behind her . . . the crowded room.

Rachel Banta sat across from her. Their gazes met, and Kirsten saw the concern in Rachel's eyes, the fear.

"We'll be all right," she said.

Rachel nodded, but looked unconvinced.

A guard had been posted near the door, and now another man brushed by him and headed to the fire, his arms loaded with wood. Kirsten saw his face and gasped. Purposely, she turned her head away and silently prayed the man hadn't seen her, that he wouldn't recognize her.

It was the man with the disfigured features. The man who had tried to murder Richard.

The women and children had become silent when he'd entered the room. Whether from the horror of seeing such a terrifying visage or the sense of danger the fellow brought with him, Kirsten didn't know. Her heart pounded so hard she was afraid the killer would hear it, that it would draw his attention to her.

Thankfully, her mother had calmed down. Now Agnes was resigned to the fact that her sobs would neither save James nor rescue her from these men. All she could do was wait and pray.

Sensing her mother's fear, Kirsten squeezed Agnes' arm. She herself relaxed slightly in doing so. The strange-looking man had risen after throwing a log onto the fire. As he moved toward the door, Kirsten felt his gaze on her. She bent her head, pretending to check her shoes, trying to be nonchalant about it.

"You!" the man said, and Kirsten gasped and raised her eyes slowly. Had he recognized her in her shirt and breeches? She released her breath in relief when she saw that she was not the object of the disfigured man's attention; it was Anna Terhune, poor girl.

"Come with me," he ordered.

The room grew loud with the murmurs of protest.

"What do you want her for?" someone asked, daring to be bold. Kirsten recognized Martin's sister.

No, Margaretha, Kirsten thought, *don't draw attention to yourself!*

The man seemed to stare right through Margaretha. "The men are hungry. We will not have to worry about this wench eating our food." He pointed toward the skinny Anna. Then he cocked his head and regarded Kirsten's cousin thoughtfully. "How about you? Can you prepare food?"

Margaretha shook her head. "My brother does all the cooking," she lied. "I was a sickly child and never learned."

He scowled as if he didn't believe her.

"I can cook!" someone said, and Kirsten was startled to realize that the words had come from her own mother.

"Moeder—no!"

Agnes rose, her face free of tears, her expression purposeful. "I'm William Randolph's sister. I'll be happy to cook for you."

There was a buzz of anger from the occupants of the room as the man nodded and Agnes followed him from the parlor. The others turned to stare at Kirsten accusingly.

"I don't know what she's planning," Kirsten said, feeling her face flush. "She's terrified of her brother, but she's worried about *Vader.* Perhaps she hopes that by cooperating she'll gain the Loyalists' confidence, and she'll be able to see *Vader*."

Rachel inclined her head and then spoke to those in the room. "She saved poor Anna here, didn't she? Let us be thankful for Anna's sake. I, for one, believe in Agnes' loyalty. For God's sake, her husband and daughter are here."

"What if she hopes to free them and not us?" someone asked.

"I'd not leave you behind!" Kirsten said sharply, stung by the remark.

"And if you've no choice?" The comment came from directly beside her, from Sarah Van Voorhees, the woman of the house.

"Then I'll get help from our men and return to free you," Kirsten said, the look in her eyes daring anyone to argue with her.

The members of the militia met back at the inn as Richard had requested. Armed with guns and swords and small knives, they were ready to rescue their loved ones.

"These Loyalists have little guns; they're experts in small arms," Richard told them. "Be prepared to use those knives—anything you can get your hands on. Such weapons could be your only hope." He paused and studied each man. "Do you know how to use those knives?"

They all murmured that they did.

"Good. Let's go then."

The men traveled by cart until they were about a half-mile from the Van Voorhees' farm. Then Captain Jonathan Hopper ordered everyone to alight and proceed on foot.

"We can't afford to be discovered, men," Hopper explained. "As I'm sure you'll agree, we've too much at stake here." As it was, they had no cover of darkness to shield their approach. The sun had risen in a cloudless sky as if to mock their efforts.

The Van Voorhees' house appeared deserted, but Richard knew better. He told Hopper and his men of Greene's fighting tactics. The Tories, he explained, would be inside, still, playing a game of bait and wait.

Crouched in the bushes at the edge of the woods bordering the Van Voorhees' property, Richard glanced at the man next to him. Jonathan Hopper, a good, able man, looked Richard's way and nodded.

"They're there all right," Richard mouthed. "I'd stake a month's pay on it."

A fierce light entered the captain's eyes, and then he rose from his crouch and raised his sword high in the signal to move forward.

Richard gripped his gun hard as he joined the advance. He hoped he wouldn't have to use the rifle, for he was afraid those trapped in the house would get caught in the gunfire. Spying an outbuilding, he ran to it for cover, offering up a silent prayer that the members of the militia had sense enough to keep their heads and stay out of sight. He was afraid that concern for their loved ones would affect their judgment. Richard understood what the men were feeling. Kirsten was inside with the captives. His sweet, spirited Kirsten.

Was she safe? Had she done something to antagonize her captors? He thought of Elias Greene, and a cold shiver of fear coiled in his belly. *Damn! I'll kill the bastard myself if he has so much as touched Kirsten!*

Chapter Twenty-two

The disfigured man's name was Phelps. Kirsten learned that when she heard one of his cohorts call out to him as he entered the parlor for the second time that morning. Her stomach lurched as memories of the man poised over Richard in the flash and fire of the storm came to her. It was all she could do to control a gasp as she recalled the fight, the moment when she'd witnessed the downward thrust of Phelps's bayonet.

She shuddered, reexperiencing the utter helplessness, the horror of watching one man purposely take the life of another. Only Richard didn't die. He might have if not for her, but thank God he'd made it.

Kirsten thought of their captors—her uncle William, Elias Greene, Phelps and the others. They were all cruel men. *God help us*, she thought. *We're at their mercy*.

She studied the women in the room with her. Despite their fear, a few had dozed off with children on their laps, too exhausted from the night's ordeal to do otherwise.

Where was *Moeder?* Kirsten wondered. She heard a burst of laughter from the next room, and she cringed, envisioning the reason for such merriment. *Oh, God, please let Moeder be all right and not the object of their sport.*

Phelps was moving about the room, staring at each woman. Instinctively, Kirsten moved closer to the person beside her, afraid that he'd spy her. She felt Sarah Van Voorhees press toward her, and the two women leaned against each other, clutching each other's hand.

Kirsten swallowed hard. The disfigured man paused over Anna Terhune, who had fallen asleep, her head propped against another woman's shoulder.

"Wake her up," Phelps growled at Rachel.

Kirsten wanted to say something, but wisely kept her tongue.

When Rachel Banta hesitated, the man got angry. "I says, wake her up!" He gave her a smirk. "Or are ya offering to take her place?"

Eyes widening with fear, Rachel shook the girl as ordered. Phelps grinned as Anna jolted awake, her face mirroring horror and fear as she realized whose attention she held.

The man reached down and hauled her up by the arm. "Come, wench!" he said. "You come with me."

Kirsten shifted uneasily as Anna grimaced, no doubt from the bruising grip on her arm and the vile odor of the man's breath.

"No, please," Anna begged.

"Leave her alone. She's not bothering anyone." Kirsten started to rise.

As Phelps looked at her Kirsten tensed in fear at having drawn his glance. He squinted his eyes as he studied her. His gaze dropping from her face to her breeches, he murmured in disgust. The air became fraught with tension as Kirsten wondered if she'd just

288

signed her own death warrant.

Phelps had seen her that night. Did he recognize her? She was dressed as she'd been then, like a boy. Would it occur to him that she and the boy in the woods were actually one and the same person? She saw that he had difficulty seeing. Perhaps he didn't recognize her!

"Are *you* offering to take her place?" He sneered, confirming her last thought. "Such generosity among you rebel women. First the old one offers to cook for her and now you're willing to . . ." With his misshapen mouth, his smile appeared more of grimace. He released Anna and came to Kirsten.

"I'm not offering anything," Kirsten replied, relieved that he'd made no connection between her and that stormy night. If she got out of this alive, she'd have to remember him, his name. Richard would surely want to know it.

Suddenly, she heard a gunshot. When Phelps turned from her to hurry from the room, Kirsten went to the window, and her heart raced as she caught sight of several members of the Hoppertown militia.

"They're surrounding the house!" she cried. "Our militia is surrounding the house! Rachel, I see Thomas and your father. Mrs. Bogert, your brother is there with your son!"

The women began talking and laughing, their hope renewed, certain now of rescue. In the excitement of the attack, the guards had left their posts for defense points. Kirsten ran to the door, thinking of escape, and found her way blocked by Elias Greene.

"So!" he said. "Just you and me . . . finally."

Kirsten laughed harshly as she glanced back at the other women. "Hardly, Greene." Rachel Banta, Anna Terhune, and Sarah Van Voorhees came up to stand behind her in support.

Eyes narrowing, Greene raised his pistol, pointed it at Kirsten's chest. "Move away, ladies, or I'll shoot her here and now."

"You'll not get out of this alive if you kill me, Greene," Kirsten said.

They were in the front hall. The outside entrance door burst inward as Thomas Banta shouldered his way inside the house.

"Thomas," Rachel called to her brother. She pointed toward the Tory leader's gun. "Get Greene!"

A flicker of emotion crossed Thomas' face as he quickly took in the situation. And then he rushed at the man. Greene cursed as Thomas managed to knock the pistol from his grip. The two men fought in deadly earnest.

With the threat of Greene's gun gone, Kirsten looked at the women and children and then assumed command of them. "Rachel—gather the children and their mothers." She fumbled on the floor for Greene's pistol; she had to back away several times to avoid being struck by the fighting men. Finally, she got a hold of the pistol's handle. "Keep them inside the house and shoot anyone who dares to threaten them," she said, giving Rachel the gun.

Rachel nodded with confidence. "What will you do?"

Kirsten never had a chance to answer. The husbands and sons of the captives came through the open front entrance, their loud voices filled with joy at the sight of their loved ones, their weapons raised against any enemy who might cross their path.

"Stay inside the room!" one man bellowed. Mrs. Banta nodded and shouted to her husband to be careful.

The militiamen scattered to all parts of the house

in search of their Tory enemies. Kirsten heard shots fired but not many. The house was alive with the sounds of battle as militiamen fought hand-to-hand to rescue their beloved families. *The Van Voorhees' house,* Kirsten thought, eyeing the destruction, the spatters of blood that stained the floor and furniture, *will never be the same.*

She left the parlor in search of her parents. She found her mother first, in the kitchen. The poor woman had been left bound and gagged on a chair near the hearth. With a horrified cry, Kirsten hurried to untie her. *Such gratitude,* she thought, *for the one who offered to cook for you.*

"Your *vader,*" Agnes said after her daughter had removed her gag. "He and George Zabriskie are in the cellar outside. I heard Dunley—"

Kirsten nodded. "You'll be all right?" Her mother was rubbing her wrists, but she assured her that she would be fine and urged her to find James. Kirsten ran outside to locate the storage cellar.

Unlike at the Van Atta home where the root cellar was beneath the house, the Van Voorhees' stores were kept in a separate cellar built underground. It had a door set into the side of a hill. *"Vader!"* she called, pulling at the iron door lock.

"Kirsten," came the familiar voice, "daughter, is that you?"

She felt a burst of joy at knowing that he was all right. "Yes, *Vader . . .*"

"Open the door, girl."

"I'm trying, *Vader.*"

An explosive noise sounded nearby, a gunshot.

"Good God!" James Van Atta exclaimed, his voice muffled through the heavy wood. "What's happening out there?"

"We're being rescued!"

"Thank God," he said. "Hurry, Kirsten, so we can help."

But Kirsten was having no luck; the lock wouldn't budge.

"Get away from that door."

Kirsten froze and slowly turned. William Randolph stood a few yards away, his pistol in hand and his eyes glittering.

"You'll never win," she said. "I told you."

Randolph cocked the flintlock. "I'll win over you. I'm going to kill you. At least I'll have that satisfaction."

"Kirsten!" her father cried from inside the cellar. "Kirsten! What's going on? What's happening out there?"

Her uncle smiled. "And then I'm going to shoot your father . . ."

"No!" The cry came from behind Randolph.

"Miles!" Kirsten gasped, stunned to see her cousin.

"Boy," Randolph said with a grin at his son, "I'm glad you're here."

Miles raised his rifle. "No, Father, I won't let you do it." His lips firmed; his hands were steady.

Randolph seemed taken aback. "This is my affair, son!"

"Don't call me son!" Miles lifted the gun higher. "And it is my affair. She's my cousin."

"No," his father said. "Don't you see? She's one of them. A Patriot. A damn rebel! They're ruining this land, boy. They're ruining everything!"

"Drop your pistol, Father."

"You won't harm me; I'm your father."

Miles sneered. "Like you wouldn't hurt me because I'm your son?" He shifted his grip on the rifle, grimacing as the fabric of his shirt stretched across the muscles of his back.

Randolph flushed. "I didn't mean to whip you that hard, son. But I had to discipline you—it was for your own good."

"And Mother?" Miles's face contorted with hate. "You had to discipline her, too?" He heard Kirsten's gasp, but he went on. "For God's sake, she didn't do anything wrong! She loves you." His voice became hoarse. ". . . Loved you." He spoke as if his mother had changed her mind.

The barrel of the rifle wavered slightly. "I should kill you now, you bastard, for all you've done to Mother . . . to me."

"No, boy!" William Randolph was visibly alarmed.

"Kirsten," Miles said softly, "take his gun."

The older man's mouth drew into a straight line, and Kirsten hesitated. Her uncle was unstable; she didn't trust him.

"Go ahead, Kirsten. He won't hurt you. He knows I'd kill him first."

Kirsten edged closer.

"And get the key to the cellar door. It's in his coat pocket." Miles moved a step nearer. "You see, my dear *father*"—he spoke with loathing—"is the mastermind here."

Kirsten reached for the gun and gasped as Randolph spun and discharged his pistol. Two shots rang out as both father's and son's guns went off. William Randolph was unhurt, but Miles fell to the ground, wounded. Thomas Banta arrived seconds later. Aghast, his face white, Randolph took one look at his injured son and then stared at Banta a moment before he fled.

"Get him, Tom!" Kirsten cried. "He shot Miles! He shot his own son!" She crouched beside her bleeding cousin.

Chapter Twenty-three

Miles was dead. Somewhere deep inside, Kirsten sensed it, but the horror of it numbed her brain. Her vision blurred until she was oblivious to everything around her. Even Miles's face. Yet, she could smell her cousin's blood, could feel it on her hands. Sobbing, she raised his head and cradled it in her lap.

"Live, Miles," she begged, stroking his forehead. "Live, please, live!"

But when her eyes cleared, she saw that Miles had been hit in the heart, killed instantly, and she knew she'd never again be the same. The war, for her, would never again hold the same meaning. *Freedom be damned! It's time to stop this senseless killing!* she thought.

Richard had been frantically searching everywhere for Kirsten. The Tories had been subdued; a few had escaped, but many had been taken. Their leader, Elias Greene, had been killed by Thomas Banta.

Richard ran from one room to the next of the Van Voorhees' house, searching for Kirsten, his heart pounding with dread when he couldn't find her. No one had seen her for some while. Finally, when he'd checked all the chambers, he went outside to check the outbuildings and the yard. Greene and his men had locked them in an outbuilding before . . . perhaps Kirsten was in the Van Voorhees' smokehouse.

His spirits fell when he didn't find her there. She wasn't in the barn or the stables either. *Dear God, where was she?*

He heard a fierce heavy pounding as he rounded another outbuilding—the summer kitchen. He saw the cellar then, built into hill and knew that someone was trapped inside.

"Kirsten," he breathed with hope. "Kirsten!" he shouted, hurrying toward the door.

And that was when he saw her. Outside. On the grass. She wasn't trapped within the cellar, but someone else was. She was so quiet, he'd almost missed her. She sat on the damp ground, crying. Her face wet with tears, she was the image of torment.

Richard ignored the thundering on the cellar door to go to her. He felt pain twisting his gut. *What did you do to her, you bastards!*

As he came closer to her, his gaze dropped to her lap, and his heart lurched.

Dear God, it's Miles. Miles, Kirsten's beloved cousin, was injured. No, dead.

Richard wanted to take her into his arms and comfort her, but the hammering on the wooden door continued, and he could not ignore it. He hurried to the lock and began struggling with the iron. "Who's inside?"

"James Van Atta," someone said.

"And George Zabriskie!" another added.

Richard stopped his struggles to hear better those trapped within. There was a quiet pause. "Are you friend or foe?" asked the one who'd spoken first.

"James Van Atta?" Richard said, his gaze straying to Kirsten. Her lifeless behavior scared him. "Kirsten's kin?"

"Her father."

"I'm a friend, although when you see me you may not believe it." Richard renewed his efforts with the lock. "I've traveled with the Tories, but I've come with your militia. I tell the truth when I say I'm not a Loyalist—a King's man—but a Patriot like you." The iron lock squeaked under his fingers, but wouldn't come free.

"Damn," Richard cursed. "Do you know where they keep the key?" A silly question, he thought, eyeing the lock with frustration.

A muffled voice came from behind the door. "William has it, I think."

A second voice—Richard thought it belonged to Kirsten's father—said, "He was here and so was Kirsten." He hesitated. "We heard gunfire. Is she all right?"

Richard stared at his beloved. "She is unharmed, but Miles is not."

"My God!"

"This William—is it Randolph of whom you speak?" Richard asked.

"Yes. Is he there?"

"No. No sign of him, I'm afraid."

There was a prolonged moment of silence.

"Check for a spare key," one of the men inside suggested. "Are there any rocks nearby? Perhaps Samuel keeps one hidden."

Richard searched the area and found nothing. "It's no use."

Thomas Banta returned from the chase. "Randolph's escaped," he gasped, out of breath from running. "Damn! The bastard got away!"

Richard nodded, understanding the man's frustration. "We'll have to break down this door. Van Atta and Zabriskie are inside."

Banta agreed. "I'll get help." He left and returned shortly afterward with two men.

Richard had gone to Kirsten's side while he waited. When help arrived and he rose to assist, one of the men—Martin Hoppe—took one look at the situation and waved him back to Kirsten's side.

Grateful, Richard did as he was bid and drew Kirsten against him. She didn't yield easily, but remained stiff, ignorant of his presence. He feared for her state of mind.

He stroked her hair and murmured to her softly. Soon, her expression changed ever so slightly, and Richard was relieved.

"Kirsten . . ."

Her tears fell in earnest now. "Richard?" she asked in a trembly voice.

"Yes, love."

"He's dead." A gasping sob. "Miles is dead."

"I'm so sorry." He ached for her. He helped her to set Miles gently on the ground. Removing his jacket, he pillowed the dead youth's head.

"Oh, God, Richard!" Kirsten turned to him then, and he inhaled sharply at the stark pain in her expression. "His own father killed him."

"Lord have mercy!"

"No!" she cried. "Not on his soul. Not on William Randolph's vile soul!"

Richard's eyes stung as he shared her grief. "His mother . . ."

"Oh, dear God in heaven!" she wailed. "Aunt Catherine!" She stood. "I have to find her. He's hurt her before, too. He's a madman. He may kill her!"

"Easy, love," Richard said softly. "I'll send someone to get her. You mustn't go yourself."

He left her to approach the men at the cellar entrance. They had managed to break in the door, and now Martin Hoppe, Thomas Banta, and John Ackerman stood back as Kirsten's father and George Zabriskie came out from the dark storage place.

Richard quickly explained the situation to them.

"I'll go," James said, and two others offered to accompany him. Richard had known James Van Atta would volunteer first, because the man resembled the woman he loved. He had the same silver hair . . . the same eyes.

James's concerned gaze went to his daughter. He approached her and touched her arm. "Kirsten dear, are you all right?"

She blinked. "I'm fine, *Vader*, but Aunt Catherine . . ."

"I know, daughter. I'm to get her."

"But, *Vader*, Uncle William . . ."

"I'll not go alone. Martin and Thomas will be with me."

Kirsten nodded and then sat down, exhausted, beside her dead cousin on the damp, cool ground. She began to stroke Miles's cooling brow. Her father frowned.

Richard came back to her. "I'll take care of her," he assured James.

Kirsten's father looked as if he would protest, but then he nodded instead, appearing relieved. "Thank you," he said and left with the other men.

"Love, come. He's gone," Richard said, hunkering down at Kirsten's side. "Miles is at peace now." Her hands were covered in Miles's blood. He coaxed her gently toward the well a few yards away. After pulling up a bucket of cool water, he washed away the blood.

Kirsten appeared to be in a stupor. Her lashes feathered against her cheeks, before she raised her eyes. "Peace?" she echoed. He nodded, and she smiled. "That's what he always wanted, peace . . . He hated the war, saw no sense in it."

Richard was beginning to feel the same way. "He's at rest now," he said. "No one will hurt him again." He kissed each of Kirsten's cleansed hands, and then he returned to where Miles lay. He bent and lifted the youth's lifeless body in his strong arms. Cradling it against his chest, he waited for Kirsten to follow him. He noted that she seemed composed.

"Peace," she murmured. "Yes, Miles dear. You're at peace. You're happy now."

Captain Jonathan Hopper came out of the house and took Miles's body from Richard's arms. The men exchanged a few words before Hopper carried Miles inside.

"Where are they taking him?" Kirsten said. She did not appear to be alarmed that someone had taken Miles away.

Unsure of her mental state, Richard frowned down at her, concerned. "Inside, love. His mother will want to see him."

Kirsten's eyes filled with tears. "Poor Miles. Poor Aunt Catherine."

Richard placed an arm about her shoulders. "Come, love. You must be exhausted. I'll see you home."

She stopped short. *"Moeder.* Where is my *moeder?"*

"According to Captain Hopper, she's fine," he told her. "She's already been taken home."

Kirsten sighed. "All right then. Let's go home."

He thought she must be anxious to get away from this place of destruction. A few families were still here. It would be some time before all could leave, for every available wagon had been utilized to take the first of the former captives home. Richard took Kirsten with him as he checked the stables.

"Oh, look," she cried. "There's Hilga. She's our mare." Her father must have taken the wagon and gelding to the Randolphs' to get Aunt Catherine.

Richard saddled Hilga. Thinking of Kirsten's upset state, he decided that they would ride together.

With the immediate threat of the Tories gone, Richard and Kirsten took their time on their journey to the Van Atta farm. The day was clear, but the November bite to the air made Kirsten shiver and burrow closer to Richard's chest. She rode sideways before him, her arm about his waist, her head against his chest. She could feel the movement of his arms as he held the reins. He was warm and strong, and she felt safe within his arms.

"What of Greene and the other Loyalists?" she asked after a time of companionable silence.

"Elias Greene's dead. Godwin and Dunley have been taken prisoner along with a few others." Richard paused. "Your uncle escaped."

Kirsten tensed and then lifted her head. "May justice be served on him soon," she said.

Agnes Van Atta was overjoyed to see her daughter safe. They hugged and tears ran down both their faces as they released each other. Richard had stood by and watched the happy reunion in silence. He felt a sudden longing for the warmth of his own family, a warmth he'd never experience again, for his family was dead.

Their greetings accomplished, Agnes suddenly became aware of the strange man with her daughter. She looked at Richard, clearly puzzled by his presence. But she was smiling, for she was glad to see any man who'd returned her daughter safely to her.

Kirsten came alive, grabbing Richard's hand. As she drew him forward, the intimacy between them did not go unnoticed by Kirsten's mother. *"Moeder,* this is Richard. Richard Maddox. He helped rescue us."

Agnes smiled and held out her hand. "Thank you, Mr. Maddox. I'm ever in your debt."

"I can't take the credit, madame. It was your Captain Hopper and his men . . ."

She shook her head. "You are too humble, Mr. Maddox."

"Richard," he invited.

Kirsten stared at him with surprise. Why, Richard could be most charming!

"You must be hungry," Agnes said to her daughter.

"A bit, *Moeder.*"

"And you, Mr.—Richard," Kirsten's mother amended with a soft smile.

"Yes, I most certainly am," he confessed without embarrassment.

"Come in then."

Kirsten and Richard sat at the tableboard while Agnes Van Atta roamed about the kitchen, preparing food.

Kirsten grew sad again. Miles was dead. A part of her was gone . . . they'd been so close. How was she to go on without him?

"Moeder," she said, her voice flat, "Miles is dead."

Agnes froze in the act of placing *olijkoecks* on a plate. "Dead," she murmured, and then continued working as if she hadn't heard.

Kirsten, watching her, was appalled by her mother's lack of emotional response. *"Moeder,* didn't you hear me? Miles is dead. Dead!"

"Kirsten"—Richard placed a hand on her arm—"I'm sure . . ."

She gave him a look that cut into him.

Agnes turned to the table, tears in her eyes. "God help him. How?"

Kirsten realized her mistake. Could her mother take much more pain? How would she react upon learning that her nephew's death was by her brother's hand? She didn't answer her mother's question.

When Agnes set the plate of cakes down on the table, the atmosphere in the room was so tense, so thick, that Kirsten felt strangled by it.

"Kirsten, how?" her mother asked again.

"He was shot." She pretended an indifference that wasn't there.

"There's something you're not telling me."

Kirsten refused to meet her parent's gaze. "It was an accident. The gun went off by mistake."

"Who?" Agnes gasped, her face paling. It was as if she'd already guessed. "William?"

Her daughter nodded, her blue eyes full of compassion as she finally faced her mother.

"Oh, my God!" Agnes swayed as if she were going to faint, and Richard sprang from his chair to support her and help her sit down.

"Are you all right?" he asked.

Agnes nodded. "I knew it would come to this, only I thought it would be James and not the boy." She held her hands over her eyes and cried. "Poor Miles . . . poor, poor dear boy!"

Richard looked at Kirsten, and she glanced away guiltily.

"Catherine," Agnes sobbed. "Oh, God help her. Catherine—does she know?" She eyed her daughter for an answer.

Kirsten shook her head. "Father went to get her.

He's bringing her here. Uncle William is gone, escaped from the fight unharmed."

Agnes' mouth became a straight line. "We will not mention his name in this household again!"

"But, *Moeder,* Aunt Cather—"

"I'll deal with Catherine," Kirsten's mother interrupted. "But as of this day, I have no brother. The man I once loved as kin is dead!"

James Van Atta came home shortly, alone. "She was gone," he said. "William must have taken her. I'm sure she went willingly, for she knows nothing of what he did."

His wife stared straight ahead, her lips firmed. At her father's questioning look, Kirsten quickly explained her mother's decision.

Nodding, James slumped into a chair, suddenly tired. "Damn," he muttered. "When will it all end, the murder and bloodshed?"

Chapter Twenty-four

The house was quiet. Grateful for his part in the rescue, the Van Attas had invited Richard to stay the night. They had a spare bedchamber and plenty of food, Agnes had assured him. It would certainly be no trouble.

And Richard had accepted quickly, without thought.

Lying in bed, studying the ceiling, he realized his mistake in staying in the Van Atta home. It was torture knowing that Kirsten was in her bedchamber across the hall, only a few feet away, while he was in the spare room, alone, in the dark . . . aching for her. He should have stayed at the inn. Martin Hoppe would have gladly given him a room.

Exhausted from their ordeal, the Van Atta family members were asleep. It didn't help to imagine Kirsten lying on her feather tick, her glorious silver tresses spread across her pillow, her lush lovely curves beneath a thin linen night rail.

Forcing desire and thoughts of her away, Richard recalled the youth Miles, and his relationship to the Van Atta family. A pain like a knife thrust pierced his breast. *Poor Kirsten. She's hurting so badly.* He would have given anything in the world to spare her grief. He sat up, fighting the strongest urge to go to her across the hall. He wanted to take her in his arms and kiss away her tears. By loving her, he would attempt to force away her torment, her bad memories.

But he knew that in fact there was nothing he could do to take her pain away. Only time would dull the hurt. Only with its passing, would her wounds heal.

Or would they? Richard grimaced in the dark, recalling how even now, after several years, the hurt of having lost his own loved ones lingered, touched him at odd moments.

He heard her crying then, soft sobbing sounds that came from the soul, and he knew he'd been mistaken to believe that everyone in the household was asleep and at peace.

Kirsten, if I come to you now, will you turn me away? Will you let me hold you, comfort you? He should have known that Kirsten's grief would overcome her body's need for sleep. The physical, he supposed, rarely triumphed over the mind. The mind was the spirit and soul of a person, *the basic core of what we are.* How could a body wrestle with such a powerful force and win?

Unable to bear hearing Kirsten's suffering, Richard rose from the bed and padded barefoot across the cold floor. He was naked but thought little of it. His only thought, his only goal, was to cross a hallway several feet wide and enter Kirsten's bedchamber.

He cared not if he'd be welcomed, nor did it occur to him that it would appear most improper should he be discovered in the middle of the night in Kirsten's bedchamber, undressed.

He opened his door silently. After crossing the hall, he gently turned the door knob to Kirsten's bedchamber, and with a slight push forward, the door swung without a sound.

The night sky was as clear as the day's had been. Moonlight filtered in through the window's glass panes, bathing the alcove bed directly across the room. He stopped and studied the bed. He'd never seen one like it. Built into the wall, it had a ceiling, three walls, and double doors closing it in. This night Kirsten had left the doors to the alcove open. Moonglow bathed the young woman as she lay, sobbing her heart out, upon the giant bed. Grief-stricken and beyond awareness of her surroundings, she remained oblivious to Richard's presence.

He hesitated, before fully entering the chamber. Suddenly, he felt as if he shouldn't have come. He was an intruder on a private moment. Everyone was entitled to a moment of privacy, and for Kirsten this time was in a sense sacred.

But he found that he couldn't make himself turn back. He couldn't leave her in such a terrible state, not without comfort, because, by God, he loved the woman.

Emotion swelled within his breast. Tenderness. Affection and desire. The urge to comfort and protect her.

Richard moved toward the bed.

"No! No!" She still couldn't believe that it had happened. *Miles dead?* Kirsten recalled her cousin's laughter, his smile . . . the twinkle in his brown eyes when he'd teased her . . . his being mischievous. Nothing had altered the deep caring they'd shown one another. Even war had not kept them apart. They'd taken chances, defied family to be together secretly. The clearing in the woods would always be their own special meeting place. Perhaps she'd go there in the morning and feel his presence . . .

The war had gone on forever, it seemed. Families destroyed. Men murdered. Innocent women molested—even raped, according to some people who had recently traveled through Hoppertown.

Why won't George's men leave us alone? The King had his people in England to contend with, why concern himself with a country that was a world away, across an ocean?

Because of greed, she thought. Wasn't that what it all came down to? Money? Coin?

Kirsten lay with her eyes closed and in her mind again saw Miles die. *The blood! So much blood!* She could smell it. Would she never be free of that scent?

Her hands had been red with Miles's blood. Would they ever feel the same again? Would *she* ever be the same?

Miles's face had been pale . . . lifeless. *Oh, dear God in heaven, he's dead!*

Grief overwhelmed her, and great sobs rattled her chest and made her gasp for air. She buried her face in her pillow, but the tears refused to stop.

The feather tick moved as a weight settled on it. The next thing Kirsten knew was that someone was lifting her, drawing her against a hard masculine chest. Words of comfort flowed over her, fingers stroked the wisps of silver blond hair at her temples. She felt the sure heat of a strong touch at her neck, down her back.

Richard, she thought, and cried even harder as she turned against him fully. Her tears continued, soaking his warm skin.

"Oh, Richard," she wailed softly.

"I know, love. I know. Let it out. It's all right. I'm here. I'll hold you."

"Why, Richard? Why did it happen?"

He was silent a moment, and when he finally did speak, his voice was deep and rasping. "I don't know, Kirsten. There's no sense in any of this anymore. I'd thought once that there was, but now . . ." His tone was laced with regret.

She lifted her cheek from his breast. Looking into his russet eyes, she saw the pain in them, the shared frustration and grief. *He is a beautiful human being,* she thought, her gaze caressing his male features. His sensual mouth was now tightened with concern, and his brow was creased ever so slightly, drawing her attention to his scar.

"You didn't go," she said.

He shook his head. "I was with Martin when the news came." He cupped her cheek, allowing his fingers to fondle her smooth skin tenderly. "At your request."

She had closed her eyes in pleasure at his touch, and now she opened them again. "You told him everything, and he believed you?" She had told him Martin would, yet she seemed awed that she'd been right.

Richard nodded. "Did you doubt Martin's faith?"

Affronted by the question, she said, "Not really, *mynheer.*"

He raised his eyebrows as he rubbed her earlobe. *"Mynheer?"* There was a glimmer of amusement in his warm, russet gaze.

"Richard."

"Say it again."

She shook her head.

"Why not?" he asked.

Kirsten frowned, the corners of her pink lips turning down into a pout, and she shifted away from his touch. "Because you make fun of my speech."

He groaned. "Good God, no, love. I wish to hear you say it, because I love the way you do so. You thrill me with the sound of it."

She blinked, startled by the admission.

"Shocked?" He smiled at her tenderly and reached out to caress her again, stroking her chin.

Kirsten shook her head no, and Richard's gaze was drawn to her lips . . . so sweet . . . pink . . . tempting. His fingers moved to trace them, enjoying their shape and texture, the way they trembled beneath his hand.

He felt a twinge of guilt for wanting her so badly, for letting physical desire blind him to her pain. "Damn!" he cursed.

"What's wrong?" She seemed alarmed by his outburst.

"Nothing," he mumbled, but he gave himself away. With a rueful smile, he looked down at himself.

Kirsten followed his gaze and her eyes grew round as she saw his manhood, thick and rising between his thighs. Within her she felt a tingle in response.

Richard set her away from him. "You're tired. You must rest." He started to rise, and she stared at him, feeling hurt. He'd been so warm and comforting, but now he was leaving her.

"Don't go!" She reached for his arm. She didn't want to be alone this night.

Richard stared at her hand before he raised russet eyes to meet her glistening blue gaze. "Love . . . have pity on me. I'm only human. I can take only so much."

"Then go ahead and take it," she murmured.

"*What?*"

"Please . . . take me. Love me—make me forget."

"You don't know what you're saying." His voice

sounded strangled. "In the morning, you'll wake up and I'll have to leave, and you'll be angry." He drew a hand raggedly through his hair, tousling the tawny-colored strands. He looked harassed, like a cat who's had its fur ruffled.

"Richard."

"Close your eyes and go to sleep."

"Richard . . ." Her voice was an invitation, purposely enticing, seductively soft.

Richard swallowed. He'd been a fool to come into her bedchamber. If he were discovered there by her parents . . .

"They sleep like the dead," she said, as if reading his mind. "They'll never know. How do you think I came to see you at the ruin?"

He felt a stirring of hope and renewed desire. His muscles tensed with the feeling; his shaft throbbed with it. His breath quickened as he sat down.

"I love you, Richard." Kirsten fell against him and wrapped her arms about his waist.

"Don't!" he said, his tone strained. "Don't say it. It'll only hurt more later."

"Say it, Richard," she prompted. "Say you love me."

The moment grew charged as she waited for the admission. With Miles gone, she felt so alone. More than ever she needed Richard's love, needed to hear him say the words.

"I do care for you, Kirsten."

"Say it, Richard." She drew back, her blue eyes glittering, her lips firm.

"Kirsten—"

"Oh, don't!" she cried all of a sudden. She threw herself back into his embrace. "It doesn't matter—don't you see? I love you so much that it doesn't matter!"

311

He groaned and held her tight. "Oh, Kirsten . . ."

They kissed, a fierce meeting of mouths that spoke of suppressed passions and emotions that were buried deep.

Richard leaned back then to study her. Everything about her fascinated him. That shining cascade of long, platinum blond hair . . . those sparkling blue eyes. Her face bore the ravages of her earlier tears, but that only heightened her beauty rather than detracting from it.

This woman cared . . . and loved deeply. She claimed she loved him. Richard felt a bit jealous of the place Miles had held in her tender heart.

Kirsten was clad in a linen night rail. The top feather tick had been shoved away during her crying episode, so his gaze swept from her lovely blue eyes to her throat, then to supple breasts that swelled and strained against white fabric. A tiny blue bow adorned the neck of her rail, it probably kept the gown closed, he supposed.

Richard's fingers went to the ribbon bow, pulled gently; and as he'd expected, the night rail parted at the collar.

She didn't say a word, hadn't moved a muscle to stop him. She neither smiled nor frowned, but just looked at him with glistening aquamarine eyes. His heart slammed against his chest muscles, and he shivered as he peeled back fabric and beheld the white, silken flesh inside.

"Are you cold?" she asked. Her face displayed concern.

He shook his head. "No. Are you?"

Kirsten sighed and closed her eyes as Richard dipped his hand inside her night rail, found and lifted her left breast. *Cold?* she thought. With Richard touching her, how could she be cold? She felt hot; her skin was tingling.

He removed his hand, and she murmured a faint protest, until she realized that he had better plans for her . . . for them. He worked to release each of the tiny buttons along the front of her night rail.

Kirsten gasped as he opened the garment, exposing her breasts to the cool, night air.

"Lovely," he said in a husky voice. "So lovely."

She smiled, glad that he found her so. Richard eased her back against the bed, following her down, warming her with his length.

She moaned. He was kissing her throat . . . her shoulders . . . the slope of her breast. He caught a nipple between his lips and nipped it lightly before laving it with his tongue. She felt the tip tingle as it hardened into a little nub.

Kirsten shifted beneath him, opening her legs until his muscular thighs were cradled in the hollow she'd created. He rose up to study her moon-lit face. His look was purely male, sensual, and the sight of his passion heightened her own.

Richard smiled, apparently satisfied by her expression, and then the smile was wiped from his face and he threw back his head, groaning. Kirsten had grabbed hold of his buttocks, had arched up against him, rotating her hips. His closed lashes hid the glaze of passion in his russet gaze, but she could hear his breathing. It came in pants—harsh, masculine inhalations and exhalations of air. Kirsten felt the growing tension in the muscles beneath her hands. She kissed his neck and closed her eyes, enjoying the scent and feel of him.

Richard rejoiced in the soft, warm hands on his back and buttocks. He groaned in ecstasy when she pushed him up so that she could tenderly handle his shaft.

"No, love," he gasped.

"Yes," she whispered. "Yes, let me."

He rolled over onto his back and pulled her up above him, setting her astraddle of his thighs. With loving hands, she touched him, for she had easy access to his points of pleasure. She fondled and touched and manipulated him until he shuddered, near the edge. He stopped her then; he wasn't about to journey alone. He wanted her with him.

"Now it's your turn," he said, his voice hoarse. And he caught the warm, fleshy globes that hung like ripe apples as she bent. Cupping a white mound, he watched with fascination as her breast responded to his fingertips. Then, with a hand at her back, he propelled her forward until her breast was a ripe fruit offering for his lips.

She shivered as he suckled her. She moaned and whimpered and made those little cat sounds that he so enjoyed hearing. Richard gave the same attention to her other breast and felt himself near to bursting as he did so. Finally, unable to bear the wait any longer, he reversed their positions and entered her.

She was ready for him, as he was for her; and as he thrust inside her, she sighed before she began to buck against him in a set rhythm.

"That's it, love," he crooned. "Reach for the stars."

He strained against her as he buried himself within her, feeling himself throb and quicken as he slid in and out of her moist sheath.

"Richard!"

"Yes, love!"

"Please!"

He pressed faster . . . harder. "Oh, yes," he grated between clenched teeth.

Suddenly, the sky opened up and the moon and

314

sun shattered, filling the dark with many, brilliant points of light. Richard exploded with sensation, with color, and a wealth of feeling he'd never before experienced.

Kirsten sobbed his name as he pushed against her one hard, last time. She gasped, shuddered, and lay still. And Richard was satisfied, for she, too, had found pleasure beyond description in their coupling.

He lay on top of her, his weight pressing her into the feather tick. He was heavy, but Kirsten didn't mind, for he was warm, wonderful, and very much alive.

Richard sat up, and her gaze caressed him as he reached out for the doors to the alcove bed. Within seconds, he'd closed them in. They were in their own little private world.

"Richard, I love you." She hadn't been able to hold back the words.

He hesitated, and then his reply came ever so softly. "Woman, I love you, too." He drew her against his side, and they lay snuggling.

"Sleep," he ordered a short time later. And she obeyed.

Sometime in the night, Richard woke. He made love to Kirsten a second time within the intimate seclusion of the alcove bed. It was a slow, tender exploration, fueled by their love, a joining of two souls as well as two bodies.

When they were done, Richard opened the doors to the alcove bed. "So I can keep a watch on the morning, love," he told her.

And again Kirsten slept within the sweet sanctuary of her lover's arms.

Chapter Twenty-five

"William, when will Miles meet us?" Catherine Randolph asked her husband. She'd been roused in the middle of the night and urged to flee from her home. The Continentals would be attacking; Miles was to be at a special meeting place where they would all stay until they were safe.

Randolph was silent as they made their way through the woods. They had traveled on foot for over an hour, first for a time along the road and then they'd left the trail for the deep, dense section of the forest.

"William?"

He paused in his steps and faced her, his features contorting with pain. He held her shoulders. "He's not coming."

She blinked up at him with those startling sapphire blue eyes that had caught his attention so many years before. "Not coming," she said. "But you said—"

"I had to tell you, don't you see?" William released her and rubbed his face as if he could wipe away the torment—the inner rage. Letting out a growl of anger, he stared at her. "He's dead."

317

"No!" she whispered. He could see her in the moonlight, the way she paled, the pain in her gaze. "Miles . . ." She gasped, swaying on her feet. "God in heaven, no!"

He grabbed her cruelly by the arms. "Get a hold of yourself, wife! Don't you realize we're in danger, too! Why do you think we're traipsing about the woods in the dead of night?"

She cringed at the word "dead." "How?" she asked, her voice choked with emotion.

Randolph turned away, unble to bear her pain. "It was the rebs that did it. Damn them! Kirsten and her cousin, Martin Hoppe."

Catherine shook her head. "No . . . it can't be."

He faced her. "Are you doubting my word?" He must convince her if they were to escape to safety together. She'd always been by his side; she would understand and remain so.

"It's doesn't make sense . . . Kirsten and Miles were close."

His eyes gleamed. "Until Miles chose sides. He was helping me, helping the King as he should and . . ." Randolph hesitated, feeling overwrought by guilt, pain, and the uncertainty of how he should proceed. He was telling her the truth, wasn't he?

His wife gazed at him, saw his expression and realized that he actually believed what he was telling her. Her fingers curled into fists. *Oh, God. Miles dead! I can't believe Kirsten would hurt him. I don't believe it!*

She noticed that her husband refused to look at her, a fact that disturbed her almost as much as a certain memory did. She closed her eyes, recalling the recent beating William had given Miles. How could a father whip his son in that manner? Until Miles's skin was striped with welts and blood.

318

Discipline, he'd said.

She'd believed him for years, but now, thinking with a clear head, she realized that the man she'd married had changed much since the start of the war.

"Let's go," he said. He started through the woods, expecting her to follow.

Catherine hesitated. If Miles were dead, then where was his body? Her chest hurt with the need to breathe. Grief was tightening her chest, making her heart thunder within her breast. She had to know. She wanted to see Miles.

She fell into step behind her husband, for she was desperate for more news of her only son. Her dead son. "Where is he?" she cried. "If he's dead, I want to see him."

His shoulders stiffened for a second, but he didn't stop walking. "I told you—the rebs got him. At the Van Voorhees' place."

She halted. "William, I must see him. I must go to him."

He jerked to a standstill. "No! You can't. You'd be killed. We'd both be killed."

She remained firm. "I'm not asking you to go."

Something dangerous appeared in his expression then, an evil light, a menacing scowl. "You are not going anywhere but with me."

Catherine ignored him, started to turn. William caught her by the arm and struck her across the mouth. *"You are coming with me, I said. Now move!"*

Catherine realized what a fool she'd been all these years to have stayed with him. She should have taken Miles away the first time William raised his fist against either one of them. Charmed by his occasional smile, she'd suffered but chosen to ignore the warnings, the streak of madness, the cruelty in

319

William. What had happened to the tender, gentle man who'd first come to court her?

Her blood froze with a horrible thought. Had William done it? Had he killed his only son? "You did it, didn't you. You killed Miles!"

The look on his face spoke the truth.

There was a soft brightening of the sky when he slipped from Kirsten's bed.

"Richard?" she said sleepily. She felt along the feather tick for him.

"I'm going to my chamber, sweet. It's near dawn; we can't have your parents discovering me here, can we?"

She frowned as she peeked out at him through sleep-drugged eyes. "I suppose not."

Richard bent down and gave her a lingering kiss. "See you at breakfast?"

Her face softened with a gentle smile. "All right," she murmured as she settled herself more comfortably on the feather-tick mattress.

"Sleep well then, my love," he said.

He ensured that she was well covered before he turned to leave the room. He paused a moment to readjust his eyesight for a sweep of Kirsten's bedchamber. Earlier, when he'd entered he'd had eyes only for Kirsten; and now he was curious to see her room, to see some more of the woman he loved.

Richard smiled as he noted the little things that were hers. A garment hung on a wall hook by the bed. A wardrobe against the back wall, no doubt holding her clothes. There was a pair of her shoes on the floor under her window. His gaze roamed. Without thought, he walked to a chair. A hat lay on the wooden seat. A cocked hat. He picked up the headwear and fingered the brim, his eyes widening as he noticed the insignia. He moved to the window and held the hat up to the softly growing light.

Sure enough, it was his hat. He recognized the familiar creases. And he'd not seen it since the day he was to meet Biv. Had Kirsten found it when she'd found him?

He replaced the hat on the chair seat. *Probably not.* She must have found it at a later date. It had blown off his head that night, he remembered, gotten lost in the storm. Did Kirsten know whose hat she had?

He grinned. Not bloody likely, he decided as he left her bedchamber and crept silently into his own room.

With the bright light of morning came the cold sobering realization that it was time for him to depart Hoppertown. As Richard dressed and then went down to break his fast, he regretted his avowal of love to Kirsten, for he knew that she'd expect more from him now. She'd want him to stay, and he couldn't do that, for nothing had really changed. There was still war between England and her colonists. Alex's killer and the traitor were still waiting to be found.

Richard had a job to finish, and there was still a chance that in completing his mission he would die.

So, while his manner toward her family over breakfast was warm, to Kirsten he was simply polite, not particularly affectionate or attentive. And the time drew near for him to leave.

Richard felt like a brute. He could see the hurt in Kirsten's blue eyes, saw her lips quiver when he refused to look at her more than a few times. But what else could he do?

Agnes handed him a satchel of food for the first leg of his journey. He graciously thanked first her and then James, who had given him a sword taken from

321

one of the Tory prisoners. Kirsten stood nearby, silent, brooding over his treatment of her.

"Where do you go now?" Agnes asked.

"To find General Washington—to let him know what has happened here," he said. He looked at James. "You will be careful? Randolph is still at large. He's a determined man, but then, I guess you know that."

He felt the sudden tension, saw Agnes' expression, and hurriedly changed the subject. "I must thank you again for giving me a place to sleep."

"We thank you for returning our daughter safely to us," Agnes said with a smile.

Richard left the house and was nearly at the forest's edge when Kirsten assailed him.

"Richard . . ." She handed him the hat; he hadn't seen her holding it earlier. "You lost yours."

He looked down at the hat. "Where did you find my hat?"

"Yours?" She seemed surprised, and he knew he'd been right. She hadn't known it was his. "I had no idea . . ." She smiled a half-smile. "I found it near the river a ways from where I first saw you. When I discovered it, I knew I had to keep it, but I didn't know why. Now, I know." Her voice grew soft. "I must have somehow sensed it belonged to you."

He didn't say anything. His throat had grown tight with the thought of leaving her, with the knowledge of the bond between them.

A long silence fell between them. *So much to say,* Richard thought, *so little time in which to say it.*

"It's better this way," he finally stated without meeting her gaze. He stared down at the hat, fingering the black felt.

"Damn you!"

He looked at her then, saw the tears in her blue eyes

and melted. "Oh, love . . . I'm sorry. I'm so sorry, but I couldn't . . . can't leave this way." He opened his arms to her, unable to pretend an indifference he didn't feel. "I thought it best, but I just can't."

"Why?" she gasped, clutching him tightly about the waist. "Why did you treat me that way? You said that you love me!"

He buried his chin in her silken tresses, inhaled her clean fragrance. "And I do," he soothed. "I do . . ."

She broke away, stared at him with reproach. "Then . . . why?"

Richard's face contorted with pain. "Because of this . . ." He touched her cheek, wiping away a tear. "My going. You know I have to leave you, and I didn't want you to be hurt. What if I don't return?"

She inhaled sharply. "We've been through this before! You will come back. And if not . . ." Her voice dropped to a husky whisper. "It's a chance I'm willing to take."

He reached out and caressed her jaw. "If I survive, then I'll surely come back, but if I don't . . ." His hand dropped to her shoulder. "How will you know? You cannot wait for me forever."

"That's for me to decide. Not you," she said.

He grabbed her then and kissed her pink lips. "I apologize then," he said when he was done with her mouth.

She nodded and smiled. Her blue eyes filled with tears, but tears of joy as well as sadness at his departure. "Good-bye, Richard."

He stroked her cheek. "I'll be back," he murmured. "As soon as I'm able." *If I'm able . . .*

And he left her . . . and the Dutch village of Hoppertown.

*　　　*　　　*

John Greene was out for blood. The rebels had killed his two brothers—first Sid and most recently Elias, his eldest kin, the one man he always looked up to. He'd make the Patriots pay—every last one of them!

He waited at the cabin as Randolph had instructed. Randolph would help him; the man hated the rebs as much as he, perhaps even more.

He and William Randolph were among the few who'd escaped the Van Voorhees' farm. Phelps had escaped, too, but he'd been unable to meet up with the disfigured man. And he wasn't sure he trusted him anyway.

It would be only Randolph with him now. Soon the two of them would rebuild their army. They'd recruit the troops needed to fight back.

John got up from the chair at the small, crudely constructed table in the center of the one-room cabin. The chamber was sparsely furnished. A single bed. The table and two chairs. A work board against a chair next to the fireplace.

There was food, though. Randolph had planned in advance, planned well. There were dishes enough and cups and a three-legged spider for cooking in. Yes, he thought, it was the perfect place for two men to hole up for a time and work out a course of action.

Wandering about the cabin, he took note of the linens and blankets, the utensils, and the broom. He heard voices. *Voices? Two?*

As he approached the door, he recognized William Randolph's deep tone, and he relaxed slightly. Randolph wouldn't bring the enemy here. Then, he heard the high, feminine reply of the one who accompanied him. Damn! Randolph had brought a woman!

John threw open the door and gazed in shock at the

lovely, dark-haired beauty at William Randolph's side. "What did ye bring her here fer?" he asked. He knew immediately that it was Randolph's wife.

"Had to," the man said with a scowl in his wife's direction. "She knows too much. Besides, she can cook and clean for us while we're here."

"Yes, but . . ."

The woman was stone-faced, unwilling to glance at her husband. Her eyes were glazed.

John stepped aside, allowing the two to enter. *Ah, so that's the way of it!* he thought. There was friction between the Randolphs. Little love, too, he decided. The woman would be no trouble. The young Greene smiled.

Catherine was silent as she entered the tiny cabin, but inside her thoughts churned. She would escape them, as soon as their backs were turned. They would have to leave sometime. William was planning something. *What?* She would find out first and then pass on the information to the Patriots.

But such hate bubbled up within her she could barely see.

Funerals were a time of sadness, but for the Dutch, they were also a time to socialize. Everyone in the community came together to share in the sorrow and then enjoy one another's company. They were day-long affairs, beginning before noon and ending at sundown. Kirsten wanted only the best day of remembrance for her beloved cousin. She did all she could to ensure that it would be special.

The funeral was held at the Van Atta home. With the Randolphs' disappearance, there was no one else to take care of the proceedings. Being close to Miles, Kirsten was more than willing to bear the brunt of the work.

As she and her mother set up the *dodekamer*, the room where Miles was to be laid out, Kirsten thought of Aunt Catherine. Did her aunt know of Miles's death? What story had her uncle concocted to convince Catherine to leave Hoppertown with him? To explain Miles's absence?

Aunt Catherine should be here, Kirsten thought. Alone, she would be accepted, Tory husband or not, for she was a good woman and everyone loved her.

Kirsten and her mother had worked hard the evening before, stitching the *dodekleed* or black funeral cloth to cover Miles's casket. James Van Atta himself had insisted on building Miles's coffin; and he was doing a fine job of it, sanding and polishing the wood to a smooth sheen. He had loved Miles, despite the boy's sire.

Friends—the Bogerts—had offered to make the *dodekoeks,* the cakes that would be served after the funeral service to all those who'd come to the gathering. Gratefully, Kirsten had agreed that Mrs. Bogert and her daughter would make the cakes, and she thanked them for their generous offering.

"In den Heere ontslapen . . ." Sleeping in the Lord.

Kirsten's eyes filled with tears as the *voorlezer* spoke Miles's eulogy. Every Patriot family had come. The Bantas and Bogerts. The Zabriskies, Van Voorheeses, and Ackermans. Even Frederick Terhune with his crooked powdered wig and his skinny daughter. And Dwight Van Graaf and his wife and son. Kirsten frowned. She didn't recall Van Graaf among the militia men who attacked the Tories or rescued them at the Van Voorhees' farm. The thought came and went quickly as the *voorlezer* continued with the service.

"Miles Randolph was a good boy," the man said with feeling. "He had no liking for this war we fight, yet he was an innocent victim. God has chosen to take him, so we must acknowledge that God in His infinite wisdom knows what is best for Miles . . . for us all . . ."

The speech seemed to go on forever. Kirsten felt more ill with each passing moment as the reality of what this day meant sank home. She gasped a sob. Through the hours of preparation, she'd been too busy working to think much, to grieve. She'd wanted things to be perfect for Miles; and while her thoughts had often strayed to Miles's mother, she'd kept her emotions at bay.

The ceremony ended. Some of the guests filtered out of the *dodekamer* for the kitchen, while others remained behind. The *dodekamer* was actually the Van Attas' parlor—the largest room, but for the kitchen on the first floor of the house. The low murmur of conversation filled both rooms as friends reminisced about the young man.

With the funeral service over, Kirsten wanted nothing more than for the day to end. She wanted to be alone, to mourn for Miles in private. She thought of Richard and longed for the warm, strong haven of his arms . . . his deep, husky voice soothing away her tears . . . his hard muscular body that was healthy and alive.

Where was he? Was he safe? Had he met up with General Washington?

She was concerned. With her uncle's escape, the danger to Richard was greater. Kirsten prayed that soon William Randolph would be found—and brought to justice for killing his own son.

Kirsten smiled, putting forth her best face as guests stayed to enjoy the treats and other food prepared by neighbors and friends and the Van Atta women. Finally, hours later, the day ended. As she helped her mother clean up the last traces of the event, she saw the strain on Agnes' face. She realized that for her mother, too, the day had been an ordeal.

"Moeder," she said gently, reaching out to take the broom from Agnes' hands. "Go up to bed. I'll finish up here." Never again would Kirsten regard a funeral day in the same light. As a child, it had always seemed a happy time, a time for socializing, but with Miles's death, the pain of such an occasion had become too real.

Agnes looked at her with relief. "Thank you. I am a bit tired."

Kirsten gave her a slight smile. "Where's *Vader?"* she asked.

"Outside with the animals. He'll be in soon."

The younger woman flushed guiltily. "The animals! I'm so sorry! I forgot."

Agnes placed a hand on Kirsten's arm. "You have worked hard enough this day, daughter." Her gaze was warm. "It is all right."

With tears in her eyes, Kirsten nodded. She'd worked hard for Miles. Miles was dead.

Chapter Twenty-six

"Halt! Who goes there?" The young soldier stood firm, gripping his flintlock.

Richard stepped out from behind a tree. He was at Washington's camp, and it was late at night. He was anxious to speak with the general and be on his way back to Hoppertown. Unless Washington had other plans for him. He hoped not.

Surprised to be discovered by one so inexperienced, he regarded the guard warily, then slowly moved forward. It wouldn't do to frighten the youth and have him fire.

"I'm a friend," he said, his gaze holding the young man's.

The soldier raised his gun to train it on Richard's middle. "Who are you, sir? And why do you travel alone?"

"I am no enemy. I work for your general. Call him and he will tell you."

The young guard looked skeptical, and Richard could guess his thoughts. *Disturb the commander in chief?*

"Suppose you are lying? What if you are a threat to General Washington?" The sentry glanced about with caution. "You've brought others with you . . ."

"No!" Seeing the man tense, Richard raised his arms as he stepped forward. "See? I come without rifle. My only weapons are this sword at my belt and a knife in my boot. Come check for yourself."

"This is a trick."

"It is no trick. I am serious. My name is Maddox. Richard Maddox."

The soldier seemed surprised. "The Mad Ox?" His gun wavered some from its target.

Richard nodded, frowning. "You've heard of me?"

"What is it, Private?" a man asked. From the tone of his voice, he was a person of authority.

"This man—this intruder—says he is the 'Mad Ox,' sir."

"Oh, does he now?"

Richard couldn't see the newcomer, for he stood in the shadow of a large cypress tree. But he recognized the voice. It was Hamilton. Alexander Hamilton, Washington's aide.

Hamilton stepped into Richard's line of vision. He stared at Richard for a long moment. Richard felt his breath slam within his chest as he wondered whether Hamilton would deny knowing him to protect the identity of the Mad Ox.

Hamilton's face cleared. "Richard!"

Richard released a sigh of relief. "Alexander." He came forward and shook Hamilton's hand. He sensed the young guard's astonishment and was pleased.

"You have come here openly—has something happened? Have you news?"

Richard nodded. "Is he awake?"

Hamilton smiled. "Does the man ever sleep?"

They found the general in his tent, bent over his lap desk, writing letters. The brown head rose at the swish of the tent flap. "Hamilton," he said with a frown. His brow cleared. "Richard!"

"General, sir." Richard had taken off his hat as he entered the tent. He came forward and extended his hand. Washington accepted the handshake and then invited Richard to sit on his sleeping cot.

Tired, Richard gratefully accepted the general's offer. Alexander Hamilton remained inside the tent, standing.

"Now tell me, Richard, why have you come?"

Richard addressed both men. "I've been to Paramus and the village of Hoppertown. You'll recall that I've been traveling with the Tory—Elias Greene?"

Washington inclined his head.

"He's been smuggling goods to the Britons in the city of New York."

"Yes, I'm aware of that, of course." The general placed his lap desk on the ground beside his chair. "You have news of this man . . . Biv, is it?"

"No, but I know of a man who can lead me to him. There's someone in Hoppertown—a disfigured man. He's the one who tried to murder me the night I was to meet Biv. He claimed he'd been sent by Biv." Richard gauged Washington's reaction, and then continued. "There's another fellow, William Randolph. I don't know why, but I have a hunch that he is deeply involved in this. I believe that he, too, knows who this Biv is."

"And you have found this man—Randolph? You know where he is?"

Richard shook his blond head. "Not at present, but I don't think he's left Hoppertown. And he's not someone you can just question. Far from an approachable fellow. An avid Loyalist. One vicious enough to betray his own mother."

331

"There must be some reason for you to feel he's involved."

"He's behind the smuggling ring taking goods to the Britons in New York. I had originally thought Greene was in charge and Randolph was merely helping, but it seems that William Randolph was the leader all along." He shifted positions and rubbed his thigh, which sometimes pained him when the weather changed. There was a dampness in the air. It was going to rain.

"Greene is dead, and Randolph's missing," Richard said. "The whole lot of them held some local Patriots hostage for a time until the Hoppertown militia rescued them. Randolph escaped the fighting, unharmed. Some of the women captives spoke of a horrible-looking man. I assume he's the one who tried to murder me. Unfortunately, when all was done, he couldn't be found. So he, too, must have gotten away."

Richard frowned with concern as he cradled his hat. "The fact that I can no longer keep an eye on Randolph worries me." He had a mental image of Miles lying on the ground, blood soaking his shirtfront, Kirsten crying over his dead body. "The man's a fanatic. I don't believe we've seen the last of his deeds—not by a long shot. He cares about little but to further his own ends."

"You actually believe this one man is a direct threat to us?" Hamilton said. "What makes him so terribly different from all the other fanatic Loyalists?"

"The man is the devil himself." Richard swallowed against the lump in his throat. "He killed his own son."

Washington and Hamilton agreed that such a man was dangerous.

"Perhaps you should go back to this Hopper-town," Hamilton suggested. "Find this Randolph. If his home is there, he is bound to return."

Richard nodded. He further explained the attack on the Tory camp by the local militia, how he was considered a traitor by Randolph. "When the Patriots attacked, I couldn't fight them. I had to choose sides. Greene and the others saw me help those of the militia who were in trouble. Randolph wasn't there at first, but he appeared on the scene before Greene's death, and Greene quickly made it known that I wasn't the Loyalist I'd pretended to be."

"Go back then." Washington said. "Go back to Hoppertown. If there is a man in my command who's a traitor, I want him exposed. If this Biv, or if William Randolph, knows who he is, I would learn his identity." He rose from his chair. "Do you need men?"

Richard gave the matter some thought. "Two perhaps, if you can spare them."

The general assured him that he could. "We will be coming that way soon. Obviously, you believe something big is going to happen there, which is why you are here."

"Yes," Richard said. "The area, as you know, is prosperous. Winter is nearly upon us, and with the rich food stores there, the enemy will come. The smugglers will start up again."

Hamilton paced about the tent. "But only Randolph remains of the smugglers."

"There are others of the group I can't account for." Richard told of the takeover of the Van Voorhees' farm. "Greene has a brother John. I didn't see him during the fighting. I couldn't find him afterward."

Washington removed his coat. "Greene and Randolph then. They would be dangerous together?"

"Deadly," Richard said.

The men left the cabin at night. They thought her asleep, but she was only pretending to be. Catherine waited a few moments and then hurried to the tiny window that faced the cabin's front. William and Greene were disappearing into the forest. Where were they going? she wondered. Her pulse raced. It was the first time they had left her alone.

For three days, she'd been locked up inside the one-room dwelling with no hope of escape. Three days and she still didn't know the plans of her husband and Greene.

Catherine didn't weep openly for Miles, although she longed to do so. She kept her mourning private. She wouldn't break down before her husband. The man had killed his own son—*her* son. She wouldn't give William the satisfaction of knowing that he was hurting her, that her feelings for him had changed. For how else was she going to learn what he was up to? How else would she get him to forget her presence and discuss his secrets with Greene?

She wasn't allowed outside alone. Everywhere she went—each time she had to relieve herself—someone went with her, either Greene or her husband. Mostly Greene. And for that humiliation alone, she'd never forgive William. Not that she would have forgiven him anyway. William Randolph was a murderer of innocent children.

Catherine thought hard. If she were to escape this prison, it would have to be at night. The black forest terrified her, but she wouldn't let that stop her. No, she had to get to Kirsten, find out the truth, and learn where they'd buried Miles.

Tears filled her eyes, blinding her. She turned from the window and felt her way back to her cot. She would wait two days, but no more. If she couldn't learn what William was up to in that time, then she would leave without knowing. Each moment spent in her husband's company increased her desire to see him pay for his crimes. If indeed he had killed Miles.

And he must have. Kirsten certainly wasn't capable of hurting him as William had claimed.

"Van Graaf!" William Randolph called as his fist struck the Dutchman's door. "Van Graaf! Open up!"

Dwight Van Graaf heard the commotion from upstairs and hurried down. "William!" he exclaimed upon opening the door. He looked faintly alarmed as he glanced about quickly. "Come in, come in," he invited when it appeared that no one was outside to see the two of them meet.

Dwight Van Graaf had been a spy for Randolph. Pretending to be a Patriot, he'd supplied Randolph with information regarding the rebels' plans.

"Are we alone?" Randolph asked as he slipped inside the house.

"At this hour?" Van Graaf shook his head. "My wife's upstairs sleeping. Fortunately, she is a deep sleeper. I could hear your call, yet she wasn't disturbed."

Randolph regarded his spy carefully. "You don't seem happy to see me, Dwight."

The man seemed flustered. "I didn't know you lived."

The Englishman gave him a cruel smile. "Well, I am alive, as you can see for yourself. No thanks to you, I'm beginning to suspect! Where were you? We could have used more men!"

"But I thought—"

"I don't care what you thought! You should have come. You knew what Greene's plans were. You should have come to help us."

Van Graaf shook his head. "And ruin my cover? How could I continue to supply you with information if the rebs were to learn that I was one of you?"

Randolph stared. "Well, I suppose this is true. All in all, I guess it worked out for the best, because now there's only Greene and I. John Greene. With your help, we can rebuild our army."

The Dutchman felt alarmed. To pass on information was one thing; to be caught by the Patriots doing more was something else. Besides, he'd been paid for the information; he wasn't foolish enough to get into a situation in which he couldn't turn a profit.

"I'm sorry, William. I wish I could help, but I don't see how."

Something about Van Graaf's manner disturbed William Randolph. He recalled the raid on Greene's camp. How had the militia learned of the camp's location? Had someone tipped them off? Van Graaf?

"I believe you can assist. Are you willing?" he asked.

"I don't know," Van Graaf hedged. "My wife—"

"You bastard! It was you that told them, wasn't it? You've been playing both sides. You told the rebs about Greene's camp! What else did you tell them?"

"I told them nothing!"

"Liar!" William went to the door and whistled softly into the night. Instantly, John Greene appeared and joined him inside the Van Graaf house. Greene's gaze was questioning. "Shoot him!" William said.

And without a thought Greene lifted his pistol and fired at the horrified Dutchman.

336

Having escaped the skirmish at the Van Voorhees' farm, Phelps wandered aimlessly about the area for days, pondering his options now that he was the only one left from the Tory army. He'd gone to William Randolph's place immediately after the militia's attack, hoping to find the man and follow his lead. It was Randolph who'd got Phelps involved in the band in the first place. They'd met in a tavern in Hackensack, where Randolph had been looking for men loyal to the English king. Phelps, while he'd given little thought to which side of the war he was on, had caught Randolph's public speech in the common room and been struck by the intelligence of the man—and most by the promise of a rich reward. Never one to pass up the offer of wealth, Thaddeus Phelps had confronted Randolph as the man was leaving the Stone Lion Inn and the two had hooked up to work together for Britain's King George.

But now Phelps was at a loss. Without Randolph, his dream of riches would never be realized. Without the Englishman, Phelps would have no place to go, no fun doing the dirty work. Murdering the Mad Ox hadn't been his first killing for the Tory army. No, that had been a snot-nosed kid, Alexander Brooks.

Randolph—or Biv, the name Randolph later took to hide his identity—had trusted the kid at first, believing Brooks a genuine Loyalist, anxious to see the King get his rightful due. But soon he'd learned otherwise. He'd found out that Alexander Brooks was a Patriot, whose only goal was to infiltrate the Tories and pass on information that would help the revolutionists win a quick victory.

But the kid wasn't smart enough to outwit Biv, Phelps thought with a smile. Brooks was one rebel who'd never help the Patriot forces again.

It was as he came across a small farmhouse outside of Paramus that Phelps recalled that first meeting with Biv when Brooks was discussed. Phelps had been away on assignment in the Ramapo Mountain region and had returned with a message from a man who was a soldier in Washington's army, a man who offered his services for he was tired and hungry and fed up with the Continental Army. The fellow, an officer by the name of Rhoades, believed that General George Washington was destined to fail, and he wanted to see a quick end to the war.

Phelps's meeting with Randolph had been at a cabin deep in a thicket a mile or so outside of Hackensack. Phelps's squinty eyes lit up as he changed directions. Randolph had no doubt gone there to hide out, to rethink his strategy for the war.

His heart pumped hard. Biv would rebuild the army, and they'd be back in business again. As long as William Randolph, alias Biv, was alive, so was Phelps's hope for wealth. Randolph had promised him land, several hundred acres of it. Phelps had no idea where this land was, but he trusted Biv and knew the man would keep his promise as long as Phelps remained loyal. And loyal he would be; no one had given the disfigured man much attention or respect before Biv. Biv appreciated him for his special "skills."

His misshapen mouth contorted in a half-grin, Phelps headed toward Hackensack and the small cabin of his leader.

The Patriot Dutch in Hoppertown were astonished. Someone had forced his way into a man's home. A fellow Patriot was dead.

338

Kirsten listened to her father's story of Dwight Van Graaf's murder. Her horror grew as she heard all the details. Pulled from his bed in the middle of the night, Dwight Van Graaf had been shot in the head and left to bleed to death on his parlor floor. His wife, having heard the shot, found him, but it was too late. Captain Jonathan Hopper of the Hoppertown militia advised all residents to arm themselves and be on watch. It was believed that Tories were responsible for Van Graaf's senseless death.

That night, when she went to bed, Kirsten lay in her alcove with a flintlock at her side. Anyone who came to the Van Atta farm would be in for a surprise, for James and Agnes were armed, too.

Chapter Twenty-seven

"Andrew?" Richard was addressing the young soldier who accompanied him. In the end, only one of Washington's men could be spared, a new recruit who couldn't have been involved in Alexander's death.

"Sir?"

"What's that you see ahead?"

"It looks like a cabin, sir."

Richard narrowed his gaze to peer through the darkness. "And someone lurking about, it would seem."

"What shall we do, sir?"

"Advance, private, and meet this person face-to-face." His hand on the hilt of his sword, he rose from his crouch and moved stealthily through the woods toward the small structure in the forest thicket. He waved a hand for the soldier to follow him.

It had been purely by chance that they'd stumbled upon the cabin. Had they passed a few feet farther away, they would surely have missed seeing it. *There could be only one reason such a hideout exists,* Richard thought. *Smugglers.*

Whoever was outside didn't want to be seen. He

kept against the side of the building, his head bent low, as he moved from the door and skirted the cabin's left side.

Richard froze, his hand halting the private behind him. The man was heading in their direction.

Catherine was frightened, but it didn't stop her from dressing in her husband's clothes and leaving the tiny cabin in the woods. She'd stayed longer than she'd expected. William and Greene had been gone for some time. Fear of their return had prompted her to move quickly, to rummage recklessly through her husband's belongings, which he'd recently retrieved from their house.

The night was pitch black. She had difficulty adjusting her eyesight to the darkness, for William had left a candle burning on the table. While the light had helped her to dress hastily, it hampered her progress into the darkened forest.

She took nothing with her, leaving behind the homespun gown she'd come in, and the few personal belongings William had thrust at her after his trip back to their house. She cared not how she looked; her only thought was to escape the man she'd married, the man who had murdered her only son.

Catherine slipped from the cabin and kept her back against the wall before she stooped low to skirt the building. William and his man Greene had headed straight away from the hut's entrance. She intended to go the opposite way to increase her chances for a successful escape.

Her destination was the Van Attas' farm. Her sister-in-law would tell her what to do. And Agnes' husband would welcome what little information she'd managed to obtain from the men who'd held her prisoner these past days.

Unsure of her location, Catherine had decided earlier to continue through the woods until she reached a road. Perhaps then she'd recognize where she was. If not, she'd follow the road until she came to a village or town—or someone who might direct her on the right path to Hoppertown. She knew she might encounter friend or foe. Her only hope was that God remained with her on her journey, directing her steps. She carried a small weapon for defense, a kitchen knife she'd unearthed from the cooking utensils William had so thoughtfully provided for her use.

There was no one about as she crept around the outside of the cabin. She could hear her heart thundering within her breast as she left the side of the structure for the woods.

It was cold. Catherine drew the edges of William's coat about herself and, with head down, moved through the tall dried grass, past thorn bushes which snagged the fabric of her breeches. With a soft exclamation, she paused to free herself before she continued on her perilous journey.

She heard the rustling through the trees and knew it was the wind, but it terrified her. In her mind she pictured wild creatures she might meet. She wasn't afraid of raccoon or deer; and certainly the rabbits, squirrels, and other small animals wouldn't harm her. But there were bears in these New Jersey forests, big monstrous brutes that could rip the flesh from a human being.

"Stop! Or I'll shoot," someone commanded.

Catherine froze, her terror blinding her. The male voice came from ahead, but she couldn't make out anyone. She heard the crunch of footsteps against dry twigs as the man approached her.

There were two of them, she saw. She inhaled a few calming breaths, her hand going to the waist of her breeches where she kept the knife.

"Don't move, fellow, or we'll kill you now!"

Her hand fell to her side. Catherine realized then that they thought her a man. *Good, perhaps I can use that against them.*

One man came forward before the other. She saw instantly that he was tall and had light hair. In the darkness, those were the only two things she could tell about him.

"Who are you?" Richard approached, his watchful gaze on the stranger's arms. He was leery of any sudden moves the fellow might make. The man didn't answer. "Private? Come ahead. Check him for weapons."

The stranger gasped. "No!"

Both men drew to a halt. The voice was most definitely a female's.

"Lady?" Richard asked.

"Don't—stay away!"

"We'll not hurt y—"

"I said, no!" Her hand moved like lightning, pulling out the knife, holding it before her to keep the private at bay.

"What is your name?"

"Are you for the King?" she asked.

Richard was silent. "Is a King's man a better man?"

"Damn the King and all that follow him!" she said.

"We are Patriots!" the private said. "Soldiers in General Washington's army."

Richard was smiling at the lady's last reply.

The knife wavered within her grasp. "Patriots?"

"Aye, mistress. I'm Private Andrew Jones. This is

Richard Maddox. Lieutenant Richard Maddox."

Richard started. It was the first time he'd been referred to by rank. "You are obviously for the cause, dear woman. For what purpose have you come here?"

Catherine lowered the knife. "I am escaping. And if you are at all gentlemen, you will tell me where I am so that I may return to Hoppertown, my home."

Richard's muscles tensed. "You are from Hoppertown?"

"I am. I have lived for many years there. My husband and I." She grew silent. "I have a husband no longer."

"I'm sorry, lady," the private said.

She drew herself erect. "Don't be. He's not dead to the world, only to me." Her voice became a whisper. "He murdered our son."

Richard stepped forward then, aware of the implication of the woman's comments. "You are Catherine Randolph. Miles's mother." He approached enough to see her face. Her eyes were wide with fear, but they held determination, too. She wore a man's clothes for protection. The sight of her dressed thus gently reminded Richard of Kirsten. Catherine Randolph's hair was covered with a dark, knit cap.

As she saw him, the woman gasped with surprised recognition. "You are—"

"I'm not what you thought," he said, referring to the time when he'd stayed at her farm as one of Greene's men. "I'm a Patriot, true enough."

Her expression had become wary. "You were with—"

"I work for General Washington," Richard interrupted. "Some call me the Mad Ox."

"I see." She looked disbelieving.

"'Tis true, mistress," Andrew Jones said. "He is

what he claims."

"I promise that the Van Attas—your niece—will vouch for me," Richard said.

"My niece . . ." Her gaze narrowed. "What is her name?"

"Kirsten."

She seemed to relax then. Apparently, she believed him. "Will you take me to Hoppertown?" Catherine glanced about as if expecting, fearing, to see her husband. "Please say yes, for my time runs out. They—John Greene and William—will return soon."

Richard grinned, his teeth a white slash in the dark night. "We will be most happy to escort you, Mrs. Randolph, for we are on our way to Hoppertown."

When Phelps arrived at the cabin, it was empty, but he saw signs that someone had been staying there recently. Guessing that Randolph would be back, he moved in and made himself comfortable.

It was in the early morning hours that Kirsten woke to the sound of gunfire. She sat up in bed, her heart pounding. There had been numerous raids of late on the Hoppertown residents. The Tories were striking without warning, without care for the women and children in the homes they'd targeted for attack.

"Kirsten!" Her mother burst into the bedchamber. "Come quickly! Grab your rifle and stay away from the windows. We're being shot at!"

Moeder! Who is it? Tories?"

Agnes confessed that she didn't know as she

346

hustled her daughter from the room.

James Van Atta was already downstairs at the parlor window, armed, his pistol raised.

"Vader?" Kirsten came up behind him, the flintlock in hand.

"Stay back, daughter," he ordered.

"But I can shoot as well as any man." She met his gaze steadily, without fear.

He nodded. "The other window then. But don't shoot until I say to."

Kirsten obeyed her father, moving to the second window, lifting her gun. She stared down the barrel toward the front yard. There was no movement, no sign of life.

A second blast of gunfire. Suddenly, out of the forest ran three people, ducking low to avoid being hit from behind.

"Why, they're seeking shelter!" James said.

"Shall I open for them?" Agnes hurried to the door.

Kirsten rose up, excited. *"Vader*—please! Before one of them gets shot!"

Agnes opened the door a crack. A few yards away, one stranger tripped, and the other two lifted him up by the arms. Kirsten's mother swung open the portal.

"Agnes!" a feminine voice said.

Agnes jerked back in surprise. "Catherine?" She shot her husband a glance. "My word, James, it's Catherine."

"Aunt Catherine?" Kirsten gasped. She stood behind her mother at the door. "Who's that with her?"

The three rose up and hurried toward the open door. The gunfire was less frequent now; there was no sign of the snipers.

Agnes moved back as Catherine bolted toward the

house, followed by the others, giving Kirsten a better view of the three seeking refuge.

She caught sight of a tawny mane, the familiar way one man moved. She froze. "Richard?" she whispered

Richard looked up then, and their gazes met briefly before he traversed the remaining feet into the house. When everyone was safe, he closed the door. Only then did he turn back to Kirsten.

"Hello, love," he said to her, and Kirsten rejoiced to see him again.

"Richard, it's you! I can scarcely believe my eyes. Where did you come from?" She set her rifle against the wall.

"From Washington's camp. We were on our way back when we came across your aunt."

She gazed at her Aunt Catherine. "Are you all right?"

The woman smiled, but her eyes were dull. "Lieutenant Maddox and Private Jones brought me."

"How?" Kirsten sputtered. "Where did you meet?"

A gun went off in the distance, and Richard frowned, joined James at the window. "I believe they're leaving, sir."

James Van Atta, startled by the recent turn of events, nodded without a word.

"Richard?" Kirsten was still waiting to hear how both her aunt and Richard had come to be here in her own home.

"William is mad," Catherine said, drawing everyone's glance. "He's kept me a prisoner these past days . . . in a cabin in the woods." The Van Attas nodded sympathetically.

"That's where we found her," Jones said. "Outside of Hackensack, where we had to stop to confer with the captain of the militia there."

Catherine turned toward her brother-in-law. "I have learned something of William's plans. He meets with others now. I don't know whom. But he has a connection somewhere. I think he's building an army."

James nodded. "He already has, if my guess is right. There have been raids on Hoppertown these past three nights. Perhaps William is involved."

His sister-in-law agreed. "We must talk later," she said, addressing the men.

Catherine then touched her niece's arm. "Kirsten, tell me what happened. Tell me about Miles."

Kirsten, knowing that the truth would only cause her aunt more pain, hesitated.

"I know," Catherine said. Her lined features hardened. "I know William killed my boy."

"Aunt Catherine—I'm so sorry."

"William, these past few years, hasn't been . . . right," she said. "I should have left him."

Kirsten's eyes stung. "It's not your fault."

Tears filled Catherine's eyes when Agnes came to her and put an arm about her trembling shoulders. "I'm sorry," Agnes whispered.

Catherine met her gaze. "Don't you blame yourself, Agnes dear. There was nothing you could have done. It was William. William did it. He alone is responsible for his misdeeds. He alone must pay."

Chapter Twenty-eight

William Randolph was extremely pleased. He waited for his men to join him in the field near the ruins of the old Van Atta mill.

Ernest Jacobs arrived first. He was one of the seven men from Hackensack that John Greene convinced to join their ranks. "Well?" he asked as Greene and the others followed.

"Terhune's place is gone, burned to the ground," John said with a grin.

"Any survivors?" William asked.

John nodded. "Two—perhaps three. I saw a man and woman fleeing."

"Ah, well, it'll teach the sorry bastard a lesson in loyalty, won't it?" Pete McGinnis said.

The men laughed and agreed.

This was William's first raid since the disaster at the Van Voorhees' farm. These past few days he'd given the commands to attack, but had not joined in and was, as a result, unable to fully appreciate their success. Tonight he'd decided to go along. Catherine slept like the dead; she'd never know he was gone. Besides, if she did she wouldn't leave, because she wouldn't know where to go. She was terrified of the forest, and at night . . .

With Van Graaf dead, the only contact William had within the rebel camp was Rhoades, one of Washington's men. It had been some time since the Patriot general had been in Hoppertown long enough for William and Rhoades to meet.

William needed to speak with him. Someone must have replaced the Mad Ox by now, and William wanted to know who that was. He'd dropped hints in Hackensack, hoping someone would rise to the bait and seek out Biv as the two spies had before. This man, Biv, it was rumored, was a man for freedom, a willing spy for the Patriot forces.

Time was running out. The British Army had to move—and soon. A post sent to Thatcher told the major of William's work in Hoppertown, of the supplies that would be waiting once William had subdued the residents and taken their goods. Thatcher was no doubt furious with him, for there had been no supply runs to New York of late, and the major sought to profit by them. *This bit of news will brighten the man's day*, William thought. In a week's time, the Tories would be making their runs again, smuggling goods to their British friends to the south. William smiled.

"Randolph," John Greene said, interrupting William's reflections. "Jacobs here says he saw some rebs on the road not far from here."

"That's right." Jacobs inhaled a bit of snuff, before replacing the pack in his coat pocket. He chuckled as he withdrew a dirty handkerchief. "Fired at 'em, we did—me and Pete. Ye should 'ave seen the way the bastards ran!"

Glancing at the two men, William frowned. "Any idea who they were?"

McGinnis shook his head. "There were three of

352

them is all I could tell. Fled to that farmhouse we seen on the other side of these old woods. Ye know, the one with the odd roof."

William scowled. There were any number of houses with Dutch gambrel roofs, but he knew which one McGinnis meant, they were on Van Atta property. "James Van Atta," he muttered with distaste.

Greene met his gaze. "The Terhunes and a servant?"

"No doubt," William said. Sheltering the Terhunes was just one more sin for which James Van Atta must suffer.

The Van Attas had gone back to bed. Catherine Randolph was in the spare room, while Andrew Jones and Richard had bunked down in the parlor.

Unable to sleep, Richard rose from his pallet on the floor.

"Sir?" came Andrew's sleepy voice.

"I'm going for a walk, Private."

"But, sir . . . the gunmen . . . shall I go with you?"

Richard paused at the door to pull on a coat. "I'll be fine, Andrew," he said. "I'll take James's rifle and scout about the house. It won't be long before I turn in."

The moon was but a faint orb covered by clouds. The air had a distinctive cold nip to it. Richard wandered to the side of the house, listening, his gaze alert for movement of any kind, his hand gripping the rifle. There was no one about. It was as if the earlier disturbance had never occurred, it was so peaceful. His steps took him toward the vegetable patch, which was nothing more than tilled, empty ground now.

Kirsten. His heart called for her. Her image haunted his every waking and dreaming moment. It had been so wonderful to see her again. Each time he returned to her, he was overwhelmed by gladness. He loved her. And he was determined that one way or another he would survive this war so that he could come back and live out his life with her.

He settled himself on a bench in the yard. Closing his eyes, he pictured her sweet face, her joy upon seeing him again. Her eyes were the most glorious shade of blue, like a fall sky on a clear day. Her lips were full and pink; they felt petal-soft beneath his mouth.

Richard's body hardened with desire. It seemed forever since he'd last held her, caressed her silken skin, although it must have only been . . . what? A week? Two weeks at most?

Time had no meaning these days. While the war raged on, weeks seemed like months, days seemed like weeks.

He lay back against the bench, and stared into the trees above, overwhelmed with frustration and anger that the Patriots weren't farther along in their quest for liberty from the King.

When will it be over? Richard wondered, closing his eyes. He sighed wearily.

Kirsten couldn't sleep. How could she while Richard was so near . . . only a few steps and a staircase away?

Their reunion had been an unsatisfactory one. In the excitement of his arrival in the company of others, there had been no time for a proper greeting. A kiss.

It was a chilly night, but Kirsten felt warm beneath

her feather tick where only hours before she'd been cold. Thoughts of Richard heated her to the core . . . memories of their loving . . . touching . . . joining. She squirmed on her mattress as a tingling invaded her private woman parts.

How long would it be before the men downstairs slept? she wondered. She wanted to slip below to the first floor and gaze upon Richard with love, to feel his presence, to be in the same room with him.

Kirsten thought of the earlier gunshots, and her body chilled. Richard could have been killed! So could Aunt Catherine and Private Jones!

She felt sorry for her aunt. How terrible it must feel to realize the man you'd been married to for years was not the same one you fell in love with but a stranger—a terrible, cruel stranger. At one time, William Randolph had been a charming, handsome young man with hopes and dreams and a winning smile. How often her mother told her of their childhood escapades. William had been her mother's protector. He'd been her champion, and the apple of many a lady's eye.

It was hard for Kirsten to see the uncle she'd heard stories about and William Randolph as one and the same man. The young William would never have killed anyone, let alone his own son!

Kirsten thought of her own beloved. Richard would never fail her. She'd accused him of lying, but he hadn't. It was just that she'd been angry and hurt because he'd been leaving. Hurt, she had wanted to hurt him back.

Everything Richard has said or done has been to spare me pain. Didn't he know that if he stayed, there would be no pain? Of course, he did! But he had a mission to finish, and staying in Hoppertown had been out of the question.

And now? Was his work done? Was that why he'd returned to Hoppertown?

Kirsten's lips firmed. He mustn't leave her again. God had brought him back to her time after time—he was meant to stay here, to do what he could for the cause on Hoppertown soil.

Suddenly, it became vital for Kirsten to speak of this to Richard. She was sure that she could convince him if only she had a chance.

But how? How could she talk with him without drawing the young private's attention?

She pushed open the alcove doors and flipped back her cover. Climbing from her bed, she gasped when her bare feet hit the cold floor. She found stockings for her feet and then changed her night rail for a heavy, long-sleeved, woolen gown of dark blue.

After silently slipping down the stairs, she crept into the parlor. The blood flooded through her veins in her excitement.

"Richard," she whispered. "Richard . . ."

No answer. The only sound was a man's soft snoring. She took another step into the room and was able to make out the two sleeping pallets on the floor. She froze. One of them was empty. Instinctively, she knew it was Richard's, and she went outside where she knew she'd find him.

He left the garden for the ruin. He knew it was dangerous to stray so far from the house, but something pulled him there. Memories of him and Kirsten?

Richard was at the cellar opening, preparing to pull away the wood blocking the entrance, when he heard a noise. He froze as he was able to make out a male voice . . . several male voices. He moved from

356

the door, and slunk around the building to peer at the other side.

His eyes widened at what he saw. He counted nine figures—all men—in conversation. Richard shuddered to realize how close they were, how easily he could have been discovered or caught.

He strained to hear them, to see who they were, but their voices didn't carry to him. He knew they were the enemy. These men wouldn't be meeting on this property secretly if they weren't Loyalists. As he moved closer to hear better, he caught one man's laughter and the raised triumphant voice of another. Richard recognized the second man as William Randolph, Kirsten's uncle.

Rage blinded him. He wanted to rush at the man, choke him for all the pain he had caused Kirsten, his family, and so many of the area's residents. Without Randolph, Hoppertown would have stayed a relatively peaceful haven during this bloody war—and Miles might still be alive.

Richard rose, clenching his fingers. Reason returned as the men moved away, and he realized that against so many his chances of prevailing was remote.

But I could kill Randolph, he thought.

And die for your deed, an inner voice said. *How will Kirsten feel then?*

Richard hunkered back into a crouch, watching with helpless anger as the Tories left. He would follow them for a time and see where they'd made their camp.

"Biv!" someone called, and Richard's breath caught when William Randolph stopped. "Where are we goin'?"

"I've a cabin . . . not far."

Richard released the air from his lungs. Having

357

rescued the man's wife, he knew where the cabin was. He felt a surge of determination, of purpose. So William Randolph was Biv . . . What pleasure it was going to give him to get his hands on Randolph and wring the truth out of him.

A dry branch snapped behind him. Startled, Richard spun, his gun raised to kill. His russet gaze glowed as he saw who had come.

"Kirsten," he murmured, lowering the rifle.

He glanced back toward the woods the Tories had entered, and knew that, if he followed his first notion and went after Randolph and his men, Kirsten would demand to go with him.

Making a quick decision, Richard set down his rifle and opened his arms. The choice hadn't been a difficult one. He knew where Randolph was heading. There would be time to find him, to capture his men. *Or perhaps it would be wiser to lure the bastard out,* he thought. But at this moment, he'd been given a blessing, granted a dream. Kirsten was here, and he'd been aching for her. His gaze flamed with desire; his body burned.

"Come to me, love," he said.

"Richard," she gasped, joy brightening her face.

And the lovers were properly reunited, flowing into each other's embrace.

Chapter Twenty-nine

When he returned to the cabin to find his wife gone and Phelps in residence, William Randolph went into a murderous rage.

"Where is she?" he demanded of the disfigured man.

Phelps gawked at him, shaking his head. "What, Biv?" he sputtered. "What d'ye mean?"

Furious at the man's inadequate reply, the Englishman drove his fist into Phelps's face, striking him again and again. Phelps had not unexpected the attack, and his nose had broken with the first punch. Still, William continued to beat him until there was blood everywhere, staining Phelps's clothing, splattering the front of Randolph's coat. The other men stared, but didn't help Phelps. They'd never seen someone so enraged as William.

"Goddamn her!" Randolph bellowed when he was done punishing his most loyal man. "She belongs here with her husband, not with that dimwitted sister of mine!" For it hadn't taken William long to figure out where Catherine had headed. Where else would she go but to the Van Atta farm? If she wasn't injured or lying dead in the forest somewhere.

"How long have you been here?" he asked Phelps.

The man cringed. He looked pathetic with his beaten, misshapen features covered in blood. His swollen nose and bruised facial parts made him appear even more disfigured. "For a few hours is all." He had difficulty speaking through his split lips.

"By God!" William shouted, smashing his hand against the cabin wall. "I'll find her! I'll force her to do her duty! She'll be a good wife to me! She must! She's all I have left now."

During this last outburst, Phelps jumped back out of Randolph's reach, and several of the men stared at their leader, unwilling to cross him yet appalled by his behavior.

Pete McGinnis dared to utter a word. "You've got us, Biv," he said in an attempt to soothe the distraught man.

The members of the Tory band knew him only as Biv. It wouldn't do if one of them got captured by the enemy and talked. Only John Greene and Thaddeus Phelps knew his real identity.

William's dark gaze glittered with wicked fervor. He stared at McGinnis as if he were going to beat a second man to a bloody pulp. But then suddenly, as quickly as it had come, Randolph's anger was gone.

"That's right," he said, his tone soft and even. "We have each other now, haven't we?" These men were at his command. He'd use them to wipe out the enemy. He'd kill James Van Atta and his family, and then he'd retrieve Catherine and make her see that her place was at his side. Miles's death had been an accident, he'd make her see this. She'd understand that it was Kirsten's fault that Miles was dead. When the war finally ended, he and Catherine would live peacefully and prosperously on whichever property in the area he claimed for his own.

"Tomorrow we return to Hoppertown," he said. "These *boers* believe they've seen bloodshed; 'tis nothing to what they'll be seeing!"

And William gathered the men around him to make plans.

The woman beside him shivered as he nuzzled her neck and ran his fingers over her bare shoulder. "Are you cold?" Richard asked.

Kirsten shook her head, but Richard thought she must be chilled. They were in the old mill cellar without blankets or bed, and the night was a cold one.

They'd chosen this spot because it was secluded and familiar. After carrying the woman he loved inside, Richard had set her down gently on her feet. A moment later, he was building a small fire. He wanted to see Kirsten as he touched her . . . loved her. Even the smallest flame would provide warmth.

"See, I kept my promise," he said, showing her the words he'd scratched in the dirt. "I did say good-bye."

"Oh, Richard . . ."

He removed his coat and spread it on the ground to cushion the dirt floor. They came together and kissed; their passion warming their hearts as well as their bodies.

It was a moment of gladness as Richard undid the front hooks of Kirsten's gown and tugged the bodice down. His eyes warmed from a russet color to a hot cinnamon as he bared her to the waist. Fondling the creamy flesh before him, he watched with pleasure as her nipples budded, then dipped his head to taste her sweetness, enjoying the soft moan that escaped her lips as he suckled her.

She smelled like wild flowers, a scent that tantalized him and heightened his desire. He knelt on the ground before her, and placed his lips to her belly. She gasped and clutched his head, and he dared

361

to move his kisses lower. He pushed her gown down over her hips, helped her to step out of it.

She stood in her naked glory, a beautiful golden goddess in the firelight. And then Richard pressed his mouth to her womanly cleft. Kirsten climaxed and cried out.

She was still trembling when Richard rose and pressed his straining manhood against her secret place. They kissed and rocked, grinding against each other.

Kirsten wanted to touch him, to feel him deep inside her, to be warmed by the heat of his flesh. She stepped back from his arms and proceeded to unbutton his shirt and slip the garment from Richard's broad shoulders. Her breath rasped as she began to touch him, to explore his muscled chest. Richard caressed her as she tugged at his breeches. She held her breath as he moved back to take them off. And then she was touching him . . . stroking him once again.

The gentle exploration became heated, then frantic. On his coat they joined, breasts touching, hips thrusting, stroking and crying out as they soared upward. Kirsten gasped; Richard groaned. For a moment, the world exploded into bright colors and wild sensation.

They floated slowly back to earth and lay in the sweet aftermath of making love. Richard, at Kirsten's side, was unable to stop touching her. He was ready for her again, and by the look in her eyes, she was willing.

He felt her shiver and moved to cover her with his length. She moaned and clutched his shoulders, her fingers splaying across his muscled back as he gently nuzzled her neck, then shifted his position to kiss the satiny skin of her right breast.

"Richard . . ." Her eyes opened to stare at him,

glistening blue orbs that shone with the flame of desire and the golden glow of their small fire.

"What do you want?" he asked. "Tell me."

She closed her eyes, arched her neck, and murmured, "For you to stay . . . to never, never go away."

He tensed above her. Her soft hands stroked him, soothing him, and he relaxed and bent to lick her pink nipple.

"Richard!"

"Yes, love."

"Richard!" she cried out as he suckled the tip and then transferred his attention to its twin, while at the same time his fingers went to the most secretive, moist part of her.

He couldn't promise her he'd stay . . . yet. But he could pleasure her, make her touch the sky and hover for those breathtaking, mind-shattering moments of ecstasy. And when he had done this, he, too, flew like a bird and descended to earth on a cloud.

They lay with limbs entwined, hearts beating as one. Lethargic but feeling good, they held each other and prayed that their time together would never end.

But all too soon they had to go. Andrew Jones might discover Richard gone, and the sun would be up soon. Without a word, Richard rose, and Kirsten followed him. They dressed in silence, then cautiously left the ruin for the house.

They didn't speak of the future, for it was too uncertain. Richard didn't make promises; and Kirsten, after that one moment in which she'd spoken her heart, didn't press him for any.

The war continued—the fight for freedom—as did the struggle to contain one's emotions in the face of dire uncertainties.

On December 4, 1778, the First Pennsylvania Regiment of the Continental Army settled in for a stay at the Paramus encampment. The villagers were pleased to see the soldiers arrive. Weary and worn, the men nevertheless looked impressive in their military cocked hats and brown uniform coats, the white linen straps of their haversacks and cartridge boxes crossing their chests. Plagued by Tories these past days, the Hoppertown residents saw an end to their torment, although perhaps only a temporary one. That night, for the first time in a long while, they went to bed without fear. The Continental soldiers would surely deter the Tories from attacking their homes.

Richard, Andrew, and the other occupants of the Van Atta household stayed awake long into the night. Unlike their Hoppertown neighbors, they knew who was in charge of the Tory band, and they believed nothing would stop William Randolph. The man was beyond logical thinking; no Continental Army would deter him from his raids.

Unwilling at first to confess that he'd seen the Tories near the ruin, Richard had not brought the matter up with anyone but Private Jones. William Randolph might be a terrible, cruel man, but he was a relative of those he stayed with. Richard feared one of the Van Attas or even Catherine Randolph might interfere with the Patriots' capture of him.

But he knew he couldn't take Randolph without help. After discussing the matter with the young private, Richard decided to speak to the family. That night, while the residents of Hoppertown slept peacefully, Richard and the others talked of seizing William Randolph.

"But how are we to lure him out? He's a cunning soul," James Van Atta said.

Catherine, who had been quietly listening for a time, spoke up. "Our house is empty. He'll return for clean garments and food. William hates to look anything but his best. In fact, it's almost an obsession with him."

Richard raised a blond eyebrow. "He's been back to the house?"

The dark-haired woman inclined her head. "At least once that I know of. He brought me some things and ordered me to make myself more presentable."

"Bastard!" Agnes muttered. Shocked, her family stared at her, but she held James's gaze steadily until Kirsten broke the stunned silence.

"Shall we go to the house and lay a trap for him?" she asked.

"You stay here with your family where you'll be safe," Richard said firmly.

Kirsten gaped at him. "And who are you to say what I can or can't do!"

A muscle ticked in Richard's temple. "I'll not be worrying about a female with some foolish notion of revenge."

"Oh? And what is your motive?" she challenged.

Red-faced, Richard ignored her comment and turned to Private Jones. "Andrew, you and I will go to the Randolphs'." He glanced in Catherine's direction. "With the lady's permission, of course." She nodded, granting it. "I'll speak to the regiment's commander in the morning. Perhaps if I explain the situation, he'll give us a man or two."

"I'd like to help," James Van Atta said.

"Thank you, but you would be more useful here where you can guard the women and report to us if William decides to come here instead of to his home."

The men in the group continued to make plans, while the women offered an opinion now and then. Only Kirsten remained silent, privately stewing over Richard's abrupt dismissal of her worth. She wouldn't be a hindrance but a help. Her uncle was out to get her, too. She could be the bait!

Near the end of the discussion, when the party broke up to retire, Kirsten asked Richard to accompany her outside. She then told him of her idea of using herself as bait.

"Absolutely not," he said, and his stern manner made her clench her fists at her sides as she stifled the urge to hit him. "I won't have you hurt. I couldn't bear it if you were."

His confession didn't make her soften. "And I'm supposed to wait here and worry about you? How many times have you come and gone now, *mynheer?* Do you think it was easy for me?"

"No," he said, his lips firmed.

"Stubborn swine!" she cried, before she stomped off to her room.

Kirsten's temper increased to the boiling point when she learned the next day that Catherine Randolph would be going with the men. Only she and her mother would be left behind.

"But she's a female," she said. "Why would it be any less dangerous for her?"

Richard's patience had reached its limit the night before. "Because, woman, she's Randolph's wife! He must be frantically searching for her by now! A few hints about her dropped in the right places, and the man will come home to get her!"

She saw the logic behind their reasoning, but was unwilling to admit it. "Please, Richard! Let me go with you."

He sighed with exasperation. "Kirsten, don't make me say something I might regret."

"Such as?"

He shook his head. "I'll not allow you to do this to me. I've been on this mission too long to let you foul it up."

"Mission?" Kirsten blinked. "Then there's a connection between your Biv and my uncle?"

Richard's teeth snapped. He didn't want anyone to know, but he had to tell her. He could see that she'd never believe him if he denied knowing. "Yes, there is. Last night, I told you what I saw, but I didn't tell what I heard. I heard someone call for Biv. Your uncle answered."

Kirsten grabbed his arm. "Richard," she said softly, "please be careful."

He nodded, his expression becoming tender.

She guiltily recalled seeing the disfigured man. She'd meant to tell Richard about Phelps, but had forgotten. Their conversation about Biv reminded her. "When we were held at the Van Voorhees', I saw that disfigured man again. They called him by name. I don't know if it will help you, but his name is Phelps." Her heart raced as he stared at her a long moment. Was he angry?

"Phelps," Richard echoed. Suddenly, he smiled. "It may help—thank you." She grinned, happy that she could assist him in some way.

They were outside in the yard, alone. The others were within, preparing for their stay at the Randolphs' farm. With an affectionate gleam in his russet eyes, Richard caressed Kirsten's cheek. "You'll stay here as I asked?"

Kirsten nodded. "You'll keep us informed?"

He nodded, then stepped away from her, his hand dropping to his side when Catherine Randolph exited the house. James Van Atta, Andrew Jones, and Kirsten's mother followed her.

"Be careful, Catherine," Agnes said.

"Of course, I will. This won't take long. I know William. I can certainly help these men get him."

"Aunt Catherine." Kirsten gave her a hug.

With tears in her eyes, Catherine smiled. "Thank you," she said, "for Miles. For everything you did for him. He loved you."

"As I loved him." Earlier that morning, Kirsten had taken her aunt to Miles's grave. Catherine, though deeply saddened, had been touched to see the care Kirsten had given to the small plot. Miles Randolph lay beneath the ground in a picturesque spot on the Van Atta property, in a clearing in the woods, near a bubbling brook. Kirsten herself had constructed the cross which marked her cousin's resting place.

With fear in their hearts, the Van Atta family watched the small party leave. It would all be over in a matter of hours . . . or days. But who would win? Richard and his men or William Randolph and his Tory band?

Help came from an unexpected quarter that same day. Washington and his troops arrived in Hopper-town, joining the Pennsylvania Regiment at the Paramus camp. Richard was at the encampment talking with the regiment's captain when George Washington and his troops arrived. He'd left Catherine at the Randolphs', in Private Jones' care.

Immediately, Richard sought an audience with the Patriot general. After he told Washington of his plans, the general offered him five men. Richard accepted the offer, and the soldiers headed toward the Randolph home. Word went out that the general himself had taken over the Randolph place.

The men selected from Washington's army were told very little about Richard's plans, only that they were laying a snare for a Tory fox and they expected their prey to appear soon.

The five soldiers along with Richard, Jones, and Catherine Randolph, who had formulated the plan, waited for nightfall—and for the fox to take the bait.

Chapter Thirty

Catherine Randolph had retired for the night. Richard and Private Andrew Jones were in the bedroom next door, while Washington's men were stationed in various places about the house and property.

It was December 7, three days since the Tories' last attack on Hoppertown, two days since the arrival of Washington's troops.

As each night passed with no sign of William Randolph and his men, Richard's frustration grew. Soon, Washington would want to leave the area, and then Richard would no longer have the assistance of five skilled Continental soldiers to help apprehend the Tories.

How many men did the Tories have now? he wondered. He didn't want to count on the local militiamen for help, for they were needed to protect their families and homes.

Richard glanced over at Andrew sleeping on his pallet on the floor. The young soldier had been a godsend to him. He reminded Richard of Alex. When they'd first taken up residence in this bedchamber in the Randolph house, Andrew had insisted that his senior officer take the bed, while he slept on the pallet. Richard did so, with some reluctance. He could tell the young private wouldn't allow him to sleep anywhere else. So, Richard had dozed these past two nights on a soft feather-tick mattress, while Andrew had slept on the hard floor.

Kirsten, Richard thought. He missed seeing her each day. She'd been to the house once since they'd come. She'd come in the daylight hours, but fearing for her safety, Richard hadn't wanted her there. The unpredictable behavior provoked by William's unbalanced mind disturbed him. What would happen if her uncle came and she was killed?

They'd had an argument—he and Kirsten—during which he demanded she return home until William was captured, along with his men. But Kirsten had stayed, insisting that her aunt needed some female company for a while. And in the end Richard had allowed it. After all, he reasoned, what harm could come to her under his watchful eye?

After the visit, which had lasted about an hour, Richard had decided that she should be escorted home in the company of one of the soldiers. When he told her of his decision, she demurred gracefully, no doubt pleased by her earlier victory in being able to stay. When she saw that it was Lieutenant Rhoades who would take her home, however, Richard noticed that she seemed uncomfortable with her escort. He questioned her and learned the reason for her uneasiness. He could see why her two previous encounters with Rhoades would cause her to be leery of the man. Private Jones, instead of Rhoades, Richard told her, would gladly take her home.

But now Richard wished Kirsten had stayed so that he could forget about Randolph and Phelps and the traitor within Washington's camp. He wanted to make love to Kirsten, to pleasure her, until all else faded from his thoughts but the silken texture of her smooth skin and her sweet womanly fragrance.

William came that night, on December 7, 1778. He'd stayed away as long as he could, but when he'd heard from a good source that Catherine had returned to their home, he knew he had to go there. Besides, he desperately needed fresh garments.

Emboldened by his previous successes, William took Thaddeus Phelps and no one else on his return trip to his house. He gave no thought to the presence of anyone other than Catherine and perhaps a servant or two, like Jims, their groom.

The house was dark when he arrived, and William realized that Catherine had retired for the night. He entered through the rear servants' entrance.

"Phelps, wait here," he ordered when he and the disfigured man reached the kitchen.

"I'm hungry," Phelps said.

William scowled. "Find something to eat then, but for God's sake, be quiet about it. I don't want to wake up the servants."

Leaving his henchman behind, William climbed the stairs to the second floor. Catherine woke up as he came into their bedchamber.

"William," she gasped, and sat up. She looked lovely and vulnerable in her linen night rail. Her eyes widened, and William was angered by her evident fear.

"You left the cabin," he said, stepping into the room and closing the door.

When he turned back, she was leaning against the headboard, clutching the bedclothes to her breast. "You didn't need me there," she said. "I was but a hindrance to you."

371

William's face softened as he approached the bed. Catherine cringed, and he halted, angered anew.

"What?" he asked. "What is it?"

"You killed Miles," she said.

"I told you—it was Kirsten."

"No." She shook her head. "No, it was you."

"You talked with her, didn't you? Damn the girl's lying tongue!"

Catherine rose up then, straightening her back. "You lied! Kirsten is incapable of hurting Miles, while you—"

He appeared flustered. "I told you—it was discipline."

"You beat him until he bled!"

He dragged her from the bed, and struck her across the head. She fell back against a night table, but he reached for her again.

In the next room, Richard heard the noise and rushed to Catherine's bedchamber. He flung open her door. "Catherine . . ." He came to an abrupt stop, his russet eyes turning an angry dark brown as he saw the other occupant of the room. "Randolph," he spat out.

William released his wife, and she fell to her knees, sobbing. "You!"

Richard drew his sword and directed its point at William's chest. "Finally, we meet again."

"Canfield," the man uttered. "Ethan Canfield."

"Wrong, Biv." Richard's smile was wicked as he aimed his sword higher, at the man's heart. He could hear Catherine crying in the background. The sound pained and enraged him. "Permit me to introduce myself. The name's Maddox. Richard Maddox." He paused. "The Mad Ox."

William appeared stunned. "The Mad Ox . . . but you're dead," he mumbled. He was tense, nervous.

His gaze kept going behind Richard toward the door. "Phelps—"

"Phelps failed," Richard said. "You can see for yourself that I'm alive!"

Phelps, who had stayed downstairs for what seemed to him a long time, decided to find William. Having found a loaf of bread, and having eaten part of it, he was ready to leave. He was angry that he couldn't eat more, but Randolph's fist had damaged his lips and jaw so, it had become painful to chew.

Because of this, the disfigured man wasn't in the best of moods as he silently went up to the second floor and down the hall to the bedchamber from which voices emanated. He came to the door and stopped.

"Biv?" he said, glancing toward Randolph and then at Richard's sword pointed at the man's chest.

William reacted. "Phelps!" he cried. "Get him! Go for his sword!"

Phelps hesitated. The sword was a lethal-looking weapon, one he'd never handled well. Besides, he was angry with William and was no longer willing to lay down his life for the Tory leader. Biv had beaten him when he had done nothing wrong. His nose still throbbed from the assault; his lips and jaw were sore.

"Phelps!" William whined. "Move!"

Thaddeus Phelps glanced at the sword before his gaze traveled to Richard's face. He blinked.

"We meet again," Richard said to him.

It was obvious that Phelps didn't recognize him. Couldn't the man see?

"You idiot!" Randolph cried. "Open your half-blind eyes and look! 'Tis the Mad Ox! I thought you'd killed him!"

"The Mad Ox," the misshapen mouth echoed. "I did kill him!"

Richard grinned. "I don't die easily, Phelps." He ordered the man from the door and called for Andrew in the next room. As he waited for the private, he kept narrowed, alert eyes on Randolph and Phelps. "Where are your men?" he asked. "Are there others with you?"

William refused to reply, but his face gave him away.

Richard smiled. "Good, for I found your wife at the cabin, so I know where to go after them." He played the sword tip across William's shirt, ripping the fabric, baring the man's chest. "I could skewer you now and feel no remorse."

"Catherine," her husband gasped. "You'll not let him kill me!"

The moon had broken clear of the clouds and its light filtered into the bedchamber. Catherine's face was expressionless. "Kill him if you want. It matters not to me."

Andrew Jones arrived then, accompanied by one of Washington's men. Lieutenant Rhoades had been stationed downstairs and had run up the steps to join Andrew as he left his room.

When William Randolph glanced toward the Continental lieutenant, his wife saw the slightest change in his expression.

"Richard," she said. "Lieutenant Rhoades—"

Realizing that he'd been found out, Rhoades drew his knife, grabbed Andrew, and held the blade to the boy's neck. "Drop your sword, Maddox, now, before I kill your loyal friend here."

"Rhoades," Richard spat out. "So it was you . . ."

The lieutenant smiled. "Who else? Who guards the general's tent. Who can hear his conversations—and those of his man Hamilton?"

"You son of a bitch!" Richard held on to his

sword, refusing to lower it. "You'll never get away with it! Fletcher and the others—"

"You'll have no help from that quarter, Lieutenant Mad Ox." Rhoades smiled, his eyes glittering with triumph. "When I saw William here entering the house, I sent them away. It seems that Tories were spotted fleeing into the woods, so you ordered the men to go after them."

"Bastard!"

Rhoades laughed. He brought the knife point higher against the throbbing pulse at Andrew's throat. His face suddenly darkened. "I said, drop the sword, Maddox—*now!*"

Richard studied Andrew's frightened face and then stared at his sword.

"A second more, and the private's a dead man!"

Sighing, Richard closed his eyes as he dropped his sword.

William scrambled to retrieve it, while Phelps watched in stunned disbelief. "Here!" Randolph handed Phelps the sword, forcing the disfigured man to move. "Watch over the Ox, and kill him if he so much as moves a step."

With a harsh laugh, Rhoades thrust Jones farther into the room and ordered Randolph and Phelps to tie all three of the Patriots up. He watched, smiling with satisfaction, as Randolph and Phelps obeyed.

Kirsten had had a feeling . . . a strange foreboding that something was to happen this night. It was this fear that kept her awake and prompted her to do something dangerous and foolhardy, escape the house and ride Hilga to the Randolph farm.

In the dark hours of early morning she tied Hilga to a tree at the edge of the property. There was no one about when she arrived at the house, not even a soldier on guard. That bothered her, so she entered the house quietly and cautiously. Once inside, in the hall, she heard voices. Furniture scraped wood as if someone was scuffling in one of the rooms above.

Her heart began to pound hard. *He's here!* she thought. *My uncle is here!* She went to the kitchen to search for a weapon and found a large, sharp knife used for cutting bread and cooked meat.

With the blade held before her, Kirsten climbed to the second floor. Her heart beat so loudly at one point it drowned out the male voices she'd heard raised in argument. She had difficulty breathing, she was so scared. She heard Richard's voice as she topped the stairs.

"You'll never make it out alive," Richard insisted as he watched Phelps bind young Andrew. "Fletcher and Harris are not stupid. They'll realize that you tricked them. They'll return to confront you with more of Washington's men."

Rhoades, who stood at the door, leaned against the threshold, his arms clasped across his chest. "But it will be too late, won't it?" He glanced toward Randolph, who was securing his wife, using one of her garments to bind her. "By the time they return, we'll have torched this place—and you and your friends with it."

"Move and I stab you clean through," Kirsten growled at Rhoades's back.

The man stiffened with surprise. He started to turn, and Kirsten thrust the knife forward to show she meant business. Crying out with pain, Rhoades obeyed.

"Now order them untied," she said, keeping her voice low.

The lieutenant trembled. "Randolph. Phelps. Untie them. Hurry!"

"Move on in . . . slowly." She urged him on with the knife's point.

Richard's eyes widened as he saw Kirsten behind Rhoades, holding a knife to his back. She grinned at him.

"Hello, love," she said in imitation of him.

"You!" Rhoades said. "Damn you, wench!"

After returning Kirsten's grin, Richard hurried to grab his sword, which Phelps had dropped to the floor in his haste to follow Rhoades's orders. He pressed the tip against Randolph's chest. William had untied Andrew but not his wife. "Untie her—now!"

The man hesitated, glaring. "She's my—"

"Damn you!" Richard bellowed. "I said untie her!"

"Richard?" Kirsten approached him, prodding Rhoades to precede her as she went. "May I?"

Their gazes met, and he nodded, moving out of Kirsten's way. Richard transferred his blade to Rhoades, while Kirsten pressed the knife to her uncle's throat. "I dare you not to do it, uncle," she breathed.

Richard's attention was momentarily distracted by his admiration for Kirsten's courage and spirit. Rhoades, seeing this, suddenly twisted away from Richard's sword. Shoving Kirsten aside and taking her knife, he grabbed Catherine and, pressing the blade to her throat, he held Randolph's wife before him like a shield.

"I don't care what you do with those two," he said. "But I'll not stay! Out of my way or I'll kill her."

Andrew had caught William Randolph's arms, and Richard held Thaddeus Phelps. Without her weapon, Kirsten could only stare at Rhoades, feeling helpless and angry.

"Love," Richard breathed out softly. "My sword."

She glanced down and spied the weapon which had fallen in the scuffle, but pretended that she hadn't noticed it as Rhoades inched toward the door.

"Don't listen to him," Catherine said. "He can kill me; just don't listen to him!"

Rhoades jerked her as he edged toward the door. "Be silent!"

Kirsten's eyes met Catherine's. Something in her aunt's gaze encouraged her to try for the sword. She moved with a suddenness that took even Richard by surprise. At the same time, Catherine, who had remained limp within Rhoades's grasp, pulled forward, allowing Kirsten to drive the sword into the man's stomach.

Rhoades made gargling noises as the blade pierced his gut. His eyes rolled back in his head, and the knife fell harmlessly from his hand before he fell backward, squirming with agony, onto the bedchamber floor, the sword still buried in him.

Catherine went to him, and stepping on his chest with her bare foot, she withdrew the sword. With a smile, she then turned toward Kirsten and held up the bloody weapon, grinning at her stunned niece.

"Now, William," Catherine said, "it's your turn." And then to the shock of everyone else in the room, she thrust the sword point into her husband's neck. William's face contorted with surprise and horror before he slumped to the floor, dead, his blood staining the rug.

Kirsten looked sickly. Reaction had set in, and she started to tremble. Richard noticed and he was aware of the now quietly sobbing Catherine. He ordered Andrew to help secure the prisoner, Phelps. Then he ushered the two women from the room and the house.

Fletcher and the other three soldiers had returned by the time Richard and the women stepped outside.

"Sir," Fletcher said, "we couldn't find the Tories. Not even a clue."

Richard nodded, his expression serious. "That's because there were none, Private, but for the three men in the upstairs bedchamber with Jones." He had his arm about Kirsten's shoulders, and he gave her a squeeze to remind her that he was by her side.

"I'll need two of you to help Jones remove the bodies," he continued, addressing the soldiers. "Rhoades is dead. He was a traitor to the cause."

Fletcher and a soldier named Martin volunteered, so Richard turned to Harris and the remaining Continental. "The stable must be checked. These ladies will want to return to the Van Atta farm. If one of you will do that, I'll send the other to alert Washington. We must have more men. There is a band of Tories to be taken, and with enough soldiers to assist that shouldn't take but a few hours."

Private Fiske volunteered to go to the general, while Harris went to ready a wagon to take Kirsten and her aunt home.

Catherine had stopped crying. Richard met her gaze. "Are you all right?" he asked. She sniffed once, but nodded. "Harris is going to take you to your sister-in-law's."

"Thank you," she said.

Richard turned to the woman he loved. "Kirsten, it's all right. Everything's all right now."

"Oh, Richard"—she sobbed—"all that blood."

He pulled her head against his chest and tenderly stroked her long platinum locks. "I know, love. I know," he murmured.

Soldiers came from the house with their prisoner, Phelps. Andrew approached Richard to give him a report. "We've removed the bodies, sir."

The women started to cry again.

"Thank you, Andrew," Richard said, his voice soft as he noted the young man's concern.

It wasn't long before Harris brought around the wagon.

"Take them home," Richard said. "I've got a job to do." He turned Kirsten so that she faced him. "Private Harris is going to escort you—"

Kirsten grabbed his arm. "No, Richard!" she cried. "You mustn't leave me!"

He stroked her cheek with his other hand, his expression tender. "I must. I'll be all right, Kirsten. *Please*, go home now." He gently removed her hand.

Epilogue

Richard climbed awkwardly onto the saddle of his horse and gazed down at his commander in chief. "I must do this, sir. It will be my last assignment but my most important one."

General George Washington nodded. "I understand, soldier. Although I'll be sorry to see you go."

The recently promoted Continental captain rubbed his leg and smiled. He'd been wounded during the raid on the Tory cabin, caught across the knee with a bullet from John Greene's gun. It had been some time since the skirmish in which the Patriots had taken the Tory camp. Richard had been staying at the Hoppe tavern; his recovery was slow. John Greene had been rewarded with death, like his two older brothers before him.

Richard set his cocked hat upon his head and took up the reins as he prepared to leave. "Andrew . . . ah, I mean Private Jones . . . is a good soldier, General," he said.

Washington smiled as his gaze shifted toward the young man. "He's a good boy. I can see that." He paused. "I'll keep an eye on him for you."

Richard swallowed against a suddenly tight

throat. "Thank you, sir," he said in a husky voice. "I'd appreciate that."

Now that Alex's killer and the traitor had been found, Richard's mission was complete. With Randolph and Rhoades dead, that left only Thaddeus Phelps. On the day of the capture, the disfigured man had been turned over to the general to await Washington's decision regarding his fate. Randolph's wife was learning to live with what had happened. As for Kirsten she was already herself again, for she knew she'd made the only choice open to her in killing a man.

"General, what of Phelps?"

Washington frowned. "I haven't decided yet, but rest assured he'll not be murdering any more of our men."

Kirsten had ridden her mare to the edge of the Paramus encampment and had entered the camp on foot. As she stood out of sight, waiting to speak with Richard, she couldn't help but hear his conversation with the general. She didn't like the topic under discussion.

She watched as Richard prepared to leave, and then hurried along the rear of the tents to intersect his path. He'd nearly reached the road when she planted herself firmly before him, her hands on her hips. Taken by surprise, Richard muttered a nasty oath and drew back on the reins to stop his mount.

"Just where do you think you're going, *mynheer?*"

He stared at her. His lips formed a straight line, and his russet eyes glowed with a strange light. "I suppose you were eavesdropping on the general and me."

Flushing with guilt, she nodded.

"So you know I'm proceeding to my next assignment," he said slowly. "A very important one." He eased himself off the saddle, his movements stiff. "A last assignment for a cripple."

Kirsten protested. "You're not crippled!"

He limped toward her and touched her cheek. "This leg may not heal. I may never walk properly again."

"So? Does a leg make a man?"

Richard's lips curved. "What are you telling me?"

She hesitated. His mission was over, but he planned to leave her again. She was hurt. She was angry. She wanted him to stay. "It wouldn't matter to me."

"You wouldn't care, let's say, if your husband hobbled about for the rest of his life?"

Her eyes filling with tears, she inclined her head.

"Good," he said abruptly. "I was hoping you'd say that, because you see, my dear, my assignment happens to be in Hoppertown." He paused. "As your husband . . . keeping you out of trouble and safe."

Kirsten blinked, startled. She was afraid to hope. Was this a dream? A hoax? It seemed not, for Richard was regarding her with flaming, golden brown eyes. The tenderness and love in his expression was real.

"I'm asking you to marry me," he said.

"But the war—"

"My enlistment's up. I'll continue to do my part—here, in Hoppertown. There are a lot of troops who'll need our help, hungry men waiting to be clothed and fed."

She melted. "Oh, Richard . . ."

He smiled. "Say it once more. I love the way you pronounce my name. I could listen to you say it over and over again. I'll never tire of hearing it on your sweet lips."

She threw herself into his open arms, and he kissed her until her head was spinning and all five of her

383

senses became alert and alive.

"Richard, I love you," she said when they'd ended their kiss to briefly come up for air.

"And I love you." His voice was husky with desire. "But will you marry me?"

Kirsten grinned up at him impishly. "I must think—"

He grabbed her, kissed her hard. She clung to him as he deepened the intimacy until she was reeling and breathless and aching with wanting him.

"Richard, Richard, yes," she gasped, "I'll marry you!"